that.
night
at the
beach

BOOKS BY KATE HEWITT

that night at the beach

KATE HEWITT

bookouture

Published by Bookouture in 2023

An imprint of Storyfire Ltd.
Carmelite House
50 Victoria Embankment
London EC4Y 0DZ

www.bookouture.com

ISBN: 978-1-80314-384-2
eBook ISBN: 978-1-80314-383-5

To Isobel, of course. Thank you, thank you for everything. I'll miss you!

PROLOGUE

I am in the place I never wanted to be. Never dreamed of being, because as mothers we never dare to delve too deeply into those nightmare scenarios, merely skirt their dark edges before quickly, gratefully, backing away.

What if... we might murmur to each other over cups of coffee or glasses of wine, and then shake our heads, not daring to put it into words. Telling ourselves it could never happen to us, as if we can ward off tragedy if we simply don't talk about it, or if we're just careful enough. If we're good enough mothers.

Yet here I am.

The steady beep of the heart monitor is the only evidence my child is alive, both soothing and terrifying in its regularity, because I am bracing myself for it to stop, holding every breath for an endless second as I wait for the next beep and then the next and the next. Let it out slowly, take another. Try, somehow, to move from that moment to this.

The doctor has already given me far too many grim prognoses. *This is very serious. It could go either way. I don't want you to get your hopes up.*

Each pronouncement is worse than the last, and yet still I

cling to hope—frail, fragile, fleeting, yet there. It's all I have now, and without it I am nothing. My family is nothing. And so I stand here, listening to that persistent beep, willing my child's eyes to open, just once. *Please... show me you're alive. Show me you're going to make it, despite all the mistakes I've made.*

I've gone over and over the last few months, second-guessing all the steps and missteps, the calculated risks and the earnest mistakes, the defensive maneuvers and the determined attacks, a series of actions and reactions that brought us teetering to this moment, wondering what I should have done differently. How I could have kept this from happening.

All I wanted was to keep my child safe.

But maybe that is where I went wrong.

CHAPTER 1

CARA

FIVE WEEKS EARLIER

"Do I have to go?"

I look up from the bowl of potato salad I've been carefully covering with plastic wrap, surprised at my son's sullen tone. He sounds like a sulky six-year-old, and he's closing in on eighteen.

"Do you *have* to go?" I repeat carefully as he shrugs, impatient, a bit dismissive. A memory flashes through my mind—Finn at four or five years old, jumping up and down in excitement, asking me to tell the time on the big clock above the stove. *How many hours till we can go, Mommy? How many now?*

How things have changed.

"Don't you want to go, Finn?" I ask, doing my best to keep my tone neutral, not betraying my alarm, and even grief, that it has come to this, at last.

He rolls his eyes, giving me the well-duh look he's perfected over the last few years. "Uh, *no*."

"Why not?"

"Because I want to go out with my friends." Spoken with a

touch of scorn, as if it is painfully obvious, and perhaps it is—
he's almost eighteen, after all, and he's eschewed his parents'
company for some time, but we're talking about the Rosses, the
family we've been friends with forever, the annual beach
barbecue we have never missed, not even when it was pouring
rain, for fifteen years. Finn and Bella, both turning eighteen in
January, have been best friends since they were in diapers.
Admittedly, that friendship has waxed and waned over the
years, from being glued to each other's sides in second grade to
barely speaking by sixth, but in the last few years, after the
excruciating awkwardness of puberty had receded, they'd
reached something of an equilibrium. Or so I had thought.
Hoped, maybe, if I'm honest, because I so want it to be true.

"Your friends," I repeat in the same neutral tone, and Finn
blows out an irritated breath.

"Do you *have* to repeat everything I say?"

"I'm just trying to understand." Another memory flashes
through my mind—Finn and Bella at five years old, coming into
the kitchen, hand in hand, beaming with pride. Bella had given
Finn a makeover, complete with lipstick, blush and far too
much blue eyeshadow. Rose, upon seeing them, had burst into
great gales of laughter; I'd smiled and chuckled along, although,
I must admit, I was slightly taken aback by the sight of my
sturdy little son in cat-flick eyeliner. Bella had been adept with
makeup even back then; hours of YouTube tutorials have since
added to her skill.

She is a gorgeous girl, and more than once I've wondered if
Finn would ever look at her like that, but, as far as I can tell, he
never has. And now he doesn't even want to see her for a single
night, or any of the Rosses, or his own family, for that matter.
He wants to go out with his *friends*.

I take a deep breath and then let it out evenly as I put the
plastic wrap away in the drawer. "Finn, this is one evening out

of the entire year, and this is the last barbecue we'll have all together before you graduate high school." The last barbecue with all four children—Finn and Henry, Bella and Elspeth.

Elspeth and Henry are fourteen, only two months apart; Rose and I spent the entire summer before they were born lying on loungers at the community pool and feeling enormous while Bella and Finn splashed in the baby pool. They've been as good friends as Bella and Finn, but in a different, less obvious way; so far, they've seemed to manage to navigate the awkwardness of the teen years, undoubtedly in large part to Elspeth's smart, snappy confidence, along with Henry's quiet passivity, his willingness to trail along after her, which I think she enjoys.

Finn pushes his lower lip out, just like he used to as a little kid. "Everyone's going out tonight. It's the last weekend before school starts."

"Yes, but you knew about this." The date has never changed—the Friday evening of the Labor Day weekend, the two families, on Westport's South Beach. When they were little, we brought buckets and shovels, boogie boards and windbreaks, made a whole day of it. Since the kids all became teenagers, we've dialed it back to a more understated evening affair—beach chairs and blankets, chips and dip and a cooler of drinks, burgers on one of the picnic area's grills.

But it's still important. It still feels like a highlight of my calendar, even—if I'm not being too melodramatic—a lodestar of my life. When everything else feels tenuous and uncertain, when children get ready to leave home and husbands become silent and surly, when parents get sick and friends drift away, there's still this—an evening under the stars, a reminder of all that is good in my life. My family, my children, my best friend.

The thought of Finn not going, of him *choosing* not to go... it makes my heart ache and my stomach cramp. I'm doing my best to get used to the idea of him going to college in a year—Michael is always talking about how he needs to get started on his applications—but I'm still not ready for our family life to change. To end, at least in a way. And I can't disappoint Rose; we've been best friends since we met at a Mommy and Me group when Finn and Bella were babies. She'd forgotten her diaper bag and Bella had desperately needed a change, was stinking up the whole room. I had provided everything for her, a little embarrassed on Rose's behalf, but she had been blithely indifferent to the other mothers' wrinkled noses, the flashes of scornful judgment I saw in their eyes. *What kind of mother doesn't bring a diaper bag to a Mommy and Me class?* After just six months of motherhood, I had already realized what a fraught world parenting could be, how quick and cutting the other women's judgments, their assumed superiority. Or so it at least seemed to me, but then I've always been so determined to do everything right, and just as afraid that I wouldn't.

"Well, you certainly came prepared, didn't you?" Rose had remarked cheerfully as I'd handed her a pack of organic baby wipes (gentler on the skin) and an eco-friendly diaper (not as effective as Pampers or Huggies, but still). "I'm always forgetting this kind of stuff. And we were only going out for an hour, but babies certainly know how to time their poos, don't they?" She'd rolled her eyes as she wiped Bella's bottom with an alarmingly expansive carelessness, considering the nature of the task. "Good thing I met you."

That simple exchange somehow sealed our friendship; Rose, in her exuberant way, started treating me as if we'd been best friends forever, pulling me easily into her orbit, and I was more than happy to spin alongside her. I'd never been particularly good at making friends; I'm too cautious, too quiet, and so having Rose take me under her rather reckless wing was a complete blessing. I've always been grateful.

I can't let her down now.

"Finn, this might be the last barbecue we have with the

Rosses," I tell him again as I put the potato salad in the fridge, next to the red cabbage coleslaw I made this morning. "Once you and Bella are in college—"

"It's not like we're dying or something," Finn interjects, an edge to his voice. "Look, I've gone every year since I was, like, *born*. Can't I just miss this one?"

I take another careful breath and close the fridge door, resting my palm against the cool stainless steel for a moment, to steady myself. "No," I state firmly. "I'm sorry, but you cannot."

Finn stares at me for a few seconds—he's six two now, with the same messy mop of dark hair that Michael had before it started thinning on top, and he towers over me. He's muscled, too, from working out, as well as playing soccer, basketball and baseball on all the school teams. Finn is what the school proudly calls an all-rounder; they think, with a little luck and a strong set of essays and personal references, he might get in to one of the Ivies.

Now he expels a gusty sigh and turns on his heel. "Fine," he says and strides out of the kitchen.

I let out the breath I was holding, grateful that I am still managing to cling to my parental authority, if only just.

I have just got out the paper plates and festive napkins when, a few minutes later, Henry slouches into the room, his bangs sliding into his face, his hands jammed into the pockets of his shorts. I tense, waiting for him to ask if *he* has to go, although the days of Henry trying to ape his older brother are long gone; they're simply too different.

While Finn is sporty and confident in school, Henry is quiet and shy, preferring drawing and elaborate board games to soccer or debating club. He found a niche for himself last year, with a few friends with similar interests; they spent an entire Saturday afternoon this summer setting some reboot of Dungeons and Dragons on the kitchen table, bent over the board, poring over character stats and game maps, while I provided smiles and snacks.

I'm glad he's found his tribe, and am grateful he seems happy, but I can't help but notice that sometimes he can seem a bit wary around his older brother. Finn doesn't always have a lot of patience for Henry; as his star has risen—captain of the baseball team this year—Henry's has bobbed along quietly, content to be in the "geeky" group, although, of course, I'd never use that word to anyone, although I know Finn sometimes does.

I recall their matching outfits and wrestling matches on the family-room carpet with a flicker of bittersweet nostalgia, back when they were both little. These days, I'm afraid, they barely talk to each other.

"What's up, Henry?" I ask as I put the plastic plates in the big, wicker picnic basket that was a wedding present and is generally only brought out for this occasion.

He hunches his shoulders. "Nothing."

"Looking forward to tonight?" I ask brightly, hoping for some enthusiasm, although I already know Henry is unlikely to give it. His tendency is to be understated about everything.

He shrugs, moderately unenthused, just as I expected. "I guess."

That's something, at least, I tell myself. Better than Finn's response, at least, and anyway, I should know better than to expect unrestrained excitement from a fourteen-year-old boy.

I glance outside at the cloudless blue sky. "I think the weather is going to be great." Although it's hot and humid, there will be an ocean breeze on the beach, and the sunset over Long Island Sound will surely be spectacular. My heart lifts at the thought of us all together as twilight settles over the sand—glasses clinking, the murmur of voices, the children's laughter, fireflies...

It really is going to be great. It has to be, although I recognize that I am probably giving what is meant to be a simple picnic far too much significance. It's only a beach barbecue, after all, and the truth is, I'm not even sure the Rosses are all that excited to go. Rose hadn't mentioned it until I'd texted her about it, and I haven't seen her since they came back from Martha's Vineyard last week.

But I want to believe it will be great, that it will somehow set my life back on track, because after a year of unspoken tension with Michael, my mother getting sick, my friendship with Rose definitely starting to drift, my oldest child soon to leave home... Can't I have this one evening?

I reach for the Tupperware of chocolate chip cookies I made this morning. Every year, Rose and I have divvied up the food we bring; she provides the drinks and the meat for the barbecue (and a veggie burger for Elspeth) and I take care of everything else—sides, salads, condiments, dessert, paper plates and napkins, forks and knives, picnic blankets and folding chairs. It's how it has always been with us, and it works.

Henry is standing by the French doors that lead out to the deck, the sunlight gilding his lanky frame in gold. He hasn't spoken in several minutes.

"Is everything all right, Henry?" I ask gently, and he shrugs.

"Yeah, I guess."

"Looking forward to going back to school?"

Another shrug.

"Maybe next Saturday you could invite the gang over to play that game," I suggest brightly. It's not called Dungeons and Dragons anymore, but something like that. "You know, the adventure one?"

"Yeah, I know." He sighs and stares out the window.

"You sure everything is okay?" I ask gently, because even for Henry, he seems a bit down.

"Yeah." He opens his mouth as if he's going to say something, but then doesn't.

I put the container of cookies in the basket. "Why don't you practice piano?" I suggest. "We're leaving at five, so you could get a good thirty minutes in."

For a second, Henry looks like he wants to protest, but then he gives a shrugging sort of nod and slouches off to the living room. A few minutes later, I hear the brisk tones of Bach's *Prelude and Fugue in G.* Henry practices diligently, and his piano teacher has remarked how capably he plays, "if without enthusiasm." Still, being capable in life goes a long way. I should know; I have spent a lot of time simply trying to be useful.

The playing continues as I finish packing our picnic and check my phone—Michael said he would text me when he left work, but there's nothing and he should be on the Metro North from Grand Central by now, an hour and fifteen minutes, door to door. Considering we leave in less than an hour, I'm starting to feel a little concerned. I think about texting him to check, but I suspect he'll be annoyed at what he'll see as my nagging and so, with some determined restraint, I keep myself from it.

As Henry continues to practice, I finish packing the picnic —cookies, coleslaw, both green and pasta salads, hummus and pita chips, carrot and cucumber sticks, a tube of Pringles and a bag of Doritos for the teenagers. I get out the picnic blankets— also wedding presents, rarely used—with their embroidered Americana designs of farmhouses and fields and baskets of apples, and a couple of folding chairs. I put it all by the front door, wondering if I can ask Finn to put it into the car, but considering his unwillingness even to go, I am reluctant to make him to do anything more, although I know I should.

Usually I would; I've always been a stickler for rules, believing that boundaries and rules are good for kids, make them feel safe. I know I certainly would have appreciated my mom caring enough to tell me to go to bed or eat my vegetables. But right now I feel too edgy for a face-off with Finn; he's in a bad mood, and asking him to lug everything out to the car when he doesn't even want to go feels like taking a match to tinder. I'm not about to set anything on fire.

Even so, the sight of all the stuff piled there in the hall gives me a warm, satisfied glow inside, the tangible proof of our family's stability, its endurance over the years, through the hard times as well as the good. At least that's how I like to see it. We'll get through this rocky time, I tell myself, although, in truth, the rockiness of it feels so nebulous—sometimes I wonder if I am imagining Michael's distance, the edge of annoyance that seems to creep into his voice. Am I being too sensitive? Too fearful, because part of me has always wondered when things will start to go wrong, even as I work so hard to make sure they don't?

Tonight, I tell myself, will be good. It has to be.

I slip out my phone and check it again; we're meant to leave in half an hour and Michael hasn't texted or called. From the living room, Henry finishes Bach's Fugue with a funereal-sounding chord before closing the piano lid with a bang.

Quickly, I swipe to dial Michael's number. He answers on the fourth ring.

"Hello?" He sounds a bit hassled, like he's busy and he's answering a telemarketer, even though he must know it's me.

"Hey, I was just wondering where you were." I try to keep my tone light, but I know I fail. I've never been able to *do* light, the way Rose does, laughing through life, greeting the trials and tribulations of parenthood with a careless shrug, an easy laugh, glass in hand, hair tumbling down her back. Everything seems to catch me on the raw, burrow down deep.

"I'm on the 4:11 to New Haven, somewhere between Cos Cob and Riverside," Michael tells me, and once again I think I hear a slight edge to his voice, as if I've asked him something unreasonable. Maybe I have.

"The 4:11... so you won't get in till after five?" I try to sound matter-of-fact, but the disappointment needles through, like holes picked in a cloth.

"Cara, I left work an hour early." Now there definitely is an edge to his voice; there's no mistaking it. "That was already a big ask."

Leaving at four on the Friday of Labor Day Weekend? I'm sure the office will be more than half-empty, and Michael has worked there for twenty years. It hardly seems like a *big ask*, but I'm not going to argue the point now.

"All right." I try to sound cheerful even though I have to bite my lip to keep from saying something recriminating. *Why didn't you leave earlier? Why didn't you call me?* "We'll wait."

"I can meet you there."

"No, it's okay," I practically chirp. "We'll go all together. Saves on the driving." Even though South Beach is only ten minutes away, I'm afraid that if we agree to meet Michael there, he will show up even later, claiming he had to change/take a phone call/answer an email/drag his feet.

"Fine."

He disconnects the call before I can say anything else, and I blink back the sudden sting of tears, annoyed that these barbed little exchanges can still hurt me after an entire year of them. I can't pinpoint exactly when Michael's attitude toward me started to change, only, perhaps, that it happened in tiny increments. When I first noticed his edginess and irritation, I put it down to stress at work; as a mid-level financial analyst at one of the big investment firms, he lost a few big clients during the economic downturn, and I know that hit him hard.

But then I started to notice that he wasn't particularly irritable with Finn or Henry, just with me. He was still Finn's champion, always ready to go out and throw a baseball around if Finn was willing, hear about his successes at school, show up for his games. And he and Henry have been doing a thousand-piece puzzle for months, dark heads bent together over a jumble of tiny pieces. Yet with me... I can't remember the last time we went out for dinner, or to a movie. The last time we shared a laugh or even a chat, or sat on the sofa, legs entwined, my head on his shoulder. The last time we made love.

Life has been hectic; I didn't notice all these absences right away, didn't count them up like a column of negative figures until more recently, when they started to become impossible to ignore. To pretend they weren't happening. The way he won't look at me while we eat dinner. The edge in his voice when I ask a simple question. How he bounds out to the yard with Finn rather than sit with me and chat about our days over a glass of wine.

A sigh escapes me, low and dispirited. A year at least this kind of stuff has been going on, and we've never even talked about any of it, which I know is as much my fault as his. I've always dreaded confrontation, that moment when someone stares you in the eye and says what you hoped they weren't thinking. I know I can't face that kind of moment with my husband, not yet anyway. And so I first pretended it wasn't happening, and then later that it would go away, if I just kept doing everything right. If I just stay the course, I've told myself, we'll get back to normal—starting with tonight.

If I tell myself this enough, will I start to believe it? Can I will it into being simply by the force of my feeling? I'm certainly hoping I can. Betting on it.

Finn comes in from the family room, slouching his shoulders, dragging his feet.

"Do I really have to go?" he asks, as truculent as a child, and Henry drifts in from the living room, his expression alert but wary as he glances at his brother.

I look at them both—my two sons, so different from each other, yet each retreating from me in his own way. Henry, with his quietness, so I never feel I know what he's thinking or feeling, and Finn, with his yearning for independence, autonomy, on the cusp of adulthood, yet still so much a little boy.

I swallow down my hurt, my anger, my fear that my life has been slowly spinning out of my control, and I give my oldest son a cheerful, no-nonsense look, the kind I perfected when he was a toddler. "Yes," I say firmly. "You do. Now let's bring this stuff out to the car."

CHAPTER 2

ROSE

"You know this is going to be an *ab-so-lute* barrel of laughs, right? One every minute, guaranteed."

My husband Brad rolls his eyes as I pull into the South Beach parking lot. As Westport residents, we get a beach pass, bypassing the traffic snaking along Compo Road. They limit the beach passes to one hundred a day for non-residents, and people park as far away as three miles, trekking in with their coolers and camp chairs, while we coast in for free, something that Brad usually gloats over, but tonight he's in a bit of a mood.

He's already had two beers at home, "to get ready," and I know by the time we get to the picnic area—when he's cracked his third and can act like the lord of his own little barbecue fiefdom, flipping burgers on the grill—he'll be his usual expansive self, full of bonhomie and largesse. But right now he's irritated and resentful, and unfortunately I understand why, at least a little. Cara and Michael aren't, admittedly, the most fun people around, especially not recently, but she's my oldest friend and that counts for something... even if my husband has had to be dragged out to these barbecues, and will be well on his way to drunk by the end of them. There's a reason why I'm the one who is driving.

"I assume you were being sarcastic, Dad, when you said that?" Elspeth's sharp voice from the backseat makes me wince, although it glances right off Brad. My fourteen-year-old daughter is too smart and sassy for her own good, always whipping out the wisecracks, picking up on the overtones. It's already landed her in trouble at school, both with teachers and friends, neither of whom always appreciate her too-smart-to-be-funny remarks, her astute and cutting assessments of every social situation. She acts like she doesn't care, but I think she must, at least a little. Although, considering she was voted "most likely to rule the world" at the end of eighth grade, maybe not.

"Why do you think I was being sarcastic, honey?" Brad calls back, giving me a glinting, sideways smile, the curl of his lip not quite a knowing smirk. Once, that devilish confidence would have made my stomach flip, but now I feel too tired to summon any kind of emotion. "I *love* the Johnstons. To pieces."

He couldn't sound more sarcastic if he tried, and that's probably on purpose.

Elspeth purses her lips and Bella, twirling a strand of honey-blonde hair around her finger, looks up from her phone. "Wait, what?" She blinks at us in confusion, unsure if Brad is serious or not.

"I love them," Brad repeats effusively, throwing an arm out for effect. He's already in lord-of-the-manor mode, and we haven't even got there yet. I try not to grit my teeth, at least noticeably. I used to love his expansive schtick, but twenty years on, it grates. "Of course I do. Our oldest friends. *Your* oldest friends." He smiles at Bella, who continues to blink at him uncertainly.

"Dad's being sarcastic, Bella," Elspeth explains in a well-duh tone. "He doesn't like the Johnstons."

"He doesn't?" she asks, startled, looking between us all. "Why not?"

"Enough of this," I say, cutting off what can only be an unhelpful conversation, considering we're going to see the Johnstons in less than five minutes.

Bella is still looking confused. My firstborn is gorgeous inside and out, and yet Elspeth can run rings around her intellectually, and often does, without her older sister even realizing.

This dynamic has bubbled up between them since they were little, when Elspeth would show Bella up in front of her friends, jumping in her with her three-year-old wisdom while six-year-old Bella would simply shrug, unperturbed, and go off with her friends anyway, leaving Elspeth behind, fuming and alone.

I give her a quick, sympathetic smile now, which she ignores, flouncing out of the car.

"Anyway," I say to Brad as I open my door, determined to swing the mood to more upbeat, even if I'm not feeling it. "You know we always have fun at these things."

Or we used to, back when the kids were small and a shovel and pail made them happy, an ice cream cone deliriously so. Cara and I could sit back with glasses of wine and watch the sun set over the Sound, while Michael and Brad talked business, their voices a rumble drifting on the salt-tinged breeze. Everything felt easy.

I miss those days. They haven't happened for a while. Too much has changed—has aged, and not all that well.

"All right, everybody." I put on a chipper voice to hide the fact that I'm dreading this evening almost as much as Brad is.

When I was younger, I had more patience with Cara, even a certain protective tenderness. I could tease her about her OCD tendencies and tone down her intensity with my own determined insouciance, but lately... not so much. She feels like a lot of hard work, and that's not how a friend is meant to feel, is it?

"Elspeth, you get the blanket," I instruct as I get out of the car, adjusting the straps of my maxi dress, the linen wrinkled from the seatbelt. "Bella, can you take the cooler? Brad, the shopping bags."

I know Cara will have packed about five times as much as I have, all of it homemade, while I bought readymade burgers, marinated chicken breasts and sockeye salmon from The Fresh Market on Post Road fifteen minutes ago. Not that she's trying to show me up, or that I even care. That's how it's always been, between us; it's only recently that it's started to feel a tiny bit annoying, although I can't even articulate why. I certainly don't want to be the one making the homemade coleslaw and cookies, and I'm grateful that Cara's willing to do it.

Everyone grabs their stuff and we head toward the picnic area on the beach, the Sound like a burnished mirror, the sun glinting gold off its placid surface. The air is warm and drowsy, and the beach is emptying out of children, sleepy and sunburned, heading home to bed. I watch a dad hoist a little girl onto his hip, and she snuggles in, nestling her head against his shoulder. I feel a pang of envy for the ease of those days, when children cuddled against you and were in bed by seven, the best of both worlds. Those days are long gone.

I scan the array of picnic tables and grills stretching down the expanse of beach; usually, Cara has already bagged both and has set everything up by the time we arrive, including paper plates and matching napkins, but it's already quarter past five and it looks like she's not here.

We dump our stuff on a free picnic table and Brad starts to fire up the grill. Bella has flopped onto a picnic bench, fingers tapping on her phone at lightning speed, while Elspeth prowls around, already restless.

"El, why don't you help me unwrap all this stuff?" I ask as I take out the packs of prepared meat and dump them on the table. "Let's get everything on the grill so we can eat ASAP." And just in case that sounds like I want to get this evening over as quickly as possible, I add with a smile, "I'm sure you're hungry."

While the grill heats up, Brad is, predictably, cracking open his third beer. He seems a little more relaxed since the Johnstons have yet to make an appearance. I can already picture their arrival—Cara striding ahead, all earnest eagerness, and Michael behind, looking mopey. Finn will do his slightly smirking, cool-guy stance, feet spread apart, collar popped, and Henry will skulk along the sidelines until Elspeth takes him in hand.

All of it, I know, is fairly normal behavior for anyone, nothing too objectionable, and yet right now it feels completely exhausting. I am tempted to join Brad and open the ice-cold bottle of Sancerre I brought, but I can already picture the slightly wounded look Cara will give me when she sees I started without her, and so I resist the impulse.

Elspeth is picking ineffectually at the plastic wrap on the salmon. "Do you know salmon farms are needlessly cruel?" she asks me with a touch of typical, virtuous teenaged accusation. "The fish have no choice but to swim in pointless circles in an enclosed space for the entirety of their miserable existences, and research has shown that despite being stunned before they're murdered, they're actually still alive and can show signs of pain, including twitching, wriggling, and gasping." *A little bit like humans then,* I think, but of course don't say. Elspeth finishes with a flourish, "It's completely inhumane, what they do to those fish. Completely unacceptable."

She has fired all of this off with such swift and certain precision that it's hard to hide my smile. I love her ferocity, but experience has taught me to be prepared for it. "This salmon," I inform her kindly, tapping the plastic-wrapped pack, "has been caught in the wild, and so I'm sure it's had a very happy life, swimming along in its natural habitat in Alaska or wherever it first spawned." Which is why it cost five times as much as the farmed alternative. "Plus," I add for good measure, smiling all the while, "The World Wildlife Fund is working with salmon farms to ensure their practices are both efficient and ethical, with responsible growth and production." Copied and pasted directly from the WWF website this afternoon, in anticipation of a discussion exactly like this one. It's nice, as well as a tiny bit tiring, to feel so vindicated.

Elspeth stares at me for a few seconds before a reluctantly approving grin quirks her mouth, lightens my heart. "All right, fair," she concedes, as I let out a little laugh. "But I'm still not eating it."

"Plant-based burger for you, sweetheart," I remind her, hefting the nearly just as pricey veggie burger I bought at the market. "And, just in case you were worried, the soya in this burger was ethically harvested in Brazil, with an acre of rainforest preserved for every acre that's used in farming." Or something like that. I didn't do all the research on the veggie burger, so my statistics might be more than a little glib, but I always try to buy ethically because I know, as always, Elspeth will be firing her environmental concerns and accusations at every aspect of a meal.

Her smile widens before she shrugs and rolls her eyes in dismissal, unable to be appreciative for more than a few seconds, lest she spontaneously combust. I suppress a laugh, knowing it might annoy her, but still enjoying her spirit.

"What about these burgers?" she demands, brandishing a pack of four, all beef. "Who eats red meat anymore, anyway?"

"I do." As usual, Brad cheerfully blunders his way into the conversation with good-natured cheer. "And it's delicious. You should try it, El. You might become a carnivore against your will."

If I said something like that she'd bite my head off, but Elspeth doesn't retort with one of her usual cutting comments, because, just like Bella, she's got a soft spot for her dad, always has. He spoils them both, expansively and unapologetically, and leaves me to be the rule enforcer, not that I really am. I grew up with enough rules and expectations to make me feel like my teenaged years had been spent in a prison cell, and it didn't help me when I finally managed to break out at college, completely unprepared for the real world in all its glory and gruesomeness.

As a result, I'd always promised myself I wouldn't do the same to my children, and I kept them as rule-free as I could, much, I know, to Cara's chagrin. Even so, I realized pretty early on in this motherhood gig that *someone* has to at least act like they are in charge, and I learned pretty quickly it was never going to be Brad. So what rules are in our house are enforced only by me.

I'm just reconsidering opening the Sancerre when Bella looks up from her phone, blinking into the distance.

"They're here," she states, sounding a little nervous; I don't think she and Finn have really been friends for years, but for an evening once a year we all pretend.

I paste a wide smile on my face as the Johnstons come trudging toward us just as I envisioned—Cara with a bright smile on her face, lugging a picnic basket and a hemp shopping bag. Finn is walking behind her, hefting a cooler, a stoic look on his face like he's enduring torture, and he probably is. Henry sidles along behind him, his hair sliding into his face, his gaze on the ground. Michael is last, head bent as he texts something on his phone. As they approach, he slips his phone into his back pocket, unable even to summon a smile of greeting.

This is going to be *such* a fun night. I reach for the bottle I'd left in the bag.

"Glass of white, Cara?" I ask as I air-kiss both of her cheeks.

"Already?" She lets out a trill of laughter as she puts down a huge wicker basket, the same one she uses every year. "Oh, why not?"

All the kids are simply standing around, looking pretty awkward and miserable; Finn's hands are in his pockets, and yes, his collar is popped, but he doesn't look as smug as I expected him to. Bella is twirling her hair, glancing nervously at everyone, and Elspeth's arms are folded as she beadily takes in the scene. It takes me a few seconds to spy where Henry has got to, half-hiding behind Michael.

I push some of the packs of burgers across the table, summoning a smile. "Why don't you open these, guys? We'll get them on the grill."

After a few seconds of stillness, they move toward the table and silently start opening the packs of meat like they're workers in a factory, heads down, expressions grim, focused on the task. I suppress a sigh as I open the bottle and pour myself and Cara two plastic tumblers of white.

"Cheers," I tell her as we clink plastic. "Hard to believe this is the last year we get to do this." As soon as I say the words, I want to take them back, just in case Cara sees this as an opening to suggest we continue, even after Bella and Finn are in college. Why wouldn't we, with Elspeth and Henry? Or maybe she'll suggest we move the weekend to earlier in the summer, when Bella and Finn will still be at home.

We've never actually said we'd stop these barbecues when they went away to college, but I feel like it had been silently agreed upon. This is the year of lasts, and when it comes to this barbecue, surely that's a good thing. We've basically been play-acting for years, and I can't be the only one who feels it.

I glance at Brad and Michael as I take a sip of wine; they aren't even play-acting: Brad is focused on the grill and Michael has got out his phone again. Sometimes it's hard to believe they were good friends once, just as Cara and I were. We used to do couples' dinners every month or so, trying out new restaurants in Westport or Greenwich. Brad and Michael even did some typical guy things together—a bike ride, a hike, a baseball game. That all ended a while back, though, probably around the time Brad got promoted to executive director and started raking in the million-dollar bonuses and Michael stayed at his safe, steady job in middle management, earning a decent enough salary but never making the kind of silly, Monopoly money that Brad did. I know Cara can be anxious about their finances, and they depend on her salary as an office manager for a pediatric practice, while it's a point of pride to Brad that I've never had to work.

It's ridiculous, really, how so many problems can be traced back to stupid money, although maybe it's not all down to that. Maybe the money just showed the fault lines that were already there.

I realize, though, that this new level of tension feels even more recent, more raw, or is it just that I have become more sensitive to it? It's hard to be sure, but what I do know—what has been painfully obvious—is that none of us have enjoyed this friendship for quite some time. Certainly not Brad and Michael, and not really Cara and me, either. Maybe it's how different our lives have become; Cara works full-time while I play tennis and go out for lunch. Or maybe it's simply that we no longer have the kids to draw us together, with Finn and Bella begging for a sleepover, or all of us spending a Saturday at the playground or zoo.

It isn't that I've wanted to end my friendship with Cara, but more that I find it so exhausting to maintain it. Cara is, in point of fact, my oldest friend, and in some ways my only real one. I cut ties with the friends I had from high school and college years ago, a determined decision to have a fresh start after graduation, and the women I lunch and play tennis with now are, for the most part, no more than shallow acquaintances, which suits me fine because I don't really want to go deep with anyone. I have my family, my beautiful girls, and they are enough.

"More wine?" I ask Cara, and she looks surprised that I've guzzled my whole cup before she's said so much as a word. I'm usually a little more restrained, or at least more discreet, but it's only a little after six and I'm already feeling ready for this evening to be over. Although, I acknowledge, if I keep up this pace I won't be able to drive home.

Cara has put down her glass to get out a tub of the red cabbage and apple coleslaw that she makes every year and none of the kids ever eat. I always put a spoonful on my plate out of duty, but maybe this year I won't. The spiky, spiteful thought makes me cringe inwardly. What's *wrong* with me? Why am I mentally sniping at Cara when I know she only means well? She's worked so hard, as she always does, and I'm here inwardly griping. I am brought up short by the sheer pettiness of the thoughts that are circling around in my head; they are not worthy of either me or Cara, my best friend for the last seventeen and a half years. Is this simply what happens with long-term friends, I wonder, the way it does with married couples? You just get *tired*, your good intentions and stamina to suffer each other petering out?

I glance, inadvertently, at Brad. I'm pretty sure my husband has gotten tired of me, and quite some time ago, not that he'd ever admit it.

Cara watches, her lips slightly pursed, as I slosh more Sancerre into my glass. "Tough day?" she asks with what I think is meant to be a commiserating smile, and I manage a smile back.

"Not really."

"Oh. Well."

I tell myself I need to rein it back in, find the kind of easy effusiveness I'm known for, the bubbly queen to Brad's benevolent king, but it seems too hard right now. I'm not up for it, and I don't even know why. I don't have an excuse; my life has been easy lately, far too easy: a month at our house on Martha's Vineyard, swimming and sailing, gin-soaked dinners at the golf club, evenings out on our deck, watching the sun set over the ocean. What on earth do I have to complain about? And yet already I know this evening really is going to feel endless.

The kids have finished unwrapping the meat, and they're now standing around, silent, each of them seeming only to endure each moment as it ticks slowly past. It's amazing how miserable teenagers can look when they want to. Does it take effort, I wonder, or do they manage it naturally?

"Hey, you guys," I say in a too-jolly voice, like they're all about six. "What about a game of Frisbee before we eat?"

Elspeth gives me one of her blistering looks. "Frisbee isn't a *game*, Mom. You don't score points or anything."

"Well, you play it, don't you?" I counter with a smile. "Come on. You brought a Frisbee, didn't you, Cara?" She always brings a big bag of sports stuff no one ever plays with anymore—Frisbees and whiffle balls, ten pins for bowling and once a whole badminton set.

Cara blinks at me, looking stricken. "Uh, no, I didn't. I didn't think... No one played anything last year..." She trails off, abject, and I do my best to rally.

"Oh, never mind, eh? Guys, why don't you go down to the water? Dip your toes in? Jump the waves."

Four teenaged faces look at me blankly. I'm treating them like they're toddlers, but, just like Cara, they're such hard work. Or maybe it's me; maybe I'm just finding everything hard these days. I take another sip of my wine.

"The burgers will be ready soon," Cara tells them placatingly, and somehow this is enough to have them drift away, towards the rippling Sound, the sun just starting its descent toward the water, turning its surface to bronze. I watch as Elspeth falls into step alongside Henry, and Bella and Finn fan out on either side, almost as if they're avoiding each other. I remember how they used to share the same towel, asking to be wrapped up together, giggling wildly as Brad would heft them on his shoulder and stagger around, pretending not to know where they were, feigning surprise when, unable to resist, they peeked out from beneath the towel's folds, their giggles turning to deep, wonderful belly laughs. Is there any better sound than the joyful and genuine guffaw of a child, bubbling up from deep within?

I didn't appreciate those days when I had them, although I thought I did. Back then, I knew, in an academic sort of way, that they were precious and fleeting, that I should savor each wondrous moment, and yet I was so *tired*, and the children's needs so demanding, that I didn't really believe it. I thought it would last forever, and then those days were gone, and I'm left blinking and gasping, wondering where they went, what's left of my life.

I glance at Brad, busy with the barbecue. Michael's not even trying to talk to him.

The kids have reached the shoreline; Elspeth and Henry have dipped their toes in, and Finn is skimming rocks, watching them bounce along the surface of the water five, six, seven times. He's good at everything, I think ruefully, not for the first time. A natural athlete, academically on top, with a charm that manages—usually—to rise above the teenaged surliness. Finn has always been charming, although in the last couple of years I've noticing the inevitable arrogance creeping in. Success does that to men, I've found. I remember how at the barbecue last year Finn spent most of the evening on his own, sauntering about, flexing his biceps, pretending to ignore the other three. This year, he seems to have toned it down a little bit, but even so, he's not even looking at any of the others.

Bella is standing off by herself, on the other side of Elspeth and Henry, her arms wrapped around her middle, her hair blowing in the breeze that has picked up, coming off the water. She looks lonely and a little sad, but maybe I'm just projecting.

I square my shoulders, stiffening my resolve as I turn back to Cara. I really need to make more of an effort with her. If friends are hard work, then that's because they're worth it. Besides, I can't pretend I'm the easiest person to get along with —scatterbrained, careless, sometimes indifferent, cuttingly so. Cara has never become tired of me, has always had my back, even when I haven't really had hers, and that says something. That says a lot, actually.

"So," I ask brightly, as if I really care about the answer, and I am determined to, *now*, "how are you?"

CHAPTER 3

CARA

I should have brought a Frisbee. And the bowling set, and the whiffle ball and bat, and maybe even the badminton set. I had it all ready to go in the big canvas bag in the garage, but at the last minute I decided not to bring any of it. Last year, I'd coaxed Henry and Elspeth into playing badminton together, but only for about ten minutes and it had taken longer just to set it up. Finn and Bella didn't touch any of the sports equipment and so it had all felt like a waste, and worse, a little desperate and ridiculous, like I was trying to hold onto the days when they were little and would have been begging to play a game, and maybe I was. Who could blame me?

Those days seem a lot better than this one. Michael didn't get back to the house until five twenty, and then he had to change, so by the time we made it to the beach, it was quarter to six. Brad had already started on the beer, which shouldn't shock me because they've always been pretty enthusiastic social drinkers, but there is something almost grim about the way Rose is slugging back the Sancerre now, like it's a dose of medicine. She's already poured her third glass, and I've barely sipped from my first.

But worse than any of that, the kids aren't speaking to each other at all. They barely did last year, so I'm not sure why I got my hopes up that somehow this time they'll all magically become friends again, in that effortless way they were when they were small, and yet I did. It's just so hard to reconcile this surly, silent Finn and quiet, reserved Bella with the two round-tummied toddlers who wrapped their arms around each other, shrieking, as they ran toward the waves.

Elspeth, at least, is talking to Henry, even if he doesn't appear to be talking back. She's probably lecturing him on one of her never-ending causes—save the whales or the rainforest or the Salt Creek tiger beetles—they were her cause of choice last year. She tends to boss Henry around, treating him like some kind of sidekick, but he doesn't seem to mind, and I don't feel I can intervene. Rose, I know, wouldn't like it. She's always been determined to "let kids be kids," no matter what the cost.

"I'm all right," I answer Rose slowly, although despite her bright smile I'm not sure she's really listening. She is gazing at the kids down by the water, her forehead slightly furrowed. "They've grown up so much, haven't they?" I remark quietly. I meant to sound proud, but it comes out more wistful. I really do miss those old days, when everything felt easy, and Rose and I laughed together, watching four little kids jump the waves.

Rose nods, her gaze still fixed on their four lanky forms, now silhouetted by the setting sun. "Yes, they certainly have. Hard to believe."

"Has Bella thought about what colleges she wants to apply to?" It feels like the sort of thing I should already know, considering Rose is meant to be my best friend, but we've barely seen each other all summer; our only real communication has been arranging this barbecue by text, and I'm not sure it would have happened if I hadn't messaged Rose first, although maybe that's unfair. I know I'm usually the organized one.

"Oh, I don't know." Rose waves a hand in dismissal. "She

changes her mind constantly, and her grades aren't amazing, to say the least, so we need to keep our expectations realistic, or so the college counselor keeps telling us." She grimaces good-naturedly, clearly not bothered by what I would find quite alarming. "Like I'd even want her to go to Harvard or something."

Bella and Finn both go to the local public high school. For a while, Bella went to a small, progressive private school, but when she was about to enter ninth grade, she begged to go to the local public, same as Finn, so they ended up in school together for the last three years, not that you'd know it from the way they act around each other, as if they are strangers. I glance toward the figures by the beach; Elspeth has turned away from Henry and Bella is walking down the shoreline, alone. Finn continues to skip stones, but I see him look in Bella's direction as he picks another up from the damp sand.

"Where is she thinking, then?" I ask Rose, ignoring the Harvard remark. I don't know if she remembers that we are encouraging Finn to apply to the Ivies, that we'd be pretty pleased if he ended up going to Harvard. I don't think she meant it as a slight.

She shrugs, nonchalant. "Oh, various places, mostly in the northeast. I can't really remember. I don't know that she's thought about it all that much yet, honestly, and I haven't asked."

I continue to be awed and, admittedly, the tiniest bit disapproving, of Rose's complete laissez-faire attitude toward parenting. It hasn't changed since the day we met, when she came to that Mommy and Me class without so much as a single wipe, and was completely unfazed by the fact that she had nothing with which to change a *very* dirty diaper.

In a culture of increasing helicopter parenting, Rose has continued to blithely orbit alone, scorning the mothers who hover, the ones who have cut-up carrot sticks in labelled Tupperware, who are sitting up straight in the first row for some third-grade music concert that she would find utterly tedious, phone at the ready to record every single second. Mothers, basically, like me.

Not that's she's been scornful about *me*. Yes, she laughs a little at my neat freakery, rolls her eyes when I tell Henry to tuck his shirt in, Finn to clear the table. But underneath that gentle mockery there has been, I've thought, a certain amount of admiration, maybe even a slight pang of envy.

Or so I've liked to believe.

Maybe Rose isn't bothered if her kids have a tantrum in public—"they're expressing their feelings"—or skip music lessons—"if they want to, they'll go"—or are on their phone for hours at a time—"I get to veg out, why shouldn't they?"—but underneath surely she's *wondered*?

Yet she always sounds so unbothered when she talks like this, so very *reasonable*, which makes me start to question, just a little, my own strict standards

But even if she thinks I'm too controlling with my children, and maybe I am, I can't help but feel just a little validated now, with Finn potentially destined for Princeton or Yale or, yes, *Harvard*, while Henry has made the Honor List every semester since fifth grade. Meanwhile, Bella has been, at best, a mediocre student with no future plans as of yet and Elspeth, although she gets good grades, has already been suspended twice for being rude to her teachers.

Admittedly, those aren't the only metrics by which you can measure the success of your parenting, of course they aren't, and if it's a competition—and it *isn't*—Rose would win hands down in terms of getting along with her kids. She's always been so close with both Bella and Elspeth, almost like an older sister to them, sharing their clothes, giving spontaneous hugs, falling about with laughter over some joke they've shared. I've never had that kind of closeness with either Finn or Henry, but then they're boys. I tell myself it's different.

Rose takes another sip of wine, and I realize she's not going to ask about Finn, or where he's applying to college. It's probably just as well; it might be awkward to mention his aspirations when Rose has basically just dismissed them for Bella. Still, I feel a little stung; she obviously doesn't care enough to want to know, and I realize that at this point, after months of pretty lukewarm overtures, this shouldn't even surprise me.

"How was Martha's Vineyard?" I ask instead. After Brad made it big, they bought a beach house outside of Edgartown, and they spend every August there. Brad plays golf and the girls take tennis lessons. I don't know what Rose does.

She shrugs, her gaze still on our children, standing by the shore. Finn has stopped skipping rocks and has moved closer to Bella, which heartens me. I think they might actually be talking to each other. Elspeth and Henry have wandered a little bit away, toward some rocks.

"It was fine. The usual."

I don't even know what that means. A few years ago, Rose made vague noises about having us come out there for a weekend. I leapt at the chance, was ready to nail down dates, but, as often seemed to be the case, it never came to anything and so we've never been. It reminds me, painfully, of how we'd begun to drift—not just over this last year, but even before then, perhaps. Friendships can slip in increments, so you don't really notice, or if you do, you can justify it—we're busy, life is hectic, the months slip past without us even realizing. It's only in moments like these that I am forced to acknowledge how much has changed. How far away I feel from Rose now.

"We had a week with my mom on Cape Cod at the beginning of August," I venture, and Rose finally turns to look at me.

"So close?" she says in surprise. "You should have come over for a visit."

I'm not sure how to reply, because while I had thought about it briefly, I'd decided against bothering Rose on her vacation—and that's what I was afraid it would feel like, *bothering*. Besides, Michael hadn't been keen and my mother can be a bit... astringent. It had all the makings of a disaster, and in the end I really wasn't sure Rose would want us to come.

"I thought you might be busy," I tell her, like an apology.

Rose sighs and rolls her eyes. "Actually, I find it all pretty boring up there. Brad plays golf *all* the time and the girls have their own thing." She smiles, the warmth of it reaching her eyes, lightening the brown to almost amber, reminding me of how she used to be, before she seemed so restless, before I started feeling like a burden. I haven't seen her smile like that, genuinely, in a long time. "You definitely should have come."

"Okay." I can't keep from sounding grateful, eager. "Next time, we will." I smile back, and Rose's own smile widens before it flickers and then dims, like a light bulb on the blink, and she looks away. Moment over.

I have never been under any delusion that Rose and I were truly equals in our friendship; she's richer, prettier, and far more popular—but when the kids were little, I felt I had more standing with her, more confidence. She looked to me to organize our outings; I was the one who brought out the Band-Aids or the diaper cream, who had enough change for vending machines or parking meters, who made sure everyone was slathered in sun cream for a day at the beach. "What would I do without you?" Rose would often say theatrically, her hand pressed to her heart, eyelashes fluttering, as I saved the day with my mini first-aid kit or half a dozen quarters. She hasn't said that in a long time. She hasn't had the opportunity.

"Burgers are ready," Brad calls, and I hurry to get out paper plates, napkins, the salads and the coleslaw. The kids come trooping up from the beach, looking marginally less sullen, which has to be a good thing. Bella and Finn are walking closer together, and Henry is smiling faintly at something Elspeth is saying. It fills my heart with hope, a ludicrous amount. *This is working*, I think, and it feels a bit like a miracle.

Maybe, I think, we can play a game after we eat—tag or hide-and-seek, something that doesn't require equipment. Or a word game, Ghost or I Went on a Picnic and I Brought A... I realize the games I am thinking of are more appropriate for six- rather than sixteen-year-olds, but I still hope they might work. Something to bring them together just a little bit more.

"Oh, your coleslaw," Rose says as she puts a big dollop on her plate. "I always love this."

"Really? I know the kids never eat it, but I always think it looks so pretty." I give a little laugh while Rose graces me with another one of her warm smiles. Usually I'm eating the red cabbage-and-apple coleslaw for a good week after this barbecue. I don't know why I keep making it; yes, it's pretty, but it's also a waste. It just feels like the kind of thing you should eat at a barbecue.

The kids load up their plates and, in one accord, move towards a jumble of rocks by the water to eat, seeming more or less happy to hang out together. Definitely a miracle, at least a minor one.

I glance at Michael to gauge his mood; he's listening to Brad drone on about something finance-related and while his expression is one of polite interest, I can sense his tension from across the picnic table, and I'm pretty sure I know its source. Ever since Brad made it big a couple of years ago, he's had a tendency to pontificate, like he's the fount of all wisdom when it comes to Wall Street and the business world. Considering he and Michael both work in finance, and both started in the same year, I can see how it could get a little irritating, especially as Michael is making about a tenth of what Brad is, or maybe even less.

Brad's tone is the perfectly grating combination of patronizing and smug; no wonder Michael has been reluctant to have get-togethers with him and Rose. He's never actually said he can't stand him, but I'm pretty sure it's true, which would sadden me, considering how much closer they were ten years ago, but I can't stand him either, not anymore. I'm really here for Rose. Rose and the kids.

She refills our wine glasses and moves to a separate picnic table from were Michael and Brad are sitting.

"Sometimes you just need a break from all that toxic masculinity," she tells me with a wink, but there's an edge to her voice that makes me wonder. Michael and I might struggle with Brad's pompous bonhomie, but I've always thought, at least in the past, that he and Rose have been pretty loved-up, often with their arms around each other, happy to touch and kiss in public in a way Michael and I never would—although maybe not so much in recent years. We haven't spent time together, all four of us, for me to really know.

Still, Brad's the kind of guy who pats his wife's butt in public, or calls her "the little wifey" like it's a joke, except I don't think it is, at least not entirely. Rose usually takes it in laughing stride, but sometimes I've wondered how she really feels about his attitude, considering the ardent feminist principles she's conveyed to me. "I want my girls to be *fierce*," she's told me on more than one occasion, usually after Elspeth has had some trouble at school.

"Anyway," she continues as we settle ourselves at the table with our food and glasses of wine, "I've been meaning to spend more time with you. I haven't been the best friend lately, I know that. I'm sorry. I should have asked about your mom." She purses her lips and shakes her head sorrowfully like some penitent sinner; Rose always did have a flair for the dramatic. I'm surprised she remembers that my mom was diagnosed with breast cancer eight months ago, but I am gratified that she thought to ask now. "How is she?"

"She's doing well. She's just got the all-clear after her last round of chemo." The trip to Cape Cod had been a celebration, although something of an awkward one, because the truth is, no one in my family actually gets along all that well with my mother, not even me, although I love her. At least, I try. She hasn't always been the easiest person to love, but that shouldn't matter, should it? No one ever said loving someone was easy, even if it's family. Especially if it, maybe. Wanting to reciprocate Rose's concern, I ask tentatively, "How are things between you and Brad?"

She gives me a sharp look, and belatedly I realize that asking about your mother is a little different than asking about your marriage.

A long time ago, when the kids were still little, Rose and I went out for cocktails—an evening of startling, intoxicating liberty in the midst of diaper changes and midnight feeds—and she asked me to "spill the secrets" of Michael's and my relationship.

"You guys are like peas in a pod, best friends," she'd said, the tiniest bit wistfully. "How do you do it?"

"Well, we are best friends," I'd answered, because Michael and I had been good friends all through college before we decided, after a rather methodical discussion, to date. It was a decision born of logic as much as love, but I've never thought that was a bad thing. "I think it's the best basis for a marriage," I told Rose, maybe a little sanctimoniously, because for once I felt like I had something that she didn't. I knew I wasn't as confident or carefree as she was; half an hour later, I was triple-checking my calculation of the tip while Rose flung a few bucks on the table, laughing at me. Story of our lives, of our friendship. So yes, I might have felt a little smug. Once.

"Better than a chat-up line at a nightclub in SoHo," Rose

had agreed with a laugh; that, I knew, was how she and Brad had met.

In any case, that conversation was a long time ago, and I don't think we've had a similar one since. Our marriages have been off limits, in some unspoken way, which I suppose makes me asking about it now all the more cringe-worthy. We talk about vacations and summer camps and the worst of the soccer moms with their fake smiles and glittery iPhones, but we haven't, I realized, talked about anything truly painful or real, at least not lately. Why did I ask?

I give her a weak smile of apology, silently offering some kind of out, but then she surprises me by answering.

"Do marriages have a sell-by date, like milk?" she wonders out loud. I can't quite decipher her tone, somewhere between sharp and playful. "Delicious when fresh," she continues, warming to her theme, "but utterly undrinkable once they go a little sour."

I open my mouth to reply, although I'm not even sure what I'm going to say, when she continues, her voice rising in stridency, although her expression is still playful, amused, albeit with a dangerous glitter to her eyes.

"Do you ever notice, with milk, that if you even suspect it's sour, the *faintest* whiff of something off, it becomes completely undrinkable? Elspeth asks me to sniff the milk when it's near the expiration date, and just the question makes me start to wonder. I can't drink it without gagging, no matter what it actually tastes like." She shakes her head, letting out a laugh that holds an edge. "Maybe marriages are the same."

I stare at her uncertainly, unable to figure out what she's trying to say.

"Or," she continues, her voice hardening, "maybe the milk really is sour, along with the marriage." She glances at me, her chin lifted, a defiant look in her eyes. "Does that answer your question?"

Um, sort of? I am perplexed as well as uncomfortable. I don't know what to do with this brittle Rose, sharp, glittering edges on display.

"Has something happened?" I finally ask, my tone cautious. Maybe it's the three—or is it four now?—glasses of wine, but Rose seems like she's in a dangerous mood.

"Does something *have* to happen?" she counters, before deflating suddenly, shoulders slumping as she stabs her coleslaw with her fork like she's trying to kill it. After a couple of attempts, she pushes her plate away as she lets out a long, weary breath. "I'm just so tired, Cara. Of everything. I'm really, really tired."

Tired? I school my expression into something like sympathy as I think of Rose's huge house in the swanky Green Farms neighborhood, in the oldest part of Westport, complete with tennis court and swimming pool. I think of the help she has, even though she doesn't have a job herself, at least not one outside the home—a cleaner comes in three times a week, and a gardening company manages the huge yard and the pool, plus she hires a private caterer for any parties or formal dinners. I think of the vacations she and her family take, several times a year—summers in Martha's Vineyard, skiing in Vail, beach trips to the Virgin Islands or Bali, a springtime jaunt to some cosmopolitan European capital. How can she possibly be *tired?*

Not that I'm actually envious. I've told Michael I wouldn't even want that much money; it certainly doesn't seem to have made either Rose or Brad any happier. I don't want Rose's life, not even a little—well, at least not *much*. I admit, it's hard not to feel a little stirring of envy when Rose texts me to cancel coffee because the girls have outgrown their ski boots and she simply *has* to take them shopping. Or she can't meet me for lunch because she's in an online queue for tickets to *Don Giovanni* at La Scala, in Milan.

I mean, if we really wanted trips to Vail or Europe, we could probably afford it, with some scrimping and saving. Last year, we went to Key West, after all, and we've got a fair amount in savings, a fact that pleases me far more than a trip to the opera or the ski slopes. I'm not sure Michael believes me, but I really do feel we have enough, more than enough: a nice four-bedroom split-level in a good neighborhood; money for a vacation every year or so; two cars; and, most of all, comfort and safety, which are more important to me than all the rest combined. After a childhood living from one paycheck to the next, the safety of that considerable amount in our savings account always gives me a warm glow of satisfaction, of relief.

"So what are you tired of, exactly?" I ask and Rose just shakes her head again, reaching once more for her wine.

"Oh, nothing," she replies dismissively. "And everything. If that makes sense. Just a general... malaise, I guess. A boredom, although that sounds too basic and blasé. Deeper than boredom, more of... an existential ennui." She lets out a laugh that makes me wonder if she's been teasing me the whole time, but then she glances up at me, a sudden, burning look in her eyes. "Don't you ever feel that, Cara? Don't you ever wonder if this really is all there is? To life? Get married, pop out a few kids, send out Christmas cards, circle stuff on the calendar, buy new clothes, eat at the latest restaurant, try to look like you're thirty-five instead of forty-eight, post it all on Facebook to prove you're enjoying every minute, rinse and repeat, *forever*."

I hesitate, not sure what the right answer is. What does she want to hear? What do I really feel? It's not, I know, a question I've ever felt the need to ask myself. I've been too busy—taking care of my kids, working full-time, and trying to help my mom, to worry about *existential ennui*. And, in any case, Rose's version of a rinse-and-repeat life is a lot different than mine.

"I..." Before I can say anything more, and I don't even know what I would say, a sudden sound has us both turning our heads. The noise was, I realize, Michael slamming his hand down hard on the picnic table while Brad looks on, bemused and more than a little drunk, beer in hand, his "Grilling Legend" apron spattered with meat juice.

"I've had enough of this crap," Michael snarls, and then he strides past us, away from the picnic tables, toward the parking lot.

CHAPTER 4

ROSE

What on earth has Brad done? Cara scrambles up from her seat as I turn to look questioningly at my husband, trying to clear my mind of the fuzziness that four glasses of wine has caused. What on earth was I blathering about to Cara?

"Michael...!" she calls, her voice turning shrill. "*Michael!*" And then she's running after him, and I am blinking blearily, because those glasses of wine really have made me more than a little buzzed, and I was the one who was supposed to be driving. Oops.

What the hell has happened, to have Michael storming off like a toddler who didn't get his favorite toy? That's not like him; he's more of a simmering anger kind of guy, keeps it in his eyes and his jaw. Brad is the one for the pointless, grand gestures.

I glance over at Cara and Michael huddled by their car, heads together, barely visible in the gathering shadows. Somehow the sun has set and I didn't even notice its rays over the Sound, the marvelous display of mauve and orange firing up the sky. I was too busy twittering about *existential ennui*, for heaven's sake. Cara probably thought I was both bonkers and annoying, and she would have been right. Too much time on my hands has made me boring, even to myself. It's hard to remember the woman I once was, before Brad, before kids, before my life derailed. I think of winning a scholarship to UConn to study marketing, of working hard, of wanting to get ahead. I feel a million miles from that stranger now, and I have for years. Decades.

I heave myself up from the bench and walk toward Brad, who is simply standing there, looking blank and not very bothered by the drama.

"What was that all about?" I ask.

"Hell if I know."

I roll my eyes at his stubborn ignorance. "*Brad.* Come on. Michael doesn't normally lose his temper like that." He usually just goes very quiet, quieter than usual, his mouth bracketed by deep lines of tension, a pot simmering, ready to boil.

Brad shrugs. "Guy's stressed about work. I gave him some advice and he didn't like it. I'm not surprised he hasn't been promoted, with an attitude like that. He has middle management written all over him. Fast train to nowhere. Or slow one. He's been there twenty years and he's still a nobody."

"And with an attitude like that, I'm not surprised he got angry." Ever since Brad became a millionaire, he's been pretty insufferably smug. He hides it with all the bonhomie and largesse, but it's there, and I'm sure Michael senses it. After three or four beers, Brad was probably more obvious—and more smug—than usual, doling out his unwanted financial advice. "Should we go?" I wonder aloud. It's only a little past eight, but it's already getting dark, and I realize I feel exhausted. I also realize I can't drive home in this state, and neither can Brad. I massage my temples, wishing I'd drunk less. Wanting to feel more capable and in control... the way, I imagine, Cara usually feels, although right now she's whispering furiously to Michael in the parking lot.

Brad shrugs and reaches for his beer. "No reason to ruin a perfectly good evening," he tells me, "now that the Johnstons are gone."

"*Brad.*"

"Um, I'm going to drive Michael home."

I turn to see Cara eyeing me, tense and unhappy, car keys in hand. Did she hear Brad's remark? I can't tell from her expression, but I think she might have.

"I'm so sorry, Cara. I don't know what happened—"

"Michael's been really stressed about work. This isn't your fault." She doesn't look at either Brad or me as she says this, and I don't think she believes it—or me. "But, you know, don't let us ruin your evening." There's a pointedness to the words that makes me think she *did* hear him say that, and I struggle not to wince. Cara nods over to the tumble of rocks where the kids are all stretched out on the sand. In a taut moment of silence, their laughter drifts on the breeze, and it feels like the only good thing about tonight. How did it all go so wrong, so quickly? "They're all finally having fun," Cara says quietly. "And that's what this is about, right? Getting them together? They were such good friends, once."

Her tone is so sad that, in my drunken state, tears sting my eyes. We've lost so much, over the years, simply to time. Or was it more than that?

"You guys stay, and they can, too," she states firmly. "I can come back and pick them up a little bit later, after I've dropped Michael off at home."

"Don't rush back," I say impulsively. We both glance again at the four of them, chatting together, the last of the sunset gilding them in gold. "If they're having a good time."

"All right." Her expression softens briefly, and I know we're both thinking about the old days, imbuing them, perhaps, with more warmth and fun than they ever possessed, but right now it's hard not to. "I can drop Bella and Elspeth back at your house when I come back, if you guys decide to leave earlier. I'll pick up all my picnic stuff then. They should be okay here on their own for an hour or so, right?"

I know this is her diplomatic way of letting me know she thinks I'm too drunk to drive, and that there is no way is she going to let her children—or mine—in my car.

"That's very kind," I say, making sure to enunciate clearly. "We might take a cab home, in a little bit. If they're having fun, the kids should definitely stay. They'll be fine." This is my diplomatic way of letting her know I wouldn't drive my kids, either. I may be a little more laidback than Cara, but I'm not insane.

She nods once, the car keys still clutched in her hand. For a second, she looks as if she wants to say something more, but then she just gives a little shake of her head and turns quickly on her heel. In moments, she is swallowed up by the darkness; a few seconds after that, I hear their car start, then the crunch of tires on gravel, and then they're gone.

"Well." I turn to Brad. "That was awkward in the extreme."

"Oh, come on, babe. Good riddance, I say. We haven't really been friends with them for years. They're both so uptight."

"That may be true," I allow, because frankly it's hard to argue otherwise, "but Cara is my friend." Talking to her tonight reminded me of how much I actually like about her. Yes, she is intense and she can be hard work, but she is earnest and well-meaning and she really listens... which is more than I can say for my husband.

"Well, Michael was never mine," Brad replies carelessly. "You kept pushing us together like we were in first grade or something, but we're too different, Rose."

"You used to do stuff together."

"Only because you made us."

I'm pretty sure my husband is engaging in some revisionist history. Back when he and Michael were both early-career analysts, on a more level playing field, they got along much better. They were never going to be best friends, it's true, but they could crack open a beer and shoot the breeze for an hour or two, easily. They respected each other, but now that Brad has positioned himself as the expert, it's no longer equal. Michael resents his superiority, and Brad resents Michael for not showing a little more awe at his success.

"What did you say to him?" I press, and Brad shrugs.

"What does it matter?" His bonhomie is fast evaporating, revealing the expected surliness underneath. "He was going to get annoyed, no matter what. It was just a matter of time. The guy's a loser."

"*Brad.*" I don't entirely disagree, but it's still not nice to say out loud. Besides, when it comes to marriages, I think Brad and I are the losers, not that he'd ever admit that, or even realize it. I'm sure Brad thinks our marriage is fine, and for him, it probably is. He's getting everything he wants, after all.

I blow out a breath as I glance towards the dark expanse of water, no more than a gentle, shooshing sound and a gleam of silver in the moonlight. My head is aching, and I'm moved from that happy-and-buzzed state to just feeling tired and old. I want to go home.

"I'll call a cab," I decide out loud, managing to keep my voice firm. "Let's call it at a night. We can pick the car up in the morning. Cara's going to pick up the kids later, anyway, if they stay here." I glance toward the water, but I can't even see them now, although I hear the distant murmur of their voices, Bella's laugh, Finn's rumble of an answer. Good. They're getting along. That's something, at least.

"Fine by me." Brad shrugs, indifferent now.

My head is starting to pound. I begin to pack up our drinks and the leftover meat, not wanting to leave it all for Cara to clean up. How did this evening go south so quickly and completely? And just when the kids were getting along, and

Cara and I were starting to reconnect. I know Michael can be hard work, just like Cara can, but I still blame Brad for starting this, whatever it turns out to be. I have no idea what riled Michael up, but I can imagine it. *What you really need to do, Mike, is…*

"Hey, are we leaving already?" Bella sounds surprised and a little bit alarmed and I turn to her with a tired smile.

"The grownups are having an early night," I reply teasingly. "But you guys can stay, if you want. Would you like that? Cara said she could pick you later."

"She can?" Bella's tone gives nothing away; I can't tell if this is seen as good news or not.

"You guys are having fun, aren't you?"

"Uh, yeah. I guess." Bella sounds shy rather than skeptical; if it wasn't so dark, I'd wonder if she was blushing. Does she have a crush on Finn, after all these years? He's a good-looking guy, no doubt, but then she's beautiful, too. The golden couple that never got together.

"All right, then," I tell her. "Knock yourselves out. Cara will be back later, maybe around ten, but you can text her if you want to leave earlier."

Bella's gaze widens. "But I don't have her number."

"Finn will. I'm sure it will be fine." Somewhat recklessly, I take a six-pack of beer from the cooler and snap off two. "One for you and one for Finn, okay? That's it, though."

She takes the beer from me, smiling incredulously. "Thanks, Mom."

I shrug, always happy to be the cool mom, the one who knows seventeen-year-olds are going to drink and is willing to accommodate them… to a degree. I doubt Cara would approve, but she probably thinks Finn sticks to Sprite when he goes out. "Have fun, sweetheart. I love you."

Bella goes skipping back to the others with her two beers,

the picture of easy, ebullient youth, and with a weary sigh, I take my phone out to call a cab.

By the time the cab comes twenty minutes later, Brad is in a bad mood and so am I. I packed up all of Cara's stuff, putting her dishes back in the picnic basket, while Brad, with ill grace, got rid of the trash, no doubt feeling put upon, although maybe that's unfair. In the dark quiet of my own mind, I tend to tar him with the worst possible motives. He was probably just feeling wasted and worn out, the same as I was. What a pair.

Whatever the case, we ride in silence back to the house; it's not even nine, but I feel exhausted, sticky from the sea breeze, my stomach sloshing unpleasantly from the wine. Back home, I put away the picnic things in the kitchen while Brad disappears to his study. All around me, the house yawns, empty and dark and foreign, even though we've lived here for four years.

When we bought this place, we hired an interior decorator to help "make it cozy," but the result is it has never quite felt like home. The kitchen is too big; a huge marble island the size of a small swimming pool, the breakfast table a good fifty feet from the fridge. Why do people need so much space? It just makes you feel more alone, stumbling through the emptiness.

The adjoining family room is Americana-themed in a way that is definitely *not* me—pillows emblazoned with American flags, black and white photographs of old pickup trucks parked in long grass, baskets of apples next to bales of hay. It looks homey, but I feel like I live in a hotel. Which, I suppose, is my fault, since I never said no to any of it—not the house décor, not the country club membership, not the tennis tournaments, not the endless dinners with business associates and their boring wives.

At the start, I made fun of it all, at least in my mind. I didn't think Brad and I would ever actually become like the people we'd once disdained—too rich for their own good, smarmy instead of smart. We were a parody of them, laughing into our sleeves, but over the last five years or so, there has been a subtle yet seismic shift, and instead of being a parody of the people we deride, we have become a parody of ourselves.

I'm meant to be free, fun-loving, a little bit wild, cheerfully reckless and always up for a laugh. That's who I became after college, when I realized being the good girl didn't get you anything except the worst kind of heartache, unbearable disappointment, and blame for things that were most definitely not your fault. That's who I try to be now, but it feels like a costume I put on, a garish, painted mask that no longer fits. Inside, I've become just another tennis-playing trophy wife, booking my Botox appointments and quietly becoming more bitter.

Maybe *that's* why I've drifted away from Cara—because I don't want her to see the me I've become. When we met all those years ago, I really was the fun one, without a care in the world, blithe and happy and free, or at least pretending to be, and doing a much better job of it. I loved having babies, as tiring as it was; I loved their exuberance, their easy love. I know I was a little bit scatterbrained about it all, but I don't think Cara ever doubted how much I loved my daughters, and how much they loved me. Love me still, although teenagers show it in such a different way, which is, generally, not very much. In any case, I don't want Cara to see me any differently now. I definitely don't want her to feel sorry for me.

And why should she, when my life looks so charmed from the outside? Not that I want her to be envious, not exactly.

It takes me a few seconds, as I stare out at the backyard cloaked in darkness, moonlight glinting off the swimming pool, to realize that I actually might be envious of *her*.

But no, that's ridiculous. There's no reason to envy Cara. Yes, Finn and Henry are paragons in school—smart, accomplished, driven, with Finn playing varsity in three sports. But so what? He definitely can be arrogant sometimes, and Henry is pretty geeky, not, of course that there's anything wrong with that. But still, I've got two wonderful daughters—smart and sassy Elspeth and beautiful Bella. I am definitely not envious of Cara's children.

And as for her marriage? Yes, she and Michael have always seemed solid, although, in truth, they were a little bit strained tonight, but maybe that's because of us. Brad doesn't even bother to hide his irritation anymore, and I don't think I did such a good job of it, either. In the past, though, they've definitely been comfortable together; they made marriage look easy, the way they'd finish each other's sentences, or exchange laughing looks like they didn't even need to say whatever it was out loud. But lately Michael can be such a downer, and Cara has started to seem so tense—and I can understand why, working full-time, taking care of her mother, getting the boys up early for piano practice or gym workouts. She's made a rod for her own back with all that, and yes, some people might think it's worth it, but that kind of grind definitely isn't for me. Maybe it isn't for Cara, either.

I take my phone out of my pocket, wondering if I should message her. *Sorry it all went south—hope you guys are okay...??* I type it out and then stare at the message before slowly, letter by letter, I delete it. I'll let Michael cool down before I message about that, I decide, although I'm not sure that's the real reason. Instead, I send a quick, bland message, letting her know that Brad and I have left and the kids will need to be picked up. I tell myself I can talk to Cara face to face when she drops off Bella and Elspeth, which is surely better than an awkwardly apologetic text.

I hope the kids at least are having fun. I'm a little surprised Cara agreed to let them stay at the beach, to be honest; she can be pretty uptight about stuff like that, but I suppose it is still early and if they're all together, they won't come to any harm. Besides, in this world it's different for boys than girls. It's not meant to be, it shouldn't be, and yet it is. I wonder if Cara will ever understand that. Not the way I do, in any case, but I'm hardly going to be worried about Bella and Finn or Elspeth and Henry tonight, not when they'd known each other practically since they were born.

I hear footsteps and I turn slightly to see Brad standing in the doorway to the kitchen, scratching his stomach, looking bleary-eyed.

"I'm going to bed," he says, with a huge yawn. "You coming?"

It's a bit early for bed, but he did have a lot to drink.

"I'll wait till Cara drops Elspeth and Bella home."

He shrugs, lets out another yawn. "Okay, whatever."

I listen to his slow, heavy footsteps through the kitchen, the hall, up the stairs, and then the creak of our bedroom door. I close my eyes. *This isn't the life I ever imagined for myself.*

The thought slips through my mind like quicksilver, swift and sly. Pointless, too, because it might not be the life I imagined for myself, but it's the life I have. I have to make the best of it, for Bella and Elspeth's sakes. At least for now.

But such noble, self-sacrificing altruism doesn't sit easily with me, the way it would with Cara, although, if I force myself to be honest, I know it isn't altruism that is keeping me with my husband; it's more like pride. I don't want to admit my marriage may have been a mistake. I don't want other people to know the ugly details of our personal lives, which would inevitably come out if we split up. And sometimes I think I still love Brad, in a weary, defeated sort of way. I remember when he was young and fun; there was an easy innocence to his exuberance, a genuineness, just as there was to me. We were good together, once.

I recall the night I met him, at that club in SoHo, the latest hotspot for upwardly mobile twentysomethings, which I pretended to be. I actually just had a lame job in marketing and a decent wardrobe, a sparkling laugh and a quick sense of humor, but that was more than enough to gain me entry into that dubious group.

I was chatting to my friends by the bar when Brad came up to order a round for his table. He gave me a look of frank admiration, no hiding it at all, and I smiled back at him, a bit of a challenge, a bit of an invitation. That was who I was back then. Who I was determined to be.

"Are you the kind of woman who lets a stranger buy her a drink?" he asked, and of all the things I could have taken away from that statement, I decided to be impressed that he'd called me a woman rather than a girl. A low bar, indeed, although, in retrospect, maybe not. I do think he was genuine, or at least *more* genuine, back then. It's hard not to shade the past with the bleak colors of the present.

The truth is, we've both become jaded, faded, and old—is that simply what happens as you age? And if it's happened to me as well as Brad, why would I leave him? Not to mention the lifestyle I resent yet whose perks I still enjoy. For all my carefree confidence, I don't feel brave enough to venture out of my own, and I've barely let myself think about it. And Brad knows I'll never leave him, for just that reason, which gives him all the license he'd ever need.

I just have to learn to put up with it all better—not in public, which I mastered a long time ago—tonight's conversation with Cara one notable exception—but in private, when it can be so much harder. For my daughters' sakes.

Although surely the last thing you want for your daughters is for them to marry someone like their dad.

A sigh escapes me as I stare out at the yard.

I don't know how long I stand there, gazing into the dark nothingness, but eventually a yellow wash of headlights slides across the adjacent dining room's floor and I hear the sound of a car door opening and closing. Bella and Elspeth are home, and I'll need to put on a friendly face for Cara.

CHAPTER 5

CARA

"I don't want to talk about it," Michael says in a tight voice as I get into the driver's seat. He's staring out the window, his face angled away from me. I remain silent as I start the car and reverse out of the parking spot. I'm not about to force a confrontation. That's something I never try to do.

"I told Rose I'd pick the kids up in an hour or so," I say once we're on Compo Road, heading home. "I'll drop Elspeth and Bella back at their house after."

"Fine."

I glance sideways at Michael; his arms are folded, his jaw tight. "Brad can be a complete ass sometimes," I say quietly. "I know that."

Michael doesn't reply, just gives a jerky little nod, but it feels like enough. I won't press now; there's no point. The evening has been completely and comprehensively ruined, at least for the adults, but maybe the kids can still have a good time. I imagine Rose and Brad will head home pretty soon, so the kids might be on their own for a bit. I wouldn't normally let them hang out at the beach unsupervised; Henry is only four-teen, after all, and he can get pretty anxious about stuff. But with Finn there, I'm sure things will be fine, and it feels important and even necessary that someone has fun tonight. That the evening is redeemed, if only a little bit.

Michael and I don't say anything else for the rest of the ten-minute drive back home. As soon as I pull into the drive, he gets out and marches to the front door; by the time I get inside, he's already ensconced in his study, door firmly closed. Once, we would have been able to laugh about something like this, or if not laugh, then at least commiserate. *He really is insufferable, isn't he? Where's the pin, because his head seriously needs deflating.* The next time we saw Rose and Brad, it would have been fine. Brad would have started pontificating once more about his expertise and Michael and I would have exchanged a silent, laughing look, defusing any tension, making it something we shared. He certainly wouldn't have blown up the way he did tonight, and I wouldn't be tiptoeing around the house the way I am now.

But it didn't happen that way, and so I drift around the kitchen, wiping work surfaces and tidying up more than I need to. The house feels so empty, although I know it shouldn't, not really, not more than usual, anyway. Finn often goes out on a weekend, although he has a strict eleven o'clock curfew. Henry rarely goes out, but on a weekend night he'd as likely be closeted up in his bedroom as not, and Michael works in his study, so I'd spend the evening alone, reading or watching TV. At least for the last year or so.

Wistfully, I think of the weekend evenings in the past when Michael and I would binge a Netflix series over a bottle of wine; sometimes Henry would join us, or even Finn. We'd sit on the sofa with our legs tangled up, relaxed and a little sleepy, sometimes offering a witty remark about the show; Michael has—or at least had—a very dry sense of humor. Where has that gone? Where has it all gone?

Eventually, I curl up in a corner of the sofa, half-watching some documentary on PBS and intermittently checking my phone. I was expecting, or at least hoping for, Rose to text either an apology or explanation, but she's just sent a message about the kids, how she and Brad have left, just like I thought they would, and thanking me for picking them up. Maybe I should have messaged first, but I don't even know what I'd say. How can I apologize when I don't even know what happened? And yet Michael was the one who lost his temper, who stormed off. Maybe I should be the one to say sorry, but for some reason I can't make myself. I suppose I should talk to Michael first, figure out what happened, but I have no energy for that now, and I know he doesn't either.

The better part of an hour drifts by without anything from the kids, and so at quarter to ten, I decide it's time to pick them up. I uncurl myself, stretch, and grab my car keys. On the way out, I tap on the study door.

"Michael? I'm going to get the kids."

"Okay, fine." He sounds distracted, and I sigh under my breath before I turn for the front door.

When I get to the beach, the parking lot has emptied out and the stretch of sand is barren, gilded in silver. I climb out of the car, scanning the shadowy rocks and dips, but the beach isn't that big and I can't see anyone. My stomach gives an unpleasant little roil; where are they? Why did I think letting them stay out was a good idea?

I walk over to the picnic area, empty now, and find my basket and bag all packed up, tucked under a table. Rose must have done that, and I am grateful for the consideration. But the kids aren't anywhere to be seen. I do a slow 360, straining my eyes in the darkness to catch sight of them, but everything is eerily still and quiet. My heart judders in my chest. *Where are they?*

Then I hear the creak of the swings, and I spin toward the

playground on the other side of the parking lot, its wooden towers and slides just bulky shapes in the darkness.

"Finn?" I call. "Henry?"

The only sound is the squeak of the swing, and it makes the hairs on the back of my neck stand up. There's something decidedly creepy about listening to that sound, while standing alone in the dark.

I walk slowly toward the playground, and the sound of the swing. "Elspeth? Bella?"

It isn't until I've reached the playground that I see who it is —Elspeth, sitting on a swing, her eyes gleaming like a cat's in the darkness.

"Elspeth." My voice comes out a little shaky as I expel a sigh of relief. "Why didn't you answer me?"

"I didn't hear you." The words are so swift and so glib, I am sure she's lying.

I've never really been able to totally get Elspeth. As a little kid, she was quiet and watchful, taking everything in. Around six or so, she started with the whip-smart wisecracks, and at that tender age they were clever and funny enough that the butt of her jokes, even if they were an adult, would just laugh it off. She loved darting into the center of attention, and then backing away quickly, once she'd fired off her repartees, leave everyone both stinging and smiling. Rose thought she was tremendous, her clever, clever girl, even if that cleverness held a hint of cruelty, or at least a cutting perceptiveness.

"Where is everyone else?" I ask her, and she shrugs. "*Elspeth.*" My voice comes out a little school-teacherish, and even in the dark I see her eyes narrow, her mouth purse. She keeps swinging. "It's late, and I'm taking you all home," I tell her, a definite edge to my voice. "Where is everybody?" That creeping sense of unease is taking over me again, pooling in my stomach, prickling the back of my neck. Am I overreacting? "Elspeth?"

She rises from the swing in one graceful movement and starts walking toward the parking lot, her long, brown ponytail swishing across her back. "I don't know," she calls back indifferently. "They were all down by the beach."

I try for a friendlier tone as I follow her out of the playground. "What have you guys been doing?"

Another shrug.

"Have you been having fun?"

"You could say that," Elspeth tosses over her shoulder, and I can't tell if she is being sarcastic or not.

"Why don't you wait by the car," I instruct, a bit severely. "I'll find the others."

"The last I saw them, they were by the rocks. Bella and Finn, anyway. I don't know where Henry went."

Why did they all go their separate ways, I wonder as I hurry toward the beach. That was definitely *not* the plan. Did something happen?

When I get closer to a jumble of rocks by the shoreline, I see them, and my stomach cramps. I'm not sure what's wrong, only that something is. Finn is slumped against a rock, his head lolling against his chest, and Bella is a few feet away from him, curled up in a ball, her back to him, her arms hugging her knees.

"Finn?" I call sharply. "Bella?"

Finn lifts his head and blinks at me blearily. "Hey... Mom," he slurs, and I stiffen in shock.

"You're *drunk*."

He lets out a laugh that turns into a burp, and his chin bobs toward his chest again.

I turn toward Bella, who hasn't moved. "Bella? Are you okay?"

She lifts her head to give me just as bleary a look as Finn did. "I don't feel well. I want to go home," she says in a small, wretched voice. I look around to see if she's been sick, but I can't tell in the dark.

"That's where we're going," I say briskly, caught between anger, exasperation, and a grudging sympathy because she really does look miserable. How much did they drink, and where on earth did they get it? They've only been on their own for a little over an hour. "Where's Henry?" I ask, and neither of them reply. "Wait here," I instruct, and then I stride off down the beach, looking for my son.

I am cross that Finn and Bella both got drunk, and angry with myself that I enabled it by letting them stay at the beach. I know what Rose would say—*they're seventeen, they're allowed to let loose a little, Cara!*—but it still goes against every parenting instinct I possess. And neither of them seems particularly happy right now, so if this is what letting loose looks like, I'll pass, and so will my kids.

"Henry?" I call into the darkness. "*Henry!*"

The only sound is the whisper of the water against the sand.

It takes me five more minutes to find him, at the far end of the beach, huddled against the pier, looking wretched.

I drop down to my knees in front of him. "Henry." I take him by the shoulders, meaning to hug him, but then I peer into his face instead, and see that it is blotchy. "Are you okay?"

"I want to go home." When he speaks, his voice is small, like a child's, and I smell beer on his breath. My concern turns to fury.

"You were drinking, too?" I demand in disbelief. He's *fourteen.*

"Finn brought a bunch of beers."

"Finn..." For some reason, I'd assumed, on a subconscious level, that Bella must have provided the alcohol, maybe because of Rose's permissiveness, so different from my own parenting. But it was *Finn*? My son? Maybe I shouldn't be surprised; he's almost eighteen, after all, and I know he's not perfect. I'm not one of those mothers who thinks their kids never steps a toe out of line. At least, I never thought I was, although in this moment my certainty is rocked. "Henry," I say, caught between being gentle, because he looks so miserable, and cross, because he drank alcohol. "You know better. Honestly. I know you do."

Has Elspeth had something to drink, too? Was that why she was so blasé about it all? A groan of frustration escapes me as I help Henry up to his feet. This was not what I'd hoped for this evening at *all*.

"Come on," I say, a little brusquely, and then try to gentle my voice. "We're going home."

Somehow, over the course of the next fifteen minutes, I manage to get all four kids and the picnic stuff in the car. Finn and Bella are both falling-down drunk, or nearly, stumbling over their own feet as I help them toward the parking lot. Bella looks near tears, Finn just out of it. Henry is silent and morose, trailing along behind me, his head lowered, his bangs sliding into his face. Elspeth marches ahead, arms folded, looking a little smug; I think she's the only one who didn't drink anything, or if she did, I can't tell, which doesn't actually surprise me. Of course Elspeth would keep her cool.

"Okay." I breathe out a sigh of relief when they're all in the minivan, slumped in their seats, miserably silent. I glance in the rear-view mirror as I head out to Compo Road; Finn is sprawled in his seat, leaning his head back, his mouth agape. I think he might actually be snoring. Henry has scooted over to the side, as far away from Elspeth as possible, looking determinedly out the window. Elspeth still has her arms folded, and she is staring out the other window, a faraway look on her face. Next to me, in the passenger seat, Bella is curled up, her head on her knees, her eyes scrunched closed, as if she is trying to make herself as small as possible.

I take a couple of even breaths as I start driving down the road. This doesn't have to be such a big deal, I tell myself. They had a few beers; it happens. They will all have headaches in the morning, save Elspeth, perhaps, so lesson learned. I'll have to talk to Finn about bringing the beers—where did he get them? The stores around here are pretty strict about checking ID. Unless he has a fake ID? The thought makes my stomach cramp. That is not who I raised my son to be, and yet Rose would probably tell me to stop being so naïve. *Of course he has a fake ID, Cara. He's seventeen!*

Like his age excuses everything.

"We'll drop Elspeth and Bella off first," I say, sounding like a tour guide, although I doubt any of them are really listening. I'll have to tell Rose that I found them drunk, although she'll be able to guess for herself soon enough. I doubt she'll even be angry or surprised; I'm the one who has absurdly high standards, who can be so easy to shock.

When I pull up in front of the Rosses' house, I see that all the lights are off, and I wonder if Rose and Brad have both gone to bed, but then Rose comes out the front door, and by the time I've gotten out of the car, she's on the driveway, next to my car.

"Welcome back!" she calls merrily, her voice a little too bright, her smile pinned onto her face. In a flash, I remember all the acrimony that led us to leaving the kids alone at the beach—Michael walking out, Brad probably being a jerk, both Rose and Brad having had too much to drink. I'm certainly not going to mention any of that now. "Did you have a nice time?" she asks the kids.

"They're drunk," I state flatly, and Rose raises her eyebrows, bemused.

"After just one beer?"

"They definitely had more than one beer." I take a breath, wondering if I should admit now that Finn brought the beer, but this doesn't feel like the right moment. We'll have to have a postmortem about this evening at some point, or maybe we won't. Maybe we'll just let it slip into the past, everything unsaid. That seems the more likely option, considering how our friendship has drifted.

"Come on, sweetie," Rose says as she helps Bella out of the car. Bella lets out a choked cry and flings her arms around her mother, burying her face in her shoulder. Rose glances at me, her bemusement turning to concern as she hugs her daughter back, although she's still trying to act easy and relaxed. "Bed, I think. And a glass of water and some ibuprofen." She rubs Bella's back the way you would a small child's and then she guides her into the house, her arm around her shoulders, while Elspeth follows alone.

I stand there for a moment, wondering if Rose is going to come back to say goodbye, but she doesn't, and after another few seconds, I climb in the car to drive home. Finn has fallen asleep and Henry is still staring out the window, determinedly staying in his own world. I am too tired to give them either a lecture or sympathy, and so we drive in silence.

Back home, I make both boys drink a glass of water each and take some Tylenol. I watch them sip from their glasses, knowing now is really not the time for a lecture and yet, despite my own fatigue, not quite able to simply let it go.

"We'll talk about this in the morning," I tell Finn, who still looks pretty out of it. "You can be sure of that." He doesn't reply, and I turn to Henry. "And you, too. Both of you should know better. Both of you *do* know better."

Still silence.

With a sigh, I hand them their medicine, watch them swallow it down, and then tell them to get ready for bed. It's past eleven now and I'm exhausted.

When I head upstairs, I see that Michael is already asleep, snoring softly. I wonder what his take on this evening will be; he's always been supportive of my decision to push the boys— music lessons, extra homework, discipline. In the past, he was more of an enforcer, but lately he's only offered half-hearted backup, although considering what happened tonight, maybe he'll come down hard. Underage drinking could, potentially, get Finn in trouble at school and suspended from the soccer team.

I strip off my clothes and pull on my pajamas, brush my teeth and wash my face and climb into bed. I wonder if I'll be able to sleep, with everything that has gone on, but I drift off almost immediately, too drained to sift through the evening's events. Everything can wait for tomorrow.

And tomorrow comes soon enough; sunlight is filtering through the curtains and Michael is still asleep next to me when I hear a hammering on the front door, jerking me wide awake. It's a little after eight, which is late for me, but I feel groggy, as if I drank as much as everyone else did.

As the hammering continues, I hurry out of bed, pull on an old sweatshirt over my pajamas and head downstairs. The boys are still asleep, their bedroom doors closed, although this racket will surely wake them up. Who on earth is knocking so loudly and long, and at such an early hour?

I open the door, surprise flashing through me when I see who is there.

"Rose..."

My friend's golden hair is wild all about her face, and her expression is one of unbridled anger, eyes flashing, chest heaving, mouth pursed. *What on earth...?* "Cara," she says, and her tone is grim, purposeful, but also furious. "We need to talk."

CHAPTER 6

ROSE

I stand in the doorway with my fists clenched as my heart races. I am practically vibrating with anger, dizzy with rage and sick with heartache. Cara, looking more bemused than shocked, nods slowly and steps aside to let me through. I came here without thinking through what I would say, how I would handle this, only feeling that I needed to do something—immediately. Right now, I want to hit something, hurt someone. I'm so angry, I feel as if I could spit or scream or grab Cara by the shoulders and shake her till her teeth rattled. Yet it's not her fault; I'm not going to blame the parents for the sins of their children.

On second thought, maybe I am.

"Come back to the kitchen," Cara says as she starts down the hall, leaving me to follow. "Everyone's still asleep. Do you want some coffee while we talk?" She glances back at me over her shoulder, eyebrows raised, like this is any ordinary Saturday morning, not that I come over to her house all that much. In fact, I can't even remember the last time I've been here; Cara always came to mine, back when coffee mornings and lazy after-noon playdates were a regular occurrence. Does she not see how furious I am? Or realize how serious this is? Her blasé attitude only stokes the fire of my rage.

"I don't want any coffee," I practically spit out.

Cara reaches for the pot and starts filling it with water. "Well, I'm afraid I do." She stands at the sink, her back to me, while I choke on my fury, hardly able to believe she can be so calm about this. She seems to be unsurprised that I am here, or even that I have something to talk about, so does that mean she knows? And if so, why isn't she freaking out, either tripping over herself to apologize, or, the more likely scenario, cowering because of my anger?

"Look," she says, her back still to me, "I'm sorry about Finn. I didn't realize... well. He told me last night what he did. And of course I don't condone it. At all." She glances at me as she goes to fill the coffeemaker, her forehead furrowed as she takes in my glare. "Although, truthfully, I didn't expect you to be so angry about it."

What? Can we possibly be talking about the same thing? For both our sakes, I really hope not.

"Not angry?" I manage to choke out. "Cara, do you actually know why I'm here? Did Finn tell you?"

She frowns and reaches for the canister of coffee. "Henry did."

Henry? He knew? *Saw?*

I unclench my fists as I force myself to speak calmly, even though my heart is still juddering in my chest. "I need you to know this is completely and utterly unacceptable and I am talking with Bella about going to the police."

Cara turns around to stare at me, an expression of complete confusion on her face, the canister of coffee forgotten in her hand. "The *police?* Rose, come on. Don't you think that's a bit much?"

I take a deep breath, let it out. She can't know, surely.

Surely. Because if this is her response… "Cara," I ask again, "do you know why I'm here?"

"Because Finn brought the beers." She shakes her head. "I don't even know where he got them—"

"I am not here because of the beers." Although I didn't know that Finn had brought some, along with the two I gave Bella. They must have drunk them all, to have been so out of it. That and then some, probably. I was as naïve as Cara, I realize, in my own insouciant way.

Cara's forehead crinkles, her eyes narrowed. "What…" Slowly, she shakes her head. "Why…"

"I am here," I state clearly, enunciating every word with cutting precision, "because last night Finn sexually assaulted my daughter."

Cara's face drains of color in a way that would almost be funny, in any other situation. It's like a cartoon, how white she goes, and how quickly, like the way you erase an Etch-a-Sketch. Her eyes are wide and dazed, her mouth hanging open as she stares at me for a long, tense moment.

"What…" The word escapes her in a long, low breath. "No."

"*Yes.* Bella told me what happened this morning. She was extremely upset, as you can imagine." To put it mildly. My poor daughter was *broken*, too shocked and traumatized even to cry, confessing what happened in shattered whispers, burying her head into my shoulder the way she used to when she was little girl.

I held her in my arms as pain and panic rushed through me, and I promised her I'd make this right. As right as I can, although I know—of course I know—the terrible damage has already been done. *Damn* Finn. Damn his unacceptable, arrogant attitude, assuming everything and everyone is his for the taking, simply because he's such a golden boy. And Cara enabled that attitude, I know she did—so, yes, maybe I do blame her. Her and Michael, along with the crazy culture that encourages this kind of behavior, the whole damned world.

Cara shakes her head, a slow, dazed back and forth. The canister of coffee has tilted, forgotten, in her slackened hand, dark granules spilling across the floor. "Finn?" she says disbelievingly. "No."

Her refusal to believe is understandable, but it still enrages me. Does she actually think Bella is lying about this?

"Yes, *Finn*," I reply as evenly as I can. "And I will do my utmost to make sure he's prosecuted."

If possible, Cara goes even paler. She puts the canister of coffee back on the counter, braces her hands against the granite. "Rose, wait. Let's think about this rationally. I know you're upset, and Bella's upset—"

"This isn't some tussle over toys, Cara," I cut across her, my voice hard. "We are talking about a criminal offense."

She takes a deep breath and lets it out slowly as she screws the lid back on the coffee. "Yes, I understand that," she says slowly. Calmly. "I do. But I'm the one who picked them up yesterday, I saw them at the beach, and they were both really, really drunk. Barely able to string two words together—"

"What does that have to do with anything?" I demand. If she's going to try to put the blame on my daughter simply because she was drinking, I am *really* going to hit the roof.

"Only that their memories might be..." Cara searches for a word, looking around the kitchen as if she'll find it somewhere. "Foggy."

Foggy? Seriously? "I think my daughter knows when someone is putting a hand up her shorts," I snap. "And lying on top of her, grinding in to her."

For a second, Cara looks as if she might be sick. She wraps one hand around her waist, as if she has to physically keep herself together. "Finn didn't do those things," she whispers. "He wouldn't."

"And yet Bella says he did."

"Yes, but..."

"*But?*" I repeat scathingly. She is *not* going to go there. I will not let her make excuses for her son's behavior, imply that Bella is lying simply because Cara can't believe her precious son is capable of assaulting a woman. God knows what else he gets up to.

Cara looks as if she might cry, blinking rapidly as if to hold back tears. "Let me talk to Finn," she says after a second, her voice choked. "There might be some explanation that we can't think of right now."

"What explanation could there possibly be, besides the one Bella gave? She woke up to Finn lying on top of her, groping her, and she had to shove him off, crying." I am trembling with my anger, my stomach roiling as I think of my daughter having to endure such an assault, frightened and alone, crying for help... It sickens me. Shames me, because I should have been there. Somehow, *somehow* I should have prevented this from happening.

And, on top of all that, it makes the memories rush up, which only makes everything about this harder.

"She woke up?" Cara's eyes, still glassy with tears, now narrow a little. "You mean she was... she was passed out from drinking too much?"

"Are you implying something?" I retort in a dangerously pseudo-pleasant voice. "Do you actually think his attack might be justified in any way, because she was drunk, just as he was?"

"No, no..." Cara's hands flutter by her sides. "Of course I don't think that, not..." She stops that train of thought, thankfully, because I think I might scream if she starts talking about how Bella might have been asking for it. "I think we need to take a step back from this, Rose," she says instead, "and think calmly, instead of just... reacting. And I do want to hear what Finn has to say... his side of the story."

"There is only one side to this kind of story," I tell her flatly. "There is absolutely no reason Finn could possibly give that would in any way justify him assaulting my daughter while she was unconscious and unable to give her consent. You *know* that, Cara. I know you do."

I know she wants to defend her son, I understand the impulse, but I also know she's a person who has always, pretty desperately, wanted to do the right thing. I hope she realizes what the right thing is now.

"Still," Cara repeats stubbornly, her chin lifting a little. "You can't accuse and convict him without even hearing his side. Or what about Elspeth and Henry? They might have seen something. Where were they when this was happening?" Her voice rises with each question, until it is uncharacteristically shrill. Now she's the one whose fists are clenched, whose body is trembling.

We stare at each other for a fraught second, two women locked in bitter battle, both of us ready to fight for our children. And yet I can't let myself admire Cara for having the same mother's instinct I do. Not now. No matter how understandable it is, she doesn't have that right.

"So it's their responsibility to keep Finn in check?" I ask coldly. I feel icy inside now, and my mind is very clear. I'm no longer angry, or at least not *just* angry; I am determined. Cara is pulling out all the old saws about how there will be reasons, excuses, for Finn's behavior, how really Bella might be to blame because she was drunk or confused or *something*, and I am absolutely not having it. I refuse to entertain the absurd and offensive notion, even for a millisecond, that "boys will be boys" or "well, if she was drunk, who knows what really happened?"

No. Not this time.

"I came over here simply to let you know we will be going to the police and pressing charges," I state, although that's not entirely true. I came over here because I was angry and I wanted to confront Cara, but now it's clear what I need to do. It's time someone paid for their crimes. Justice *will* be served.

"Rose, *please*," Cara whispers. "Can't we just... hold on for a minute, before you go rushing to the police? I haven't even talked to Finn about this—"

"I don't care what he has to say," I snap and, for the first time, anger flashes in Cara's eyes, turning them from brown to gold.

"Aren't you being a little high-handed about this?" she demands. "You're taking Bella's word for everything. She was *drunk*. She might not remember things exactly as they happened, you know. Events are probably fuzzy. She might have lied—"

"*Lied?*" I spit the word, enraged again. "Why on earth would she lie?"

Cara shrugs, throwing her hands up in the air. "Because that's what girls do sometimes, when they're panicked or scared or when they regret their own actions—"

"Stop right there." My tone is deadly. "I do not want to have this conversation with you. I will *not* have it. I believe my daughter, Cara. End of story."

"Well, it's not the end of the story for me," she flashes back. "I'm as invested in this as you are, and the repercussions for my son are worse than those for your daughter, if you're actually thinking about going to the police—"

I let out a hard huff of disbelieving laughter, although nothing about this situation is remotely funny. "What is this, some sort of sick one-upmanship? Finn *assaulted* Bella—"

"You don't *know* that—"

I take a deep breath, force myself to stay calm. We're going around in circles here; I realize there is no point continuing this conversation.

"Talk to Finn," I tell Cara as levelly as I can. "See what he says. Maybe he'll do the right thing and admit he's guilty."

"You don't even know if that's the right thing or not, because you don't know that he's guilty!" Cara's voice is rising to a shriek before she forces herself to calm down, scrubbing her hands over her face and then dropping them. "Rose, please, come on." Her voice lowers, trembles. "This is Finn we're talking about, not some random teenaged boy you've never laid eyes on before. *Finn*, whom you've known since he was a baby. He's slept over at your house, you've cuddled him in your arms, he and Bella were best friends for *years*. Can't we just take a step back and think reasonably about this? Remember that these are two kids we've known and nurtured forever, two kids we both love?" Her voice wavers, breaking as she gazes at me pleadingly, her hands clasped together in front of her.

I know she's trying to appeal to my sympathy, our shared history, but right now I don't love Finn. I feel like murdering him. And, in any case, the history Cara is pleading for me to call on is over a decade old. Finn and Bella haven't been best friends since they were about seven. Maybe eight. For the last few years, it has seemed as if they've done their best to avoid each other. They're not those cute little kids holding hands anymore, and they haven't been for a long time.

"Talk to Finn," I say again, wearily this time. "I don't know what else to tell you."

"Please—please don't go to the police just yet." Cara's voice wavers and then breaks. She draws a shuddering breath. "Please let's just talk about this a little more before we... we involve outsiders."

"This isn't something that can be resolved with a conversation, Cara." The words are a warning. I am not going to roll over and say this was all just the usual teenaged stuff, too many beers, *whoops*, so let's not bother with the police. No way.

"Still," she persists, her voice hardening a little. "For the sake of our friendship, our children's friendship, will you at least give me the courtesy of telling me before you go to the police? So we can be prepared?"

I give a terse, grudging nod, although the truth is that right now I don't feel like being even that reasonable. "Fine."

Cara swallows hard. "Thank you," she says, and I can tell she doesn't want to say the words. She doesn't mean them. I'm pretty sure she's feeling as angry as I am, and she doesn't deserve to. She is not in the right here. She does not get to feel the kind of rage I do.

I turn on my heel and walk out without saying another word.

Back at home, everyone is still asleep, including Bella, who has drifted off after our painful conversation this morning. I feel exhausted, and it's only nine o'clock. I head to the kitchen, to make coffee; I need a cup, after all. This day feels like it's going to be very long, and it's barely started.

I sit at the table with my coffee, cradling my hands around the mug as I stare unseeingly out at the yard. It's another perfect summer's day, not quite so hot now that it's September. The girls start school on Tuesday. Last week, we did a big back-to-school shop and I felt nostalgic about buying Bella pencils and notebooks for the last time. It felt so innocent, and now I feel like that's been wrecked. There is no more innocence, no more easiness, and I fear that there might never be again.

I think of my conversation with Bella this morning, how broken she seemed. I'd come to check on her with a glass of water and another couple of ibuprofen, a smile on my face, ready to tease. I wasn't going to be like Cara, all stiffly disapproving just because she'd had a few drinks.

But when I poked my head around the door of her bedroom, I was jolted by the way she looked—curled up in a fetal ball, arms wrapped around her knees, eyes open but staring, unblinkingly, at the wall.

"Bella?" I asked uncertainly. "Sweetheart?"

She didn't reply. Didn't even blink.

I took a step into the room. "Bella... I brought you some more ibuprofen. And some water." I proffered them both, but if I was hoping this would rouse her, it didn't. She still didn't move, and I was starting to get alarmed.

My first rather shaming thought was that she'd taken something. You hear horror stories about what kids get up to these days; it's not a casual joint at a party anymore, it's ket at a night-club, snorting coke in someone's bathroom. Overdoses and addictions and kids dealing hard drugs in the locker room. The world is a crazy, scary place, especially for teens, even in a protected place like Westport, a haven of wealth and privilege.

My heart started to race as I put down the water and medi-cine and dropped to my knees in front of her. "Bella... sweetie... what's happened? What did you—"

A single tear snaked down her cheek, silencing me, splin-tering my heart.

"Bella... whatever happened, it's going to be okay. I prom-ise." Of course, parents can't make those kinds of promises, and yet still we can't help ourselves. We will make our children's worlds safe. We will right every wrong. Whatever it takes. *Whatever it takes.*

And so, when after another five minutes of coaxing, Bella finally whispered the truth, my heart both broke and hardened. "It's about last night..." she mumbled, drawing her knees even tighter to the chest. "I was drunk, I know I was, but Finn..." Her voice broke and she closed her eyes as another tear squeezed out.

Finn? My whole body tensed as I gripped her shoulder as gently as I could, even though a deep, abiding anger was starting to rush through me, because I knew what was coming next. Of course I did.

"What about Finn, Bella?" I asked. "What happened with Finn?"

"He... he..." Her voice trembled and she closed her eyes.

"Did he hurt you? Touch you?" I already knew. I could hear it in her broken voice, the way she curled into herself, as if she wanted to disappear.

A thousand memories rushed through my mind like shards of broken glass, catching and cutting, drawing blood. I pushed them away to focus on my daughter.

Slowly, miserably, her eyes still closed, she nodded.

"Tell me what happened, sweetheart. Please." I tried to speak calmly, even though I was practically vibrating with a dozen different emotions—sorrow, grief, anger, pain. *Memory.*

"I don't know exactly," she began, the words hesitant. "I was passed out, I guess... I know I shouldn't have... and then I woke up and he was on top of me... He was so *heavy*..." She shuddered and my stomach roiled with nausea at the image of my daughter being treated that way, like meat, like a carcass. "I tried to push him off... His hand..." Her voice choked on a sob. "His hand was under my shorts, like, *really* under my shorts. And I felt like I couldn't breathe..."

"I'm so sorry, sweetie. So, so sorry." I gathered her in my arms as she finally broke down and wept, and iron entered my soul even as my heart felt as if it were no more than a handful of splintered glass. My Bella... my beautiful, golden Bella. This would *not* be swept under the carpet, I promised myself, my daughter, an uncomfortable little mess tidied neatly away. It wouldn't be explained or justified or be treated like some regretful peccadillo—*oh, well, you know, they were both drinking, and things probably got out of hand, it happens, doesn't it, really too bad...*

No. *No.* Not when my daughter was here, shattered, and I

would be the one who would have to, lovingly and painstakingly, put the pieces of her back together.

I am startled out of my memories and thoughts by a noise, and I look up from my coffee to see Bella standing in the kitchen door, her hair tangled about her face, one leg winding around the other.

"Hey, sweetie." I try to smile, but my lips tremble. I feel as if I could cry, but I can't, not in front of Bella. I have to be strong, for her sake. "Let me get you something to eat."

She shakes her head, hair flying about her face, her shoulders hunched, as if she is trying to hide herself. "I'm not hungry."

I fight the urge to insist she force down at least a piece of toast—I'm not Cara, after all—and nod instead. "How about a cup of coffee, then? Or herbal tea?"

Bella shrugs, and I decide to take that as a yes.

As I get up and move about the kitchen, finding tea bags, filling the kettle, I decide to keep my voice brisk. "So, I went over to the Johnstons' this morning."

Bella's breath is an indrawn hiss. "You didn't!"

"Yes, I did, Bella." I turn to face her, determined to be calm, even though part of me still feels like shouting, weeping, moaning. "I talked to Cara and I told her what happened."

"*Mom*." Her face is splotchy now, her lips trembling. "I didn't say you could do that."

I squelch the flicker of guilt I feel at her protest. All right, yes, I should have respected her wishes, but—"Bella, she has to know. This is not something we can keep secret. It shouldn't be."

She presses her lips together as she shakes her head. "But I don't want to tell people. *Anyone*. I just want to forget it even happened."

I understand that sentiment all too well, but it's not the right one.

"Bella," I tell her steadily, "what Finn did was wrong. Very wrong. He can't get away with it. He shouldn't. We need to tell the police—"

"The police!" She steps away from me, her eyes flashing. "You had no right to go talk to Cara," she declares, her face twisting with anger—an anger that shakes me, because I'm on her side. I'm fighting her corner, I'm being her champion. She has to realize this—

"Bella—"

"I mean it," she spits furiously at me. "I told you because I was feeling sad and I thought you'd... you'd understand, but then you have to go rush off and handle it your own way, do what *you* think is best. Well, *I* don't think it's best! I don't want people knowing, talking about me, getting all up in my business." She shakes her head, violently this time. "You had no right," she chokes out. "*No right.*"

And then she whirls around and runs out of the kitchen, leaving me shocked and reeling in a whole other, awful way.

CHAPTER 7

CARA

The slam of the front door as Rose storms out reverberates through both the house and me, a shudder that goes through my whole body. I am still standing by the coffeemaker, frozen, numb, unable to make sense of any of what she said. Not wanting to.

Finn... Bella... *assault*.

I cannot believe it. I will not.

A choked sound escapes me, and for a second I feel as if I could crumple, sink right down to the ground, forehead on the floor, and stay there. Underneath my frozen numbness is a wild terror, a deep, seething grief, because already I know everything has changed, forever. Even if we somehow get through this, if I manage to prove that Finn didn't do what Bella said he did, that he *couldn't* have, my relationship with Rose will never be the same. So much will never be the same... this stain covers all of us.

And if he did do it...

But he couldn't have. No. No way. I cannot believe my son would do something so completely and unequivocally wrong. I will not let myself consider it for a second. And yet... he was drunk. Bella was drunk. Can I really say what Finn might have done when he was out of his senses? When I picked them up last night, he could barely string a sentence together. He might not even remember what happened, what he might have done.

I need to talk to him, a conversation that I know will be the most painful and difficult I've ever had with my son, but first I have to tell Michael what has happened.

Slowly, my body aching, I walk upstairs. Michael is still asleep, the pillow over his head. Bright sunlight streams through the curtains I forgot to close last night. I stand in the doorway for a few seconds, bracing myself, summoning my strength, although already I feel as if I am reeling, staggering, hopelessly weak. I want to go back in time, to yesterday afternoon, when my biggest problem was Finn's reluctance to go to the damned barbecue—*why* was he reluctant? And why I make him go? That was all I had to worry about, that and a bit of tension with Michael. Those problems seem easy now. *Easy.* I want them back. I want them to be my only ones, but they're not and I have to face this. Deal with it.

"Michael," I say softly.

He snores.

"Michael." Louder this time.

Still nothing.

I reach over and pluck the pillow from his head, throw it on the floor, feeling annoyed that he's not waking up even though I know it's not his fault he's a deep sleeper. "Michael, wake up. Something has happened."

He blinks me into focus, standing over him, looking so grim, and then with a start, he sits up, rubbing his eyes. "What is it? Is it your mom?"

My mom has only been clear from cancer for a few weeks, so I understand his alarm. I shake my head. "No, no, it's... it's not that."

I must sound truly wretched because Michael peers more closely at me, his face paling. "Cara...?"

"It's... it's Finn."

"*Finn?*" He gulps, leans forward, his hands bunching on the sheet. "Did something happen last night? Why didn't you wake me?"

"I only found out this morning."

I perch on the edge of the bed, take a steadying breath, although now that I have to tell Michael, the reality of it is slamming into me, leaving me breathless. *Assault. The police. Finn.* I realize I am simply sitting there, staring into space, *reeling*, because Michael grabs my arm.

"Cara, *tell* me—"

"Rose came over this morning and said Bella has accused Finn of sexually assaulting her last night." I speak in a numb staccato, the horror hitting me all over again. My shoulders slump.

Michael stares at me for a beat, his jaw slack, his eyes blank, the words not seeming to compute. Then, in complete disbelief: "*What?*"

"They were both drunk," I explain stiltedly. I feel as if I have to search for the words, as if they are hard to find, or perhaps I just don't want to find them. Say them.

"Drunk," he repeats, absorbing that fact. "How did they manage that?"

"Finn brought some beers, apparently. I don't know where or how he got them." Liquor laws are pretty tough around here; I was carded until I was thirty. I don't like the idea of Finn having a fake ID, but I have to acknowledge that it's not outside the realm of possibility, everything else considered.

Michael blows out a breath, raking a hand through his hair as he slumps against his pillow. "And the... the assault? The alleged assault," he amends quickly, and we share a guilty look, as if it's not right to say that. Maybe it isn't.

"Rose said Bella was passed out and woke up to Finn on top of her... groping her. Quite... intimately." It's distasteful to say, unbearable to envision. I close my eyes, then force them open. "She said Bella pushed him off her. When I arrived, they were both pretty out of it, sitting about six or so feet apart. Neither of them said anything about it..." I stop, because I'm not sure any of that is relevant. I feel like I'm walking through a minefield, and this is just with Michael. What about when we talk to Finn, or, heaven forbid, the police?

Michael shakes his head slowly, still processing. "Have you talked to Finn yet?"

I do my best to suppress a small stab of irritation, even hurt, that he assumes I would be handling something as enormous as this on my own, that I would manage it, present it to him as a problem solved. "No, I thought we should do that together," I reply, trying not to sound too pointed. I hesitate before I tell him the rest. "Rose told me she intends to go to the police. To press charges."

"What?" Michael shakes his head again and then swears softly. "This will kill his chance at the Ivies. If there's even a *hint* of scandal..."

That's his reaction? And yet, I acknowledge fairly, it was more or less mine. Neither of us want this to ruin Finn's future. "I told her to tell us before she does anything," I inform him. "We need to talk to Finn, get his side of the story." I think of Rose furiously declaring that there was only one side of the story to something like this. But surely that can't be completely true. What if Bella somehow remembered it wrong? It sounds pretty feeble, even to my own desperate ears, even though they were both drunk.

"The likelihood is that they were fooling around, and Bella regretted it after," Michael says, his tone both weary and decisive, as if he's made up his mind, as if he already knows.

It's what I basically suggested to Rose, but somehow it

sounds worse, coming from Michael in such a certain tone. Does Bella really deserve that doubt? I picture her waking up groggily, blinking in confusion, feeling those grasping hands... but the hands of my *son*? No.

"We don't know what happened," I say quietly, "which is why we need to talk to Finn."

"All right." Michael starts to climb out of bed. "Let's talk to him, then." He reaches for a T-shirt.

"He's asleep. And if we wake him up to demand answers, he'll feel ambushed and defensive." Which is not the right way to start what is going to be a very difficult conversation. I shake my head. "Let's think about this first. Be deliberate about it."

Michael pauses, his T-shirt in his hands. "Okay," he agrees after a moment. "That sounds sensible. What do you suggest?"

It occurs to me, in an awful sort of way, that Michael and I are working together in this, presenting a united front, for the first time in forever, or at least in recent memory. Did it really have to take something like this for us to be on the same side? Could this somehow draw us closer together? It's a small silver lining on an otherwise very dark cloud.

"Why don't you wake him up, and I'll make him breakfast," I say after a few seconds' thought. "We'll let him eat, have a cup of coffee and maybe a shower. And then we'll talk to him in your study, the door closed so Henry doesn't overhear. I don't think we need to involve him in any of this." Henry would just get anxious, and Finn angry at having his brother overhear what to him will probably feel like a grilling. Better for both of them to keep it private. Separate.

Michael nods slowly. "All right," he says. "Good idea."

And, improbably, considering the situation we're in, I find myself smiling, because I can't remember the last time Michael gave me any praise. Maybe this really could help us to turn a corner.

In the kitchen, I put the coffee on that I forgot about before, and set about making Finn's favorite breakfast—oatmeal with bananas and brown sugar. There is something steadying, even strengthening, about stirring the oats, slicing the bananas. This I can do; it is a physical, tangible evidence of my love for my son. My capability and success as a mother. I can make him breakfast; I can support him, no matter what he might have done.

My hands slow as I realize sickly, that part of me is bracing myself for Finn having done exactly what Bella said he did. As much as I want to deny every bit of it, as much as Michael seems determined to, I am readying myself for the possibility that it is actually true. That this situation will only get bigger, worse, more devastating.

As I stir the bubbling oatmeal, I acknowledge for the first time that some small part of me actually believes Finn is capable of such a thing. It both shames and scares me, that I think that, that I *know* I think that, even if it is no more than a tiny, treacherous flicker of doubt I do my utmost to extinguish. But I have noticed—and this is something else I haven't been willing to acknowledge before, even just to myself—that Finn has become a little arrogant in recent years. I've seen it in the way he sometimes swaggers or sprawls in his chair, his chin tilted, master of his every domain. I've seen the disdain visible on his face when Henry and his friends are playing one of their board games at the kitchen table, all of them too geeky for him. I've heard it in the second's hesitation when I ask him to do something, the exasperated breath before he saunters away. Nothing too big or awful, but little changes that I haven't wanted to see, never mind accept.

And I even understand why they've come about. Making varsity in three sports, captain of the baseball team, celebrated by the school, told by just about everyone that the world is his oyster... it would be hard, at seventeen, not to start to feel a little bit superior. Invincible, even. Like anything is yours for the taking, as long as you want it.

Even Bella...

A shudder goes through me, and I twitch my shoulders in an anxious shrug, as if I can banish these terrible doubts in that simple movement. As if I can pretend I never had them, because I don't want to have. What kind of mother thinks that way about her own child?

And what does it say about me, that I might have a son capable of that kind of assault?

I wanted to be such a good mother. From the moment I found out I was pregnant, I tried to do all the right things. Prenatal vitamins, folic acid, absolutely no alcohol, Kegels and breathing exercises for labor and every other suggestion found in the hallowed pages of *What To Expect When You're Expecting*. I was so diligent about it all. Michael used to tease me about forgetting my folic acid. "One missed day isn't going to hurt, I promise," he'd say while I fretted I'd done something irreversible. And then he'd hug me and kiss the top of my head... I miss those days, in so many ways.

My fervor to do things right—perfectly, even—only increased once Finn was born. I fed on demand for the first six weeks and then I religiously kept to a schedule that had us both thriving. He slept through the night at two months, was potty-trained before he was two, spoke his first word at eleven months, his first sentence at seventeen...

A gasp escapes me as I realize how ridiculous I am being. As if these infantile accomplishments are somehow proof that I am a good mother, that Finn is a good son. That they show that I succeeded, when now my son, who is almost a man, might be charged with a criminal offense. I taught him to talk and pee on the potty, but it seems I might not have taught him how to respect women.

But maybe he didn't do it.

Still, my shoulders slump and I fold in half over the pot of oatmeal, tears stinging my eyes as I feel as if I could break in two.

Please, please, God, he didn't do it.

"Mom?"

I straighten with a jerk, whirling around to see Finn standing in the doorway of the kitchen, still in his T-shirt and pajama bottoms, hair ruffled, blinking sleep out of his eyes, looking like a little boy.

"Hey, honey. I'm making you some oatmeal. Bananas and brown sugar, your favorite."

His eyes narrow suspiciously at my over-bright tone, but he doesn't say so much as thanks as he slouches to the table, flings himself down and takes his phone out of the pocket of his pajamas.

"Did you have your phone in your bedroom last night?" I ask sharply, because we have a very strict no-phones-in-bedrooms policy, enforced mainly by me. Henry and Finn both have to deposit their phones in the kitchen to charge at 9 p.m. every weeknight, eleven on weekends, no exceptions. I try to do the same, to set a good example, and Michael usually agrees to as well, although not always.

But I realize I forgot last night.

Finn shrugs his assent, obviously uncaring, and I feel a slow burn of anger. I wanted to be reasonable this morning, matter-of-fact and calm and *caring*, but already I feel myself on edge, fury bubbling up although I desperately don't want it to.

"Finn." I do my best to sound calm. "You know the rules."

"I'm *seventeen*," he replies without looking up from his methodical scroll. He doesn't, I acknowledge, seem like someone with a guilty conscience—but maybe he doesn't have one. Maybe he doesn't think he did something wrong... even if he did.

"So what if you're seventeen?" I demand, my voice rising a

little, although I am trying my best to keep it level. "Our house, our rules. You *know* that."

He just shrugs, dismissive, and driven by an anger deeper than the phone rule breakage, I cross the room and twitch the phone from his fingers before he can react.

"I'll take that until further notice," I tell him smartly.

He glances up, glaring at me, anger, and worse, derision, simmering in his eyes. "You know I'm going to college in less than a year, right?" he drawls. "And then I can do whatever I want, whenever I want?"

There is a challenge in the words, as well as an innuendo. I force myself to ignore both, although considering the situation we're in right now, his remark is painfully ill-timed. Did he do whatever he wanted, whenever he wanted, last night?

"A year is a long time," I reply shortly as I pocket the phone. "While you're under our roof, you'll obey our rules. And one of them is no phones after 11 p.m. on weekends, as you very well know."

He lets out a long, gusty sigh as he sprawls back in his chair. "Dad doesn't care about your stupid rules."

There is an unfortunate grain of truth in that statement, at least of late, and it makes me angry with both Finn and Michael. I have always been the main enforcer, but at least he has backed me up, although apparently not enough.

"They're *our* rules," I state flatly and then I go to dish up his oatmeal. The supportive mood I was aiming for is ruined now; tension is thrumming between us as I sprinkle the bowl of oatmeal with the bananas and brown sugar and then bring it to him, without much grace.

He pushes the bowl away before he's so much as glanced at it. "I'm not hungry."

Rage flares in me, high and hot, before I can tamp it down. "No?" I reply sarcastically and then, without any warning, I grab the bowl and dump the contents down the garbage disposal.

"*Mom*." Finn has straightened in his seat, staring at me with a shocked, hurt, little-boy look—he would have actually eaten the oatmeal, I know—before his expression hardens and he rises from the table. "Fine." He starts to walk out of the room.

"Don't go anywhere just yet, Finn." My voice rings out, enough for his determinedly indifferent stride to falter. "Dad and I need to talk to you."

He hesitates, and then slowly turns around. "Is this about last night?" he asks, derision audible in his voice. "Because, trust me, it's no big deal, Mom—"

"Yes, it is about last night, and yes, it is a big deal." My voice pulses with anger. This is not at all how I wanted this conversation to go. I was going to be calm, unflappable, supportive, caring. Instead I've been angry and reactive and made Finn feel the same way. *Complete* failure. I take a deep breath, desperately trying to claw back some control, but I am too far gone. "In Dad's study," I manage tersely. "Now, please."

Finn lets out a weary, long-suffering sigh before he walks slowly, dragging his feet, letting me know how tedious he finds this, to Michael's study.

I take another few breaths, clenching and unclenching my fists, trying to calm down. I don't know if I want to scream, cry, or hit something. Maybe all three.

Michael comes into the kitchen, eyebrows raised. "Did Finn eat already?"

I shake my head, more a negation of the question than an actual answer. "He's in the study. We should talk to him now."

Michael frowns, opens his mouth to ask something, but I cut him off.

"He knows something is going on. Let's just talk to him now, get it over with."

"Okay," he says slowly, and for a second I think he is going to reach out to me. As I walk past him, he raises one arm as if he's going to touch me, hug me even, but then he doesn't.

We both walk in silence to the study, where Finn is waiting, sprawled in Michael's desk chair, spinning around like he doesn't give a damn about anything.

Michael closes the door behind him with a decisive click. We both sit down. Finn glances at us both, and for a second his weary, louche mask of indifference drops and he almost looks scared. Small. My heart aches, but then his expression hardens once again and he says, "Is all this drama about me bringing a couple of beers to the barbecue?" He sounds so skeptical, so scathing, that I tense right up.

Before I can think to reply, Michael does, his voice deep and even.

"No, Finn, it's not about that, although that is definitely something we will discuss. But this is about something more serious. A lot more serious."

Finn's mask drops once more, and he looks both surprised and more than a little scared. "Wait... what?" he asks uncertainly, his gaze darting between Michael and me.

We are both silent for a second, glancing at each other, wondering who will be strong enough to put it into words. Finally, Michael does, and I am so grateful, because I'm not sure I have the strength to say it.

"Bella told her mother that you sexually assaulted her last night," he says. His voice is low, level, but I see how he's gripping the armrests of his chair and I know how hard this is for him. For both of us.

Finn's lips part, his mouth opening soundlessly, closing again. "Wait, what..." he says again, barely a breath this time.

"Do you remember what happened last night, Finn?" Michael asks steadily.

Finn shrugs, licks his lips. "Yeah, I mean... I was kinda out of it, I know, but I remember. I definitely remember."

We wait, and he looks wildly between us, his voice rising, getting stronger as he straightens in his chair.

"I remember everything," he states firmly, "and I definitely did not assault Bella. No way. *No way*."

CHAPTER 8

ROSE

I hear Bella's bedroom door slam and I close my eyes. I thought she'd be glad I was on her side, fighting her corner, *believing* her. I thought my words, my certainty, would be a comfort as well as a strength. Clearly, I had that completely wrong, and yet I still mean what I said. I still want to go to the police. But I know I can't unless Bella wants to. Somehow, I have to convince her, help her to have enough strength to do the right thing.

I walk slowly back to the kitchen table, take a sip of my coffee, even though it's now cold. I need to talk to Brad, which I didn't even consider before now, which says something about my marriage as well as my family, I suppose. I also need to talk to Elspeth. What if she saw something? Although, if she had, wouldn't she have said something already? And what about Henry? Where was he when all this was happening? Will Cara talk to him? My mind spins in circles, going nowhere. These are all conversations I need to have, and yet I dread each and every one.

But I recognize, even though I don't want to, that I need more information. Bella's heartbroken confession roused my righteous rage, as well as my latent grief, and while I believe her

—of *course* I believe her—Cara's reaction reminds me that not everyone will. That a lot of people, maybe even the police, will ask those unfair and insulting questions, questions that feel like another assault, all over again. *How much did you have to drink? What were you wearing? Do you have a sexual history with the accused?*

As if any of that actually matters.

And yet, for Bella's sake, I need to know more. I need to know exactly what happened, the how and the why, at least as much as she is able to tell me.

I take another sip of coffee and then I toss the rest in the sink. A headache is starting to throb at my temples and my stomach churns. I feel exhausted, drained, even though the day has only just started. The righteous rage that propelled me to Cara's, that filled me with a determined energy and purpose, has left me, and right now I only feel defeated and sad.

I ache for Bella, hating that she must be battling shame and fear, that awful sense of feeling dirty, no matter how clean you try to get. I remember scrubbing myself raw and red in the shower, with a desperate, sobbing fury, and then I force the memory away. This is not about me. Not this time.

"Hey, babe."

I turn slowly to see Brad shuffling into the kitchen, scratching his stomach absently, blinking sleep out of his eyes, his hair mussed. Even though he's put on a bit of paunch and his face is reddened from decades of "social" drinking, he is still a handsome man. His blond hair is thick but now lightly stranded with silver, and besides the slight paunch, he is well-muscled, his shoulders powerful. He cuts an imposing figure, especially in his natty business suits or even his requisite summer wear: a pair of Nantucket Red dockers and a Polo shirt with a popped collar, the silver and gold links of a Rolex flashing on one thick wrist.

He doesn't make my stomach flip anymore, hasn't for a long

time, but that isn't nearly as important as the knowledge that I can't trust him, even though he would insist that I could, at least about what matters. Our difference of opinion on something so fundamental has created an ever-widening fissure in our marriage, and there are times now when I think it is a chasm impossible to cross. I don't even want to try. I don't want to tell him about Bella, but I know I have to.

Brad wanders over to the coffeemaker while I simply stand by the sink, silent and unmoving. He pours himself a mug, yawning hugely, his back to me, indifferent to the despair I am feeling, even though it feels like a miasma surrounding me, oozing from my pores.

"Pass me the milk?"

Wordlessly, I go to the fridge, which is as close to him as it is to me, take out the milk, hand it to him.

He finally clocks my bleak expression. "You hungover?" he asks with a grimace of sympathy. He obviously is.

"No, I'm not hungover," I reply, my tone terse. At least, not very hungover. Why did I drink so much wine? I usually stick to a couple of glasses, max, but last night I was on edge. I was anxious about seeing Cara, having to navigate the tensions that have sprung up in our friendship, but that seems ridiculous now, in light of last night. I was dreading nothing more than a little awkwardness, and yet what happened is so, so much worse. Our friendship is surely ruined, a drive-by casualty of a far greater offense, and yet right now I can't feel more than a flicker of regret about it, if that.

Brad pours milk into his coffee and then leaves the container on the counter. I grit my teeth as I pick it up and put it in the fridge.

"Brad, we need to talk," I say, my tone so grim and purposeful that he has to realize how serious this is.

My husband looks startled for a millisecond and then, with

a sigh, he rolls his eyes. "Is this about Bangkok again? Because I told you—"

"No, it's not about Bangkok." I speak through gritted teeth. Bangkok was last month's offense—*everyone does it, Rose, what's the big deal?*—and I've done my best to move on from it. I don't even know why I mention these infractions anymore; why I want him to tell me about them. Am I keeping a list? Maybe, but that doesn't matter right now. "It's about Bella."

"Bella?" He sounds nonplussed, not particularly concerned, taking a sip of coffee, his eyebrows raised over the rim of his mug. "What about her?"

"Last night, Finn assaulted her."

"*What?*" Brad puts down his mug hard enough that I wince. It's easy to break a cup or plate on these stupidly unforgiving marble counters. Drop something and it instantly shatters. "Are you kidding me?"

"No, of course I'm not kidding you," I reply, struggling to keep my tone even.

Brad shakes his head slowly, reminding me of a big, sleepy, shambling bear. "What do you mean exactly, *assaulted*? What happened?"

"He sexually assaulted her." I speak flatly, trying to keep the shaking emotion out of my voice. "He was on top of her, pawing her, putting his hand up her shorts."

Brad grimaces, and I see the reactions chasing across his features—distaste, anger, pragmatism, acceptance. All in the space of about ten seconds. "Well," he says after another moment, "what's the whole story?"

"Does there need to be more to the story than that?" I retort before I can help myself. Picking a fight right now won't help me—or Bella.

"Come on, Rose." Brad picks up his mug and takes another sip of his coffee. "All I'm asking is to hear how it got to that stage."

I take a deep breath, let it out slowly. Try to stay calm, even though I am both battling tears and fury. "I don't know all the details. Finn brought some beer, they both got drunk. Bella passed out and woke up to Finn on top of her."

"Okay." Brad nods slowly, absorbing—*accepting*. "Okay."

"*Brad*." I can't keep the emotion from my voice now; it trembles. "Are you not at least a little heartbroken for our daughter?"

For a second, Brad looks annoyed, then his expression morphs into a grudging sort of sympathy. "Of course I am, I mean, *obviously*, but teenagers—they get up to stuff. You know that as I well as I do. Stuff happens, they might or might not regret it. And if they were both drunk..."

I shake my head, despondent now that my husband is thinking this way about his own *daughter*. If even Brad can justify Finn's assault so easily, then I am pretty sure a lot of other people will, too. No wonder she doesn't want to go to the police.

"If someone is drunk, are they not still responsible for their actions?" I challenge. "Would you say as much to a drunk driver who hit and killed someone?"

"Come on, Rose. It's not the same."

I tilt my chin, meet his gaze, ready to be angry again. To come out swinging. "Why not?"

Brad lets out a long, weary sigh and puts his mug down on the counter, gently this time. "Okay, look. I know this is clearly a very difficult situation, but I think your past history might be coloring your perception of this situation."

I swing away from him, not wanting him to see the expression on my face. *My past history.* I told Brad about it a long time ago, when we got engaged, wanting him to understand, longing finally to share this damaged part of myself. And, to his credit, he responded in the way I wanted him to at the time—he hugged me, reassured me, was impotently angry on my behalf. I felt vindicated, heard in a way I hadn't been before, grateful that he cared enough to summon that much emotion. But now I wonder if they were just words; if Brad, as smooth and assured as ever, was just reading from some internal script. How to be a sympathetic boyfriend. And, more significantly, how to get what you want.

But maybe that's too cynical; I know he's changed over the years, just as I have. Maybe, back then, we both meant what we said. We loved each other, after all, at least in the beginning. I know that much.

"If anything," I tell him, keeping my voice level, my back turned, "my past history gives me a better understanding of what Bella is going through."

Brad is quiet for a moment. I stare out at the yard until the bright green grass blurs and my eyes water. "Bella... she wasn't raped, though, was she?" he finally asks, choosing each word with care. I know he's trying to be sensitive, but it still hurts. Angers me, too, because already I know he will never understand.

I turn around. "She was assaulted. Intimately, if you know what I mean. Very intimately."

He grimaces, more in distaste than anything else, and my fists bunch. I wonder why I expected more from him, considering that he sees his own infractions as worthy of only of a shrug. But Bella is his *daughter*, his darling princess. Why isn't he swelling in fury on her behalf? Why isn't he storming over to the Johnstons' the way I did, and punching Finn in the face? Not, of course, that that would be the right or appropriate thing for him to do, but I still want him to do it.

"So what do you want to do about it?" he finally asks, in a tone that suggests there is nothing to do. "Talk to the Johnstons? To Finn?"

"I already talked to Cara. I told her we were planning on pressing charges."

"Pressing charges?" Brad looks alarmed, which is almost

comical, because it's not an expression he wears often, or well. His bloodshot eyes widen, his cheeks sag as his mouth gapes. "Rose, really? I mean, I get it." He speaks quickly, placatingly, holding up one hand to keep me from saying anything—or flying at him, which is what I feel like right now. I am almost on my tiptoes, poised for flight. "Bella's upset, naturally. You're upset. I understand that. Of course I do. But they were both drunk, it happened, it was awful, yes, and we should talk to Finn and his parents, definitely, make sure they realize the seriousness of what occurred. An apology is certainly in order, at the very least." This is offered as if he's generously granting me a concession. "But then we can—we *should*—put this behind us. We can all move on, for Bella's sake. This is an important year for her. We don't want to distract her or mess it up." He gives me a faint, hopeful smile. "At least we won't have to go to any of those damned barbecues again."

I glare at him, icy with disbelief. "Well, that's one hell of a silver lining," I say coldly. "You really think sexual assault is a *distraction*?" Why am I surprised?

Brad sighs, like I'm being tedious. Childish, even. "I'm just saying, there's not much we can do in a situation like this. It's a case of 'he said, she said'—"

"I don't know that Finn will deny it."

Brad rolls his eyes. "Of course he will."

Because all guys deny it? Because it's so easy to blame the woman, the victim, for a man's own callous actions? I am so angry at his attitude, but I also feel as if I could cry. Nothing ever changes.

I think of my mother's censorious tone: *You can't tell your father. It would break his heart.*

And forget about mine.

"As it happens," I tell Brad, "right now, Bella doesn't even want to go to the police. But we could talk to Elspeth, to Henry. They were there, they might have seen something. They could be witnesses. That would change things, so it wouldn't be a he-said-she-said situation, after all."

Brad rakes a hand through his hair, already shaking his head. "Do we really want to drag more people into this? Our children? Rose, these things get so ugly. Bella would be blamed." He holds up a hand to keep me from saying anything. "I'm not saying it's her fault, I'm really not, but you know that's the way the world works. Unfortunately. People would ask all the usual questions—how drunk was she? Had they been fooling around? What was she wearing? Do you really want to go through all that? Do you want Bella to?"

I think of what Bella had been wearing—a pair of cut-off denim shorts and a T-shirt, a string bikini top underneath. The T-shirt was loose and a little see-through, the shorts just covering her butt. Is that enough to justify Finn assaulting her, in people's minds?

In some people's, yes. I know it is, and it makes me sick.

"That stuff shouldn't matter," I say staunchly.

Brad's expression droops sorrowfully. "It will matter to Bella."

"Going to the police is the right thing to do," I insist. I believe that, utterly. "If everyone just keeps to the status quo, never daring to question or challenge anything, teenaged boys will continue to assault—"

"Fine, yes," he cuts me off, wagging his head theatrically, "but do we really want our daughter to be the poster child for some kind of campaign? Are we going to sacrifice her for some alleged greater good, some political agenda that will just hurt her in the end?" Brad sounds so reasonable, and it just makes me even angrier.

"How do you suppose anything changes, Brad?" I demand, and his expression gentles.

"This is Bella's life, Rose, not yours." He sounds both quiet and firm. "If she doesn't want to go to the police, then we have to respect that. It's her choice."

"And it suits you too, doesn't it?" I retort bitterly. "You don't want the publicity, the gossip."

"No, I don't," he agrees without a shred of shame or remorse. "Do you? Really? Westport can feel like a small town sometimes, and Green Farms even more so. Do you want all our neighbors wondering what Bella gets up to, whether it was really her fault? Because that's exactly what will happen, no matter what your intentions."

I know he's right, and I hate it. "And what about Finn?"

Brad shrugs. "I can go over there and scare the crap out of him, tell him if he touches Bella again, I'll take care of him myself." He raises his eyebrows. "Is that what you want?"

It is, a little bit, and I can tell Brad doesn't actually mind that image of himself—the fearsome protector, the big man throwing his weight around. He'd probably like to scare Michael, as well, put the whole family in their place. That would make him feel good.

"No, I don't want you to act like some sort of vigilante," I tell him tiredly. "I don't want to scare Finn. I want him to face justice. Properly."

Brad shrugs. "Well, face it, that probably won't happen, even if you go to the police."

He's so pragmatic, it hurts. "And you're such an expert?" I retort snippily, and he just shrugs again.

We both know how this world works. People might post about justice on social media, put their pithy sayings on Instagram about awareness and respect, fill the world with entreaties to "be kind," but it's all just lip service. It costs nothing; it hurts —or helps—no one. When it comes down to it, the reality is this.

"So, what?" I finally say, and now I sound as defeated as I feel. "We just leave it, let Bella get on with her life as best as she can? Let Finn do his own thing?"

Brad shrugs, spreads his hands. "Lesson learned, I guess?"

"What lesson?" I demand. "Not to trust guys she's known since she was in diapers? Not to fall asleep, in case a guy climbs on top of you, puts his hand in your pants? Are these lessons we really want her to learn, Brad? Are these the messages we want to send to our daughter?" My voice has risen shrilly with each question until I am practically screeching, vibrating with rage and, more than that, with pain.

Brad was right; my past *is* coloring my perception. It's bringing it all back. The suffocating sense of fear, of shame. The hopelessness, the helplessness, the knowledge that I was naïve and somehow that was my fault. The realization, over the years, that no matter how hard and deep you push something down, it's still there. It will always be a part of you, no matter how much you try to distance yourself. Be someone different. Someone who is street-smart and savvy, confident and carefree. *You* know it's all a façade, a cheap mask. Strip it away and you're still that frightened girl, and you always will be.

I *can't* have that for Bella. I won't let her do what I did, and ignore it all, be a good girl and stay quiet, because I know it doesn't make it better, only worse. So much worse.

"Rose." Brad has taken me by the shoulders; I realize I am shaking. "*Rose.* It doesn't have to be like that, okay? Let's talk to Bella together. We can still show her sympathy and support. *We're* not judging her, okay? We can still be there for her, even if we don't go to the police. Get her some therapy, help her to talk through it. I don't want to hang our daughter out to dry, believe me."

He folds me in his arms and I let him, because in this moment I am desperate for comfort, for someone else to be strong. He's not actually right, I know he's not, but right now I am weak and frightened enough to simply rest in his arms, a place I haven't been in quite a while.

"It'll be okay," he tells me, his tone soothing and sure. It's the same voice he uses, I realize, when he's closing a deal. "It'll be okay." He rubs my back and I close my eyes.

I don't believe him. I know too much to let myself be lulled by such false promises, easy words. But for a few seconds I simply stand there, my cheek resting against his shoulder, and wish that I could.

CHAPTER 9

CARA

"I filled your prescription, Mom."

I put the brown plastic bottle of pills on the kitchen counter while my mother lifts her gaze from the TV for a few seconds before returning to it with a "hmmph," which I know is meant to pass as a thank you.

I take a couple of steps into the boxy living room of her two-bedroom ranch house twenty minutes north of Westport. We bought it for her ten years ago, because she'd been living in shabby rentals her whole life and had never been able to afford a down payment, never mind a mortgage. We got a "hmmph" for that, too. I know she has trouble owing people anything; she's lived an independent life, earned everything herself. Words like *thank you* or *I'm sorry* come reluctantly, if at all. I've taught myself not to mind.

"Is there anything else I can get you? Do for you?" I ask and this time she doesn't lift her gaze from the TV screen.

"The trash needs putting out, I suppose. Since you're here."

"Tomorrow's Labor Day, so it won't go out till Tuesday."

"Hmmph." This is not a thank you, I know, but an expression of her disapproval that I came on the wrong day.

I lean against the kitchen counter, aching with tiredness, my heart so heavy, it feels like a bowling ball suspended in my chest, weighing me down. It's Sunday afternoon, just a day and a half since Rose came storming into my house, since Finn denied assaulting Bella. Since my world broke apart, pieces scattering, so I don't know if I can even find them anymore.

Not much has happened since we talked to Finn; we've been existing in an awful, tense limbo, waiting for the worst. When we pressed for details about what had actually happened on that night, he stormed out of the study, hurling accusations about us not believing him, and went upstairs, slamming his bedroom door hard enough for the whole house to shake.

"I believe him," Michael said after a moment and I let out a huff of sound—something between despair and a fleeting, fragile hope that this could somehow all go away. That Bella could be mistaken, and realize it. But already I knew that was impossible.

"Why would Bella lie about it?" I asked wearily.

Michael shrugged. "Maybe she's not remembering it right."

I prickled, even though I didn't want to. "She couldn't have just made it up, Michael."

The fragile solidarity we'd been feeling snapped like a thread. "So you're taking her side?" he demanded. "Against our son?"

"*No.*" But neither did I want there to be sides. "I just want to get to the truth, whatever that is." I stared at him in challenge, even though I felt defeated. "Don't you?"

"There isn't always going to be one objective truth in a situation like this, Cara," Michael told me, his tone turning both weary and severe. "There's going to be what happened, what Finn thinks happened, what Bella thinks she remembers. It's complicated."

"And if Finn didn't touch Bella like he said he didn't, then how is it complicated?" I replied, my voice rising. I didn't want to fight; I have always avoided confrontation, much preferring to placate and appease. But I was tired and scared and I wanted someone to comfort me; I wanted Michael to put his arms around me and tell me it was all going to be okay, and I knew he wouldn't.

He shook his head. "He didn't say he didn't touch Bella. He said he didn't assault her."

"He made it sound like he didn't touch her at all," I pointed out, thinking of Finn's vehement denials that what Bella had said had definitely not happened.

Michael shrugged, as if the point was negligible, even though it seemed pretty important to me.

"So what do we do now?" I asked.

"Let Finn cool down a bit. Maybe ask Henry what he saw, if anything."

"When I found him on the beach, he was pretty far away from Bella and Finn. And he'd been drinking, too." I remembered Henry's quiet misery; I wondered if Finn had told him to get lost, so he could be alone with Bella. Or had Henry just felt like a third wheel and taken himself off? Why hadn't he hung out with Elspeth instead of going off on his own? Although Elspeth can be sharp and snappish at the best of times; I could understand why Henry might have wanted to be on his own. "We should talk to him," I agreed with a weary sigh, even though I was reluctant to get him involved. "Although I have a feeling he won't tell us much."

And he didn't. When he came down to breakfast a short while later, already wary, no doubt from hearing Finn's door slam, he stayed practically mute when we asked him if he'd seen anything—no mention of the assault accusation, not yet—simply shaking his head and mumbling that he'd been off on his own for most of the evening because he'd felt sick from the beer.

"How many drinks did you have, Henry?" I asked, trying to keep my voice gentle, even though I was appalled. He was *four-*

teen. No way he should have been drinking. I was ashamed and guilty that I'd let it happen, that I'd unknowingly facilitated it. I felt the condemnation of the invisible chorus of other mothers shaking their heads at me, exchanging wide-eyed looks of shock and horror. They follow me everywhere, those women of my imagination, like the chorus of a Greek tragedy, with their narrowed eyes and pursed lips of judgment. I will never be a good enough mother for them, no matter how hard I try. No matter how hard I try not to be the kind of mom I grew up with.

"So anything else besides the trash, Mom?" I ask. "I could clean the bathroom, if you like." This is said in a coaxing tone, like it's something I want to do if she'll just let me. I am forty-nine years old and I am still seeking my mother's approval, even though I know full well she'll never give it, because she never has. It's not even that she disapproves of me, at least I don't think she does. It's more that she's lost the capacity—if she ever had it—to care.

"You can do the bathroom if you want," she tells me with a shrug, and I go to get a dish towel and some cleaning spray.

As I tackle the limescale in the toilet, the rest of yesterday's conversation with Henry comes back to me. He insisted he'd only had two beers; Finn and Bella had each had three, and Elspeth didn't have any.

"Three beers?" Michael repeated skeptically. "And Bella passed out from that?"

"*Michael.*" I didn't really want to debate Bella's ability to hold liquor.

He shrugged and Henry said in a mumble, his shoulders hunched and his gaze on the floor, "I think Bella might have brought something else. A flask of something."

"She did?" Suddenly, I didn't feel so guilty about Finn being the one to bring the beers.

"And Rose had given them some beer, too," Henry added, and my interest sharpened like a razor blade, poised for the cut.

"Oh, really?" Something she failed to mention that morning, although I recalled her saying something about "only the one." Now that made more sense. She wasn't exactly forthcoming, though, and it made me wonder what else Rose—or Bella—might be hiding. Maybe the evening wasn't as straightforward as Rose wanted it to be, after all. The thought made me feel guilty, but it also gave me hope.

Henry looked up, his expression turning panicked. "I don't want to get anyone into trouble."

"Henry," Michael assured him, "you aren't. And you will never get in trouble yourself for telling the truth."

If this was supposed to make him feel better, it obviously didn't, maybe because we all knew it was one of those placating promises that really amounts to a lie. The reality is you can often get into trouble for telling the truth, which is why people often choose not to.

Is that what Bella did? Finn? Rose?

"And you really didn't see anything?" I pressed, and Henry shook his head, firm now, resolute.

"No. Nothing. Elspeth and I did our own thing."

"Together?"

He shrugged. "For a little bit. Then she went to the playground and I wasn't feeling too great, so I just hung out by the pier, where you found me." He ducked his head. "Sorry, Mom," he mumbled, and my heart melted, a little.

"It's okay, Henry," I told him quietly, even though it wasn't. He still needed reassurance, and I know he isn't to blame for any of this "So, you didn't see Finn or Bella after that?"

He shook his head, and I had the feeling that even if he had seen something, he wouldn't necessarily be telling us now. Over the last five years or so, his relationship with Finn has become complicated, sometimes fraught; Finn can be a little dismissive of Henry, and in return Henry is a bit wary around Finn. It's not the dynamic I ever wanted my children to have, and I hope they might still grow out of it. When he goes to college, Finn won't be the big man on campus and might be taken down a necessary notch or two; without his brother around, Henry might grow into himself, gain confidence. They will equalize, balance each other out. I hope.

But those kinds of dreams feel further away than ever, in light of yesterday's bombshell. Right now, I'm hoping my son doesn't face criminal charges, never mind learn some valuable life lessons while away at college.

I pause in my scrubbing of the sink, resting on my elbows, my head bowed, pain pulsing at my temples. From the living room, I can hear the tinny sound of some game show on my mom's TV. She won't thank me for cleaning her bathroom, I know, or taking her to her chemo and doctor's appointments, or inviting her over for dinner, or any of the things I do to show her I love her, because, in spite of everything, I actually do. Love isn't always about what a person does for you or how they make you feel; sometimes it's simply about who they are. She's my mom, so I love her. And Finn is my son.

A long, low breath escapes me and for a second I sag, my knees buckling so I feel as if I could sink right to the floor. If I do that, I might never get up. With a gust of breath, I heave myself upright, gather the cleaning supplies, and walk out of the bathroom, my mind still hashing over what I know, and all that I don't.

Rose hasn't called the police yet; at least I hope she hasn't, since she said she'd tell me first. Maybe Bella is reluctant, or revisiting her memories, having second thoughts. Maybe this still can all go away, at least for Finn. As for my friendship with Rose? I have a feeling that's gone forever, but in the privacy of my own mind, I can be honest enough to acknowledge that might have been happening anyway. Rose had been growing tired of me long before this. I know that.

As I come into the living room, my mom looks up from the

TV, a vague expression of guilt and resentment flashing across her features before she schools them into something slightly more welcoming. I know she struggles with needing my help; all through my childhood, she was self-sufficient, a single mom working two jobs just to make ends meet, often too tired to do more than slump at the kitchen table after work while I got my own dinner, packed my own lunch. I don't blame her for it—how can I?—and yet it still has the power to sting, after all these years.

"You finished?" she asks.

"Yes, is there anything else I can do?"

She just shrugs.

I go into the kitchen to put away the cleaning spray, throw the dirty cloth into the washing machine. Michael has, on occasion, suggested I stop visiting my mom. "You don't really have a relationship," he said, his tone so reasonable. "So why keep going?"

That stung more than it should have, because despite every evidence to the contrary, I like to think we do have a relationship. It was just my mom and me for so long, after my dad walked out when I was five. He never got in touch again—not for birthdays or Christmases, nothing. He never sent any money, either, which made things all the harder for my mom. But when I was little, my mom and I were close, or at least closer. She'd sometimes read me stories at bedtime, or fall asleep while lying next to me, exhausted after working two eight-hour shifts. I remember waking up in the middle of the night to her beside me, comforted by the warm solidity of her body next to mine, her deep, even breathing steadying my own.

There were occasional hugs, tired smiles, sometimes a chocolate bar she'd brought home from the grocery store where she worked the checkout, offered like a prize after dinner. I felt that, in her own way, she loved me, even if she was often too tired or stressed to show it.

At least I think that's how it was; memory is a funny thing. We remember some things in hazy hues of goodwill, and others with painful precision, and I don't know if either is really accurate. What I do know is that at some point, over time, my mom stopped with the affection, the interest. The best way to describe how it felt was as if her love was a faucet that drip-dripped its way to dry, until there was nothing left. It was already on its last drips by the time I married Michael; she had no interest in my wedding, and did nothing more than show up. By the time Finn and Henry came around, my mother's indifference was an accepted fact; it's telling, I suppose, that it was Rose, herself eight months pregnant at the time, who I asked to watch Finn when I went into labor with Henry.

Maybe a mother's love can be finite; eventually, over time, it might run out. Is that how it will be with me and Finn? I don't want it to be; in every way, I've wanted to be different to my mother. I want to be energetic and invested and interested, giving my children opportunities, support, firm guidance and loving affection, always present, loving and firm.

I know Rose has always thought I'm too strict, but when I was a child, I craved for my mother to care enough to be strict. Setting boundaries and keeping rules is *hard*. Words are cheap and easy; being both tough and tender, walking that tightrope, is the harder, stronger way to show love.

But if Finn did assault Bella... if Rose goes to the police... if Finn goes to *jail*... I know I'll still love him. My mother love won't run out like a well that runs dry, I'll make sure of it, but already I know it will be tested. Loving Finn through this is going to be *hard*. Harder than anything I've done before, any boundary I set, any rule I made.

"What are you just standing there for?" my mother asks, an irritable note creeping into her voice as she glances up from her show, toward the kitchen.

"Sorry." I feel as if I am always apologizing with her. "I was just zoning out for a minute. It's been a long weekend."

If I am inviting my mom to ask why it has been, she, of course, doesn't. She just shrugs and turns her attention back to the TV.

I stare at her for a few moments, wishing I could tell her about Finn. Wishing she would care. Wishing she had some sympathy or wisdom to offer; I know I could use both. Desperately.

But she doesn't ask, and I don't tell her, and after promising I'll be back next week, I say goodbye and walk out of the house.

The humidity has broken and there is an autumnal crispness to the air, which I suppose is appropriate since school starts in two days. My stomach cramps to think of Bella and Finn facing each other across a classroom or hallway; I know they're in the same homeroom, although they don't share any classes. Finn has all AP subjects, and Bella doesn't take any.

Will they ignore each other? Will Bella tell her friends what Finn has done, so everyone whispers? I imagine the rumors, the gossip, the judgment. Westport can feel like a very small town sometimes. If the school gets wind of it, they might cut Finn from one of the schools' sports teams or discipline him in some way—although are they even allowed to do that? Isn't it innocent until proven guilty, even in this much-needed #MeToo era?

But what if Finn isn't innocent?

My head aches with all the questions as I climb into my car and head back to our house.

I left Finn and Henry with Michael, but when I get home, he is out and Henry is slumped at the kitchen counter, picking his fingernails, skimming one of his manga comics. Finn is nowhere to be seen.

"Where is everybody?" I ask, keeping my voice light as I drop my purse on the island.

"Dad said he had some errands to do." Henry's head is

lowered as he studies his book, flipping a page, his bangs sliding into his face. He needs a haircut, but there isn't time before school starts. I am annoyed with myself; I'm usually so much better about that kind of stuff. I'm on top of everything, appointments scheduled months in advance, circled on the calendar, typed into my phone, but I missed it somehow this year and right now I feel as if I am stuck at the bottom of a well, staring up at a faraway slice of sky.

"Errands?" I do my best to moderate my tone, although I am a little irritated that Michael left them alone, considering recent events. "And what about Finn?"

Henry shrugs, his gaze still on his comic book. "I don't know where he is."

Which isn't all that unusual, but I still feel uneasy, maybe even alarmed. I want to know where Finn is. I want to keep tabs on him, now more than ever.

After a few seconds, I reach over the counter to touch Henry's hand; he flinches and draws away.

"You okay, Hen?" I ask gently. I gesture to his fingers, which look sore. "Don't pick your nails, sweetheart. You know it's not good for you." He's had raggedy, bleeding cuticles more than once, due to anxiety.

He drops his hands into his lap, his head still lowered. "What's going on?" he asks in little more than a mumble. "Is Finn in trouble or something?"

I hesitate, unsure how much to reveal, yet knowing it might all come out anyway. "He's not in trouble, not... exactly." I pause, studying my son, wishing he could shed some light on that night on the beach. Should I ask him again, press him for more information, or is that unfair to him? He really shouldn't have to be involved. "Why do you think he is?" I ask instead.

Henry finally lifts his gaze to give me a typically teenagerish *well-duh* look. "Because you and Dad were talking to him in the study and then he was yelling and slamming his door and stuff.

Plus, he's been in a really bad mood." His mouth tightens and his gaze darts away; when Finn is in a bad mood, he has the occasional, unfortunate tendency to take it out on everyone else, especially his little brother, snarling, shouting, shoving until he's worked it out of his system. When he's lost a soccer match or a baseball game, we all tend to stay out of his way—not the healthiest way to deal with conflict, I realize, but I really do hate confrontation. So, it seems, does Henry.

"Things are a bit difficult and tricky right now," I tell him, and he gives me another one of those looks; I'm clearly only stating the utterly obvious. "It's about the night of the barbecue... are you sure you don't remember anything that happened then?"

He eyes me uneasily. "Like what?"

"I don't know. Between Bella and Finn, maybe? Did they... argue?" I know I am stumbling through the dark, but I am reluctant to use the words *sexual assault* in relation to Finn, and to Henry's face. He is only fourteen, after all.

"No," he answers after a hesitation. "They weren't *arguing*."

The emphasis gives me pause. "What were they doing, then?"

Henry shrugs, looking away.

I reach over and touch his hand again, this time clasping it in my own, stilling him, although I sense he wants to pull away. "Henry, please. I know you don't want to be involved in all this, and you shouldn't be, but it could be important. Were Finn and Bella... were they getting along?"

His mouth twists and he tries to pull his hand from mine, but I keep holding on, trapping him, although my grip is gentle, if firm. I need him to answer.

"*Henry.*"

"They were definitely *getting along*," he says at last, and then, with effort, he pulls his hand from mine and buries his nose in his book.

My mind spins, whirls. "What do you mean... they were..." Stupidly, I can't make myself say it, although I think I know what Henry is implying. Of course I do.

"Yeah," Henry says, and then he stands up from the counter so hard that he sends his stool skidding across the floor. "They were making out, like, really obviously. It was gross. That's why Elspeth and I left."

His face is mottled, his expression almost angry in a way I don't understand. Is he annoyed that I pushed him to say it? Is he angry that Bella and Finn ruined the evening by getting together? Or is it just typical teenaged embarrassment, to have to say something like this?

"Thank you for telling me," I say finally, and Henry gives a twitchy sort of shrug.

"Why did you think they were arguing?" he asks after a moment, his gaze on the floor.

"There are just some different views on what happened," I say carefully. "They'd had a lot to drink, so..." This is so *hard*. Everything I say feels wrong. "It doesn't matter," I finish, which has to be the least true thing I've ever said.

"So Finn's not in trouble?" Henry's expression is caught between anxiety and hope.

"I don't know," I admit. "But we're trying to figure it all out." I'm trying to sound reassuring, but Henry doesn't look convinced. "You'll tell me if you remember anything, Hen, right?" I say, and he nods, his eyes downcast, before he grabs his comic book and hurries from the room.

I know there must be more to what happened that night, maybe more to ask Henry and make him answer, but I've said enough for now, and I don't think Henry or I can take much more conversation right now. As I stand there, staring into space, Henry having disappeared upstairs, it takes me a moment to realize what I am feeling—something almost like relief.

If Bella and Finn had been together earlier in the evening—

consensually—then surely the sexual assault that supposedly happened later on has to be at least a *little* bit more complicated? There are shades of gray when Rose wants to make it glaringly black and white.

I know, I *know* sexual history isn't supposed to matter when it comes to assault, of course I know that, and yet... two drunk teenagers, making out earlier in the evening, groping each other when drunk. It puts a different complexion on it, at least a little bit... doesn't it?

But I'm not sure how to explain that to Rose, or if I even should. Does it really change anything, when it comes down to it? And, more importantly, more painfully... should it?

CHAPTER 10

ROSE

Bella is doing her best to avoid me, which just about breaks my heart. I want to be her champion, her staunchest defender, and instead she sees me as some sort of threat, almost an enemy, sliding me warning looks anytime we're in the same room. It's absurd, and yet I understand it. She's scared. She's ashamed, even though she shouldn't be. It doesn't change the fact that I want her to go to the police, but she won't give me a chance to talk about it again.

We limp through the rest of Saturday and Sunday, all of us exhausted, distant, fragile. Bella pretty much stays in her room, and Brad does some work from home, closeted in his study, doing his best to absent himself from everything. Elspeth lies on the family-room sofa, watching TV or on her phone, while I drift around the house wishing I had something to keep me busy, a hobby or a job, but I don't. I haven't for years, beyond the minimum of household maintenance, the social life I don't even like. I want to bustle around importantly the way Cara does, but I can barely drag myself to the kitchen to make coffee.

That's the perk of having a husband who makes millions. I literally don't have to lift a finger, but I've never felt so aimless, so restless, so *bored*, as I do now, with all four of us in this huge house, spinning resolutely in our own lonely orbits. It's taken this upheaval to make me realize just how long I've been feeling this way.

A friend calls me about a tennis tournament in September, mixed doubles, and I find I couldn't care less. I see on the calendar that there's a cocktail party next weekend—a back-to-school celebration for Green Farms families—and the prospect fills me with a swirling dread. No one knows what happened on the beach, but I'm afraid it will leak out, an invisible poison, a toxic gas. People will gossip, wonder, judge, whispering behind their hands, darting glances at me over their gin and tonics. They certainly will if Bella goes to the police like I want her to. Never mind her, am I prepared for that? For all it will undoubt-edly mean.

At first, it was the price I was more than willing to pay, but as the days pass, my resolution wavers, and I begin to wonder. Doubt.

In any case, Bella is doing her best not to speak to me right now, and I can't go to the police on her behalf, although I don't know that I would, even if I could. The blazing, righteous certainty that fired me a few days ago is burning itself out, hour by hour. I feel tired, as well as dispirited, remembering just how hard this all is, and it hasn't even begun yet, not really. If Bella does go to the police, the scrutiny will start. The skepticism. The judgment. I remember how that goes, and even now, over twenty-five years later, I remember just how gut-churningly awful it felt.

And yet the silence was worse.

The morning of Labor Day, I sit at the kitchen island nursing my second cup of coffee, wondering if I can coax Bella out of her bedroom to do something fun—not the beach, no, but maybe a gentle hike or bike ride, or a trip to Cranbury Park, or the aquarium in Norwalk? Or maybe Brad could borrow a colleague's sailboat? We're not the hardiest of sailors, but we've done it before and it could be fun. Different. Get us out of our heads, or at least me out of mine. I want to have a normal day, if it's still possible; I want to smile and mean it.

And yet every option feels like too much effort, so much *work*, and it's easier simply to sit here and stare into space. I think back to the days when the girls were little and they were always up for things. The trip to the library was a cause for great excitement; going to the pool was like winning the lottery. They'd practically dance out to the car, squeal with joy when I tickled them as I buckled their seatbelts. Now it's hard to get them out of bed, off their screens, and if we go out, they'll huff and sigh the whole day, checking the time on their phones and asking when we can go home. It makes me not want to do it at all.

I sigh, knowing how pointless such a lament is, the one parents of just about every teenager has. My kids aren't little anymore; they aren't innocent or fresh-faced or full of wonder. I need to accept that, move on. Figure out how to deal with the now, in all of its pain and complication.

Reluctantly, yet with determination, I heave myself off the stool, dump the dregs of my coffee in the sink. We'll go to Cranbury Park, I decide. It's not too muggy out and Bella has always liked the wooded trails there. At least, she used to. I'll drag Elspeth along too, even though she'll probably resist. We could pack a picnic, have it on the great lawn of the Gallaher mansion. Make a day of it, even, although realistically I know two or three hours will be stretching it.

Yet just as I am formulating these plans, steeling myself to rouse the girls from their beds, Bella saunters into the kitchen with a full face of makeup, dressed to go out in a denim miniskirt and navel-skimming top. The scent of the Miss Dior Blooming Bouquet perfume I gave her last Christmas wafts on the air.

"Bella." I stare at her in a mixture of dismay, alarm, and a wary hope that she might actually be okay; she's no longer sidling along the walls of rooms in her pajamas, hiding behind her hair. Or is it all a façade? Surely it must be? "Are you going somewhere?" I ask.

"Meeting some friends in town." She grabs a banana from the fruit bowl on the island, inspects it, puts it back.

"What friends?"

She gives me a darkly suspicious look; she's still angry with me, that much is obvious. "Just friends. Why do you care?"

Despite her anger, there is no real hostility to the question; more a slightly irritable curiosity. I don't normally ask who she goes out with; my parents insisted on full names and telephone numbers of anyone I socialized with, and I wanted to give my own children more freedom than that. More trust.

But right now I want to know who Bella is seeing.

"Just wondering," I tell her lightly. "I was thinking about heading out to Cranbury Park."

Bella gives a careless sort of shrug. "Okay."

I try for a smile, even a laugh. "I meant with you. And Elspeth. It's the last day before school starts. I thought we could spend it together."

A look of guilty regret flashes across my daughter's face and she nibbles her lip. "Oh, right, well..."

I feel a rush of love, because I know Bella always means well. She hates disappointing anyone, and even though she's angry with me, she doesn't like letting me down. I can see all of that in her face, the widening of her eyes, the nibbling of her lip. It gives me the strength to smile, to shrug as if it's all no big deal.

"It's okay. You go out with your friends. Have a good time." I make my smile meaningful as I lower my voice. "I'm glad you're getting out, seeing people, Bella. That's good."

Her expression turns guarded. "Yeah, okay..."

"Have you thought anymore about what I said? About going

to the police?" Now I am trying to sound matter-of-fact, practical, my tone turning like a switch being flicked, a dial I spin. "I know it's hard, but it's really important guys like Finn don't get away with their behavior, Bel. You know that, right?" I try for a we're-in-this-together sort of smile—*let's go, team!*—but Bella's expression has closed right up, her mouth pursed, her eyes narrowed and flashing.

"I told you, I really don't want to do that, Mom. Can't you just drop it?"

"Will you tell me why you don't want to?" Back to being gentle, trying so hard to hit every note exactly right, because that's what you have to do as a mother. No matter how laidback you try to be, it's all an act. It has to be, because you care so much.

"I just *don't*. I mean, it's my life, my body, right? Isn't that the whole point of being liberated or whatever?" She flings the words at me like a challenge, a taunt. "I get to choose. Well, I choose *not* to go to the police. Not to make a big drama out of it. Okay?"

I take a deep breath, keep my gaze lowered as I say quietly, "He hurt you, Bella. I don't want him to get away with that."

She is silent, and I risk a look up. My daughter is biting her lip hard now, blinking rapidly, and my heart aches. No matter how she's trying to get over this, she can't. I know how that goes. Part of healing has to be getting justice, surely. "Bella, sweetheart..."

"Don't, Mom. Just don't." She whirls away, her hair flying about her shoulders, her body vibrating with tension.

She swipes her keys from the counter and I curl my hands into fists, feel my nails bite into my palms before I make myself flatten them out, take a deep breath. "When will you be back?"

"I don't know."

"For dinner?" It's barely ten in the morning. Surely she won't stay out for that long?

"Maybe." She pauses by the kitchen doorway, her back to me, the car keys clenched in her hand. "I'll text you to let you know, okay?"

This, I know, is a concession, practically an apology. I let out the breath I've been holding. "Okay."

And then she is gone. I hear the sound of the garage door open, and then Bella's car starting. Brad bought her a huge, ridiculously priced SUV with a sunroof for her seventeenth birthday. It's a nicer car than mine, not that I care about that, but sometimes the sheer excess of our lives makes me cringe. Wonder, too, whether it's actually good for our children, to have so much. To take it for granted, because how can they not? No one ever thinks they're entitled. But Brad is all about the presents and perks, and I haven't resisted because like with so many other things, it feels like too much effort. In any case, there are bigger battles to face now.

"Is there anything for breakfast?"

Elspeth slouches into the kitchen, dressed in an oversized sweatshirt and shortie pajama bottoms that barely peek from beneath its ragged hem, her hands hidden in her sleeves.

A gusty sigh escapes me before I can suppress it, summon a smile and a cheerful tone. "I think we've got some granola and yogurt. Do you want me to make you something?"

Elspeth gives me a suspicious look, because the truth is, I'm not really the kind of mom who *makes* something. I'm not Cara, who pureed her own baby food, made healthy cookies with agave nectar and carob chips, nutritious casseroles with lentils and chickpeas. On school mornings, I usually let the girls get their own breakfasts; since Elspeth started high school, I might not even get up until after they've left at seven-thirty.

But right now, in the aftermath of that night on the beach, I feel the need to *do* something. To make hearty breakfasts, warming soups; to gather my chicks under my wings and shelter them, the way I didn't that night.

I am jolted by the thought; for the first time, I acknowledge my pervading sense of guilt. I should have been there that night. I should have protected my daughter. I know it's not entirely reasonable; Bella is seventeen, after all, and she is going to be independent, and yet I feel it all the same. That old, relentless mother guilt. Somehow, I am to blame.

"I'll just have a banana." Elspeth grabs the same banana from the bowl that Bella did, inspects it, puts it back. Clearly the one tiny brown spot on it renders it inedible.

"Let me make you something," I persist. I feel an urgent need to care for my child, to prove something to her, or maybe just to myself. "We haven't had pancakes in a while." Years. "Why don't I make some pancakes?"

Elspeth's look is one of blatant incredulity. "Pancakes," she repeats disbelievingly, as if I've suggested making something outrageous, extravagant, a tart or soufflé.

"Yes, Elspeth, pancakes!" I try for a jolly tone. "I used to make them, you know, back in the day." When the girls were small, they were a Saturday morning treat, every so often. I was more present then, always up for fun—pancakes with whipped cream, making forts in the family room. I was the mom who didn't mind upending every sofa cushion in the house. When did that enthusiasm slide into apathy? Well, I can choose to be different now.

I start opening cupboards without waiting for Elspeth's reply, determined to do this. I find a half-empty box of Bisquick, goodness knows how old it is, but this kind of stuff doesn't go bad, surely? Elspeth, warily accepting, slides onto a stool.

I dump Bisquick into a bowl, smiling almost maniacally now. Eggs, milk, oil. Elspeth props her elbows on the counter, watching me. I realize I must look more than a little unhinged, but I feel desperate to create—something. Normality? Happiness? The illusion that life is good, that I'm a good mother?

It feels like something is writhing painfully within me,

because I always thought I *was* a good mother. I always believed —truly, utterly—that I didn't need to be like Cara to be a good mom. I wasn't going to stand over my children while they practiced piano, or bark at them to put their dirty clothes *in* the washer, not next to it. No finger wagging, no stern tone or frowning eyebrows, no air of constant, low-grade disapproval, no silent sighs of not-good-enough. Not like my parents.

But for some reason—and I'm reluctant to think about this too closely—the whole situation with Bella has thrown me into confusion. Made me doubt whether I've been a good mother after all, whether something like this would have happened if I was. If I'd been more like Cara... and yet it was *her* son who did this, so clearly her method of parenting didn't work. I still don't feel vindicated, though. I wish I did.

"I think it's mixed, Mom."

Elspeth's tone is a strange mix of sardonic and gentle as I look down at the frothy, churned-up batter. Yes, it is mixed.

I take a deep breath, lay my hands flat on the marble for a few calming seconds.

Elspeth's eyes narrow. She's not dumb, not by a long shot. She knows something is going on, but how much?

We haven't told her about Bella yet, we haven't mentioned assault. I haven't even asked her what she saw that night, if anything, because I'm not sure Bella would want her to know any details.

But Bella isn't here, and I need information, for my own sanity, if nothing else.

Another breath. I bend down to get a frying pan out from the cupboard. Turn on the stove, drop a pat of butter onto the pan and stare blindly as it sizzles and smokes.

"Mom?"

"Right."

I dollop batter onto the pan, and within a few seconds the comforting, homely smell of pancakes cooking fills the kitchen, making me wonder why I don't do this sort of thing more often. I have plenty of time. Too much time, really, and that's part of the problem. My life is one of inertia, in every regard, suspended in the emptiness.

"Here you go, sweetie." My voice is over-bright, yet with the revealing threat of tears behind it, thickening in my throat. The plate clatters onto the counter as I hand it to her.

Elspeth prods the pancake cautiously with a fork as I hunt in the fridge for a bottle of Aunt Jemima, expiration date unknown, the top crusted with glinting shards of crystallized syrup. I find it in the back of the fridge and brandish it victoriously.

Elspeth blinks at me slowly. "Mom... are you okay?" Her tone is dubious, a little reluctant; there's only one answer to that question, because do children ever want to hear that their parents aren't okay? No, they do not.

I take another deep breath, try to smile. "Yes, I'm fine. Absolutely fine." She ignores the bottle of syrup, picking up the pancake and tearing a piece off with her fingers. "I'm just a little worried about Bella," I confide, choosing my words with care, watching her expression closely.

I see the flash of something like irritation in her eyes, the way her lips tighten before she swallows her piece of pancake. "Bella?" she asks, tearing off another piece. "Why?"

"She's seemed a bit down recently." I have an awful feeling Elspeth can see right through this pretense of ignorance, but I persevere, hoping to glean something from her. "Since the barbecue, actually." I pause as Elspeth concentrates on ripping strips off her pancake, saying nothing. "Do you know if anything... happened that night?"

"Happened?" She speaks scornfully. "Like what?"

"I don't know." I shrug, widening my eyes as if I am truly mystified. This little charade is absurd, but I don't know how else to find out what Elspeth knows. I can't tell her outright, although I'm not even sure why. Is it for Bella's sake, or my own, or maybe even Finn's? Everything feels complicated, more than it should be. The truth isn't something to simply bandy about. "Was everybody getting along that night, Elspeth?" I ask.

She shrugs, her gaze on her pancake, which is now a pile of torn-up pieces on the counter. She picks up one and nibbles it.

"I know they were drinking," I tell her, like it's no big deal. "And emotions can run high when there is alcohol involved."

Elspeth rolls her eyes. "Save the PSA for your friends, maybe? Or the school?" she suggests, and I try not to wince. This is not how I usually talk; I'm the mom who is down with the kids, who knows their lingo, who belly laughs over the vines they show me online, although, come to think of it, vines are already pretty passé, and their slang changes at lightning speed. I recently used the word *yeet* and that caused both Elspeth and Bella a major cringe. I'm not down with the kids at all, and Elspeth certainly knows it.

"You know what I mean," I say with an attempt at a little laugh that sounds more like a cough. "Finn and Bella were both drunk. I know that."

Elspeth just shrugs.

"Did they argue?" I press.

"Finn and Bella?" There's a note in her voice I can't quite decipher; it's something between scorn and anger, maybe both. "Hardly."

"Hardly?"

Her lips tighten again, and she pushes away the pathetic little pile of ripped-up pancake. "They weren't arguing, Mom, trust me."

"What do you mean, Elspeth?" My voice sharpens. I'm pretty sure I know what she means, and yet I need to hear it.

"They were all over each other," Elspeth snaps. "That's why Henry and I left them to it. It was, like, *gross*. I mean, do you really want to be doing that with an audience? I don't know, maybe Bella does." Her eyes flash and her lip curls, yet for a second it almost seems as if she could cry—my Elspeth, my tough cookie, sharp as a tack, seeming almost near *tears*? What is going on?

"When was this—" I begin, my mind racing down blind corners, hitting dead-ends. If Finn and Bella got together earlier in the evening, it doesn't change anything. I know that, and yet I feel a shameful twinge of uncertainty.

"Who cares?" Elspeth cries, her voice rising shrilly. "Why do you want to know so much? So Bella and Finn hooked up. What's the big deal?"

"It seems like a big deal to you," I reply quietly. Right now I am thinking about Elspeth rather than Bella, and why she is being so emotional, so unlike her usually sassy self. It feels like more happened that night than what I'm already worried about, and I'm not sure I have the emotional bandwidth to deal with it right now, yet I know I have to. It's all part of the puzzle, the tangled mess that a single evening has made of our lives. "Why are you so upset, Elspeth?"

"I'm not upset," she snaps, and then sniffs. "I'm just tired of everything being about Bella."

I absorb that statement for a few seconds, trying to figure out if it's a genuine complaint or more of a distraction technique.

"If there's anything you know about that evening, you need to tell me," I state firmly, which I realize as the words leave my mouth is the exact wrong thing to say at this particular point in time.

"Oh, and why?" Elspeth demands, folding her arms. "Because Bella got her feelings hurt? What, Finn wasn't as into her as she thought? She was trying her hardest to pull him, I saw *that* much."

"No, it's nothing like that," I reply quietly, determined not to rise to her goading. "But I still don't understand why you're so angry about it."

"Because!" She slams the counter with the flat of her hand, the loud noise surprising, I think, us both. "You and Dad always treat Bella like she's Miss Perfect, but she's never done anything to earn it. She's not on any sports teams, she's never gotten even above a C, her teachers all think she's dumb as a rock, but the truth is, she just doesn't study. And you don't even *care*. You just keep thinking she's the most amazing person in the world, and she's not. She's just a shallow, stupid bit—"

"*Elspeth*." I speak reprovingly, but I'm not even sure what to say. Where did all this come from? All right, yes, I've known Elspeth was envious of Bella on some level, of her popularity, but I had never imagined this type of vitriol, of pain. "Dad and I love you both," I tell her, and even to my own ears, although I mean it utterly, it sounds feeble.

Elspeth must think so too, because she curls her lip in contempt. "Oh right, thanks for that," she jeers. "Like I even care."

"You must care, to be speaking this way. And I'm sorry, very sorry, if the impression you got from either Dad or me was that we... we cared more about Bella than we did you." It feels wrong simply to put it into words, to somehow make it a possibility, if an entirely improbable one. I love my daughters equally, if in different ways. Bella's gentleness and Elspeth's sass are like two sides of a coin; I love them both, I need them both.

"Whatever," Elspeth dismisses, and yet I can tell, from the wild glitter in her eyes and the way her chest heaves, that she feels this all very strongly. Even if she is trying to act as if she doesn't.

Have I, in some subconscious way, favored Bella over Elspeth, the cardinal sin of any parent? I don't think I have, but, painfully, I recognize that I don't actually know. Bella has always been easygoing, Elspeth prickly, and perhaps that has made a difference to how I treated them. More of a difference than I might have realized, but I'm hardly going to acknowledge that now.

"It's simply not the case, Elspeth," I state with gentle firmness. "I promise you, we love you both equally, and very, very much."

Elspeth huffs as she bends her head over her pancake, nibbling the edge of a strip, and frustration and sorrow swamp me. For a second, I feel as if I don't have the strength to stand up. I sag against the kitchen counter, braced on my elbows, my head lowered so my hair swings in front of my face. I need to do my roots, I realize dully, and then I almost laugh—or maybe sob —at thinking such an idiotic, inane thing right now. Right now, even though I know Elspeth is hurting, and that is important, I have to focus on Bella—and Finn, and what Elspeth has told me about them.

Wearily, I lift my head. "Is there anything else you can tell me about the night of the barbecue?"

Something flashes across Elspeth's face and I know I have said the wrong thing—again. "What are you, Scooby Doo?" she sneers. "No, there isn't. Bella was flirting with Finn, like, *so* obviously, and they started making out. Henry and I left, because, *gross*. That's it." She tilts her chin up, her eyes still glittering.

"You didn't see them for the rest of the evening? Till Cara picked you all up?"

"*No.* How many times do I have to tell you? If you're so worried about what happened between Bella and Finn, why don't you ask one of them?"

And with that, she whirls away, stomping out of the kitchen in a swirl of sweatshirt and tangled hair.

I stand there, slumped, my mind reeling with what Elspeth has said—and shown, with her wild flares of fury. So Bella and Finn got together earlier in the night, and it made Elspeth angry? Did she have a crush on Finn herself? It seems unlikely, considering how she's disdained the whole popularity thing, but I know that might only hide envy. And Finn is a handsome guy, with the dark, rumpled hair, that cocky grin. At fourteen, Elspeth's tender heart could easily have been swayed. And maybe Bella knew it... and still took Finn for herself? I know I'm making wild suppositions, and none of it really matters compared to what happened later in the night, but it still feels important, part of the puzzle. Or am I just trying to find a piece that fits?

And, I remind myself dully, what about Elspeth's accusations towards me and Brad?

I really don't think we favor Bella, but maybe I am blinded by the fact that she's always been so easy—hardly ever argues, happy to help, drifting along. Yes, I've always known she wasn't the most studious of pupils, but so what? There are more important things in life. But with Elspeth so sharp, maybe we did favor Bella unintentionally, because it was easier. And Elspeth, being Elspeth, of course noticed.

A sigh escapes me, gusty and despairing. It feels as if the more I try to unpick the tangled mess of that night, the more knots are exposed and the more complicated everything seems. And while I know I need to focus on what happened between Bella and Finn, I can't just act like Elspeth's obvious hurt is a mere drive-by casualty. I will talk to her later, I promise myself. Maybe we'll have a girly day together—afternoon tea, something at a spa. I have a feeling Elspeth might turn her nose up at such a suggestion, but don't the parenting books all say that what kids really want is your attention? I can give her that. Soon.

But first I have to deal with Bella—and Finn. Although, the truth is, I have no idea what to do now.

CHAPTER 11

CARA

The morning of Labor Day, I lie in bed, my eyes closed against the sunlight, as my mind drifts through a sea of memories. I am recalling a Saturday when Rose and I went out together to the aquarium in Norwalk, with all four kids. It was spring—pale blue skies, that first breath of warmth in the air, like a kiss. Buds on the trees. A rising sense of hope. How old were the kids? Finn and Bella were eleven or twelve, maybe. Not quite teenagers, not the full adolescent angst, but hints of it, the occasional scuffed foot or scowl, hands jammed into pockets as they avoided each other's gazes, not enough to make us worry.

Rose and I laughed about it, I remember. When the kids all went off to dip their hands in the pool with stingrays, she bought us both coffees and we sat on a bench in the sunshine, watching the four of them skim their hands along the water.

"What are they going to be like in a couple of years?" she asked, her voice rich with laughter, with a comfortable certainty that whatever they were like, we'd be able to handle it. "Bella is doing her best to act like Finn doesn't exist, and yet last summer they had a sleepover together." She shook her head slowly, her smile ebbing. "It changes so quickly, doesn't it?"

"I know." I felt a pang of bittersweet sorrow that they had to change at all. If I could have kept them as giggling, chubby-cheeked toddlers, I would have, even though that stage had been exhausting. Already Henry was becoming shy, ducking his head, going quiet, while Finn had developed a bit of a swagger. He'd made the county's twelve-and-under baseball team the week before; Henry, in tears, had begged Michael not to have to play in the local club this year.

"Although who knows, maybe they'll get married one day." Rose turned to me, her eyes dancing over the rim of her cup. "They'd be perfect together, don't you think? Bella needs someone to believe in her and Finn needs someone who won't take him so seriously." I frowned a bit at this, trying to figure out if I agreed with it, if there was some implied criticism of my parenting hidden in the honey, but Rose continued blithely on, "I never thought I'd be an advocate of arranged marriages, but, you know, there's some merit to it."

I knew she was joking; in previous conversations she'd talked about her daughters never feeling pressured to marry, to conform, and yet I couldn't quite the hide the look of eagerness on my face. I would have loved it, if Finn and Bella got married. If we could have joined our families that way, forever.

"Who knows," I said, trying to sound nonchalant, and then Elspeth marched over to us, arms folded.

"Can we go see the sharks?" she demanded, and with a laugh, Rose tossed her coffee cup in the trash and said of course we could.

I open my eyes, blinking in the sunlight, as the memory fragments and drifts away, like wisps of smoke, a spattering of droplets. I've probably misremembered it all anyway; did Rose really say that about them getting married? Maybe I'm wishing the whole thing happened that way, because of how low I feel now.

The question tormenting me, I realize—almost as much as

how Finn could have done what Bella said he did—is how could my friendship with Rose collapse so completely? Because already I know it is over. I think of the lackluster response to my peppy reminder of the annual barbecue—*a Johnston/Ellis tradition!* I'd actually used those words, with an emoji, maybe even several. Clearly I felt vulnerable, desperate, trying to remind Rose of what we'd once been to each other. And now it's all over.

The door opens and Michael comes into the room, dressed in workout clothes, walking with purpose. I resist the urge to roll over, curl up on my side and close my eyes against everything.

"You're still in bed?" He speaks with surprise rather than censure; I'm usually the one who is up first, making coffee, getting things done before the household erupts into activity.

"I didn't sleep well," I mumble. Michael, heading into the bathroom to brush his teeth, doesn't hear.

"I thought I'd take Finn to the gym," he says as he comes out, holding some floss. I let my eyes drift shut.

"What about Henry?" I ask.

"What about him?"

This is so typical, and today it gives me a sudden surge of fury. *Is he supposed to mooch around all day while you and Finn bond over training circuits?* I don't say it, though. I just sigh as I open my eyes. "It would be nice if you could do something with him, too."

"Finn has pre-season training tomorrow." Michael says this like it's a reason, an absolute.

I close my eyes again. I'm too tired for this. Michael has always lived somewhat vicariously through Finn—his sporting successes, his academic ability, his easy popularity. Neither of us were that type in school, both shy even in college, first bonding over, of all things, a love of crossword puzzles. I think we have both been surprised and gratified by Finn's trail of successes, that he's one of *those* kids. How did we, two uncertain introverts, create him?

And yet we did, and we are proud, as if we had something to do with it, more than a mere contribution of genes. And maybe we did; maybe the piano practices and diligent discipline paid off, at least in that regard, and yet it has created a dispiriting dynamic, because it makes Michael eager to bask in Finn's reflected glory, while Henry too often remains in the shadows.

"I'm just saying," I tell Michael wearily, "it would be nice to include Henry in whatever it is that you're doing. He's anxious about everything that's going on too, you know."

Michael is silent, and when I open my eyes to look at him, I see he is holding a pair of gym socks in his hands, looking a little annoyed.

"Henry doesn't like to go to the gym." He states this like it is an insurmountable obstacle, and perhaps, to Michael, it is. He clearly had his heart set on working out with Finn, and I'm basically asking him to go to the library instead. Henry will probably refuse to go anywhere with them, anyway; he hates tagging along, a third wheel to the dynamic father and son duo. Not, I acknowledge fairly, that this happens all the time. Michael is a good dad; he makes time for Henry, too. They've almost finished that huge jigsaw in the dining room, and last spring they went to some two-day manga convention in the city. But it still isn't the same as his bond with Finn.

In any case, there's no point in arguing about this now. There are far more serious things to consider. "Michael," I say, my voice heavy with import, and he stills, looks at me intently. "Yesterday, Henry told me that Finn and Bella were... together —earlier in the evening."

"Together?"

"Making out, or something." I can't keep from grimacing a little. It all sounds so puerile, and yet so sordid.

"They were?" Michael nods slowly, a gleam of something

like satisfaction entering his eyes. "Well, that changes things a bit, doesn't it?"

"Yes, it does." And not necessarily in the way I initially thought, *hoped*, when I had that treacherous flicker of relief. When we asked him about it, Finn acted as if he hadn't laid a single finger on Bella, as if the whole thing had to be completely made up. But surely it can't have been, if they were together earlier in the evening? Finn certainly didn't mention *that* fact, and the accusation of assault can no longer be considered outrageous, utterly outside the realm of possibility, because they have history.

If Finn and Bella had already gotten together once that evening, it made it all the more likely they'd got together again, that Finn would think they could. Maybe Finn misread the signals, or maybe he was oblivious to the fact Bella was passed out—a possibility that makes my stomach churn—but whatever happened, it most likely happened. Finn's *no way* holds less weight now.

But Michael doesn't seem to understand that—or maybe he understands it all too well. "Look, Cara," he says, sitting down on the edge of the bed, "I feel sorry for Bella, I do. If she wasn't... on board with whatever she and Finn were getting up to, that's..." He searches for a word and I fill in, my voice spiking.

"Wrong?"

His eyes flash and he lets out an exasperated breath. "Okay, yes, wrong. Of course it was wrong, very wrong, *if* it happened that way. I do believe that, you know."

I stare at him, wondering if he realizes how blinded he is by belief in his son. Wanting Finn to be absolved. Needing him to go to Harvard or Yale or wherever he's been hoping he'll get in. "You still think Bella might be making it up?" I ask. "How?"

"Having second thoughts, more like," he replies carefully.

"Or maybe just forgetting how it actually happened. Maybe she was awake when it started but then passed out later..."

"And Finn just kept going?" My mouth prunes up with distaste. "I don't see how that's much better."

"He was drunk too—"

"I know, but that's not an excuse."

"Still, it's a consideration, isn't it?" he presses. "Why does Finn have to be responsible for his actions but Bella doesn't for hers?"

"She didn't *have* any actions," I burst out. "Michael, she was passed out." As much as I long to find mitigating factors, these are not them.

He sighs, contrite. Mostly. "I know, I know. I'm just trying to see it from both sides. But anyway, that's not really my point." He leans toward me, across the bed. "If Bella pursues this, it could be disastrous for Finn, no matter what happened that night. You know how the world works these days, Cara. The politicians and celebrities whose careers have been ruined because of a single whisper, an unsubstantiated rumor—"

"*Michael.*" I shake my head, sickened that he's saying these things, even though I've thought them myself, admittedly in a vague, inarticulate way. We're both so afraid for our son, but that doesn't change the reality of how this world has worked. "For centuries," I tell him, "*millennia*, women have been mistreated and oppressed in the most horrible of ways. You *know* that. And now the moment the tables turn ever so slightly, it's all a gross injustice—for men?" I shake my head again, harder this time. "Come on. That's not fair. Think beyond Finn for a second. Bella deserves to be believed."

He sighs again, this time in defeat, even apology. "All right, yes, you're right. I'm sorry." He runs a hand through his hair, shoulders slumping. "I know I probably sound really unfeeling," he explains quietly, "but I'm just trying to find a way through this thing. Finn's not a monster, Cara. We both know that."

I swallow past the lump that has formed in my throat. "Yes. I know."

"A lot of those guys, those celebrities, whatever, were in the wrong, absolutely," he continues. "Maybe all of them. *Probably* all of them. And genuine sexual assault should be prosecuted, absolutely. Completely." He grimaces. "I'm not trying to justify a crime. I'm not a monster either."

"I know you're not." The lump in my throat is getting bigger, and I reach for his hand. To my surprise gratification, he takes it, and for a few seconds we simply sit in silence, united, at least in our grief and confusion. I feel like we're on the same side again, but it's always so fleeting, and I'm still afraid to ask why he's been so distant from me. Now is definitely not the time.

"But Finn..." he continues, his voice choking as he looks down at our joined hands. "*Finn*. You don't think he did something like that, do you? That he's capable of it? Out-and-out *assault*?"

For a second, I imagine Finn as he was—a rumple-haired toddler, with that impish grin, ruddy cheeks, flinging himself into my arms with a giggle that comes from deep down in his belly... But that was when he was three. He's seventeen now, practically a man, with a low rumble of a voice, needing to shave every day, muscular and confident, with an assertiveness and even arrogance I can't deny, even if I want to.

"I don't want to think he's capable of it, of course not," I say slowly, heavily. "But neither of us knows what happened that night, Michael. We can't. And while we want to protect our son, we also need to find out the truth. For his sake as much as anyone else's."

"His sake?" Michael's lips twist in something close to a sneer, except he looks too sad for that. He almost looks as if he could cry, and I ache for him, for Finn, for all of us. How did we get here? Was it a single moment, a careless mistake, or something more—a series of steps that led us to this awful, awful place?

How much do I blame myself?

"Yes, his sake," I repeat, as staunchly as I can. "I don't want to raise a son who doesn't respect women, who is capable of assault—"

"You sound as if you already think he is guilty."

"No," I say, but my voice wavers.

Michael yanks his hand from mine and rises from the bed. "You could at least give him the benefit of the doubt," he states coldly, shaking his head, and then he walks out of the room without another word.

I fall back against the pillows, close my eyes as I feel the hot press of tears against my lids. *I didn't mean it like that*, I want to cry, but I don't, because Michael wouldn't hear, and in any case, I'm not even sure it's true, which is an awful thing to think, to feel, and yet right now, in a tiny, dark corner of my mind, my heart, I know I do.

I believe, at least in some small part, that my son might be capable of this kind of sexual assault. Not grabbing a stranger in the street, heaven forbid, nothing like that, but on a night out, with a woman he knows, has been friends with? Taking what he thinks is his when he's had too much to drink, when he's high on his own success, not to mention the hormones flying around? Yes. Yes, I think he might be capable of that.

Does that make me a bad mother? Or an honest one?

Or maybe it makes me a good one.

The truth is, I don't know anything anymore, and I realize I can't keep floundering around in my ignorance. I need to talk to Rose. Not in anger or accusation, but in honesty and trust. We were best friends for a long time; I have to believe in that friendship now, even if it's been wavering in recent months, or even years. I have to act on the foundation we once had, even if we're on shaky ground now, in so many ways. Surely we both want to find out what really happened that night. And surely we have enough history to talk about it together—seriously, sensitively, sensibly.

Feeling encouraged for the first time since the barbecue, I get up from bed and take a shower. I even hum as I soap my hair, fired with a new purpose. I dress, dry my hair, put on the minimum amount of makeup, mainly to hide the dark circles under my eyes. Then I go downstairs, checking around for Henry; Michael has already gone out with Finn. Henry's lying on the family-room sofa, scrolling on his phone in a desultory sort of way, barely scanning the Instagram feed, or whatever it is he's looking at.

"Hey, Henry," I practically chirp, determined to be cheerful. As I glance around the kitchen, I decide to make a load of banana bread to take over to Rose, a peace offering. I start getting out bowls and measuring cups. "You okay?"

"Yeah, I guess." His head is bent over his phone, his fingers determinedly swiping.

"You seem tired," I remark, and he shrugs, not replying.

I never finished the conversation we had yesterday, when Henry told me about Finn and Bella. I don't really want to get into it now; the last thing Henry needs is to be the unfortunate conduit of information about the evening, feeling like some sort of spy. Finn certainly wouldn't appreciate that.

And yet he seems more morose than usual, and my heart twists in sympathy. Is he hurt that Michael and Finn went out together? I picture them leaving with a jangle of car keys and friendly punches to the arm, while Henry watched, silent, ignored.

"Do you want to help me make banana bread?" I ask, because he has enjoyed helping me bake in the past; when he was younger, we'd get out the chocolate chips and the rainbow sprinkles and make a giant cookie, a triple layer cake. Something ridiculous and over-the-top just because we could, and because that was the kind of mother I wanted to be. I remember his giggles, slipping out of him like bubbles, the way his eyes danced as he spread glittery sprinkles, face alight. "Henry?" I ask again, gently, with a smile. "It could be fun."

He glances at the mixing bowls I've put on the counter, a sack of flour. For a second, I think he's going to agree, that we're going to recapture a little bit of what we once had. I want a few minutes of that—the ease, the fun, the feeling that things could be simple. Then he shakes his head, turns back to his phone. "What are you making it for?"

I hesitate for a second before replying, "To take over to the Rosses."

He looks up, his expression indecipherable from across the kitchen. "Why?"

Another hesitation as I think of what words to choose, how much to say. "Things have been a little tense between us since the barbecue. I wanted to make up for it."

"You mean because of Dad storming off the way he did?" I'd actually managed to forget all about that, in light of other revelations. I suppose I should ask Michael about it again at some point, although it hardly seems to matter now. Brad was being annoying, most likely, and Michael snapped. "Why does he hate Mr. Ross so much, anyway?" Henry asks.

"He doesn't hate him," I answer automatically, disquieted to hear him say such a thing, and so matter-of-factly.

"Elspeth says he does."

"Does she?" I've never considered how the kids talk about us, but I imagine Elspeth has made a few pretty shrewd remarks, a prospect that makes me feel distinctly uncomfortable. What has she said about me? About my friendship with Rose? Already, I can picture her, hands on hips, head cocked, lips twisted. She never misses a trick. "Well, hate is a rather strong word," I tell Henry carefully. "They're different people, that's all." I start measuring flour. "Anyway, it's not about that."

I decide, recklessly, that I need to be at least a little honest. "It's about Bella and Finn."

Henry scoots up to a seated position on the sofa, his hair rumpled, his cheeks flushed. "Bella and Finn? What about them? Is it about what I told you? Because I don't want to get anyone in trouble—"

I hesitate again, wishing now I hadn't brought it up. What on earth was I thinking? How can I explain it in a way that isn't awful? "There's been some upset about what went on between them that night," I finally say, my gaze on the bananas I am now mashing with determination. "Romantically, I mean." Although romantic is hardly the right word, I know.

"But I told you what happened."

"Yes, but..." Telling Henry clearly was not a good idea. I cannot see a way out of this conversation without telling him more than I want to—and yet, if Rose makes Bella go to the police as she's said she will, Henry will have to know, along with a lot of other people. "It's a bit more complicated than that, Henry. Feelings are running high. We need to talk it through."

"And so you're making *banana bread*?" He sounds incredulous, and when he says it like that, I realize it seems a bit... token. Offensively so, even. Yet what else am I supposed to do?

Resolutely, I reach for the eggs, crack one hard against the side of the bowl. "Yes," I tell him firmly. "I am."

CHAPTER 12

ROSE

I know it's Cara simply by the way she rings the doorbell—one firm press, held a second too long. I stifle a groan. Bella has been out all day and since our painful conversation this morning, Elspeth has retreated to her room. I've done precisely nothing; I haven't even cleaned up Elspeth's destroyed pancake, and yet I feel utterly exhausted. I'm not ready to face Cara.

She rings the bell again, another long press. This time, the groan escapes me.

I walk slowly to the door, steeling myself for whatever lies ahead, although I don't even know what that might be. Will Cara be repentant on her son's behalf? Angry at the way I threatened the police? Maybe she's consulted a lawyer and is brandishing the big guns, fighting fire with fire. It could be anything, and I don't feel prepared for any of those options.

"Cara." Her name escapes me wearily as I open the door.

She is standing there, looking determined, holding a loaf-shaped Tupperware which she thrusts toward me. "I brought you some banana bread."

Okay, what? I take it, simply because she is still holding it out, her arms completely straight, her expression fierce.

Somehow I can't make myself say thank you. "Why did you bring me banana bread, Cara?" I ask after a few seconds have passed when neither of us has moved.

"As a... a peace offering, I suppose."

I feel like hurling the loaf right on the floor. "You think some banana bread makes up for what Finn did?" I demand, my fury rushing back to the fore. Can she possibly be serious?

"No, no, of course not," she replies in an unhappy rush. "Rose, no. I was just hoping we could talk." The avidity of her expression drops and she nibbles her lip, apprehensive yet hopeful. "Honestly, I mean, as... as friends. We are friends, aren't we?" She looks at me pleadingly and I struggle to find the words.

Are we friends? We were, but both Cara and I know our friendship has been on the wane, even if we never said as much to one another. And yet... I have a sudden, piercing memory of Cara fourteen years ago, after Elspeth had been born. Henry would have been less than two months old. She'd come over with no less than three casseroles for the freezer, a "big sister" present for Bella—a My Little Pony, I think, which she'd been crazy about at the time—and a bottle of champagne for Brad and me. She'd cleaned the kitchen while I'd nursed Elspeth, had played with Bella while I'd slept for the first time in what felt like days.

"Rose?" she prompts hopefully. "I know this is a very..." She blows out a breath as she searches for the word. "Difficult and explosive situation. But I think we both want the same thing—"

"Do we?" I interject tiredly. Somehow I don't think Cara wants her son in jail for assault.

But is that what I want?

For the first time, I acknowledge that I'm not actually sure what I want from this situation. Prosecuting Finn will not change the fact that the man who assaulted *me* got off scot-free, that hardly anyone even knew what he did. Making Finn face his crime doesn't change the fact that my attacker did not, and never will.

A shudder goes through me, and I almost drop the container of banana bread. Maybe Brad was right, and my personal history *is* coloring my perception. But sexual assault is reprehensible regardless, so does it even matter?

"Rose?" Cara asks again.

Once more, I picture her back then, scrubbing my kitchen counters with Henry strapped to her chest. I step aside from the door. "Yes, of course you can come in," I tell her, although, the truth is, I don't want to have this conversation.

She follows me into the kitchen. I toss the banana bread onto the island, and the Tupperware skids across it, almost falling off the other side.

Cara looks around the kitchen, blinking slowly. "I can't remember the last time I was here."

Despite my poignant memories, I cannot have *that* conversation now. I don't think I can take Cara's puppy dog eyes on top of everything else, the silent accusations that I haven't been a good friend. I know I haven't, but right now that isn't the important thing. It can't be.

"What exactly do you want, Cara?" I ask, keeping my tone neutral. "Have you talked to Finn about what happened?"

"Yes."

"And?" Now my voice turns hard. Already I know what he must have said, simply by the flash of guilt across her face, the way her gaze slides away and she bites her lip again. He denied it. Of course he did. I think of Bella's eyes full of tears this morning, the bravado of going out with her friends, and my resolve hardens again. Maybe I actually needed Cara to come over, to remind me of what I was fighting for. How important it is.

"I think it's more complicated than either of us realize," she says after a moment, rushing on before I can reply, "Please, can we talk about it, without making any accusations? Just... discuss?"

I throw my arms wide, a parody of expansive acceptance. "All right," I say as I drop them. "Let's talk."

I saunter over to a stool and slide onto it, knowing that everything I do bristles with hostility. I can't help it; I feel too raw, too broken by everything that has happened—both to Bella and to me. Dealing with this, I know, has brought up my own history in painful detail. Something I am not about to explain to Cara right now.

After a second's pause, she sits on the stool next to me, folds her hands on the island counter like she's at a board meeting. "Did you know Finn and Bella were... intimate... earlier in the evening?" she asks quietly.

I stare at her for a good ten seconds, my gaze boring into hers, and to her credit—or not—she doesn't look away. "What does that have to do with anything?" I ask levelly.

Cara blows out a weary breath. "Come on, Rose—"

"No, seriously." My voice hardens, rises. "What does that have to do with anything?"

She shakes her head slowly, her expression turning the tiniest bit obdurate. "Surely you can acknowledge it might make something of a difference? It doesn't take away from what Bella experienced, or remembers. I'm not saying that at all. I'm just saying..." She pauses and I wait, wondering how she's going to dig herself out of this one. "There may have been... miscommunication. Misperceptions, perhaps..."

"Bella was passed out and woke up to Finn pawing her. Intimately. His hand under her shorts, *touching* her." I keep my voice steady, even though inside I am shaking. "How is that a miscommunication, considering she wasn't even able to talk at the time?"

Cara glances down at her folded hands. In the silence, the ticking of the clock above the stove sounds unnaturally loud.

Ominous, like a bomb about to go off, a countdown to something even worse than this. "I... I don't know," she whispers at last. "It's true that Finn has denied it. He said there was no way he assaulted Bella. And the way he said it... I believe him." She looks up quickly, eyes wide with something like panic. "I mean, I believe he believes what he says. That he really does think that, he's not just saying it to get out of trouble."

Her wide-eyed gaze pleads with me, as earnest as always, so desperate to do the right thing—except, right now, I'm pretty sure we have entirely different ideas of what the right thing is.

"Maybe he thought Bella wanted it," I suggest sarcastically. "But she just couldn't *say*."

"Rose—" Cara sounds anguished.

"I can believe Finn might have thought something like that," I continue spitefully, knowing I probably shouldn't but saying it anyway, because I'm angry. "He's always been something of an arrogant little jerk, hasn't he?"

"*Rose.*" Her eyes widen with hurt, and I feel a flicker of regret for being cruel. Even so, I press on.

"Come on, Cara. You know he has, at least for the last few years. That swagger. That sure-fire cockiness. Making all the sports teams, president of this, captain of that. He thinks a lot of himself, doesn't he? And you and Michael do, too, so proud of your golden boy. It's obvious."

My words are laden with disdain, and her eyes flash not just with hurt, but with anger now. "Is it so wrong to be proud of our own child, for his accomplishments?" she asks quietly, and then continues, her voice sharpening, "Or maybe you don't know what that feels like."

I almost let out a laugh. Cara, being catty? She never is, and yet I know I drove her to it. "I'm not desperate to get my child into Harvard, no," I reply with a defiant shrug. "Maybe that's affecting your thinking here. I know you both are panting to get him into an Ivy, with all those varsity sports on his transcript."

Her cheeks flush and I can tell I've hit the nail right on its smug head. Of course they care more about where Finn goes to college than doing what's right. Than about things like justice, or equality.

"So you think it's wrong to be concerned for Finn's future?" she asks.

"Above all other things, yes. He committed a crime, Cara. An act of—"

"You don't know that for sure. You can't, whatever Bella says." She leans forward, her intense gaze boring into mine. "You may take your daughter's word for it, Rose, but I don't have to."

"And why should I believe an arrogant little ass like Finn over—"

"You're talking," she interjects, her voice shaking, "about my *son*."

I lean forward, my hands gripping the counter. "And you're talking about my *daughter*. If Finn didn't assault Bella, what do you actually think happened? Tell me." I lean back, expansive again, but with an edge. "Tell me exactly what you think happened, if it wasn't assault. She lied? She forgot? What?"

"I don't *know*." Her voice turns ragged and I feel a sudden, surprise surge of sympathy for her, because this has to be so very hard, and I'm certainly not even trying to make it any easier. It has to be as agonizing, in its own way, as my situation is, and maybe even more so because, as a mother, Cara has done everything right. At least, I know that's how she would look at it. She did everything you're supposed to as a mom to safeguard against disaster, and I did basically nothing, and yet here we are. She doesn't deserve this. But then neither does Bella.

Still, it's enough to make my breathing even as I lower my voice. "What did Finn say happened, exactly?"

"He didn't. He just insisted that he didn't do it, and then he got really angry and upset and accused us of not believing him."

She takes a gulping sort of breath. "But Henry said they had been... you know, making out earlier in the evening, and I just wondered... with all that they'd drunk... maybe some wires got crossed?" She glances at me hopefully, and my sympathy withers. "There really might have been a misunderstanding of some sort, at some point..."

"Maybe Finn misunderstood that you can't grope someone without their consent, and making sexual advances on someone who is *literally* unconscious constitutes assault," I reply evenly. "Maybe that's where the misunderstanding was, Cara."

She bows her head, her eyes closed, a penitent, and I am reminded that this isn't actually her fault. If I were in her place, maybe I would be looking for reasons, too. Excuses. Brad would tell me to take a step back from this, from my own roiling emotions, but I can't, and I'm not even sure I want to. The seesaw of my feelings toward Cara, sympathy and anger pinging back and forth, is exhausting along with everything else. It would be easier simply to blame her, hate her, but I can't.

"Well?" I ask when Cara simply sits there, her head still bowed, saying nothing.

Slowly, she raises her head; the look in her eyes is bleak. "Finn really seemed like he believed he hadn't touched her that way," she states quietly. "Maybe we need to talk to him again."

"Maybe you do."

She blinks back sudden tears, and I feel a reluctant thawing toward her. I really should not be taking out my anger on Cara, and yet... "How is Bella?" she asks, and in that second, I know we are both realizing she should have asked that first, long before she launched into everything else about Finn.

I think of Bella defiantly going out, the tears in her eyes, the tremble of her lips. "She's struggling," I reply, "and trying not to. But when she first told me... she was broken, Cara. Absolutely broken."

"I really am so sorry..." The words are whispered, pointless.

"I wish I'd never suggested they stay at the beach," she exclaims suddenly, and while I agree with her, I am also annoyed. The problem wasn't that they stayed at the beach. The problem was Finn. As mothers, we want to protect our children, orchestrate events to keep them from harm. And yet what if they are the harm? What do you do then?

I realize I don't actually know what I would do if I were in Cara's situation. March Finn to the police station? Maybe. But maybe not.

It's enough to make me say to her, only a little bit grudgingly, "I might as well tell you she doesn't want to go to the police. She just wants to forget this ever happened, and move on."

"*Oh...*" Cara is trying to hide it, but I hear the palpable relief in her voice, see the glimmer of hope in her eyes that this can, after all, just go away. But it won't go away for Bella, and it shouldn't for Finn.

"But I don't think that's the right thing to do,'" I continue, my voice coming out hard again. "I know it isn't."

I've never told Cara my history, the way I told Brad, way back when. I'm not even sure why; I suppose I didn't want to poke holes in the persona I'd constructed for myself, that bright, breezy woman Cara believed in so ardently. She looked up to me, and I enjoyed it. I didn't want to give her a reason not to, and the truth is, that's what people do when you mention words like *rape* and *assault*.

Oh, they might try to hide it, act all shocked or sympathetic, but you can see the truth of it in their eyes, that flicker of skepticism, the questions they won't ask even if they are almost certainly thinking them—*Yes, but what did you do? What were you wearing? How much had you had to drink? Did you flirt? I mean, he wasn't a stranger, so...* Women can be just as judgmental as men, maybe even more so. *That never happened to me*, they might think, *so why did it happen to you?*

Would Cara have responded that way? I realize there is only one way to find out.

"You know," I tell her, my voice turning brittle, "I was assaulted when I was just a little older than Bella. Raped, actually, by a guy I went on a date with." Her eyes widen and her mouth parts silently. "I know I've told you how protective my parents were," I continue, "way too much."

I'd, somewhat laughingly, told Cara about all the rules—a ten o'clock curfew on weekends, only going out with friends whose parents they'd met, phone numbers always having to be given. Dates alone with boys completely forbidden, not that anyone asked me, because the whole neighborhood knew about my parents, hard-working Catholics who took everything so seriously. I'd joked about it all to Cara, rolled my eyes, never letting on how stifled it made me feel, how *scared*, like one misstep was all it might take... and, as it turned out, that was true.

"It made me naïve," I tell her now, "and so when I went on a date my first semester of college, I didn't actually realize..."

I stop, because that's not what I meant to say. What was I supposed to *realize*? That guys expect sex on the first date? That if you kiss a guy while lying on your bed in your dorm room, he thinks you're up for anything and everything, and he's justified in doing so? That when you push his hands away, mumbling because you're embarrassed, he'll laugh and keep trying, more insistent this time, his body heavy on top of yours, his hands reaching, grabbing, hurting? And when you push him away again, a little scared now, he'll become exasperated, and call you a tease? And when you are mortified and confused and near tears, having absolutely no idea how to handle this moment, he will take this as consent and rape you while you close your eyes and try to disappear?

Was that what I was meant to realize?

"Rose, I'm so sorry." Cara's voice is hushed, and I realize

I've simply been staring into space. "I had no idea you'd gone through that. I wish..." She stops, starts again. "I really am so sorry."

"It was a long time ago." I'm not sure why I say this; I know full well that assault is not something you just get over. Time is not that great a healer, as it happens. "But," I continue, forcing myself to sound brisk, "maybe you understand why I want justice for Bella. My rapist never had to deal with the police. He was never even accused, because everyone told me not to bother." Including, first of all, my own mother, when I confessed to her in tears and shame.

"Finn didn't rape Bella," Cara whispers, her voice hushed, appalled. "It's not the same..."

"Right, so the sentence won't be as severe," I reply crisply. "But he assaulted her, and that's still a crime, as I'm sure you know."

Cara's face is ashen. "If you really did go to the police, and you insisted on prosecution, a trial, all that... Rose, it would ruin his life. I know you think worrying about where he goes to college isn't important, and on one level, maybe it isn't. Not like... But, *Rose*." She leans forward. "You know it would affect him, his whole future." She shakes her head, despondent, disbelieving. "Do you really want my son to go to jail? When you consider all the circumstances?" She flings a hand out before I can reply. "I *know* what Bella experienced was devastating. I know she'll need to recover, heal..." She trails off, a silent *et cetera*. "But she can still go to college, live a full life. She won't have a criminal record. She—"

"She won't have a criminal record because she didn't commit a crime," I interject. "Do you see the difference?"

Cara's face is bloodless now, her hands clasped in front of her. "Please, Rose. Can't we talk about this all together? Figure out a way forward that makes sense for everyone? If Finn really did what Bella said he did, then he should apologize to her. Of *course*. Whatever you want, a conversation, some way to make amends... *yes*. But do we really have to involve the police? Turn it into some big, public spectacle that will hurt everyone?"

"And Finn most of all," I finish sardonically. Of course.

"Why," Cara asks, her voice shaking, "do you blame me for wanting to support my son? If Bella had done something wrong, would you stop loving her?"

"I'm not asking you to stop loving Finn," I return. "But maybe the best way to love him is to make him face up to his crimes. Isn't that what real love is? Tough love?"

"And there are different ways of doing that. Ways that—"

"Don't have consequences?" I finish, cynical now. We're just going around in circles, having the same conversation, never seeing the other's perspective. Never wanting to. I understand why Cara came over here, but there's no point in continuing this. "I told you, Bella doesn't want to go the police," I remind her, wearily. It's exhausting, to go through all this emotion, both mine and Bella's, over and over. "But I am still going to try to convince her to go," I tell Cara. "That much you should know. I want her to report this to the police, and I want the police to investigate it, and I don't think I am in the wrong about that."

Cara stares at me for a long moment, blinking slowly, before she slides off the stool. "Then is there nothing more to say?" she asks bleakly.

I stare back at her for a few seconds, her shoulders slumped, her face pale, everything about her defeated, and again I feel that flicker of sympathy. This isn't her fault. "I'm sorry, Cara," I say. "Truly I am, because I can only imagine how heartbreaking it is to be in your situation. But that doesn't change the facts, or what is actually the right thing to do here." I speak as calmly as I can, hoping that even in the midst of all this emotion, Cara can see the rightness of my cause. "I hope you can appreciate that, even if it's hard."

"Hard?" she repeats. "You think this is just *hard*?" She

stares at me in disbelief, and although I don't want to, I find I have to look away.

I feel guilty, and it infuriates me. I'm not in the wrong here —but then, neither is Cara. I open my mouth to say I'm sorry— for what, exactly, I'm not sure—but before I can form the words, Cara, shaking her head slowly, walks from the room. I hear the front door click behind her, and I know our friendship is over forever.

CHAPTER 13

CARA

That Tuesday, the first day of school, I leave with the boys to get to work. I'm the office manager of a small pediatric practice in Norwalk, and while I have enjoyed my job, it tends to be frantic. I don't have the mental energy to think of anything else when I'm at work, and yet I know I have to. I have to figure out a way to deal with all of this.

Yesterday, I told Michael that Rose was going to try to convince Bella to go to the police, how firm and resolute she was about it. I kept it short, because it hurt too much to talk about. To remember the way Rose looked at me, like I was the enemy, or worse, like I was suggesting something abhorrent and vile, for saying the things I did. For trying to make sense of our situation, of *Finn*, a boy she's swung up into her arms, whose tummy she's tickled, whose face she's covered with kisses, and, all right, yes, that all happened a long time ago, but isn't that the point? We have history, and she doesn't even want to acknowledge it. She won't let it make a difference.

"Why is she on such a vendetta?" Michael asked wearily when I told him, and I stayed silent, not wanting to tell him about how she'd been raped. That felt too private to share, and even now I am reeling in shock over it. I can't believe Rose never told me such an important thing about herself; absurdly, perhaps, that hurt, along with everything else. Did she not trust me with that secret? Were we not as good friends as I thought we were, even back at the beginning, when I thought we shared everything about ourselves? Or at least, most things.

It's true I've never told her about my mom, not really. I've never explained how I always feared I was unlovable, until I met Michael, or how I try to do everything right so he—and everyone else—will keep loving me. I know it's not healthy, I've worked through it, or tried to, but I've never felt brave enough to tell Rose, just as she, I suppose, was never brave enough to tell me about her past. It makes me wonder what sort of friends we really were.

"Why does it matter?" I said instead to Michael, deciding not to debate the questionable use of the word *vendetta*. "The point is, that's where she's coming from. We need to talk to Finn before the police do, and figure out exactly what happened."

"He told us what happened—"

"Come on, Michael. He said 'no way,' that's it. We need details, all of them, or at least as much as he can remember." Even if I dread the conversation with every fiber of my being.

"All right, fine." Michael nodded, his expression turning grim. "Let's talk to him tonight."

But events overtook us—it was the night before school started and Henry couldn't find some books he needed and Finn was stressed about his pre-season soccer training, a match on Saturday—and so we didn't sit down and have that serious talk as we'd promised. We ate dinner, and found stray sneakers and notebooks and a backpack with a browning banana in it that hadn't been aired out in three months, and tried to get ready for going back to school and work, all of which felt strangely overwhelming, like a mountain I'd never climbed before, even though I've done it every year, usually with a color-coded calendar and a neatly ticked-off to-do list. And I thought I was on top of everything. Clearly that was, in so many ways, nothing more than a mirage.

This morning, I try to tell Finn that we need to have a talk after school, but he's distracted and harassed and he doesn't really listen. I walk them both to the bus on the corner and then I drive to work in Norwalk without even saying goodbye to Michael; somehow we slipped past each other without noticing. I feel exhausted and numb, but at the same time my mind is racing, racing, looking for some escape hatch I've missed. Some way to resolve this situation without it ruining my son's life.

I think of how resolute Rose was, how determined to see justice done. She doesn't care if Finn's whole life is torpedoed, if he can't get into college, if he has a criminal record for doing what so many other boys have done. And that's *if* he did do it, which I'm not entirely sure he did, no matter that I have admitted to myself he might have been capable of it. *Still.* Does he deserve to have so much taken away from him, for a single slip?

I know that's not the right way to think. I know if I voiced these kinds of thoughts out loud to friends, or, heaven forbid, on social media, I would be utterly excoriated. Canceled, if a nobody like me can even be canceled. But if I tweeted something indiscreet, would I lose my job? Be suspended? Something would happen, surely. None of it bears thinking about, and yet I have to. I have to find a way to save my son that makes sense. First, though, I have to figure out what he did or didn't do.

At work, I am catapulted into busyness, thankful that after the Labor Day weekend, the practice is heaving with appointments for childhood vaccinations, wellness checks and summer cases of swimmer's ear, so I don't have time to think about anything else. I am processing invoices, dealing with insurance claims, reviewing and then forwarding a new HR policy to the whole staff, even manning the front desk when Susan, our receptionist, goes on break. As office manager, I do a bit of everything, especially when staff tend to be in short supply. We lost our business manager last year and haven't yet replaced him, so I now have to deal with the clinical and administrative budgets on top of everything else. I like being busy, feeling competent, and I'm usually happy to be nearly rushed off my feet for most of the day, but right now I am too fragile, too worn out and on edge. Everything is exhausting me, and my brain feels as if it is working on half-speed even as my mind races.

When lunch comes, I decide to take a full half-hour, more than I usually do, and get a sandwich from a café down the street. I am so distracted that I am already taking my sandwich and turning away after I've swiped my card, only to have the teenager at the register say uncomfortably, "Um, ma'am? Your card was declined."

"What?" I turn back to stare at him blankly. "I used it just a few days ago." I can't remember when, but I am not the type of person whose credit card is ever declined.

The teenager shrugs and I feel the impatience of the line of people behind me, holding their sandwiches, wanting to pay. Someone shifts from foot to foot; another person mutters under their breath.

I feel my face heat as I tuck my sandwich under my arm and fumble with my purse. "Okay, let me try another one."

Fortunately, my debit card is accepted and with a silent sigh of relief, I hurry away. I'll have to figure out what happened with the card later; I keep track of all our credit and debit cards, the whole household budget, while Michael deals with our life insurance and pensions, that sort of stuff. It's been an arrangement that works out well, and I can't believe that I may have dropped the ball and missed a payment or something. Or what if it's a case of identity theft?

I push the problem away for later as I sit outside on a park bench, unwrap the sandwich I don't even want, and try to think what to do. My mind feels stalled out, like I've come up against an enormous mental brick wall and I don't know how to navigate it. There's no going around it; do I tear it down brick by brick with my bare hands? How do I fight this? Should I fight it? If Finn is guilty... Rose certainly seemed to think she knew what the right thing to do was. I wonder if she'll be satisfied with anything other than Finn behind bars.

Of course, he wouldn't actually go to jail for what he did. At least I don't think he would, considering the circumstances of the situation. But his reputation would be in tatters. He might be kicked off his sports teams, or even out of school. Would Rose be satisfied with that? Would she feel he'd paid enough, for that single transgression?

After a few seconds of simply staring into space, I finally swipe my phone. I hesitate for a moment and then, resolutely yet with trepidation, I type in the internet browser's search box *teenaged sexual assault*. The first result that comes up is on a website about parenting, and it helpfully includes its key takeaways in bullet points at the top of the article. They are: *sexual assault is a serious crime; sexual assault is any unwanted sexual behavior that happens without consent, including touching, kissing, and penetration; if your teenager decides to report sexual assault, there are people specially trained to help them through this process.*

I put down the phone, my stomach churning. Where is the help for the boys—and their parents—who have been accused? Or do those websites not exist?

I pick up my phone again and swipe the back button, then type into the search box *teenaged boy accused of sexual assault*. This time, the first result that comes up is a horrible story written by an anonymous mother, whose fourteen-year-old son was accused of assault after a girl in his class sent him a topless photo of herself, and they then met up and made out.

How it got to an accusation of assault is a rabbit trail of fear and intimidation—the girl's mother got hold of her phone, called the school, who, it seems, overreacted and suspended the boy without so much as a conversation. The gossip and judgment that followed forced him to leave the school, depressed and suicidal, seen as a rapist even though he had believed all along the situation had been consensual. I wonder if the girl, terrified of being similarly pilloried, stayed silent. Is this what we've come to? Is that the kind of future Finn faces?

I click on the next link, and this time it's a far worse story of a fifteen-year-old girl who got drunk at a party, was raped by three boys from her class, who filmed it and sent the video around the school. She killed herself while they have yet to face any kind of justice.

I feel sick, utterly sick in both my stomach and heart, that these terrible things happen, that this is the world in which we live. And yet what can I do about it? I'm not some social justice warrior; I'm not about to *campaign*. I just want to protect my family. They are the ones I have to care about right now.

And yet still, perhaps as some sort of punishment, I continue to swipe. I read story after story of both boys and girls who are victims and aggressors. Girls who have been assaulted, humiliated, shamed and judged, with no justice to be found at all. Boys who are terrified to so much as speak to a girl, lest they be seen as someone capable of assault or worse. And boys, so many boys, who swagger through school, believing every girl is theirs for the taking, *and taking them*, because that is how the world—their world—has always worked and no one is telling them otherwise.

Then I stumble upon a site that is nothing but a place for girls to post anonymously about the assault they have experienced, a virtual wall where they can share their stories, finally be heard. The stories are short, bleak, uncompromisingly matter-of-fact and yet filled with pain. I scroll through a few of them, my mouth slack, as I read of girl after girl—child after child—who was forced to do something she didn't want to do. Not by strangers in the street, but the men they trusted— friends, boyfriends, first dates.

He pushed my head down and I couldn't move. He was on top of me and I couldn't breathe. I said I didn't want to and he said as his girlfriend it was my responsibility.

I close my eyes, bile rising in my throat, and then I force myself to read more.

He bought me a drink, so I felt I had to. I never said no, so it can't have been rape. I just closed my eyes and waited for it to be over. I was passed out and when I woke up, my underwear was around my ankles, and everyone was laughing.

Finally, I thrust the phone away from me. I can't bear to read anymore. I can't bear to think that Finn might have been on the other side of something like that. Michael and I have got to talk to him tonight, I resolve shakily. We have to get to the bottom of this, no matter how hard it is. No matter how much it hurts us—or Finn.

By the time I get back from work, Finn and Henry have been home from school for over an hour. In the past, we've had strict rules about this unsupervised hour of limbo before I get home from work: piano practice and homework only, screen time is for later. The only food they can eat is the snacks I left out that morning—carrot sticks and hummus, a can of Pringles because I'm not a monster. I know Rose thinks this sort of thing is ridiculous, and my standards have certainly slipped as the kids have got older. It feels a little absurd telling a sixteen-year-old he's got to finish his cut-up apple. And yet it worked. Didn't it? Clear boundaries and strict rules *worked*.

Except now that we're in this situation, I wonder if they did at all. Surely if they worked so well, we wouldn't be here, facing this. In any case, I forgot to leave out a snack this morning, and judging from the state of the kitchen, they've helped themselves. Toast crumbs litter the counter, the butter and jam are both out, along with a half-gallon of milk, now lukewarm. It all feels like some kind of taunt to me, that they don't have to obey my rules anymore, that they know it. And maybe even that they never cared about them anyway.

I know Rose, and even Michael, and probably most other people, would just shrug and roll their eyes. *Teenagers*, they'd say. *You know how thoughtless and self-obsessed they can be. They'll grow out of it.* And maybe that's true, but do I really want to take that risk as a parent? And *will* they grow out of it, if I just ignore it all?

And so I don't. I walk upstairs, rap firmly on Finn's door, and then Henry's. "Boys, there's a mess downstairs and it needs cleaning up. Now." I keep my voice brisk, not angry, and I turn around and walk downstairs without waiting to see if they will follow. In the kitchen, I put my purse away, charge my phone, my heart starting to beat hard, because what if they don't come down? Am I prepared for this battle right now, when I know there is a much, much bigger one to face?

Thankfully, they do. Henry slinks into the kitchen first, followed by Finn. Neither of them makes eye contact with me or each other as they clean up the kitchen—Henry putting the milk away, Finn the butter and jam. I watch them for a few moments before I tidy up the loaf of bread and sweep toast crumbs into my hand.

"How was school?" I ask as I deposit my handful of crumbs into the trash.

Henry shrugs.

"Fine," Finn says.

I want to ask if he saw or talked to Bella, but not while Henry is here. I also want to tell Finn that we will need to have a talk with him tonight, since I don't think that registered this morning, but again, not while Henry is here.

In any case, I'm not given the chance to say anything. They both slouch out of the room before I manage a word. As I hear the thud of their footsteps upstairs, I reach for my phone to call Michael.

"Cara?" He sounds alarmed, and I wonder if he's bracing himself for bad news. This is all going to get worse, I know, it's just a question of how much, but not quite yet.

"I just wanted to make sure you were on board with talking to Finn tonight. So we can really figure out what happened that night at the beach." I try to sound brisk, but I think I fail. I recall everything I read during my lunch hour, and I suddenly feel as if I could cry, although I'm not even sure for whom. For my son, for myself, for those poor girls on that site, their words like drops of blood on the page, spilling out their pain?

"Yes, I know," Michael says. He sounds resigned. "Has Finn said anything more to you?"

"No, but there hasn't really been the opportunity."

We are both silent, and I have a sudden urge to ask him what happened, not during that night on the beach, but to us. *Why have you become so distant? Did I do something wrong?* This whole situation is forcing me to confront people and problems in a way I never have wanted to before, conversation after painful conversation, and yet I'm still afraid to ask my husband about the state of our marriage. Instead, I focus on the mundane, the trivial.

"My AmEx got declined this afternoon," I tell him. "I was wondering if I was late with a payment, but I don't think I was. Has your card been okay?"

"My card?" Michael sounds nonplussed. "Yeah, I think so."

"All right." I sigh, the sound too heavy for dealing with the petty irritation of a canceled card. "I guess I'll look into it."

"I'll try to be home early," Michael says. "By five at the latest."

And yet you complained about being home by five for the barbecue? Funny how our priorities shift. I can't help but now wish, futilely, that Michael had come home a lot later. Maybe then none of this would have ever happened. Maybe we could have avoided all this heartache and hurt, if Michael had missed his train. Maybe... the most pointless word in the world.

"Okay," I say, and we end the call.

The next few hours feel like a bizarre facsimile of normality, a close copy but not quite an exact reproduction of what a happy family is meant to look like. I make dinner—spaghetti and meatballs. I tell Henry to practice piano, so the strains of Chopin's *Prelude in B Minor*, hauntingly beautiful, drift through the kitchen as I fry onions, giving the most mundane of activities a strange and terrible poignancy, as if we are actors in a play, on a stage, a captivated audience watching our every unknowing move, aware, as we are not, of how it will all soon end in tragedy.

I shake my head at my own melodramatic thoughts as I prod the onions; I am not usually so fanciful. I prefer to be practical, no-nonsense; flights of emotions can be dangerous. Rose was the careless dreamer, not me. She's the one emoting all over the place, effusive, extravagant. I've seen the flip side of that now, I realize. She is just as over-the-top in her anger as she was in her cheerfulness. I suppose I should have expected her to be, and yet her hostility still takes me by surprise, grieves me along with everything else that has happened.

From the living room, the music suddenly stops, and I am

brought back to reality, without its accompanying sorrowful soundtrack, with a thud.

"Do I have to play anymore?" Henry asks, standing in the kitchen doorway, and for a second, I am struck by how tall he's grown over the summer; I have one of those breath-catching moments when you can see your child not just as himself but as others might observe him. His shirt is too small, the sleeves too short so his wrists, bony and thin, are bare for a good two inches; his hands dangle down, long and elegant, piano player's fingers for sure, a man's hands on a boy's body. He must only be a couple of inches shorter than Finn, I realize with a ripple of shock. He really does need a haircut.

"No, you don't," I tell him with a smile. "But you can set the table."

Wordlessly, without any protest, he goes to the cutlery drawer and collects forks and knives with a rattle of silver. I watch him, wondering if I am imagining how abject he seems. He's always been a bit morose—a true melancholic, as Rose has said, with a sympathetic smile—but he's usually a bit more energetic, more animated. Is he worried for Finn? Anxious about the unknowns?

I think back to when he was little, and he needed to know everything that was happening the next day. *Yes, but when will we go to the library? Will we return all our books? Will I get a new one? What will we do after?* It had been charming, in a bittersweet sort of way, and I'd always done my best to answer each question matter-of-factly, to offer him the reassurance he so clearly craved. Unfortunately, I can't do that now. Still, I try to engage him.

"Are you okay, Henry?" I ask quietly as he starts setting the table.

He shrugs, his gaze on the knives and forks.

"Is there anything bothering you?" I press.

Still nothing, and so I grasp the nettle.

"Is it this situation with Finn?"

"What *is* this situation with Finn?" he asks, a bit belligerently, as he turns to me. "Did something happen with him and Bella? Because I feel like no one is telling me anything, and yet something massive is going down."

I hesitate, my gaze returning to the onions. "We're still trying to figure it out."

From the corner of my eye, I see Henry frown, and I know he is registering that I did not deny the massive remark.

"What is there to figure out?" he asks.

"You know they were both drunk." I pause, but he doesn't say anything, just stares at me. "They... remember things differently."

"You mean..." He swallows. "How they were, you know..."

"Yes."

A blush is spreading up his neck, along his cheeks as he keeps his gaze on the table. "They both seemed pretty into it," he half-mumbles. "I'm pretty sure about that."

"Well, unfortunately, because they'd both been drinking alcohol, their memories of what happened are somewhat hazy." Somehow, when I say it like this, it doesn't sound so bad, and it's almost reassuring. They were drunk. Stuff happened. Does every teenaged fumble have to become a case of assault?

But then I think of Rose, and all those heart-breaking stories online, and I feel stomach-churningly guilty for thinking that way for even a second.

"We're going to talk to Finn tonight," I tell Henry. "Try to get to the bottom of this. And my hope is that it will all be sorted out soon." Which makes it sound like a simple misunderstanding, and part of me still hopes that it is. Surely a desperate, futile wish, and yet I say it with as much conviction as I can muster. "But, you know," I continue, "this doesn't need to affect you, Henry."

He gives me a look of incredulity. "You think my brother

being accused of something like this doesn't affect me? Everyone will be talking about it in school. Not to mention," he adds under his breath, "that Finn can be a big jerk when things aren't going his way." He slams a knife onto the table, his one act of rebellion.

"Have people been talking about it in school?"

Henry shrugs. "How would I know? I'm not in Finn's crowd." He speaks matter-of-factly, without bitterness; I don't think Henry has ever wanted the kind of popularity Finn receives as his due. He prefers animé and gaming to sports and parties; he has a couple of good friends, they all do the same geeky stuff together. I'm especially glad of that now, and I hope that he can keep away from the gossip that is surely rising like a tide, coming for us in a flood.

"Okay." I nod slowly, accepting, ready to leave it there for now. I don't want to dig for information about Finn with Henry; that isn't good for either of them. Answers can wait until tonight. Hopefully, *hopefully*, we'll get them then... from Finn.

It's like a repeat of the first time we talked to Finn, in Michael's study, with Henry upstairs in his room. Even though I think Michael and I are trying to be both relaxed and matter-of-fact, authoritative yet calm—what a tightrope parenting is, I can't help but think—the mood is tense, and Finn looks sulky before we start.

He is sitting in the chair in the corner this time, and Michael is at his desk, fingers steepled like some CEO. I have brought in a kitchen chair and sit in the corner across from Finn, so we make an abject triangle, all of us silent, waiting.

"Finn," Michael says finally, fingers still steepled. "Talk us through that night. Tell us what happened with Bella."

Finn shrugs, already defiant. "What, you want *details*?" There's a hint of scorn, even disgust, to his voice, like we're creepy voyeurs, wanting to know what he got up to with a girl. And yet we have to know.

"Yes," Michael replies steadily, and I'm grateful for his calm because I can't seem to find mine. Maybe I shouldn't have looked all that stuff up online. I feel like shrieking, screeching. I want to take Finn by the shoulders and shake him until his teeth rattle; I want to hug him tight to my chest and never let him go. I'm not used to all this emotion; the force of it frightens me. I perch on my chair, my hands hidden in my lap, clenched together so hard my knuckles hurt.

Another shrug from Finn. "We were all just hanging out."

"And the beer?" Michael asks. "Where did that come from?"

Finn lets out a long sigh, like this is all so tedious, scraping his feet along the floor as he sprawls back in his chair. "From a friend."

"Not a fake ID?"

He rolls his eyes. "Is that really important?"

"It would help, to know you're telling the truth about one thing, in order to be able to believe you about another," Michael replies. "So, what was it? A friend or a fake ID?"

For once, Finn looks a little chastened, hanging his head. "A fake ID," he admits in a half-mumble. "I bought the beer earlier and had it in my backpack."

I let out the breath I was holding as quietly as possible. I'm glad he told the truth, even if I don't like it. I wonder if I should have mentioned Bella bringing a flask of something to Rose, but I am pretty sure it would have just incited her ire, and she would have shrugged it off anyway. What does it matter, really, who brought the alcohol?

I glance at Michael, who seems to be struggling to figure out our next steps. Neither of us wants to start asking who put their hand where, how Finn and Bella got together.

"And you and Bella..." I finally prompt. "How did that start?"

"Do you really need to know this?" Finn bursts out. "Because it's really—"

"Yes, Finn, we do." This from Michael, sounding severe. "Bella has alleged you assaulted her. We need to know *exactly* what happened."

Finn looks between us, and just like before, his defiance drops and he starts to seem scared. "Is this, like, really, serious?" he asks, and his voice suddenly sounds small. "Because you guys are acting really weird."

"Yes, Finn, it is serious," Michael replies in the same severe voice. I see how his hand is clenching the armrest of his chair, how white the skin around his mouth is. "We told you before what Bella accused you of—"

"Yeah, but—"

"What we didn't tell you," Michael cuts him off, "is that Mr. and Mrs. Ross are encouraging her to go to the police with an accusation of sexual assault."

"What..." The breath escapes him in a rush as he looks between us again. "The *police*? But..." He trails off, dazedly, and I realize in that moment he has not remotely envisioned something like this; he thought, perhaps, that we were coming down too hard on him, the way he feels we often do, with our curfews and rules about phones and all the rest. He didn't realize, just like Rose suggested so scathingly, that what Bella said he did was actually a crime. Here is his misunderstanding, and it both infuriates and grieves me. How could he *not* think it was serious, after everything that has happened?

"Look, I didn't assault her," he says, speaking quickly now, leaning forward in his chair, everything about him urgent and focused, as if he can clear this up with just a few words. "I mean, yeah, we messed around. We'd both been drinking—Bella brought some vodka, it wasn't just me—and we were laughing and, I don't know, somehow we were talking about how we'd never got together. Bella started it," he remembers, his eyes lighting up with the seeming importance of this detail. "She was asking if I'd ever had a crush on her. And I laughed it off, said of course I had, I mean, when I was a *kid*, and then Bella said maybe we should kiss. She said it, not me." He looks at Michael wildly, and then me, as if we can confirm this, as if our expressions will clear and we'll both say, *oh, okay then...* "So we did," he finishes, "and then Henry and Elspeth got, I don't know, annoyed, and they both left. And we were alone, so..." He trails off, shrugging as he spreads his hands wide.

"Did you have sex with her?" Michael asks matter-of-factly, while I try not to wince, cringe.

"No." Finn's face is pale and he is sitting up straight now, gripping the sides of his chair. "*No.* I mean, yeah, we fooled around. A bit. Maybe more than a bit. Like..." He swallows, and when he speaks his voice cracks. "Do you really need to know all this?"

"These are the questions the police will ask, Finn," I tell him quietly. "Like Dad said, we need to know exactly what happened." Even if I dread hearing any of it.

He doesn't reply; his face is even paler, sweat breaking out on his forehead as he clutches the arms of his chair.

"Okay," he says on a gulp, "well, we, you know, kissed. And stuff. I mean, not... not like, *that* much." He flushes, twisting in his chair, so clearly uncomfortable. "Do we have to go into this? Like, completely?"

Michael and I glance at each other; *do we?* This is already excruciating. How many more details do we really need?

"Bella is saying you assaulted her later in the evening, when she was passed out," Michael states. "So I suppose after the events you've just described. She says..." He pauses, swallowing, before continuing, managing to keep his voice steady, "She says she woke up to you on top of her, kissing her and touching her. Intimately, under her shorts." Michael stops abruptly, swallowing hard. I feel both numb and wild, frozen in place, my stomach churning.

The silence in the room feels like concrete poured over us. I look down at my lap, blinking slowly as I try to keep my breathing even. I think this might be the worst conversation I've ever had to endure.

The silence ticks on, endless, excruciating, second by second. Then Finn makes a sound, a hitching of his breath. When I look up, his face is crumpling, full of panic and fear.

"After? But..." He gulps. "I didn't... I mean, I don't *think* I..." He gulps, scrubbing at his cheeks, blinking hard. "I was really drunk, Mom. Dad." He swings between us, as if begging us to find answers, to make it all better, and I so, so wish we could. "Maybe... I don't know... I really don't think... but... I can't remember everything exactly..." Another gulp. "When you told me about it the other night, I thought you meant *before*. You know, when we were... and that was definitely... she was... she was into it, then." He stares at us both, eyes wide and panicked, his Adam's apple bobbing as he gulps for air. "I know she was, then, definitely. But after... I mean, I was out of it. I know that. But I don't think I would... I really don't... but I can't remember... I don't know. *I don't know.*"

And then he starts to cry, like a little boy, like a frightened child. My frightened child, with shoulders shaking and sobs he chokes back in, pressing his hands to his eyes.

And as his childish bravado, his swagger and defiance, drop away, my love expands, encompasses us all. I drop to my knees as I put my arms around him and bring his head to my shoulder. He doesn't resist; he clings to me, his arms tight around me and I ache with both love and regret. My boy. *My boy.*

"It's going to be okay, Finn," I say gently as I stroke his hair, which is a promise I know I can't necessarily keep, but I want to.

Oh, how I want to, and I will do everything, *everything*, in my power to make it true. "We're going to make this okay."

And then, to my surprise, I feel Michael's arms around me, me and Finn. He doesn't say anything, just holds us, holds us both, and with amazement, with hope, I wonder if this is the thing that will finally bring the two of us back together.

CHAPTER 14

ROSE

When Bella comes home from school that first day, she grabs an apple from the fruit bowl and hurries upstairs without answering my pseudo-bright query, the plaintive lament of every mother, *How was your day*? I've long thought it was a pointless, absurd question, demanding only the most dismissive of answers, and yet I continue to ask it. To hope it will somehow engage my children, who move like flashing shadows so quickly through the kitchen, the supposed heart of our home, to somewhere more important—and private.

In this case, Bella's bedroom.

I hear her bedroom door close as Elspeth comes into the kitchen after her, flinging her backpack to the floor as she saunters over to the fridge.

"How was your day?" I ask, and this time I sound dispirited.

"Fine." Elspeth is taking each yogurt container out one by one and sniffing them suspiciously before putting them back. I bought the pack three days ago; I'm pretty sure they're all fine. Well, four or five days ago, now that I think about it, but who cares?

"How did Bella seem to you?" I ask, even though this

doesn't feel like a question I should ask my younger daughter, especially in light of her revelations yesterday. Still, I can't keep from asking it. I need to know, and nothing escapes Elspeth. I'm pretty sure she knows exactly how Bella is doing.

She shrugs, her bony back to me. "I don't know," she replies in a bored voice. "The same, I guess?"

As I look at her, riffling through the contents of the fridge, I am struck by how tall she is, and also how skinny. She doesn't have any curves yet; her legs are like pipe cleaners, her chest as flat as a board. I was the same, the proverbial late bloomer; I remember just how hard it was to look like a tall twelve-year-old in tenth grade, especially when other girls were filling out their C cups.

I take a deep breath, decide to lay it all on the line. "Do you remember what we were talking about yesterday, about Bella and Finn?"

Elspeth lets out a long, bored sigh. "Uh, yeah? Since it was, like, yesterday?"

I ignore the snark to cut to the chase, because I can't keep talking around it all. I need to *know*. "Bella has accused Finn of sexually assaulting her on the night of the barbecue." I leave it at that, waiting for her response, watching her closely.

Elspeth turns around slowly, a yogurt in one hand, her eyes narrowed, her expression thoughtful yet unsurprised. Did she know more than she told me before? Did Bella talk to her about it? I wait her out as she cocks her head, her gaze sweeping slowly over me.

"And?" she finally asks, and I realize I have no idea what to make of that. Why isn't she horrified?

"Did you know?"

She shrugs. "It's been obvious something was going down. You and Dad... Bella... I'm not dumb, you know."

"I know that very well." I try to smile, but my lips tremble, just a little. "Elspeth, I have to ask again, now that I've told you about the assault. Did you see anything that night? Between Finn and Bella?"

"Besides them with their hands all over each other? No."

"But later, when Bella... when she'd drunk too much, and passed out."

"She passed out?" Elspeth smirks. "Typical."

"*Elspeth.*" I am as horrified by her level of unsurprised acceptance of such events as by her apparent callousness toward her sister, and yet considering how angry she was before, should I really be surprised? Clearly Bella and Elspeth's relationship is more difficult than I've ever let myself acknowledge.

Elspeth's chin tilts up a notch. "Sorry, Mom, but you really do have this image of Bella like she's this angel baby of yours, and she's not. I mean, she's not *horrible*," she concedes, despite what she said before, "but she's not who you think she is, that much is for sure."

"And who do you think I think she is?" I ask, curious as to her meaning, despite my desire to keep this conversation on track. "Because, I assure you, I don't think either of you are *angel babies*." I try to lighten my tone, smile, but Elspeth is unimpressed.

"Well, you definitely have an inflated view of Bella and you always have," she states matter-of-factly. "You think she has this heart of gold, not a mean bone in her body, just wants the best for everyone, couldn't hurt a fly, yada, yada, yada." She rolls her eyes, but I hear the hurt in her voice, and I wonder if this is more about how she believes we love Bella more than we love her.

"I don't think Bella is perfect," I say, although I know there is a grain of truth in what Elspeth has been saying. But Bella *is* kind. Elspeth is the one who always picks the fights; Bella always seems to be looking out for her friends. Yet looking at the world-weary certainty on my daughter's face, I wonder if I have been naïve. Or is Elspeth speaking from her distorted view? "But yes," I concede, "I do think she is a kind person—"

"There is a difference," Elspeth cuts across me, "between being kind and just wanting everyone to like you."

I reflect on this for a few seconds. "Is there something wrong with wanting people to like you?"

It's a genuine question, but the sudden flash of scorn on my daughter's face makes me want to retract it. "I'd rather have integrity than do whatever I could to get in with the in-crowd," she snaps, which is surely a different sentiment than wanting people to like you. Isn't it?

"So what does Bella do that bothers you so much?" I ask. "What does she do to get people to like her?"

Elspeth hesitates, and on her face I see a look of mingled guilt and hurt, and I think I know what this is really about. This is about Bella not caring what Elspeth thinks. Not even considering it. When the girls were little, they were closer; at least I think they were. Bella could be motherly to Elspeth, although, as I recall, Elspeth didn't particularly appreciate it, because she wanted to do things herself. She didn't want Bella to cosset her; she wanted her to respect her, even as a little kid. This isn't about Bella being unkind, I realize, not really. It's about her being indifferent, which, to Elspeth, is worse.

"You wouldn't get it," Elspeth finally says, dismissively. "She's just so fake, busy being Miss Popular. Whatever, okay? I don't care."

I'm pretty sure Elspeth does care, and I am determined to do something about it, but right now I need to take control of the conversation. "That may be," I tell her, "and we can talk about it another time, because I care what you think, Elspeth." She stares at me, nonplussed, as I continue, "But right now I need to know about that night. You didn't actually tell me whether you saw anything, you know, later. After you and Henry had gone... Where did you go, anyway?"

Her mouth tightens. "To the playground. Henry went over toward the pier."

"You didn't stay together?"

She hesitates, and then shrugs. "No, he was kind of upset."

This is new, and everything in me perks up. "Upset? Why?"

Another shrug, this one more disinterested. "Because Finn was making fun of him."

"He was?"

Elspeth rolls her eyes. "Yeah, like he always does, calling him a geek and stuff." Her expression darkens. "Finn can be a real jerk sometimes. And his parents don't see it, just like you don't see it with Bella."

"Don't compare Finn to Bella," I reply swiftly, and Elspeth raises her eyebrows.

"Why not? Because you think he assaulted her?" She tilts her head back to look down her nose at me. "Well, I certainly didn't see that." She slams the door of the fridge and turns to walk out of the kitchen, a yogurt in her hand.

I stop her with a ragged plea. "*Elspeth*. Why are you being so... so callous about this? I heard what you said yesterday, about Bella... I know you're angry, and I think I understand why, but..." I am grasping at straws, each plea more pathetic than the one before. "You and Bella usually get along okay, don't you?" I sound as if I am begging her to tell me that they do. "Don't you... don't you care that she was assaulted?"

Elspeth hesitates, torn, it seems, between wanting to trash-talk her sister some more and, perhaps, tell the truth. "Of course I do," she says at last, relenting reluctantly. "I take sexual assault very seriously, Mom, thank you very much." Now she sounds like a teacher, lecturing me. Like I don't take it seriously. "But Bella was all over Finn earlier in the evening."

"You know that doesn't actually make a difference, don't you?" My voice sharpens even though I'm trying to keep it level. I take a deep breath, force myself to sound calmer. "You know, I hope, Elspeth, that being intimate once with someone doesn't give them any rights over your body?" I have had these conversations so many times with my daughters, have made it all so *clear*, and yet Elspeth is still coming out with this? Where did I go wrong? "It's really important," I finish, "that you know that. That you believe it, for yourself as well as for your sister. Your body is your own. Always—"

Elspeth shrugs, already dismissive. "Well, yes, I know that in *theory*," she says as she peels the lid off the yogurt and then licks it. "I mean, everybody does." She crumples up the lid and tosses it toward the trash can; it misses. "In theory."

"But it's not a theory," I reply, my voice rising in frustration. "At least, it shouldn't be."

Elspeth dips a finger into her yogurt and then licks it clean, and distantly I wonder why on earth she couldn't be bothered to get a spoon. "Well, yes," she concedes, the vocal equivalent of a pat on the head. "But, you know, it's different, Mom, in the situation. Bella was totally flirting with Finn, like a *lot*. Really coming on to him. Wanting him to kiss her." She grimaces in distaste, or maybe something deeper.

"Is that so wrong?" I ask quietly.

"She was just trying to prove she could pull him," Elspeth snaps, and I shake my head.

"Prove to whom?"

"To me," she cries, and then she flounces out of the kitchen.

I slump back onto a stool, trying to process everything Elspeth said. *Prove to her?* So Elspeth did have some kind of crush on Finn, as I'd thought? Is that why she's so angry? And yet she's always been a bit disdainful of him, of his high-school jock persona, the way she just called him a jerk... and yet, I know that doesn't really make a difference to a teenaged heart. What if Elspeth was just acting dismissive to hide how much she cared... about Finn?

It seems laughable, and yet, based on what Elspeth just told me, the way she was, I can't help but wonder if it's true. And then I wonder if Elspeth is right, and Bella flirted with Finn simply to prove something to her little sister, always seeming so much smarter than her. If that's the case, then I understand all the more why Bella would have been horrified to wake up to him on top of her. Yet, it hardly puts her in the most flattering light. And neither does it reflect well on Elspeth, whose callousness is motivated by jealousy, pure and simple. No one, I realize, is going to come out of this situation looking anything like an *angel baby*. But, I remind myself, that shouldn't matter to the rights and wrongs of what Finn did.

This time, though, I wonder if I'm being not just naïve, but stubborn. Stupid, even. Getting justice might be a terribly tragic and Pyrrhic victory for Bella, for me. I know, as much as anyone, how costly going to the police can be, how the supposed cure is worse than the disease. I understand completely why Bella wants to stay silent, even if she doesn't think I do.

And yet I believe—I *have* to believe—it's still the right thing to do. Because what is the alternative? That girls—women—just have to put out and shut up? That boys—men—like Finn can do what they want, whenever they want, and no one will bat an eyelid, no woman allowed so much as a squeak of protest? Or, if they do, they'll be seen as troublemakers, drama queens, liars and sluts?

No. I am not going to stick with that abhorrent status quo. I just have to convince my daughter to be brave enough to speak out... the way I never did.

I head upstairs, determined to talk to Bella. Be honest, *real*, the way the parenting books are always telling you to be. All around me, the house is hushed, a mausoleum of a place, everything hushed and expectant. Upstairs, the plush carpet sinks under my feet. As I near Bella's closed bedroom door, I hear her voice floating from within.

"Yeah, I know, right? *So* lame..." I stiffen, and then she lets out a laugh, a careless, carefree sound, like a blossom floating on a breeze. "So, who do you have for English? Mrs. Ellis? Oh, right..." She trails off then to listen to whoever she is talking to, and as the conversation continues in all its pleasant banality, I realize how unconcerned she sounds. How *happy*. And then I realize I don't know how I feel about that.

After a few more minutes, realizing she could be chatting for a while, I tiptoe away, back downstairs. Of course, I'm happy she's happy. I'm *relieved*. Maybe she can move past the assault. Maybe, in today's culture, where kids are putting everything online, where sexting and nudes and Tinder and all the rest of it are par for the course, this isn't really as big a deal as I seem to feel it is.

And then I can't believe I'm actually trying to talk myself out of doing something. That I'm justifying an act that, in any frame of reference, in any society or world, is heinous.

Slowly, I walk into the kitchen, open the fridge. I stare blankly at the contents—some readymade meals, fresh pasta, a tub of marinara sauce. Easy dinners, because I don't really cook. I don't really do anything.

After a few seconds, I close the door and simply stand there. When, I wonder, did I become so *passive*? In every aspect of my life, I am a drifter, a spectator, and have been for years. I haven't worked since before the girls were born, and even then, it was a banal, entry-level job in marketing that I didn't care about. As a stay-at-home mom, I silently (or not so silently) mocked the ever so earnest mothers who insisted on everything organic, learned baby sign language, did all the toddler classes with an absurd amount of zeal. I turned up my nose at crafting parties and Zumba classes and Mary Kay makeup evenings. I was never going to make a wreath, or run a 5K for charity, or be on the PTA, and I was *fine* with that. More than fine. But now I wonder what the hell I've been doing for nearly twenty years.

Is that why I am becoming so proactive about this? Because

I want to finally *do* something? And surely there is nothing more important, more crucial, than seeking justice for my child?

I open the fridge door again, take out the pasta and sauce. I will, at least, do this. I will make dinner, even if it's no more than opening tubs and packets and dumping their contents into pots and pans.

As I work, I wonder how much of what I'm feeling is about Bella, and how much is about me. I think back to the eighteen-year-old I was, naïve and hopeful and shyly pleased when a guy showed just a little bit of interest in me. My parents were working-class Catholics, as strict as they come, sheltering me from the world even as they were always suspicious that I was secretly being enticed by it. I wasn't—not until later, anyway. Not until I realized none of it actually mattered. You could be the biggest goody-two-shoes in the world, do everything right and proper and perfect, and no one would care or even believe you. When I realized that, I decided to welcome the whole wide world in. I went wild, chased every heady pleasure, determined to be defiant and reckless, even as part of me hated myself for who I'd become. I loved to shock, and to act as if I didn't care, when all the while I did. Desperately. It was no way to live, to be, and it is a road of self-destruction I do not want Bella to go down—not one mile, not one inch. Not if I can help it.

And so, with supper simmering on the stove, I go back upstairs, tiptoeing like I'm in trouble, or maybe like I'm scared. I knock on her door, two tentative taps. I should have thought of what to say, how to frame it, but my mind is spinning. Should I tell her about my own experience? Explain why I feel so strongly about this?

The questions evaporate from my mind when she tells me to come in, because her voice is muffled, clogged with tears. I open the door with trepidation, to see her huddled on her bed, clutching her knees to her chest, her face red and blotchy. Half an hour ago, she was laughing, insouciant. Was it all an act?

Don't I know how that goes?

"Bella." I crouch by the side of her bed, rest one hand on her shoulder. "Bella, what's happened, honey?" Although don't I already know what has happened? There doesn't need to be anything more. I know that, too.

Bella sniffs and burrows her head into her knees, as if she is trying to hide from me.

"Sweetheart..." Gently, I squeeze her shoulder. A shudder rips through her, and I stay crouched there, my hand on her shoulder. I don't say anything, because in this moment I realize there is nothing to say. I'm not going to press her to go to the police. I'm certainly not going to tell her it's all going to be okay. I'm not going to tell her my story, either, because right now she has enough of her own pain to be dealing with.

What I am going to do, what I know is the right thing to do, is simply sit here and offer my daughter the love and comfort she so desperately needs. That, right now, is the most important thing, the only thing, for me as her mother to do.

After a few seconds, Bella looks up from her knees, tears trickling down her cheeks, and tries to smile. "I don't know why I feel so sad," she tells me with a ragged attempt at a laugh. "I want this to be no big deal. I just want to get *on* with my life."

"I know." It was exactly the way I felt.

"And sometimes it doesn't feel like that big a deal. Like, Finn took advantage of me. Whatever." She shrugs, rolling her eyes even as another tear slips down her cheek.

I hesitate, only for a millisecond, because I know I need to ask about earlier in the evening, but now is not the time.

"And then?" I ask instead, gently.

"And then I feel angry and stupid and, I don't know, *used*. And I hate feeling like that. And maybe it's my fault—"

"No," I say quickly. "*No*, Bella." I slide my hand from her shoulder to her hands still wrapped around her knees and squeeze them, wanting to imbue her with my strength. My certainty. "No, it is *not* your fault. At all."

"I shouldn't have drunk so much..." she whispers.

"No matter how drunk someone is, it's not a license for anyone else to assault or abuse them," I tell her steadily. Firmly. Believing it utterly. "There is no way that Finn assaulting you is your fault. Not in any way at all."

She stares at me, wide eyes, her expression full of hunger and hope, like she's desperate to believe but she just can't make herself. My heart aches for what I know she's feeling, what I've felt myself. The guilt that cripples and strangles you, the constant self-doubt and second-guessing, and all the while feeling so *dirty*. So used, just as Bella said. Like someone just threw you away.

"We'll get through this," I tell her with another squeeze of her hands. "Day by day, hour by hour. Minute by minute, if necessary. We will, Bella."

"I don't want to go to the police..." This said like an apology, and maybe it is one.

"I know." I take a deep breath, let it out slowly. "And you don't have to, if that's really how you feel. I'm not going to force you to do anything you don't want to do, Bella, I promise. That's not what this is about." At least, I don't want it to be.

Relief suffuses her face and I feel a flash of guilt because I've clearly pressured her, along with disappointment that she really doesn't want to go.

I can't keep myself from adding, "But if you change your mind, Dad and I will support you one hundred percent." I will make sure Brad does, if I have to script his lines myself. "We're on your side, sweetheart. We're here for you. Always."

The smile she gives me is tremulous, fragile, and the most beautiful thing I've ever seen. "Thanks, Mom," she whispers, and then she throws her arms around me and hugs me tight.

CHAPTER 15

CARA

The next week passes by in a surreal sort of normality, so I almost can believe it might last, even as I am bracing myself for something else, something terrible. Finn and Henry go to school, come home. Henry practices piano and Finn starts looking into college applications. I go to work, make dinner, remember how to breathe. My credit card works again, the next time I try it; it almost feel like some cosmic reset button has been pressed. Nothing bad happens, for seven whole days, and I do not take that for granted, at all.

Normal life feels like a miracle now, the mundane become precious. To brew coffee, to put out the trash, to have the greatest problem be finding Finn's cleats... all these things feel wonderful, because there is nothing worse. I am trying not to let the unknown loom; I want to live in this easy moment, I want to believe in it.

Even the distance between Michael and me doesn't seem like such a hard thing as it once did; I almost wonder if I've been imagining it all. Menopausal oversensitivity, maybe, or perhaps he's had something of a midlife crisis that is now starting to pass. Deep down, I know it can't be either of those things, at least not *only* those things, but, in any case, things certainly seem better between us. We are united in—not grief, not yet, but perhaps in fear, which we are keeping at bay, and in love. Love for our son.

Michael comes into the kitchen while I am wiping down counters and the boys are upstairs doing homework, the house feeling peaceful and still. He walks over and puts his arms around me, and I stiffen in shock at the feel of him, because it has been so long since we've actually hugged—a reminder that I *haven't* been imagining it, but right then I just want to enjoy the moment, the sensation, for what it is. I press my cheek against his shoulder and close my eyes as I relax into him. He smells of aftershave and laundry detergent, and his chest is hard and solid and comforting against me.

"This whole thing..." he says in a low voice, cautious, hopeful, his arms around me. "It seems to have blown over."

I nod slowly against his shoulder. "Yes... maybe."

"Has Finn seemed okay to you?"

"Ye-es..." I sound uncertain now, because Finn has definitely seemed more like himself, if with a bit less of the swagger, the brash confidence, which, all in all, is no bad thing, but is he *okay*? Do we really just get to walk on from this, put it in the past, the end? As much as I long for that, it doesn't feel entirely right.

"I know it's not that simple," Michael tells me, as if he can guess the nature of my thoughts, and he probably can. "For Bella, anyway. But if they've decided not to go to the police after all..." He trails off as we both silently finish that sentence. That would answer all our prayers. Keep Finn on track. Save us all.

"I haven't wanted to ask," I admit. "I haven't talked to Rose at all since I went over to her house." And while a week's silence isn't that unusual for us, especially in the last few years, I feel it more this time. I wonder how long it will last, and what will finally break it. "Maybe I should text her, just to check in."

I say this tentatively, because after our last conversation, when she was so angry and so sneering, I am really not looking forward to another round.

"Maybe better to just leave it," Michael advises, and then he drops his arms and steps away from me, and I can't help but feel a little bereft. "She'll get in touch when she wants to."

He speaks confidently, but I'm not so sure. What if Rose is expecting to hear from us? What if our silence fuels her own determination to go to the police? I hate that I'm thinking this way, like this is a game of chess and I need to make the right move. I want to do what's right, not what is merely expedient. "I was thinking, though," I venture hesitantly, "that even if nothing happens, if they don't go to the police... at some point, we should address it. Finn should apologize to Bella, at least—"

Michael jerks back. "And admit his guilt?"

"If he did do it," I remind him quietly. "Then—"

"But he isn't sure he did," Michael cuts me off, "and neither is Bella."

I frown, because that isn't exactly true. "Bella seemed pretty sure, even if she didn't want to go to the police, Michael. She never said she couldn't remember, the way Finn did." At least as far as I know, but I haven't even talked to Bella about it.

Michael sighs, the sound turning into a grimace. "Even so... do you really think an apology is the right course, especially if they aren't even asking for one? Let's not jeopardize anything right now, Cara. The last thing we want to do is make things worse for Finn."

I want to argue, but I don't, because I realize Michael might actually be right. My banana bread didn't go over all that well, and who knows if an apology would just make Rose angrier, as if we think a simple sorry can make it all better.

Like sticking a Band-Aid on a stab wound, don't you think? I can hear her voice, vibrating with fury, already, as she gears up for another fight. *This isn't some playground mishap, Cara. Your son assaulted my daughter.*

Yes, I can imagine her saying something like that.

But then it occurs to me that saying sorry—genuinely and sincerely asking for forgiveness—might be as important for Finn as it is for Bella. Maybe even more so. I don't want an apology to be just another chess move, a way for us—and Finn—to get what he wants. The end game isn't for Finn to get into Harvard, the way Rose made it sound as if it was. It's so much more than that.

"This isn't just about Finn not getting into trouble," I tell Michael slowly, feeling my way through the words. "It's about doing what's right—for him as well as for Bella. I don't want to teach our son the lesson that if he just stays silent and holds his nerve, he can get away with something."

"I don't think Finn thinks he got away with anything," Michael replies, his tone turning censorious. "A week ago, he was in tears, remember?"

"Yes, I remember." And holding my son in my arms, with Michael holding me, made me realize how much I want to do the right thing by him. By all of us. "But this can't be just about Finn getting into an Ivy," I say. "Or staying on the soccer team. It's about making sure he does the right thing. That we teach him how to be a good person, the kind of person who acknowledges the mistakes he's made, who apologizes for them, who is forgiven. Don't you think those things are important?"

Michael's gaze slides away from mine. "Yes, I do..."

"But?" I prompt, because he sounds pretty hesitant, and I don't want him to be. Not about this.

He swings his gaze back to me resolutely. "It's just at what cost, Cara? There's a lot riding on Finn's future right now. And, for the record, I don't think he's some arrogant punk of a kid who thinks he can treat women however he wants. He got drunk. His memory is hazy, and so is Bella's. The whole situation is complicated, and Finn apologizing for something he might not have even done could open up a whole new can of worms that we really do not want to deal with right now. Maybe in time... when things have settled down... but we don't even know if Finn did anything, remember. He might not have."

That feels like such a slim chance I don't bother replying to it. In truth, part of me agrees with what Michael is saying—and part of me really, really doesn't. I don't want to be the type of person who thinks saying sorry is too much of a risk. And yet isn't that the world we live in? Everyone's ready to point a finger, to cancel and to condemn. There's a sort of gleeful frenzy about it, especially online, an unfettered, demented joy in writing people off, in feeling so smugly vindicated in your anger, in smirking and saying "not good enough" when some celebrity or other does offer a groveling apology. I can see Rose saying that—shaking her head, pursing her lips, asking Finn if he really thought a sorry would do it. Maybe apologizing *is* too dangerous.

And yet thinking that way still feels like a cop-out, and a shameful one at that.

"I don't know," I say, and it isn't until I say it that I realize that is a cop-out, too.

Michael nods, satisfied, and I feel my certainty slipping away from me. "Let's give it a little while," he says, and I wonder just how long that is.

As it turns out, it is no more than two weeks, and Michael, nor any of us, is in charge of the timeline. Still, it's a lovely two weeks, a respite from all the drama and uncertainty, when the weather is mild but with a crispness to the air, and the birch leaves are turning ochre, the maple leaves russet. I love this time of year, when everything feels fresh and new, even as the nights draw in and the leaves drop from the trees. I love the normality of life, days passing in a hopeful haze of comings and goings.

My boss talks about hiring a new business manager, to ease my burden. Finn says he's interested in Princeton, and Michael and I look at the application questions online with him, even laugh about the quirkiness of some of them: *What brings you joy? What is your favorite word?*

Henry is enthusiastic about a new afterschool club for drawing cartoons, showing me some of his drawings of dragons and orcs, which I duly and happily admire. Michael sits next to me on the sofa, his shoulder touching mine, as we watch the news one night. On Friday, he even opens a bottle of wine; we drink it together, talk about nothing important. That night, he reaches for me, and afterwards we lie together, my head on his shoulder, both of us silent, sated, the only sound the deep evening out of our breathing.

So many lovely, little, normal things. I cherish them all, every last one.

That Saturday, we all head to the school field for Finn's first big soccer game, against a team from Darien. Football is really the school's big fall sport, with the stadium filling up most Friday nights; the school has come at the top of its league for years, but Finn never wanted to try out for the team. Baseball is the game he really loves, but soccer is close second and so we're all there to support him—Michael, me, Henry.

The sky is a deep, solid blue, the air crystalline, the sun warm, the leaves rippling with myriad colors. I pack a picnic basket—not the big one from the barbecue—and make a day of it, with a thermos of apple cider, homemade cookies, sandwiches. We spread out a blanket at the side of the field, wave to a few families we recognize, although with our work schedules we've never been able to socialize as much as they all seem to, cocktails and dinners and weekend trips to wineries.

"It's a young team," Michael remarks as he surveys the field. "Only two seniors on it." If there is a slight edge to his voice, I know why; Finn was not chosen as captain, even though he's the only one who has been on the team since ninth grade. I told Michael that maybe it was because he'd already been selected to be captain of the baseball team, and they probably wanted to spread the roles and responsibilities around. I'm not sure he was convinced.

We haven't spoken about Bella or the accusation of assault since we agreed to wait it out, and while I've been happy enough not to think about it for a few weeks, especially when life actually seems sweetly simple for once, it still skirts the fringes of my mind, a cloud looming on my mental horizon that I keep pushing away. I can't help but consider what our responsibility is—to Finn, to Bella, to the Rosses, to the world. It isn't just about surviving something, getting to the other side. Is it? Or is it wrong to sacrifice my child to some abstract principle, no matter how noble it is?

In any case, I am determined not to think about any of that today, as I hand out paper cups of cinnamon-spiced cider, the sun shining down on us all, the players warming up on the field.

"All right, Henry?" I ask as I hand him his cup. He has a book resting on his knees but he hasn't opened it. I lean forward to glance at the title; it's some sort of animé thing. "Good book?" I ask lightly, and he shrugs. I know this whole thing with Finn has hit him hard, even though he's trying to hide it. I've seen him watching Finn sometimes, frowning, cautious. I wonder if he's remembered something, or if he's simply worried about what might happen. He's never liked change, not even good change; he wore the same winter coat for three years, even after he'd outgrown it, because he didn't want to try the brand new one I'd bought him. By the time he finally agreed to wear it, it was too small.

As for bigger change, the cataclysmic kind that shifts the dynamic of our family, the earth under our feet... well, I don't even want to imagine how he'd react to that. He and Finn might not be as close as I wish they were, but I know Henry is still concerned for his brother. It both heartens and alarms me, because it means I worry about Henry as well as Finn. What has happened has, in very different ways, affected both of them.

Even today, I can see that Henry has been picking the skin around his fingernails again, which is red and raw. I want to put my arm around him and tell him that maybe, just maybe, it's all going to be all right, after all. That we'll get past this, all of us, together. I settle for a smile, and then the coach blows his whistle and the game starts.

The team wins, and Finn stays out to celebrate, although that makes me a little anxious—where is he going? Who with? What might happen? Still, I tell myself he'll be careful, of *course* he will, and Bella doesn't hang out with the soccer players anyway. But I know I wouldn't have worried like this before the barbecue; I would have assumed he would stay sensible, safe, and follow my rules, naïve as that might have been. Now I realize I really don't know.

I try to keep from overreacting as Michael, Henry, and I all watch a movie together, some silly superhero thing, and it feels nice. More sweet normality, although I don't realize it's the last thing that will feel normal for a long, long time.

As Henry gets ready for bed and Michael finishes a few things in his office, I tidy up the kitchen, set the coffeemaker for the morning. I realize I am humming; I feel, if not happy, no, not quite, but something close. *We can get back to where we were*, I think, *or maybe even some place better. We're already on our way.*

Then the front door opens, and I turn to see Finn coming into the kitchen. His face is pale, and my first thought is he has had too much to drink. Again.

"Finn?" I say, a bit sharply.

He takes a breath, swallows. His hands are jammed into the pockets of his jeans and he lowers his head so I can't see his face as he mumbles, "Something's happened."

I freeze, terror coursing through me already, although I try not to show it. "All right," I say evenly, grateful that I am able to sound calm even as my mind races through worst-case scenarios. "What is it?"

He looks up, anxious now, a pleading look in his eyes. "I didn't do it."

Another statement to freeze my heart, this one worse than before. "What is it that you didn't do, Finn?" I ask steadily, although part of me is thinking, *There seems to be a lot of things you didn't do*.

He sighs heavily, raking a hand through his hair. "Some stupid Instagram reel. I don't know who posted it. They made an anonymous account, tagged practically everyone in our class."

"A reel?" I know about Instagram, of course I do, but I don't know much.

He shrugs impatiently. "Just like, a short video thing."

I take a breath, nod. "And what is it of?"

A hesitation, long and telling. "Of Bella. And me."

What? How? I stare at him slackly. "You mean..."

"Not anything like that," he says quickly. "But about it. About us." He looks miserable as he admits, "Basically, it looks like I'm bragging that I... that we got together, but I wasn't. I didn't. I haven't even told anyone about it."

And yet someone posted about it? My eyes narrow as I stare at him, the way his gaze slides away. He is six years old and he's just lied about who broke the vase in the hall that Michael and I received as a wedding present. There's a soccer ball on the floor...

But he isn't six, I think, and this is far, far more serious.

"You haven't told anyone at all, Finn?" I ask. "Are you sure?"

A slight blush touches his cheeks. "Well, I mean I did tell a couple of guys that we, you know, got together, but not like that." For a second, he looks hurt. "I didn't brag about it or anything. I'm not a jerk, Mom."

"Can I see it?" Again, he hesitates, and I hold out my hand. "I want to see it, Finn."

Reluctantly, he takes his phone out of his pocket, swipes a few times, and then shows me. It's a carousel of photos—first Finn in his baseball uniform, posing with a bat, eyes narrowed against the sun, some publicity shot for the school. And then it's a photo of Bella, looking like a prom queen, blonde and beautiful, a photo taken from her own Instagram feed, perhaps. There's a soundtrack of some pop song I don't know, and the final photo, to my shock, is of Bella sprawled on the beach, long, golden legs tangled in front of her, her top riding up and her shorts unbuttoned to show a slip of skin, her expression unfocused. And written in a neon-pink scrawl above are the damning words: *Guess who tapped this.*

I thrust the phone away from me, back at Finn. He takes it, abject, repentant, and I feel icy inside, icy and terrified, but also angry. "You said it wasn't of that night."

"I meant it wasn't of the two of us, together—"

"Who took that photo of Bella?" I demand in a low voice. "Because there are only three people who could have, Finn, as far as I know, and I really don't think it was Elspeth or Henry."

His expression is miserable, wretched. "I took the photo."

"What..." Even though I suspected it, it is a shock to hear him say. Instinctively, I take a step back from him, and his face crumples into hurt.

"*Mom...*"

"You took that photo of Bella when she was passed out?" Like some sort of *trophy*? I feel sick inside, and it must show on my face because Finn holds his arms out to me, a supplicant.

"She wasn't passed out!" The words explode from him in a panicked cry. "It was when we were messing around. She took a bunch of photos of me, too. We showed them to each other. It was just for fun, a joke..."

So how did they get on Instagram? "And then?" I ask levelly.

"And then, I don't know! I didn't send it to anyone." He pauses, hanging his head, his voice lowering into a mutter. "At least, I don't think I did."

I feel like taking another step back, distancing myself from all this, from my own son, but I manage to hold my ground. "You think there's a chance you might have sent that photo to someone?"

"I don't know!" He sounds angry, but I know it's really fear. "I mean, we were messing around on social media, laughing about how if people found out..." He trails off and I feel like there's something I'm missing.

"Why would it be such a big deal if people found out, Finn?"

He looks startled, and then embarrassed. His cheeks go pink again. "Because Bella's, like, the ice queen. She never hooks up with anybody."

"She doesn't?" Does that make a difference? It definitely doesn't help Finn's cause, I think, even though I know it's unfair. I press one hand to my head, which has begun to ache. "So why did she get together with you?"

He shrugs. "I don't know. I thought maybe she liked me." His gaze slides away from me. "But not that much, obviously."

Because if she did, she wouldn't have accused him of assault? Is that how he thinks this works? My head hurts. My heart hurts. "Are there any more surprises?" I ask my son.

"No. I mean... I'd forgotten about the photos. They weren't a big deal. If you looked at her phone, you'd see some of me." I definitely do not want to see similarly styled photos of my son on Bella's phone.

"But this person didn't post that kind of photo of you," I

point out as reasonably as I can. "Why is that? And why did they make it about you bragging?"

"I don't know. I really don't, Mom." He looks earnest now, like if I just believe him, it will make a difference. But already I know it won't. If Rose sees this... if it gets people gossiping...

I shake my head. "Can you see on your phone if you might have sent it to people? On text messages or whatever?"

The look Finn gives me is mingled scorn and pity, along with regret. "Nobody sends text messages anymore, Mom."

"So how do you send photos?"

"Snapchat, mainly. They disappear."

Except this one damned well isn't disappearing.

I take a deep breath, try to think calmly. What are we supposed to do now? If Finn didn't make the reel, there's nothing we can do, is there? I really do believe that he didn't make it; cynically, perhaps, I think he wouldn't have told me about it if he had. The trouble is, I don't know if any of this will make a difference.

"Well, thank you for telling me about this," I say finally.

"It doesn't... change things, does it?" he asks. "I mean... the Rosses aren't actually going to go to the police?"

I glance at him sharply. "I don't know if they're going to the police or not."

"But it's been, like, weeks." There is something about his tone that is both hopeful and calculated, and it fills me with dismay, with dread.

"Finn," I tell him, "they could still go to the police. There's not a time limit on it."

"But, I mean... it's less likely, now, isn't it?" he says, and I realize just how much he has moved past this—more, perhaps, than he should have.

"I don't know whether it's likely or not. But, Finn, it's not just about whether they go to the police." I hesitate, because if my husband didn't like it when I said something like this, I know my son will even less, and yet even so, I feel the need to say it. "It's about doing the right thing."

His face settles into stubborn lines, his lower lip thrust out just like it was the day of the barbecue, when he asked me if he couldn't go. How I wish now that I'd told him he didn't have to.

"And so what am I supposed to do?" he asks, a bit sulkily.

"I don't know," I admit. "Maybe, at some point, you should apologize to Bella."

"But I don't even know if..." He takes a breath, lets it out. "Fine. I mean, if she's willing to speak to me, I'll say sorry." He shrugs. "If it makes a difference."

I'm not sure it will, at least not enough, but I'm grateful he's willing.

I glance back down at the phone as I hand it back to him. "Do you have any idea who might have posted that?"

He starts to shake his head and then stops, first looking uncomfortable, and then guilty, like he's been caught with his hand in the cookie jar, crumbs around his mouth. "Well, I mean, I guess... anyone on the soccer team could have," he half-mumbles. "I mean, only as a joke... it's not like it's that bad, is it? I mean, the last photo? Bella saw it and thought it was okay."

And while I'm horrified, I also get it. The photo of Bella on the beach isn't as racy as what most girls put on their own feeds. I've glanced at Bella's phone when she's mindlessly scrolling, and her friends' pages look can sometimes look like porn shots, sexily posed, scantily clad. Not that I'm judging, but a single undone button isn't the same thing, surely. And yet the message, the unabashed gloating. And the music—the words of the pop song registering for the first time in my shocked consciousness.

"What was the song that's playing on the reel?" I ask, and Finn looks pained.

"Just some lame song," he says, like an apology, and I can't keep from letting out a groan, because I heard at least one word in the song—slut.

"*Finn...*"

"I didn't do it!"

Realization thuds through me. "That might not matter."

"But it should," he insists, and I can't argue against that.

"Do you know how many views it has had?" I ask instead.

He glances down at his phone. "Five hundred," he admits in a low voice. "And it was only posted an hour ago."

Five *hundred*? There are less than two thousand students at the high school. What if the entire school has seen it by morning? Part of me wants to insist this could still not be that big a deal; far, far more intrusive and incendiary things are posted on Instagram all the time. And yet. *And yet.*

If Bella had decided she didn't want to go to the police, I'm afraid this just might convince her otherwise, and if not her, then certainly Rose.

CHAPTER 16

ROSE

Bella doesn't show me the photo at first. She doesn't tell me anything. We get through the first weeks of school in a way that almost feels normal, although I know I am hovering, fluttering, useless. I try to get her to eat breakfast; I tell her I'm always available to talk. She gives me fleeting smiles that don't reach her eyes and walks away. I try with Elspeth, too, suggesting a Saturday together, maybe going to a spa. She looks scornful, as I knew she would. She's too smart not to realize I'm trying to make it up to her, but is that so wrong? What else am I supposed to do? I decide to leave it, ask again later, but the moment never comes.

Then, three weeks into the school year, Bella rushes in off the bus, into the house, runs upstairs and slams the door to her bedroom so hard it feels as if the whole house, all five thousand square feet of it, shakes.

Elspeth comes in after, her backpack trailing behind her, looking uncharacteristically subdued.

"What's happened?" I demand without preamble.

For the last two weeks, I have been as gentle and involved as I can be, as loving and accepting, attentive and *there*. I have made dinner every night. There have been snacks when the girls come home from school. I've asked Elspeth about her homework, her afterschool club on the school newspaper. I've told Bella I am always here to talk, or really, just to listen. I am trying to do everything right, but in this moment, when I can hear Bella's noisy sobs from upstairs, it all evaporates in a single puff of smoke, and I am back to being both aimless and stressed, never knowing what the right steps are but blundering onward anyway.

"Elspeth?" My voice is sharp when she doesn't answer. "What's happened?"

She shrugs, letting go of her backpack as she sidles towards the fridge. "I don't know."

"You must know something," I insist.

She avoids looking at me as she opens the fridge, as she always does every day after school, studying its contents with more concentration than surely is necessary. She seems reluctant to impart any details, and that makes me nervous. I think I'd almost prefer her spark, her fire.

"Elspeth?" I ask again.

"People are talking at school."

"About Bella?"

"And Finn."

"And what are they saying?" Already, my hands are curling into fists, nails digging into palms. Of course, I know what they are saying, or at least what *kinds* of things they're saying. What kinds of things they always say.

Another shrug, her gaze fixed on the fridge. "You know. Stuff."

"*Elspeth.*"

She sighs and closes the fridge, then turns to face me, her arms folded, her expression stubborn and closed. "They're calling her a slut and stuff. For getting together with Finn."

So damned typical, I think. The girl's the slut, the guy's the player. Always.

"How did this happen?" I ask. "How did people find out?" Did Finn say something, bragging even because he thought he'd got away with it?

Elspeth's gaze slides away from mine and she hunches her shoulders, not saying anything.

"Elspeth," I say again, trying to gentle my voice. "Please tell me what you know."

"I don't know anything," she declares, and now her voice is high and thin as she turns back to glare at me. "Why would I know anything?" she demands, her voice ratcheting even higher. "Why do you keep involving me, asking me stuff? Why don't you ask Bella?" And then she runs out of the room, up the stairs, and slams her bedroom door just like Bella did.

I close my eyes. After the reprieve of the last two weeks, it all comes rushing back, leaving me breathless, flattened. There was no *reprieve*, I realize. There was only waiting.

Slowly, my legs leaden, I walk upstairs. I stand in the hallway and listen, but all is ominously silent. Who to talk to first? I think of what Elspeth said and I choose Bella.

There's no response as I knock on her door, but I open it anyway and peek in. Bella is in the corner of her room, knees drawn up to her chest, her cheeks streaked with tears, her hair in a golden tangle about her flushed face. Her expression, though, is one of grim resolve.

"Bella?" I ask. I close the door behind me.

She doesn't look at me as she responds. "I hate school," she states, her lips pressed together. "I hate it."

I take a few steps toward her. "Is this because of what people are saying?"

She glances at me sharply. "Who told you what people are saying?"

"Elspeth."

Bella lets out a shuddering breath. "Even Elspeth has heard about it?"

There's a very slightly sneering tone to her words, an incredulous edge, a certain dismissiveness. I doubt Bella even hears it, but it gives me a second's pause, because it matches what Elspeth has revealed.

"What happened, Bella?" I ask after a moment, keeping my voice gentle. "Why are people talking about it now?"

"Because some stupid jerk posted some photo on Instagram." Her face sets into even grimmer lines. "It's *so* unfair."

"Someone posted a photo?" These days, words to chill my heart, considering what kids get up to online, what can be posted, shared, turn viral. "Was it Finn?"

"I don't know. Maybe? But I didn't think..." She hesitates, her face crumpling as her breath comes out in a ragged rush. "I know this is stupid, but I didn't think he'd do something like that."

And what is there to say to that? "I know, sweetheart. I'm sorry."

I slide down to sit next to her on the floor, my arm around her. She burrows her head against my shoulder and for a second we just sit, Bella leaning against me. I wish I had words of comfort to offer, but I know that I don't, not really. Will it get better? Eventually, yes. Will people forget? Mostly, but some will always remember. Is it fair? No. Absolutely not.

"Why are guys such jerks?" she asks finally, the words mumbled against my shirt.

"Not all guys," I tell her, but then I think about her father, and I wonder if I should take it back. I don't have a lot of sterling examples to offer. "I'm sorry, so sorry, sweetheart, about all this."

Bella eases back from me, wiping her cheeks. "Everyone's talking about what a big man Finn is, how he's *scored*." Her lip curls in disdain even as her eyes flash hurt. "He's treated like some hero and I'm slut-shamed, even though there are plenty of girls who have done so much more. So much *worse*. But nobody cares. They're all whispering, giggling. Someone wrote 'slut' on my locker, in *Sharpie*. It's so *wrong*."

I simply nod, knowing she needs to vent, raging silently on her behalf.

"How could he do that?" she demands, her voice breaking. "How could he *brag* about it, when he knows how it happened? What he did?"

"Because he got away with it." The words slip out before I can fully think them through. I am thinking about the man who raped me. I only saw him once, after it happened. We walked by each other at UConn, in a stream of students heading to their next class, and as he went past me, his lips twitched in a small, knowing smile and his gaze raked over my body. I ran to the nearest bathroom and threw up. I transferred to another UConn campus the next semester.

"I don't want him to get away with it," Bella declares, and her voice comes out hard, sounding like a stranger's. "It's not fair. It's not right. I didn't want to go to the police before, because I didn't want to make a big deal of it. But now he's made it a big deal, and everyone's joining in. I mean, do you know how many girls do stuff, way worse than I did? And yet I'm the one with 'slut' on my locker." She shakes her head, furious now, fierce. "Everyone just needs someone to hate, and Finn is the one who made it be me." Her eyes glitter as she turns to me. "I want to go to the police now. I'll tell them everything."

My heart leaps with both hope and trepidation. This was what I wanted, justice for my daughter, but now that it might come to pass, I am terrified for her, for the scrutiny she'll have to endure, the shame she won't be able to help feel. "Are you sure?" I ask, and she nods, one firm up and down of her head.

"Yes. I'm sure."

I reach for her hand, hold it tightly. "Okay," I tell her

quietly. "We can go together. Dad and I will support you, one hundred percent, Bella." Another squeeze as I try to imbue her with my strength, strength I didn't have at her age. "I'm proud of you, sweetheart."

We go that very evening. Brad is stuck at work—entertaining some Japanese clients at some steak-and-sushi place—and so it's just Bella and me. When I tell Elspeth where we're going, her face pales.

"Really? But why? I mean..." Her gaze darts from Bella to me and back again, and I feel a flash of guilt for leaving her alone at home.

"Bella has decided it's what she wants to do," I state.

Bella stands next to me, hunched and silent. Is she having second thoughts? I can only imagine how scary this must be. I never even got this far, but I'm so glad Bella has.

"We shouldn't be too long, Elspeth. You'll be all right on your own for a few hours? Don't answer the door to anyone," I instruct, even though I know she knows that already. "Any problems, call or text me, okay? Dad shouldn't be home too late." Which, I realize, is more or less a lie, if he decides to take his clients to a strip club after the steak and sushi, but maybe, all things considered, he won't. I did text him to tell him what we were doing, but two scotches into the evening, he probably won't check his phone.

"Okay." Elspeth folds her arms, looking uncertain. "I... I hope it goes well," she says. "If these things can go well."

I feel a rush of love for my spiky daughter, trying to soften.

Bella doesn't even reply, but I guess she's distracted.

I don't know what to expect from the police, although I certainly had some vague but sure hopes that things would have moved on from thirty years ago, when my mother and my resident assistant at UConn both told me to just let it go. *You have so much going for you*, my RA said earnestly. *Don't let this define your life.*

Unfortunately, that wasn't entirely my choice.

But since I never even made it to the police—after being fed horror stories of shame, skepticism, and sneering—I really thought they'd be different now. And they are different, in that they tick all the boxes. They follow the rules. But the flicker of doubt in the sergeant's eyes is exactly the same as the one in the RA's, in my mother's.

"My daughter wishes to make a report of sexual assault," I state firmly to the desk sergeant as Bella squirms silently next to me.

"Okay." He seems unimpressed. "Did this happen tonight?"

"No, on the Saturday of Labor Day weekend."

There's that flicker. "Okay." He glances at Bella. "We can take a statement in private. Would you like to speak to a rape crisis counsellor?"

"I wasn't raped," Bella whispers, so quietly that the sergeant doesn't hear her.

"Sorry, what was that?"

She speaks a little bit louder. "I wasn't raped."

He hesitates and then says dutifully, like he's reading from a script, and he probably is, "If you believe you have experienced any type of sexual assault, you have the opportunity to speak to an officer specially trained in dealing with sexual offenses."

Bella glances at me, and I can see from the panic in her eyes that she is regretting this already.

I take control again. "Yes, we would like that, thank you."

He turns to Bella. "Would you like to speak to the officer alone?"

I stiffen, bristle at the seeming rudeness of the question, as my daughter, without looking at me, nods. "Yes, please."

And so I spend thirty minutes in the waiting room while Bella talks to a woman in her thirties who is their specialist for sexual offences. I tell myself there is absolutely no need to be offended or hurt by her decision, that the woman will have to ask a lot of invasive questions about what exactly happened that night, and Bella understandably doesn't want me listening me in while she describes just how far Finn's hand went up her shorts.

Still, I can't hide it from myself. I *am* hurt. I wanted to be there with Bella, to hold her hand, be her staunch supporter—as much for my sake as hers. *I* needed this closure, and the realization humbles me. No matter how many times I tell myself this isn't about me, it seems I still need the reminders.

Just as Bella is coming out from one of the interview rooms, looking pale and shaken, Brad texts me. *The police? Now?? I'll be home late.*

So he is going to a strip club or something similar. I don't have time to think about that as Bella walks toward me and I stand up, sliding my phone into my pocket.

"Bella—"

"Let's go," she says woodenly, and the officer gives us a sympathetic smile.

"We'll be in touch," she says, and then Bella is marching out of the police station, and I have no choice but to follow her, and I feel like this wasn't at all what I wanted it to be.

"You want to talk about it?" I ask as we get into the car.

Bella sits in the passenger seat, her arms folded as she stares straight ahead. "The woman was nice, but it's all basically a big joke," she states flatly, and then, in a mimicking sort of voice, says, "'Are you sure you are remembering it that way, honey? I know this is painful for you, but we all do things we regret when we've had too much to drink, don't we? But it's important for you to know that no matter what, this is not your fault.'" She lets out a sound of disgust as she shakes her head.

"That seems like some really mixed messages right there," I tell her quietly.

I turn out of the station parking lot, and we drive home through the darkness, Bella fuming all the while.

"They said they can open an investigation, but unless there are witnesses it's just a case of 'he said, she said,' and there isn't much they can do."

Which is exactly what Brad said. I hate that he was right, that he knew he was right.

"What does it mean," I ask, "to open an investigation?"

Bella shrugs. "She didn't say."

So, write a few words in a file, then call it a day? Frustration boils through me. I wish I'd been in the room with Bella; I would have stood up for her, made sure they listened, but it's too late now.

Bella turns to look out the window. "I wish I didn't come here," she says in a low voice, and guilt follows frustrations, a rushing river of it.

"I'm sorry, Bella."

She shrugs. "People will stop talking about it eventually," she tells me, trying to sound nonchalant and completely failing. Her lips tremble before she presses them together and stares determinedly out the window. She brushes her fingertip with her eye to catch a tear, and my fingers tighten on the wheel.

I feel like screaming, shrieking, breaking down and weeping. I want to drive over to the Johnstons' and punch Finn in the face. I want to stomp through the school and scream at every stupid student there, who lives off the gossip, the vindictiveness and the hypocrisy. Most of all, I want to gather Bella into my arms and protect her from everything and everyone in this world that stomps on you and doesn't care. But none of those things would actually help, and Bella wouldn't want me to do them anyway.

And so I do what I can, and I give her a smile as I reach over and touch her hand, hoping to convey my love, my support, as we drive the rest of the way home in silence.

Elspeth is waiting by the front door as we come in, looking anxious.

"How did it go? What happened?" she asks, and I wonder when she started caring so much. A few days ago, she was completely dismissive of Bella's assault claim, but now she looks invested. Worried for her sister's sake.

"The police won't do anything," Bella tells her as she heads upstairs, defeated. "Not without witnesses."

"Witnesses?" Elspeth says the word sharply and I do a doubletake. *Did* she see something, and she just hasn't said? She glances at me and then quickly looks away, and before I can say anything, she heads upstairs, following Bella, so I am alone, wondering what any of us can do now.

CHAPTER 17

CARA

The police come for Finn while he's at school, during the last week in September. No warning, nothing at all, just a call from the school's principal, his words guarded, as if he is already distancing the school from their once superstar student.

"Finn has been taken to the police station for questioning in relation to an allegation of sexual assault," the principal, Mr. Wood, tells me, his voice somewhere between censorious and matter-of-fact. "Naturally, the school takes this type of allegation very seriously, and we will be working in full cooperation with the police, as well as reviewing the situation ourselves." He makes it sound like Finn has already been found guilty, sent to jail.

I close my eyes, draw a breath as I taste bile. I've been so afraid of this exact scenario unfolding, and yet I am still completely unprepared for this moment. "It's an *allegation*," I remind Mr. Wood, a man who has always been jovial with me in the past, positively chummy, beaming fondly at Finn. Now he sounds like he is trying to forget both our names.

"And we take such allegations very seriously, Mrs. Johnston," he repeats, as if I need reminding. I know what he's really scared of—this whole situation going viral, the school made to look bad. In one of my internet deep dives, I read stories of schools that had been vilified by both parents and press for not taking such allegations seriously. They were accused of protecting their football stars, worried more about a home-coming victory than the safety of their female students. And when I read about it, it all sounded awful, hideously unjust, but this is my *son* and it feels different. It is different.

But not for Mr. Wood.

As soon as I finish that call, I make another. I'm at work, I'm not supposed to make personal telephone calls, but this is clearly an emergency. I call Michael.

"Finn's been taken to the police for questioning," I tell him before I've even said hello. He draws his breath in sharply. "I'll go over there now."

"I'm about to go into a meeting, I can't just leave—" He sounds panicked, and I do my best to reassure him, even though my heart is thundering and my palms are clammy.

"I'll go, it'll be okay. Maybe... maybe this can be cleared up quickly." I'm just saying words without thinking them through, much less meaning them, but Michael takes me at my word.

"Okay," he says shakily, as if I can promise such a thing. We both know it's not going to work like that. "Keep me updated."

My boss is not impressed with my unexplained emergency —I'm not about to say exactly what has happened with Finn— but since I haven't had any emergencies in the ten years I've been working there, he lets me go. If he didn't, I suppose I would have just walked out, and maybe lost my job on top of everything else. It hardly seems to matter now. All I can think about is Finn.

Finn, as a pink-cheeked baby, with dimples in his elbows and knees, giving me his gummy smile. Finn at three, a deter-mined tornado, tackling life with scabbed knees and a gap-toothed grin. At twelve, his voice cracking, his Adam's apple emerging, all uncertainty and bravado. At fourteen, spending twenty minutes in front of the mirror with a tube of hair gel, trying to get his style right for the first day of ninth grade. Finn, now being taken for questioning by the police. I feel utterly broken, and yet I don't have the luxury of letting myself fall to pieces. I have to pick myself up, hold myself together... for the sake of my son.

I don't remember the twenty-minute drive to Westport's police station, an innocuous-looking brick building across from the library, in the center of town. My mind is a blur of panic, a constant sound of static as I think of Finn as he was and not as he is, or as I need to be, facing this moment. I need to consider everything very carefully, and yet mere syllables elude me.

When I get to the station, Finn is in one of the interview rooms, being questioned. I am told I can't go in.

"I'm his mother," I insist, my voice trembling, rising. "And he's a minor."

"He's seventeen, which is an adult in terms of criminal law," the sergeant replies.

What? I never knew that. Can that really be a thing? I don't even want to think about the words *criminal law* in relation to my son.

"In any case," he continues, "the police are allowed to question a minor who may be involved in a crime without parental permission or presence."

"But if Finn requested—" I begin, full of fire, but the sergeant shakes his head.

"He didn't. He's been completely willing to answer our questions." He relents a little, gives me something close to a smile. "This is just procedure," he says, and I don't know whether that's meant to be a comfort.

Why did I not google any of this, when involving the police seemed a more likely possibility? Maybe because I didn't want to tempt fate. Press my luck—or Finn's. But the result is I am now standing in a police station, having no idea what to do, or what my—and Finn's—legal standing is. I should have told Michael to call our lawyer. I should be able to spout facts, insist on legalities, but I don't know what they are, and all I have now is my cell phone with patchy service, wondering if I need to call Michael again, call our lawyer, but afraid to take those terrible steps. Maybe I should just trust the sergeant, and assume this is nothing more than *procedure*... whatever that means.

On shaky legs, I turn from the desk and take a seat in the waiting room. I tell myself not to act like the principal and assume this means Finn is guilty, that he will be charged, prosecuted, whatever. They're just asking *questions*, I tell myself. There's no proof of anything; they have no evidence. This might go no further than today, and I need to keep that in the forefront of my mind.

And then I wonder if I am thinking like a criminal, like a guilty person. I realize I feel like one, and I think Finn must, too. Just being questioned is surely bad enough, having the sergeant give me that weary, unsympathetic look, like I'm the one who has done something wrong.

Twenty minutes later, Finn emerges, looking shaken, his hair rumpled where he's clearly driven his fingers through it repeatedly, his eyes dark in his pale face, as he walks unsteadily toward me, an officer behind him. I rise from my seat, my heart lurching into my throat at the sight of him.

"Finn..."

"We'll be in touch," the officer says, like Finn has just left a job interview.

I have a thousand questions, but I don't want to ask any of them right now. I don't think I want to know the answers, not yet. I walk toward Finn and then, on instinct and out of need, I take him in my arms and hug him tightly. He hugs me back, just as tightly, his arms wrapped around me, his head bowed to my shoulder, the way he hasn't since he was a little boy. *My little boy*. For those few precious seconds, all I want to do is absorb his pain, take it deep into myself. Isn't that what a mother does? Aren't I supposed to protect him from this?

And yet he's a man, or as good as, in the eyes of the law. Some things are beyond a mother's duty, a mother's love.

Slowly, I release him, and we walk in silence to the car.

I don't speak and neither does Finn as we start the drive home. My mind and stomach are both churning, and yet I also feel numb. I don't want to move on from this moment, even as I desperately wish we were already far, far past it.

"Can you tell me what happened?" I finally ask quietly, when we are halfway home.

Finn shrugs, turning to look out the window, his expression hidden from me. "They asked me a bunch of questions about that night," he tells me in a low voice. "What I did, what Bella did." In his raggedy tone, I hear a throb of pain, a tremor of fear.

"Do you know how it got to this?" I ask after a moment. I am struggling to know how to handle this moment, what the right words are to say. Maybe there simply aren't any. "Did Bella..."

"She went to the police a few days ago." His voice comes out in a flat monotone now. "She made a report and they said they have a legal obligation to investigate it." It sounds like he is quoting verbatim.

"Okay." I flex my arms, forcing myself to loosen my death grip on the steering wheel. "Did they say what the next steps would be? If there are any?"

Finn jerks his shoulder in a semblance of a shrug. "I don't know. They didn't tell me much, just asked me a lot of questions. And they took my phone."

"Your phone..."

"Because of the photos. And I guess because they think I sent that post." He presses his forehead against the window, and then, none too gently, rears back and hits it against the glass— one, two, three times, each making an awful, smacking sound.

"*Finn.*" I am frightened, as well as far too close to tears. I've never seen him like this before, beyond despondency, beyond even despair. "Finn," I say again, steadying my voice. "We'll get through this, I promise. We will."

"They said they'd spoken to witnesses." He has stopped hitting his forehead against the window, thank goodness, but his is still pressed against it, his eyes closed.

"Witnesses..." my mind whirls. "But who..."

"Who do you think?" he snarls, his eyes still closed.

"You mean... Elspeth?" It must be, and yet I am startled. Would Elspeth really go to the police? Yet if she saw something, why shouldn't she? "Henry said he didn't see anything..." I trail off, because surely Henry wouldn't have gone to the police without telling us.

"Yeah, well, maybe Elspeth did. Or says she did." He draws a shuddering breath. "I feel guilty, and yet I don't even remember doing anything. I'm not sure I *did* do anything, not anymore. But I know Bella can't be lying. I mean, why would she lie? She wouldn't do that to me."

Something about his voice, the intensity of it, the *hurt*, makes me ask, "Finn, why didn't you want to go to the barbecue?" He doesn't reply and I continue, "Why did you ask me if you could skip it, right before?"

Another long silence; this one I wait out. Finally, he says in a weary, defeated sort of voice, "I'd messaged Bella the night before. She left me on read."

"On read?" I've heard the term, but I'm not entirely familiar with it, or its significance now.

Finn lets out a gust of something almost like laughter, although it's too sad-sounding for that. "Get with the kids, Mom. I mean, she saw my message and didn't reply."

Which doesn't sound so bad, but then I think of the messages I've sent to Rose over the last year or two that she waited days or even weeks to reply to, if she replied at all, and I remember how much that hurts.

I also acknowledge how much it must hurt if Finn's message to Bella was personal, or somehow risky, maybe even asking her out... or whatever the terminology is for teens these days. And yet I had no idea he had any interest in Bella. I didn't even think they were friends, not anymore.

"The message you sent her..."

"It wasn't anything bad." He speaks wearily, like he doesn't care anymore, and yet I know he does. He must. "I just said I was, you know, looking forward to seeing her."

Doubtfully in that slang-less terminology, but I know what he means. He showed his interest, and that made him, school superstar that he might be, feel vulnerable.

"You liked her?" I ask, and he shrugs, which is answer enough.

"She didn't even answer, so I figured she wasn't into me. And so, I didn't want to go."

"But at the barbecue," I say slowly, "she was the one who..." This feels so odd, to talk about this with my son. So very uncomfortable, and yet it's necessary. "I thought she was the one who... expressed interest first." I sound like such a prude. I am, I suppose, when it comes to my children. Isn't every parent, more or less?

Finn lets out a sigh, his head still against the window. "Yeah, well, it doesn't matter anymore, does it?"

No, I don't suppose it does. I don't suppose it ever mattered, in terms of the allegation of assault, and yet I am saddened in a whole other way, a way I haven't been before—grieving for the relationship Finn and Bella might have had.

I think back to that balmy day at the aquarium when Rose and I joked about them getting married. *Bella needs someone to believe in her and Finn needs someone who won't take him so seriously.* I had bristled slightly at the time, searching for the faint criticism hidden in those words, but now I wonder if Rose might have been right. If Finn could have given Bella, so pretty and yet so quiet, the confidence she needed, and Bella would have kept Finn from the brashness he's been prone to.

Of course, it's all utterly impossible now, and I shouldn't really spend a moment thinking about it. I need to think about my son, and how to help him through this.

We drive the rest of the way home in silence; it turns out there isn't that much to say. We have to wait to hear back from the police and I wonder again if we should talk to our lawyer.

As we walk into the house, weary and dispirited, Henry comes into the hall, his eyes wide. "Were you... were you at the police station?" he asks. His voice wavers.

"Yeah, I was." The defeated despair I heard in Finn's voice in the car is gone, replaced by something that is turning hard and even ugly. "Were you one of the witnesses?" he demands. "Did you speak to the police?"

"Finn," I protest quickly, unthinkingly. "Of course Henry didn't..." My voice trails away as I watch Henry's face drain of color, his lips part soundlessly. The truth is written right there, and yet I can't let myself believe it. *He went to the police? He turned in his own brother?*

In contrast to his brother's white countenance, Finn's face flushes angrily, his hands balling into fists. I realize that although he made the accusation, he didn't actually expect it to be true. He is blindsided by his brother's betrayal, and his jaw slackens for a mere second before it bunches. "You *fu*—"

"*Finn.*" I intervene, swift and panicked. "Wait a minute—"

But it's too late. Finn has launched himself at his brother, and Henry, too shocked even to duck, topples hard to the floor, Finn on top of him. I'm so shocked that for a few terrible seconds, I watch, helpless, horrified, as Finn starts punching Henry, in the face, in the stomach, his face contorted in anger, in hurt. Henry tries to ward off the blows, but his arms are pinned to his sides by Finn's body and blood blooms on his lip as he turns his face away, crying out, while a shrill, shocked note reverberates through the hallways—me, I realize distantly. I am screaming.

"Finn. *Finn!*" I am crying now, as well as screaming, as I try to pull one son off the other. He is so heavy, far stronger than I am, and I can't do it. "*Finn—*" I tug on his shoulder hard, but he barely notices. I am sobbing now, and Henry is curled on his side, blood trickling from his nose. Then the front door opens and Michael is there; he is pulling Finn away from Henry, flinging him to the floor, his voice thundering.

"Get off of him!"

Finn, breathing hard, blinks up at his father as if coming out of a trance. "He... he turned me in," he gasps out, and then, while Henry retches and weeps, one hand to his bloody nose, Finn begins to sob, deep, guttural sounds torn from his body, tearing my heart.

My family is being destroyed in front of my very eyes.

Above our two sons, Michael's and my gazes meet—both of us bewildered, devastated. Then Michael walks over to Henry, and pulls him up to his feet and into an embrace.

"It's okay, Henry. It's okay."

On unsteady legs, I walk to Finn and tentatively put one hand on his shoulder. He runs his wrist underneath his nose, scrubs at his eyes, and then jerks away from me as he gets to his feet.

"Finn..." I have no idea what to say. "We're a family," I finally tell him, all of us, my voice breaking. "We can't let this tear us apart."

No one replies.

"Please," I say.

Henry gives Finn one bleak, terrified look and then bolts upstairs. Finn scrubs his face again and then walks away from us, his back taut, into the kitchen. Michael and I stand there, silent and appalled.

Finally, after what feels like endless minutes but is probably only a few seconds, he lets out a low breath. "Maybe give them a chance to cool down, and then we'll talk to them. Separately, for now."

I nod, grateful for the suggestion. I, who almost always have a plan, have no idea what to do.

"Why," Michael asks, "was Finn so mad at Henry?"

I close my eyes. "I think... I think Henry went to the police. As a... witness." I can't believe it, even though it was written all over Henry's face. How did he even get to the police? It must be three miles from the school to the station. Then I remember that the police came and took Finn from school. Did they talk to Henry then? I can hardly bear to think about it all—the shock, the fear, the whispers, the condemnation, as Finn was marched from the school. And Henry offered himself as a *witness*. It wasn't the wrong thing to do, I know, and yet it feels like it was.

I open my eyes to see Michael staring at me in shock. "*Henry* did?"

"I think so, yes." I swallow; my mouth tastes of acid. "The police told Finn they had witnesses. And that seems to be Henry and, I suppose, maybe Elspeth."

Michael shakes his head. "But he said he didn't see anything."

I swallow again, my stomach swirling. I'm afraid I might actually be sick. "Maybe he did."

His face darkens. "And so he turned in his *brother*?"

"Michael..." I am about to remind him that just a few weeks ago, he told Henry you could never get in trouble for telling the truth, when I stop. Now isn't the time to argue about whether Henry was right or not. We need to see to our sons. "I'm going to go talk to Henry," I tell him instead. "Maybe you should talk to Finn."

He nods slowly, still shaken, and on wobbly legs, I head first to the kitchen, to get an ice pack. I glimpse Finn standing in the backyard, his hands on his hips, his back to the house as he stares out into the trees. Michael glances at me as he comes into the kitchen, and then he heads outside. I go upstairs.

Henry is on his bed, his back to me, his knees tucked up to his chest. I perch gingerly on the edge of the bed and offer the ice pack. "Put this on your nose," I tell him gently. "Or maybe your eye." He has a black eye, a bloody nose, and a split lip. Tears streak his face and he ignores the ice pack, twisting away from me.

"You didn't tell me that Finn assaulted Bella *later*."

"What?" I blink, trying to absorb this statement, and why it is phrased like an accusation. "It's true I didn't go into details, Henry—"

"I thought Bella was accusing him of you know, *during*. When we saw them." He hugs his knees tighter. "I wouldn't have gone to the police if I'd known it was later."

"You wouldn't have?" I lean over to put the ice pack against his lip, and reluctantly he takes it. "Why wouldn't you have?" I press gently.

"Because... because I didn't see anything then!" he bursts out, one arm hugging his knees even tighter, the other pressing the pack to his lip.

I simply sit there, trying to understand what he isn't saying. "Why did you go to the police at all?" I finally ask, and then I add hurriedly, when I see him stiffen, "I'm not saying it was the wrong thing to do. Of course it wasn't. If they had questions... of course you had to tell them what you knew. Your dad and I will always support you telling the truth, Henry." *Just like we said we would.*

Henry doesn't respond for a long moment. I wait, willing myself not to say anything more, not to jump in with requests or even demands. *Tell me what you know. For the love of God, Henry!* I stay silent.

"Elspeth said we should," he finally says, the words coming slowly, reluctantly. "She said we had to tell the police what we'd seen."

"But what had you seen? I mean... from what you told me before..."

"I *know*!" he bursts out. "I thought... I thought it would be a good idea to go to the police, to tell them that Finn didn't do it. That Bella was, you know, into it."

"Is that what Elspeth wanted?" I am feeling more and more confused, trying to sort out the truth from what all the different parties want the truth to be.

"I don't know," he admits in a mumble. "She seemed like she wanted to get Finn in trouble. I thought... I thought if I went too..." He trails off miserably. "But I don't know what she said. We were interviewed separately."

"At the police station?"

"No, at school." He hugs his knees again, his eyes closed. "But then they told me that Bella was saying Finn had assaulted her *later*... when neither of us were there. I didn't realize that." He opens his eyes, his expression anguished. "I never would have gone if I'd realized... if I'd *realized*..." He trails off, his face full of misery, and I pat his shoulder.

"It's okay, Henry," I say, the words coming automatically even though I'm pretty sure nothing right now is okay at all. "It's okay," I say again, because I don't have any other words, and I so, so want these ones to be true.

CHAPTER 18

ROSE

In the days after we go to the police, I expect Bella to be despondent; I am ready for it. I think of how broken she seemed, the tears in her eyes, and I want to overwhelm her with my mother's love. And so I make oatmeal and toast for breakfast, which she doesn't eat; I give her bracing smiles and quick, tight hugs, which she duly accepts before twisting away. I tell her I'm here for her, and she smiles distractedly as she scrolls on her phone.

It occurs to me that I am not as important to my daughter's wellbeing as I think I am. As I want to be.

When she sails out of the house to school a few days afterward, I am the one who is left feeling lost, bereft, wondering what the future holds. Bella, strangely, seems fine, or at least determined, her chin held high, a glitter in her eyes. I am glad of her strength, but I wonder what it hides. The Instagram post, I know, will blow over, eventually, for everyone else, probably sooner than anyone would expect as the next drama takes precedence. But for Bella? The hurt and betrayal won't be forgotten, along with the painful memory of the assault. Those kinds of things don't just leave scars; they change your DNA, the very essence of who you are. No matter how much you try for them not to.

In any case, I have other things to worry about, or at least consider, picking at my thoughts the way you would a scab, knowing you shouldn't, that it will only make you bleed. The night we went to the police station, Brad came home after midnight, smelling of whiskey and cheap perfume and sweat. What a cliché of the philandering husband, and yet Brad doesn't even think of himself that way, which makes it all the harder to bear, even as I've chosen, time and again, to bear it.

The first time I found out about what went on during his business trips was four years ago, right after his big promotion. There was a cocktail party for directors and their spouses; another wife, pretty drunk at the time, made some joke about how she liked it when they took business trips because it meant her husband left her alone at night for weeks after. We all tittered uncomfortably, but I felt a stab of pity for her, a flicker of disgust. *Who thinks that way,* I thought, and *if you did, why would you stay married?*

Back then, Brad and I were pretty solid, or at least we *seemed* solid, although, in retrospect, of course, it was all a sham, and I think I always knew that on some level. I think, looking back, that even though I was shocked, I wasn't actually surprised.

As we drove back from the city, the lights of the George Washington Bridge streaming by in a yellow and orange blur, I mentioned the conversation to Brad.

"What a creep," I said of the woman's husband. At the time, I thought we were speaking in solidarity; only later did I realize I was testing him. Brad didn't reply, and I turned to look at him. "How many of the guys do that sort of thing?" I asked, sounding both curious and more than a little disapproving, and Brad shrugged and then cleared his throat. "Brad?" I pressed, and with his eyes on the road, his mouth tightening, he replied:

"It's just business."

I stared at him, the yellow lights from the bridge washing across his face, turning it a sickly color. I saw the tightness of his jaw, how his eyes had narrowed, and I realized he was annoyed with me for bringing it up. In his view, this was a discussion that we never should have had to have; I hadn't realized we had agreed on that, without so much as a discussion, but I knew right then that Brad thought we had.

"What exactly," I asked, "is just business?"

He gave a sigh, the sound of impatience. "*Rose.*"

"No, seriously. Tell me. I want to know."

He shifted in his seat, uncomfortable and clearly not wanting to be. Wanting to dismiss this, and for me to, as well. "Entertaining clients is part of the deal. You knew that."

Did I? We'd never discussed it, not the way he seemed to be implying, like we'd had some negotiation, struck a Faustian bargain, laid it all out, signed and sealed.

"I thought entertaining meant steak dinners and cigar bars," I replied after a moment, my voice wavering. He simply stared at the road. "*Brad.*"

The silence ticked on as we drove through the darkness. Then: "What do you want me to tell you?"

"The *truth.*"

"Really?" He glanced at me then, an eyebrow arched sardonically. "It's not a big deal, Rose, but you're clearly wanting to make it one. And if I give you details, you'll just freak out, I can tell. It's how we entertain clients, that's it. Seriously. No. Big. Deal."

He was staring at me like I was a child having a tantrum, and yet I'd barely raised my voice, and I was his *wife.* I was too hurt to feel angry, too shocked to realize how differently we viewed our marriage, our marriage *vows.*

I turned to the window and stared blindly out at the road,

the lights of the other cars blurring before me. We didn't speak for the rest of the way home.

Eventually, later that night when I sat with him in the kitchen, gritty-eyed and aching, I got the details out of him; in a rare show of temper, he spat them at me, one by one, like I was the one who was being unreasonable: The lap dances, the "happy ending" massages, the high-end call girls booked for private parties. He told me he didn't always participate in whatever was going on, like that was meant to make me feel better. "But sometimes I have to," he added, warningly, "for the clients' sake. It's about keeping them happy, that's it."

"And keeping you pretty happy too," I replied bitterly, and he just shook his head, exasperated by my seeming unreasonableness.

"Other wives understand," he told me, and I felt like throwing something at him. Something heavy and hard.

"I'm not other wives," I replied, my voice shaking. "*We're* not other couples. We're not like that, Brad."

Except, it seemed, we were.

That argument was the only time we have ever truly talked about it, although sometimes, mostly to torture myself, I still ask. Back then, as now, Brad was completely immoveable on the subject; as far as he was concerned, it was not even worth discussing. It was part of his job, he had to do it, and as his wife, with all the perks and luxuries that useless role entailed, I had to put up with it—or else.

Not that he ever said the "or else," but he didn't need to. The warning was clear, and lay heavily between us. He was not going to change his attitude or his behavior, so it would be up to me change mine. And the truth was, I wasn't willing to push it, or maybe I was just scared. In any case, I did put up with it, although as the years have gone by, I've wondered more and more why I have. I don't remember making an active decision to do so, only feeling that I had no choice. At the time, Bella was thirteen, Elspeth ten, and I hadn't held down a job in over fifteen years. Not that I even got so far as thinking like that. I just assumed I *had* to put up with it, that that was the only option available to me.

Why, I still don't really know. I don't care that much about being rich. I grew up working class, won a needs-based scholarship to UConn; I've certainly known what it is to do without, and the big house, the country club membership, the designer clothes—I haven't cared that much about any of it, even if I act as if I do. The love I once felt for Brad—and I did love him, when we were young and he was fun and he made me feel both safe and special—has trickled away to a weary sort of tolerance, if that.

The love I felt for him back then, I realize now, was based on the shakiest of foundations; you don't love someone just because they're fun to be around or make you feel safe. You love them because of who they are. And I'm not sure I ever loved Brad for that.

But even so, I never left. I never even thought of leaving.

So when he came home, reeking of booze and perfume, not even asking about Bella going to the police, I expected to do what I always did—which was ignore it. I was already in bed, although I hadn't been able to sleep. My mind kept replaying too many memories—both of Bella and myself at almost the same age. Remembering the futility and fury, the heartbreak and hopelessness. Hating that Bella was going through the same kind of thing I did.

"You're not even going to ask about Bella?" I asked Brad as he shucked off his suit and reached for his pajamas.

"She made a report?" He didn't sound particularly interested, but maybe he was just still drunk. His voice was a little slurred; he'd taken a taxi from the train station, at least.

"Yes, she did."

He let out a sigh as he headed toward the bathroom. "I

suppose you'd have texted me if it had made a difference."

"It would have been nice to have you there, for your support," I replied shortly when he came back into the bedroom, the smell of mint layered over the stale smell of cigarettes and whiskey.

"I support Bella," he replied as he climbed into bed, "but I don't particularly support her going to the police. We should have just drawn a line under the whole thing, Rose, right after it first happened. Bella was doing better. She has other things to focus on, like getting into college. You making a meal of this at every opportunity is hardly helping her."

I sat up in bed, gaping at him, too shocked to be angry, the same as all those years ago. "You're blaming *me*?"

"I'm just saying, let's all move on."

"If the police open an investigation—"

"What are they going to find?" he cuts me off. "That two teenagers drank too much and got up to no good, something that happens every single weekend, all over this country, without much fuss." He adjusted the duvet, turning over on his side so his back was to me. "I feel sorry for Bella, I understand she's upset, I'm sorry for it, but that's life. Unfortunate things happen. The best thing we can do for her now is help her get over it, not keep milking the situation, which you seem to want to do." He paused, and then gentled his tone, although grudgingly. "I do understand why you would, considering your own history. But as I've said before, Rose, this isn't about you." And with that, he switched off the light, discussion over.

I didn't reply. I had no words. I lay there and stared up at the ceiling, and realized I was sharing a bed—a life—with a man who had just been to a strip club, or worse, without so much as a shred of remorse, who had justified his daughter's sexual assault, who had dismissed me and his daughter in every possible way. No. Big. Deal.

I'd allowed him to say it to me all these years, but I wouldn't allow it for Bella. She deserved more from her own father.

The next morning, when Bella seemed so bright, my late-night resolutions predictably began to falter. When Brad hugged her goodbye before school and promised to take her and Elspeth to a "dad-and-daughters" dinner at some ritzy steak-house in the city—with a veggie burger for Elspeth, of course—I was reminded how much Bella adored her father, daddy's girl that she always has been. I saw her at two, three years old, fresh from the bath, being tickled before bed. At eleven, shy and proud at a father-daughter dance at school. Thirteen, and not too big to curl up on her daddy's lap. Seventeen, and accepting the keys to a new SUV incredulously, a kiss for her father's cheek.

As for this? Cynically, I couldn't help but wonder if Brad's suggestion was a calculated move, because he realized he'd come across a little harsh the night before. He hadn't suggested one of those dinners in months, if not years.

And, even more cynically, I wondered why he was trying to keep from losing me—I didn't actually do that much, besides pick up the dry-cleaning, order the groceries, and stay on top of the girls' lives, with the occasional wearily offered sex. But all that, I realized, was probably enough. Besides, he liked the image of himself as the genial family man; divorced dad prob-ably didn't have quite the same ring. And then, of course, there was the whole issue of alimony—in a no-fault divorce, I'd get a hefty chunk of whatever Brad managed not to squirrel away. He wouldn't give it up willingly, I knew that much for sure.

All of it made me feel completely hopeless, jaded. Was there no way out of this? The far worse question, insidious, treacherous, *wrong*, slipped inside my mind—did Brad, in his clumsy, callous way, have a point? Bella did seem happy again, or almost. The thing with the police clearly wasn't going to go anywhere. Maybe it would be better if we all moved on... if we could.

Then Elspeth comes home, about a week after we'd gone to the police, and announces, "The police came today and took Finn in for questioning." She sounds strangely satisfied, which surprises me, because she hasn't exactly been on Bella's side before this, although admittedly she was concerned when we went to the police.

"They did?"

"Yup. At lunch, so everybody saw. But everybody knew about it all, anyway."

My stomach churns as I imagine the whole school gleefully gossiping about my daughter. "Because of that Instagram post?"

Something flashes across Elspeth's face, too quickly for me to decipher what it is. "No, because of Bella's post," she says. "Everyone's read it."

"Bella's post?" This was the first I'd heard of it. "What did she post about?"

Elspeth lets out a sigh, like I'm being thick, and maybe I am. I don't really understand, or like, this world of social media, where teenagers live their whole lives online, the unforeseen repercussions rippling through their reality. Where they're willing to offer it all up as entertainment, to be absorbed or spat out, feted or judged or joked about.

"About the assault, of course," Elspeth tells me, rolling her eyes.

"She posted about it?" I say cautiously. "Where?"

"On a page for women who have been assaulted or harassed to tell their stories anonymously."

Elspeth reaches for her phone, swipes a few times, before proffering to me, although when I reach for the phone to see it better, she typically doesn't let me hold it.

I end up squinting at the type, trying to make it out.

On Labor Day weekend, something terrible happened to me, and ever since it happened, I've felt like it was my fault. I'd

*gotten together with some family friends for a beach barbecue,
and after the parents left, we all had a few beers. It was meant
to be fun, and it was, and yes, I flirted. We kissed. It felt sweet
and innocent and promising, and then I woke up a couple of
hours later to him on top of me, his hand under my shorts, his
face against mine, and I couldn't breathe. It was only a few
seconds, but it felt like forever. I felt trapped, frozen, like I
couldn't think or move. Finally, I pushed him off and rolled
away from him, wanting to forget it happened. Wanting to
forget. But the thing is, no matter how much you want to, you
can't. I started having nightmares, and that was when I could
get to sleep. A lot of nights I couldn't. I felt paranoid, like
everyone was looking at me, especially after word got around
and I was immediately labeled a slut. What was he labeled?
You tell me. I'm writing this because I want to get it out. I
want people to understand how it feels—like I'm dirty, like I
deserve to be shamed. Are you going to ask what I was wearing, or how much I drank, or whether we had history? I've
been asked all those questions and more, but the reality
remains: I was asleep, and I woke up to someone treating my
body like it was their possession. And somehow that's
supposed to be my fault. I deserved it. I asked for it. Well, I'm
telling you now, I didn't and what happened was wrong. It
was a crime, even if I'm the only one who has the guts to call it
what it is.*

I ease back, feeling both shaken and moved, because it's so
painful and raw, and I can imagine how it all happened, and I
don't want to. Bella. My baby. My poor, poor little girl. And yet
she had the strength to say all that, to proclaim it in public, to
announce to the world "this is wrong."

"That's very eloquent," I finally say quietly.

Elspeth pockets her phone. "I helped her write it."

"Did you?" Again, I am surprised by Elspeth's about face.

"You seem very supportive of Bella now," I remark as neutrally as I can. I should be gratified by my daughter's change of heart, but I can't help but be suspicious too, and I'm not sure why. Maybe it's just because I know Elspeth; she always has an angle, and just a few weeks ago, she was completely disdainful of Bella. What, exactly, has changed?

"She was *assaulted*," Elspeth replies, with scornful emphasis.

"Yes. I know." I take a deep breath, let it out slowly. "I'm glad Bella has been able to tell her story." But I am still surprised at how disquieted I feel, at the thought of Finn being taken out of school by the police, in front of everyone. I can't imagine how frightening that would have been, how humiliating. Cara will be in pieces.

But why do I care? Finn needed to be questioned. These are the necessary consequences of his behavior. It was the right thing to do, I *know* it was, and yet I still feel unsettled.

Later, I go upstairs to talk to Bella about it. She's on her bed, texting on her phone and twirling her hair. She sits up when she sees me, her expression turning a little guarded. I realize how serious I must look.

"Mom?"

"Elspeth showed me what you posted online," I tell her as I sit on the edge of her bed. "That must have been a hard thing to do."

She ducks her head. "I just wanted people to know what it feels like."

"Yes, I understand that." I smile at her, through the haze of tears that rise unexpectedly, when I think of what she's been through. "I'm proud of you, Bella."

She looks up quickly, surprise flashing across her features. "You are?"

"Yes." I pause, deliberating, deciding. "I wish I'd had the courage to do something similar."

Confusion crinkles her forehead as she nibbles her lip. "What..."

"I was assaulted when I was just a little older than you are now," I tell her quietly. I'm not going to go into too many details; Brad was right when he said this wasn't about me. "And I never told anyone about it, not really." Because the two people I did tell told me to keep it quiet, not to break my father's heart by knowing his daughter had been dirtied. *Try to forget.* As if.

"Wait.... What... you were?" Bella looks flummoxed.

"Yes." I swallow, surprised to feel the lump in my throat, the way my heart pounds. Thirty years later and the telling isn't any easier. "Maybe I should have told you before," I say to Bella, "but I didn't want to take away from what you were experiencing. I want you to know, though, that I understand. And I'm proud that you've been brave enough to tell people what happened. I wasn't."

"What..." She searches my face as if she can find the answers there. "What happened to you?"

"Something similar to what happened to you." I swallow again, amazed at how hard this is, *still.* "I went on a date, and the man involved thought that meant he had a right to my body." I look down at the bedspread, smooth the creases out with one hand. "When I told... people, they said I should forget about it. That it was hard and sad, but these things happened, and I still had my life to live." I don't want to tell Bella that it was her grandmother who told me that. Although I haven't been close to my parents in years—since then, really—we still visit them a few times a year, keep up the pretense that everything is okay. Bella effuses about my mom's classic style—pearls, twin-set, and a full face of makeup for every occasion. Maybe it's unhealthy, but I'm not willing to take something else away from my daughter right now.

"That sucks, Mom," Bella says after a moment, her voice quiet, almost hushed. "I'm sorry."

I nod jerkily. "Anyway, the point I wanted to make was I'm proud of you for speaking out. I know it can be scary." I pause, because Bella doesn't look scared. "What has the response been?"

To my surprise, her face lights up. "People *get* it," she said. "I think they really do. I only posted it last night, but so many people have read it. And they've texted me and said I was brave and that it was the right thing to do, which has been amazing."

"They have?" I am surprised, and gratified, and yet a little disquieted, too. I don't even know why. This can only be a good thing—raising awareness, telling the truth, receiving support. Why am I resisting it? Is it some masochistic impulse, the last vestiges of self-doubt, thinking I didn't deserve to be believed, and so Bella must not, either? I hate that I wonder, even if for a second.

"My English teacher, Mrs. Reese," Bella continues, "gave me a hug in front of the whole class. And Mr. Wood did this assembly on speaking out when you need to. He didn't mention me, but everyone said he basically was."

"Really?" These things should both please and gratify me, and yet somehow they don't. Not entirely, anyway. As far as the school is concerned, I suspect it is just the usual, useless virtue signaling of every institution these days. They're terrified of being vilified, of something going viral, and so they'll do all the supposedly right things while nothing actually changes. Will Finn be disciplined? I doubt it.

But maybe I'm being too cynical.

"And how do you feel, Bella?" I ask.

"I'm glad I did it," she says firmly. "But it does feel a little... I don't know, revealing." She shrugs, ducking her head. "I didn't think it would all be such a big deal. I just wanted to get it all out... I didn't really think about people actually reading it."

Which is true of most teenagers, I know. They put their innermost selves online and then seem surprised when it becomes public knowledge.

"And Finn?" I ask after a moment.

She tenses, turning guarded again. "What about him?"

"Elspeth said he's been questioned by the police?"

"Yeah." Her expression falls as she chews her lip. "That was weird, when they took him out of the cafeteria. Everyone was just, like, silent. And he didn't look at anyone. Just kept his head down." She sounds regretful, but she doesn't need to be.

"It was the right thing to do," I tell her—and myself. "He needed to be questioned. That is part of the process. It has to be."

"Yeah." She nods slowly, not looking entirely convinced. "Yeah."

We are silent for a moment, both of us imagining the scene —or maybe it's just me. I am the one who is picturing a pale-faced, fearful Finn walking out of the school, flanked by two burly policemen, wondering why the image makes me feel so uneasy. I think of Cara appealing to our shared history, how Finn and Bella used to make forts, have sleepovers.

I have a sudden, piercing memory of bringing in Bella's birthday cake when she was seven or so, and Finn was standing right next to her, grinning hugely. Bella said he could blow the candles out with her, but he didn't, just let her do it by herself, watching with a mingled look of both pride and affection.

Suddenly, I feel overwhelmingly sad, a sweep of grief that rushes right through me, too encompassing to understand, and I wonder if Bella feels it, too.

"Bella," I ask, "have you talked to Finn at all since this happened?"

She shakes her head. "No, I couldn't. I don't even know what I would say to him."

"And he hasn't tried to talk to you?"

"No... he looked like he was going to come up to me once, on the first day of school, but then he didn't, and I walked away." She glances down at her fingers, pleated together. "I actually liked him, you know? And I thought he liked me. But I guess that's all ruined now."

I have no reply to that, no reassurance I can give, because it most surely is ruined, and while the last thing I want is my daughter to date someone capable of assault, I still feel sad.

"Did you ever find out who posted that on Instagram?" I ask. "Was it Finn?" I want to believe it wasn't, that he wouldn't do something like that, even though the evidence is to the contrary. If he was capable of the assault, he's surely capable of boasting about it.

"I don't know," Bella replies. "No one does."

Is it a mother's instinct that makes me press, that deep, maternal sense that something isn't adding up, isn't right? I'm not even sure why I asked about the post in the first place, and yet I hold out my hand. "Can I see it?"

Her eyes widen and she bites her lip. "Why?"

"I just want to see it." I don't actually, but I think I need to. I raise my eyebrows, gentle my tone. "I'm sure the police have seen it, right?" Along with most of the school.

"It's been taken down..."

"And you don't have a screenshot or something?" I would be surprised if she didn't. It's evidence, after all, and kids always screenshot stuff these days, for so-called posterity, don't they? Always keeping a record, even as they insist on believing posts and pictures can disappear into the ether, that they can post what they like and not have it matter. The paradox, or perhaps just the naiveté, of today's youth.

"Yeah, but..." Bella trails off, looking decidedly reluctant.

How bad is it? I wonder. Do I even want to see it?

But maybe I need to.

"Bella, please."

Slowly, reluctantly, she swipes a few times on her phone and then hands it to me. There is a picture of Finn first, looking so handsome and yes, a bit smug, in his baseball uniform, like he's about to swing his bat, and then a photo of Bella, shining and golden in a strapless dress of pale pink, taken from the eleventh-grade prom. She went, I recall, with a bunch of girl-friends. It all seems so painfully innocent now. Mocking pink hearts have been drawn around each of them, before the final photo of Bella sprawled on the twilit beach, shorts unbuttoned, looking sexy and tousled and out of it, with the bright pink script: *Guess who tapped this.*

"There was music, too," Bella says, a quaver in her voice, any bravado vanishing in an instant. "This pop song that was basically calling me a slut."

"Oh, Bella." I reach out to touch her hand, and to my surprise she clings to my fingers for a second before she draws away. I am filled with helplessness, with despair, because it's all so awful, so unfair, and I can't bear to see my baby suffering like this. "I'm so sorry."

She gulps and nods and I look back down at the phone, the photos. My breath escapes me in a long, shuddery rush. It's all horrible, *horrible*, and yet, I am forced to acknowledge, it could be so much worse. I've seen Bella's friends post mirror selfies that are way more provocative and explicit. There is something weirdly, unsettlingly innocent about these photos, the pink hearts, no matter how much it hurts Bella; oddly, they contain a certain amount of restraint.

And then, with a sickening rush of realization, I know who must have posted these photos. Both the cutting mockery and the weird innocence of it make me almost certain. It wasn't Finn or someone on his soccer team who somehow got hold of the photo, like Bella has suspected.

It was Elspeth.

CHAPTER 19

CARA

"Finn, please."

I am standing in the doorway of Finn's bedroom, trying to keep the tears from my voice as he lies in bed, staring up at the ceiling and not saying a word. It's seven-thirty and school starts in twenty minutes. Henry has already left to meet the school bus, although Finn usually drives him in, in the second-hand car we gave him for his seventeenth birthday.

"You need to go to school," I tell him, not for the first time. I've been trying to get him out of bed for an hour.

His gaze doesn't move from the ceiling as he answers, "What's the point?"

It's been three days since the police interviewed him. Three painful, cataclysmic days, and some of the worst of my life—and Finn's.

It started when the principal called us into school, the morning after Finn was questioned. "We'd like to talk things over," he said, his voice smooth, too smooth, hiding deeper and darker currents. My stomach cramped.

"I wasn't aware there was anything to talk over," I replied

numbly, without any real spirit. "We're waiting on the results of the investigation..." I trailed off, already afraid, ashamed.

"The situation has developed," Mr. Wood stated. "For the safety and wellbeing of our students, I'm afraid measures need to be taken."

Which made it sound like we were dealing with a nuclear threat rather than a seventeen-year-old boy who might or might not have acted inappropriately. Yet what could I do but agree? We were at the school's mercy, and we all knew it.

Michael came back from work; I took the afternoon off. Finn met us in the principal's office, already seated, his gaze on the floor. Mr. Wood sat behind his desk, florid, firm. So much for his superstar, headed for the Ivies. It was clear he was doing his best to distance himself from Finn.

"I'm afraid," he said, his manner both grave and pompous, "that this situation has escalated."

"Escalated?" Michael's voice rose, already on the attack before we'd even sat down. "How has it escalated?"

"I'm sure you're aware of the current climate," Mr. Wood said. "And the growing awareness, much needed, I should add, of sexual assault in a culture that has been silent on these issues for far too long—"

"What does any of that," Michael interjected, "have to do with our son?"

Mr. Wood bristled slightly, annoyed at being interrupted in the middle of his politically correct spiel. "Some of the student population has indicated that, due to recent events, they no longer feel safe in school," he told us after a pause. "And, as I am sure you understand, I have to take that very seriously."

For a second, there was nothing but silence, the kind you feel between the flash of lightning and the crack of thunder, absolutely electric. I was staring at the principal, my mind frozen with shock, with fear.

"Are you kidding me?" Michael finally demanded, half-rising from his chair as he let out a huff of disbelief. "Are you *kidding* me?" he said again, his voice rising to something between a screech and a roar.

"Dad," Finn said softly.

"Mr. Johnston, I am going to have to ask you to lower your voice and conduct yourself in a civil manner, if we are to continue this meeting." Mr. Wood sounded as severe as if he were talking to a seventh grader throwing spit balls.

Michael sat back down with another huff. The silence coated us like ice; I felt frozen, unable to move. Unable to speak. A week ago, we'd been looking at the application questions for Princeton. *What brings you joy?* I wanted to cry, but I was too numb. Finn was *not* a danger to the girls in this school. That much I knew.

"So what are you suggesting?" Michael finally asked, still sounding angry, a throb in his voice that made me squirm, and Finn let out a breath, running his hand through his hair, scuffing his feet.

Mr. Wood hesitated, and I knew he was wondering just how to walk the tightrope between being seen as making an effort and not inviting a lawsuit. If he suspended Finn without any evidence of wrongdoing... I knew I didn't have the strength to sue, but I thought Michael might. But, meanwhile, who knew how many young women were clamoring for something to be done, for the school to show it took sexual assault seriously.

Why did my son have to be the poster child for it, though? I could only imagine how many boys in this school had done what he'd been accused of, or worse, much worse, and yet the school was utterly silent on those. I remembered Rose telling me that the football team had some party last year where they locked the door and said the girls couldn't leave until they'd all hooked up with someone, whether they wanted to or not. We were both horrified, but the rumor drifted on and no one so much as lifted a finger. Why this? Why now? *Why Finn?*

"Until the investigation concludes, Finn will not participate in any soccer matches or any other sport," Mr. Wood stated like he was reading from a script, a proclamation.

"What?" Michael leaned forward in his chair as he gripped the armrest. "This is his last season. The investigation could go on for weeks."

"We cannot have him representing the school in any capacity until this is completely resolved." The principal managed to look both obdurate and nervous.

"Michael," I said quietly. Now was not the time to argue.

"This is ridiculous." Michael sat back, still furious. "Utterly ridiculous. Finn is one of your star students—"

"I'm hardly going to make exceptions," Mr. Wood interjected stiffly.

"You don't even know if he is guilty—"

"*Dad.*" Finn's voice sounded more strident. "Please. Just leave it, okay? I don't even care."

Michael glanced at his son, and then, with one last huff, he subsided. We filed out of the principal's office a few minutes later, like penitents.

"This whole thing is outrageous," Michael told me later, when we were at home, Finn upstairs in his bedroom. He hadn't wanted to go back to classes, and we hadn't had the heart to make him. "They have no right—"

"I think," I interjected, "we need to seem as if we're cooperating."

"We're going to be complicit? Really?"

"Michael, the mood has changed." I had felt it as we'd walked from the principal's office to the car, like a miasma in the air. Last week, everyone was calling Bella a slut; this week, Finn is an abuser. I wasn't sure if anyone truly believed either narrative; they just liked the excitement, gossip, the outrage, without caring who it hurt.

"The police are going to drop this investigation," Michael

stated. "It's not like they can put Finn in jail. They're going to drop any charges, if they even make them in the first place, but it won't be before the damage is done."

I couldn't argue with that, and yet, just a day after Finn had been questioned, we had no idea of just how much damage there would be. The next day, we made Finn go into school, even though he was deeply reluctant.

"Why can't I just stay at home until this all dies down?" he complained, hiding his fear behind irascibility.

"You need to show your face," I insisted, while Michael told him to "hold his head up high."

He lasted all of two hours. I got a call from Mr. Wood while I was at work, informing me that Finn had left without permission.

"All things considered, perhaps a few days off would be wise," Mr. Wood suggested, in an attempt to be diplomatic that I didn't appreciate, even less so when I found out what had happened.

It was Henry who told me, after school that afternoon. I'd called Finn myself, just to make sure he was safely at home, and promised we'd talk when I returned from work. When I got home, Finn was up in his room, and Henry was in the kitchen, mooching around.

"They formed this brigade in front of his locker," he told me, without prompting, before I'd even put down my purse.

"A brigade? Who did?"

"A bunch of girls. They wouldn't let him get into his locker. And they called him stuff, until Mr. Wood came and told them all to go to class."

My stomach swirled with acid and unhappiness as Henry looked at me miserably.

"Is he... is he going to be expelled?"

"No." I spoke more firmly than I felt. "People just like to take sides, Henry, that's all." Except, of course, that wasn't all.

"Sexual assault is wrong," I tell my son stiltedly. "We still don't know what happened, because Finn can't remember, but even if he did... what I'm saying is, he might have made a big mistake, and he's really sorry for it. But, unfortunately, these are some of the consequences."

"But if he really doesn't remember..." Henry licked his lips. "What if... what if he didn't do it?"

"But Bella remembers," I reminded him gently. I was coming to accept that Finn had done what Bella had said he had, even if he couldn't remember it. It didn't, however, make him a monster.

"What if she remembered wrong?" The look Henry gave me was full of both yearning and fear. "What if it didn't happen the way she thinks it did?"

"I don't think Bella is lying, Henry." A weary sigh escaped me. After everything that has happened, all the conversations had, I know this to be true. "I really don't."

"Not lying," he corrected in a half-mumble. "But maybe, you know, mistaken."

Something about his tone made me ask, a bit too sharply, "Why are you saying this, Henry? Do you know something? Something you haven't said?" To us, or to the police? I was so tired of not knowing what had actually happened. I wondered if I would ever find out the truth, if it could ever actually be known.

"No, no." He spoke quickly, with a touch of panic. "I was just wondering, you know, *if*."

And then he backed away, clearly not wanting to talk about it anymore.

That evening, Michael and I agreed we needed to give Finn a break. We let him stay in his room, even though my heart ached for him, and we let him skip the whole next day, even though I didn't think moping around did him any good. I took half a day off and made him breakfast—another bowl of oatmeal with bananas and brown sugar, this time one he morosely picked at—and then washed his sheets and tidied his room, futile gestures of a mother's love. I wanted to comfort my son, but I didn't think he'd let me, and so I could only offer these mindless tasks of tidying.

This morning, though, has been different. Michael and I agreed that Finn can't miss any more school; it's not good for him, and it's not good for the school. Regardless of what he did, he needs to show his face. He can't be vilified forever, treated as some dangerous threat.

"Please, Finn," I tell him again, uselessly, because he's not budging. He's wearing his clothes from yesterday, and even though I washed his sheets less than twenty-four hours ago, his room smells rank. He does. When did he last shower? I have no idea. I need to get to work; Michael has already gone, but I don't want to leave my son alone.

Finn doesn't take his gaze from the ceiling as he answers me. "I'm not going."

"This will blow over eventually. And you'll still have your life to live. If you stay away, it looks like—" *You did something wrong.* I can't say that, because I'm more and more afraid that he did. And yet I can't help but feel he doesn't deserve this.

He doesn't bother to reply, and after a few futile seconds, I leave him alone. We'll give him another day, I think. It can't hurt that much.

I email the school and ask them to put aside his work, so he can at least keep up with his classes. And then I go to work, because I don't know what else to do. I try to concentrate, but my mind is both buzzing and blank; I can't hold onto a single thought. How will this end, I wonder, without any idea of how to answer that question. When will it end? And when it does, who will be satisfied?

Then, during my lunch hour, Finn calls me. "The police gave me back my phone," he tells me dully. "And they said they're closing the investigation, because there isn't enough evidence."

"They... are?" My heart leaps with wild hope even as I register my son's flat tone. "That's good news, isn't it, Finn?" To have it be resolved so quickly... I press one hand to my racing heart. We can get back to normal now, I think in dazed, incredulous gratitude. Finn can go back on the soccer team, we can think about Princeton again. *What brings you joy?* This, surely. *This.*

"I guess." He does not sound at all relieved or pleased, which alarms me.

"Finn... this is great news. Really great. It's *over—*"

"It's not over, Mom." He speaks flatly, matter-of-factly, with complete resignation. "Everyone at school thinks I'm this... *criminal*. They all hate me."

"Not everyone—"

"Bella does," he says, and I wonder if she is the only one who really matters.

"You could still talk to her," I suggest gently. "Apologize to her." Because no matter what the police say about it, Bella surely deserves an explanation, an apology. Something.

"For what?" For the first time in the conversation, Finn's voice rises. "I've gone over and over that night since it happened, and you know what? I really don't think I did do what she said I did."

"*What...*?" My mind spins, racing to absorb this new information. "But... I thought you couldn't remember..." I picture Finn huddled in Michael's chair, looking so scared. *I don't know. Mom, I don't know!* Now he does?

"I know I was drunk," he states, "but I don't think I was *that* drunk. I mean, I think I'd remember something like that, especially if she'd pushed me off and was, you know, upset or something. And," he finishes, hurt spiking his voice, "I don't actually get off on feeling up someone who is comatose, you know?"

I have no idea what to say to any of that. "We'll talk about this when I get home," I tell him, and for the rest of the afternoon the hours creep past as my mind whirls. *If Finn didn't do it...*

I realize, in this moment, that I never actually ever doubted that he did, not seriously. Not at *all*. Miscommunication, yes. Wires crossed when they were drunk, not realizing, maybe, just how drunk she was, that she was passed out, unable to consent, until she pushed him off... All of that, unfortunately, yes. But not that he was actually innocent. Completely innocent. That he never even touched her.

How could that be possible? What if Bella *was* making it up? I feel guilty for even considering the possibility, because I have never truly deviated from the belief that Bella should be believed. That anyone who says they were assaulted deserves to be taken seriously, and treated with compassion. Yes, I once grasped at straws, hoping Bella might have misremembered. But what if she actually *lied*? But then, why would she?

Yet what other alternatives are there, if I want to believe my son?

And then I think of Henry telling me not that she was lying, but mistaken. *How...?*

As I head home that night, I am no closer to answering that question, and I don't know that talking to Finn about it all over again will shed any further light on it.

Back in Westport, I stop at the overpriced Fresh Market, where I don't usually shop, to pick up some essentials. I've dropped so many balls lately—housework, cooking, paying bills —all the little ways to keep our lives running. I need to get back on track. We all do.

"Sorry, your card has been declined."

I stare in shock at the middle-aged woman giving me a bored stare. *Again?* I reach for my AmEx. "Sorry, I forgot that card was..." I mumble, a lie I can't even finish. I slip the card back in my wallet and pay with my ATM card instead.

"Sorry, this card has been declined, too."

What? I stare at the woman, who is no longer looking bored, but stony.

A flush creeps up my cheeks as I realize I have no way to pay for the items on the conveyor belt—a gallon of organic milk, a block of cheddar cheese, some wholewheat pasta, overpriced free-range chicken, a bottle of wine, a half-gallon of freshly squeezed orange juice. All of it looks ridiculous, far too elitist and expensive, considering I have about five bucks in my wallet.

"Can you try the ATM card again?" I ask, a bit desperately.

She does. It is declined. Again.

There are three people behind me in the line, including someone I know vaguely from school. Just like in the sandwich shop, they are shifting, sighing, looking away, like I'm an embarrassment. I feel like one.

"Do you have another way to pay?" the woman asks, her tone flat.

I shake my head, feeling utterly humiliated. "I have five dollars..." I say, looking at the items on the belt. The only thing under five dollars is the pasta. I pay for it while one of the baggers starts loading my stuff off the belt, into a spare cart. "Thank you," I whisper, and then I hurry out of the shop, to my car. Why, I wonder numbly, does one thing have to get worse just as something else is getting better?

Right now, all thoughts of Finn have flown out of my head. Why were *both* my cards declined? What on earth is going on?

CHAPTER 20

ROSE

I don't want to believe it's Elspeth. *Elspeth*, throwing her sister under the bus? Posting that mean-spirited photo on Instagram, making her the subject of vile gossip, the butt of cruel jokes? I don't want to believe it, and yet I'm afraid I do. But how can I possibly talk to her about it? I can't bear to come out and accuse her outright—what if I'm wrong? I *hope* I'm wrong... and yet I know, with a leaden feeling in my gut, that I'm not.

I don't know if it's a mother instinct, or maybe a deep-seated fear finally realized, but I'm absolutely sure Elspeth made that post, and yet still I stay silent.

I'm a coward, I acknowledge bleakly, in so many ways. I avoid Cara, have done for years; I do the minimum to keep my husband happy and my marriage stable, even when I chafe against both bonds. I pretend to be a good mother, when in fact I think I might just be a lazy one. So much of my life is characterized by inertia, and as much as I blame myself—and I *do*—I also blame my past. That one night that ripped my life, my very self, in two, and paralyzed me in so many ways, kept me frozen in fear, unable to move forward in any way that matters.

Or am I just finding the easy out, making excuses, playing

the victim? It's been thirty years, after all. I've married, had a family, built a life, even if I don't really like it anymore. I haven't actually been *paralyzed*... even if I feel like I have.

My mind goes round in circles, until I feel like I don't know anything anymore. Maybe I never did—except I do know that Elspeth wrote that post. And I have to talk to her about it... at some point.

A week after Finn is questioned by the police, Bella drifts into the house, melancholy and uncommunicative again. Her moods are giving me whiplash, and making me feel exhausted, constantly on emotional high alert, wondering what's coming next.

"How are you doing, sweetheart?" I ask as she flings herself on the sofa in the family room, dropping her bag and curling up into a ball. Elspeth lurks in the doorway, silent, watching.

"I don't know." Bella presses her face into her knees. I stare at her, concerned but also so, so tired. I don't know what the right words to say are, and I don't have the energy to look for them.

"What's going on at school?" I finally ask, coming to perch on the sofa opposite her, because I have to try.

"Nothing."

Now what?

I glance back at Elspeth, who is still standing in the door-way, one leg wrapped around the other, twirling a strand of hair around her finger. "How about you, Elspeth?" I ask. "How was school?"

She shrugs. "Fine."

I really should know better. Does that question *ever* get another answer? If it does, something has to be really, really wrong. And yet here Bella is, curled up on the sofa, her face pressed to her knees. Something *is* really wrong. Again. Still.

"Bel?" I put a hand on her shoulder. She doesn't respond, just tightens her arms around her knees. "I'm sorry you're hurting," I whisper, because those are words I can say, words I desperately feel.

"I know," she mumbles into her knees.

I glance back at Elspeth, but she's disappeared, which is probably a good thing.

"Do you want to talk about it?"

"No."

"Is Finn back at school?" I ask. I know, from Elspeth, that he didn't show up to school after the whole thing with the police. "Are you having to see him—"

"I don't *care* about seeing him," she bursts out and I fall silent, waiting for more. She takes a shuddering breath, lifting her head from her knees so she can speak, but still not looking at me. "This doesn't feel the way I thought it would," she says after a long moment. "The way I wanted it to."

"This...?" I venture cautiously.

"You know, after," she says. "When I wrote that thing online, it felt... *good*. Like I was taking control. Like, this thing happened to me, but I could switch it around, change the narrative. I could choose how to respond, how it affected me." Her words are heartfelt, even if they sound like the sort of pithy sayings people post on Instagram; perhaps they are.

"But?" I prompt, because surely something else is coming.

"But it's all *changed*," she bursts out, a tremor in her voice. "And I don't feel in control anymore."

"Has Finn—"

"This isn't about *Finn*," she cuts across me, sounding angry. "Not anymore." She presses her face back into her knees, as if to block out the world, or maybe just me.

I wait, hoping that by giving her a moment, she'll tell me more. Explain what she means, because I really don't understand.

After a few seconds, she does. She lifts her head once more, and, without looking at me, says flatly, "Today Finn was at soccer practice and these girls came out onto the field and refused to leave until he stopped playing."

"Why—"

"They said they don't feel safe having him at school, and it's not fair that he's been let off the hook. Even though the police finished their investigation." Something I found out from Elspeth a few days ago. I wasn't surprised, but I was still disheartened.

"Well..." I begin, and then stop, because I don't know how I feel about any of it. Those girls have a right to protest, especially if they don't feel safe, but at the same time they shouldn't *harass* Finn.

"They don't even know him," Bella bursts out. "Or me. They're not my friends, they don't actually care about what happened to me. They're just using this whole thing as a way to be—I don't know—alternative. Like, wow, you're *so* brave, marching onto a field. Good job." She shakes her head in disgust, while I sit back, surprised at this turn of events, even though I know I shouldn't be. Isn't this what happens when you put your life on social media? And yet I'm still glad Bella was brave enough to be honest.

"What did Finn end up doing?" I ask, and she sniffs.

"He left the field. The coach said he didn't have to, but he said it was too much of a distraction."

The note of something almost like pride in her voice gives me pause. "Bella," I ask slowly, "do you still have feelings for Finn?"

She shoots me a look that is half guilty, half defiant. "He's the *only* guy I've ever had feelings for."

"What?" I stare at her blankly. "You mean you liked him before the night of the barbecue?" How did I not know this? How did I not figure this out over the last few weeks?

Bella rolls her eyes. "I've liked him, like, forever. I just never had the guts to tell him."

"But that changed, that night?" I am still reeling from learning all this.

Bella ducks her head, turning shy. "He sent me a text the night before, joking about it being like old times. And it gave me the confidence... but I wasn't sure..." She bites her lip. "And now it's all been ruined. And these stupid girls are making it all about them when it isn't. Plus," she adds, a tremble entering her voice, "some people are still calling me a slut, and a girl was raped by her boyfriend last weekend and no one even *cares*."

"What!" I sit up straight, instantly alarmed. "Who? Has she told the authorities—"

"No, she doesn't want to tell anyone. I only found out because she was crying in the bathroom when I went in there." Bella hunches over her knees again. "It's all just so *unfair*. Guys get away with so much and there's nothing we can do about it, and even when you try to change things, it still goes against you. And I'm just really *tired* of it all." A sob escapes her, and she presses her head to her knees once more as her shoulders shake.

"Oh, Bella. Oh, honey." I rub her back as she weeps, everything in me aching—for Bella, for the nameless young woman who is scared to speak out, for all the women and girls I know who are trapped by the system, damned if they come forward, and forced to suffer in silence if they don't—and for me. For me, the eighteen-year-old who had to grow up way too fast, while never actually growing up at all.

"I just wish none of it ever happened," Bella says after several minutes, her voice clogged with tears. "I wish I hadn't gone to that barbecue. Hadn't flirted with Finn. Hadn't..."

"Bella," I remind her softly. "This is not your fault. You were not the one who had to prevent this. That was never on you."

"I know." She sniffs, running her wrist under her nose as she looks up at me with pain-filled eyes, her lashes spiky with tears. "I know."

But I wonder if she really does, if she *believes*. If any woman can, when the world is relentlessly determined to insist otherwise.

Slowly, she uncurls herself from the sofa. "I'm gonna go have a shower," she mumbles, and I nod and let her go.

I know I should go upstairs and talk to Elspeth, but after having one draining conversation, I'm not up for another. Instead, I go into the kitchen, to the little desk built into the cabinets that Brad says, somewhat patronizingly, is my office. The detritus of our lives builds up there in drifts of paper— forms I forgot to fill out, coupons I never clipped, invoices and statements that need to be filed. I search through it all for my laptop, which I hardly ever use, and take it back to the family room.

As I settle on the sofa, my hands hovering over the keys, I'm not sure what to type. I feel a sense of determination, of purpose, and yet it lacks focus. Finally, after a few seconds, I type "marketing job charity sector New York." I click on a link, holding my breath, expecting—what? The absolutely perfect job to be magically right there, waiting for me, a click away, now that I'm finally thinking about jumpstarting my life?

It isn't, that much is clear, but as I scan the offerings—a development officer for an interreligious charity, donor relations assistant for the NYU School of Law—I realize I don't need the perfect job. I'm not going to wait to simply stroll into something amazing; I'm going to be proactive and make it happen myself. It's enough, right now, that I'm even looking. It's more than I've done in years, decades, and I'm not going to wallow in the what-ifs, the relentless regrets. I'm going to face the future, and I'm going to help my daughters—both of them— do that, too.

Of course, it's all easier said than done. I spend forty-five minutes browsing various jobs, most of them requiring more experience specific to their field than I have: *Must have at least three years in the charity sector. Experience with the housing industry preferred. Must know how to use Raiser's Edge.*

I don't even know what Raiser's Edge is, although a quick search shows me it's some sort of fundraising cloud-based software I've never heard of, much less used. Trying not to feel dispirited, I head into the kitchen to make dinner—in this case, stone-baked pizzas fresh from their plastic wrappers. I can feel guilty about only so much.

As I slide them into the oven, Brad comes in the house with his usually cheery hello, and Bella ventures downstairs, already in her pajamas, her damp hair pulled back by a scrunchie. I still haven't seen Elspeth.

"Hey, honey," Brad says, pulling Bella into a one-armed hug, as easy and careless as ever. No real heart-to-hearts between him and Bella, but then she's never looked to her dad for those.

Maybe she won't miss him so much if he's gone.

The thought slides into my mind slyly, but without surprise. When I was looking at those jobs online, I wasn't just thinking about a career move. I knew that, even if I didn't acknowledge it to myself.

"What's for dinner?" Brad asks me, and before I can respond as any good housewife should, there is a thundering knock at the door. Bella, Brad, and I all look at each other, mystified, alarmed.

Another hammering, and then a voice. "Open this door!"

Brad's forehead crinkles in confusion, and even Bella doesn't recognize the voice, but I do.

I take a step toward the front door, and then stop. "It's… Michael," I say.

CHAPTER 21

CARA

It is frightening, how quickly things can spiral out of control, especially when I was so hopeful that they might start, *finally*, to go well. For things to get back to normal, which is really all that I have wanted. All those petty little problems and irritations, worries and grievances that I nursed before that barbecue —I'd take them all back now, in a heartbeat. Gladly. They seem like nothing compared to what comes next.

And I tell myself, I insist, that it can happen; normality is still within our grasp. The police investigation has been concluded, no charges made, never mind dropped. Finn can go back to school; he didn't even miss a single soccer game. All in all, a terrific result.

Except it doesn't feel that way. At all.

When I come back from the Fresh Market with my single packet of pasta, my mind is reeling. I know I need to check in with both Finn and Henry, make sure they're okay, but I go straight to my laptop and try to log in first to AmEx, then to our joint checking account. The passwords to both sites have been changed, and I can't get into either. The red text that comes up like a sneering admonition has me staring, incredulous and yet at the same time unsurprised.

A shiver goes through me and for a few seconds I simply sit there, my hands hovering over the keys, wondering what on earth has happened. Is it a case of identity theft? Has someone hacked into our accounts, taken all our money? But if that were the case, surely we would know. The bank would tell us if there had been suspicious activity, unusual withdrawals…

Another shudder goes through me. I don't want to think what this could be. What it could mean. And I don't have time, because the door opens and Michael is home, breezing in on a buoyant mood, because Finn texted him earlier that the police have dropped the investigation. Just as I did, he thinks it's all over.

And I guess it is, even if Finn doesn't seem to feel like it is.

Dinner is a morose affair, despite Michael's determination to only see the positive; Finn is monosyllabic, Henry completely silent. I thought he would be relieved, along with Finn, that the terrible drama in our lives has finally come to an end, but neither of my sons seems particularly pleased. They toy with their food, they eat with their heads down. Conversation is painfully stilted. After a few jolly attempts, Michael too falls silent.

We just need to recover, I tell myself. *We need a little time, that's all.* I want to believe it so badly.

When the boys have drifted upstairs, I turn my mind to the problem of the accounts, even though part of me doesn't want to bring it up—a realization which brings only more alarm. Why wouldn't I want to talk to Michael about this?

"Something funny happened today," I tell him as he clears the table and I stack dishes in the dishwasher. He hands me a plate, his eyebrows raised, his expression neutral. "My AmEx and my ATM card were both declined at the Fresh Market," I say, and I wonder why I am using this light tone, why I feel like

I have to manage the situation. I am playacting, and I don't know why. "And when I went to log onto the accounts," I continue, "the passwords had been changed." I pause, waiting for him to jump in with exclamations or explanations, but he remains silent. "Do you know what has happened?"

"I changed the passwords," Michael says. He's over at the table, clearing dishes, his back to me. "I'd got locked out for some reason, maybe I'd mistyped the password too many times or something, but I thought it was easier to change them." He turns around, a plate in his hand, his expression bland. "Sorry, I should have told you."

"But why would both my cards be declined?" I ask, hating that I feel uncertain, suspicious—and why? Simply because Michael has been distant for the last year, and I am wondering if money has something to do with it? What could it have to do with it?

He shrugs. "You know how tricky banks can be, always checking your identity, making you verify it a dozen different ways. Maybe changing the passwords set up an alert or something."

"But my AmEx was declined a few weeks ago, too. Remember?"

Annoyance flashes across his features. "What can I tell you, Cara? I don't know."

"So what are the new passwords?" I ask after a moment, because I'm not sure what else to say.

Michael hesitates. "I wrote them down somewhere. I'll email them to you."

Email? "Michael..." I can't leave it like this. "You would tell me, wouldn't you," I say slowly, "if we were having some sort of financial difficulty?" I am embarrassed to realize how little I actually know about our financial situation. Yes, there are always fairly healthy amounts in our checking and savings, but Michael manages the life insurance, the pension plan, the ISAs and whatever else. I don't even know where most of our money is, or how much we actually have. It's been enough for me to know there is enough to pay the bills, as well as some saved.

"Difficulty?" he repeats, sounding a bit aggrieved. "No, of course we're not having any *difficulty*. I've just moved some money around, put some into one of our ISAs for a tax thing." He shrugs, defensive now. "If you want to look on the accounts, I'll go get the passwords now."

I am fully aware that he is deliberately turning the tables on me, making it so I seem unreasonable for wanting the passwords now, for demanding to see the accounts we share. I open my mouth to say yes, actually, let's just look at them now, but then Henry comes to the door.

"Mom? Can I talk to you?"

I glance at Michael, startled by Henry's serious tone, by the way he's looking at me, so grimly determined. He's picking his fingernails, the skin around his nails red and raw and weeping. "Sure, Henry," I say after a moment.

"I'll just finish this," Michael says, gesturing to the half-cleared table.

Henry and I go into the living room, a room we hardly ever use as a family, with its stiff-looking sofas and the piano Henry practices on, now covered in dust. He hasn't played in over a week, I realize. Another ball I've dropped without even noticing.

I perch on the edge of a sofa, try for a smile, a friendly tone. "Well, Henry? What do you want to talk about?"

He stands in front of me, his hands clenched into fists at his sides as he takes a deep breath, lets it out. "Finn didn't do it."

I blink at him. "What?"

"I saw them, then, at the beach. I know he didn't do it. He'd didn't assault Bella or whatever."

"You saw them?" I am confused at the about-face, and the way he's telling me, spitting the words at me like bullets, his fingers scraping at his poor, damaged skin. "What do you mean, you saw them, Henry? For the whole evening? You couldn't have—"

He nods mechanically, cutting me off. "Pretty much, yeah."

"But when I found you," I say slowly, "you were over by the rocks. You couldn't have seen them then."

"I know, but by then they were both passed out." His voice rises, full of aggravation. "Just trust me, Mom, okay? He didn't do it."

"Okay," I say after a moment. "I believe you." I let those words fall into the stillness.

Henry nods slowly, his breath coming out in something close to a shudder. He doesn't look any happier, as far as I can see.. Why did he tell me this now?

"I'm not sure how much it matters now, though, Henry," I say gently. "The investigation has already been dropped. Finn isn't going to be charged or anything like that. You don't need to worry anymore."

"I know, but Bella... and other people at school... they still think he did it."

I nod, deflated by this unavoidable truth. "I'm not sure how we can change their minds, except to give it time." I let another pause hover between us as I feel my way through the words. "If Finn didn't do anything, Henry... what do you think happened?"

He shrugs, the movement jerky. "I... I don't know. I think Bella maybe was just really out of it."

"You think she imagined it?" Why would any woman imagine something like that?

"I don't know." He shifts from foot to foot. "Maybe someone else came along. Someone we didn't see."

A *stranger*? That seems so much worse, although I know either option is a terrible violation. It is possible it happened that way, I suppose, and yet something still feels off. Wrong.

And, with an awful settling in my stomach, I realize I'm afraid I might know what it is.

"Henry..." I begin, hardly able to put what I'm thinking into words, but he shakes his head to keep me from speaking.

"Look, that's all I wanted to say. Finn didn't do it. I went to the police because I was trying to help, even if he won't believe that. But he didn't do it, Mom, okay?"

"Okay," I say, because I know there's no other answer to give right now. Henry is too distraught and high-strung, and before I can try to keep the conversation going, he nods and then hurries out of the room, up the stairs.

I lean back against the sofa and close my eyes. I don't have the energy to confront either him or Michael about their strange behavior right now; it's cowardice, I suppose, but I only have so much strength, and enough has happened already today. Tomorrow, I tell myself, I'll deal with it all. I'll ask Henry what he meant, why he's saying what he is, get to the bottom of whatever is bothering him.

When I go back in the kitchen, Michael doesn't repeat his offer to go over the accounts, and I don't remind him.

Several days pass in a haze of cautious tiptoeing; I go to work, I come home, I make dinner, I do laundry, I ask Henry and Finn how they are, they say okay, and I choose to believe them. I choose to believe that with a little time, some patience, our lives will return to normal. And just as before, nothing terrible happens. I choose to trust in that, to rest in it, just for a little while. I don't feel strong enough to do anything else, and if the police investigation has been dropped, this really is the end, I tell myself, repeatedly, as if I'll believe it more, the more I hear it. We really do just need some time to find our equilibrium again.

I do rouse myself enough to check the AmEx and checking

accounts, after Michael, with a somewhat wounded air, gave me the passwords. He hovered over my shoulder while I checked them, and just as he'd said, he'd moved money around to various stocks and ISAs, but the balances are fine and I tell myself not to be worried, even as I know that I am.

Then, over dinner one night, everything starts to fall apart as the flimsy façade I really knew it was all along. Michael comes home in a good mood, because Finn has a big soccer game that weekend. Henry is, as he has been all along, quiet and withdrawn, even more so, toying with his food, not meeting anyone's eye. I tell myself—again—that I'll talk to him tonight.

"So, Saturday," Michael says, grinning, to Finn. "Big game."

Finn looks down at his plate without replying. The mood, which had been buoyant if fragile, pops in an instant, like a soap bubble.

"Finn?" Michael asks.

He is still looking down at his plate as he answers. "I quit soccer."

There is a beat of silence, of incredulity, as Michael simply stares at him. "What?" he finally says, and there is a sort of desperate confusion to his voice; he wants so badly to believe he misheard, but I know he didn't. I look at my son and I realize, with a sickening rush of guilt, that these last few days haven't been fine at all. Finn is not okay, and neither is Henry. Why did I lull myself into pretending they were, even for just a little while? Am I that weak, that desperate?

"I quit," Finn says again, raising his head, meeting Michael's eye. "I don't really care about it anyway."

"Finn..." Michael shakes his head, at a loss. "Why would you quit now, your senior year, your last season?"

He shrugs. "It's too much of a time commitment, and I have to do all these college applications anyway, right? Princeton has, like, *seven* supplemental questions—"

"They're a hundred words each," Michael protests, looking

winded. "Finn, you can't quit now. The team depends on you—"

"They really don't," Finn says quietly.

"And what about those college applications?" Michael asks, his voice rising. "It's not going to look so good on them, is it, that you quit a team sport midway through a season—"

"So what if it doesn't?" Finn replies, and now his voice is rising, too. We are in pitched battle territory, with Henry and I silently watching, stricken bystanders. "I don't even care about those stupid colleges. You're the one who wants me to go to an Ivy, Dad, not me." He pushes away from the table in one abrupt movement, but then doesn't rise from his chair, and I see so much dejection under his anger, so much despair.

Michael sees it too, for after a second's tense silence, he asks quietly, "What's really going on here, Finn? Is this about Bella? Still?"

Finn, his gaze lowered, shakes his head.

"Finn?" Michael presses, his voice rising once again. "Why are you quitting soccer? Has something happened at school?"

"No." A mumble, his chin tucked towards his chest.

"*Finn.*"

"A bunch of girls came out to the field at practice today," Henry blurts, his voice high and thin. "They kept the team from practicing."

Finn looks up to glare at his brother. "Shut *up*—"

"What girls?" Michael asks sharply. "Why?"

"Henry—" Finn interjects warningly, but Henry is on a determined roll now, his panicked gaze darting between Michael and me.

"Just girls," he says. "I don't know who. They said they didn't want Finn to be on any sports teams. That he shouldn't represent the school."

A flush is creeping up Henry's neck and he ducks his head while Finn continues to glare at him.

"And what happened?" Michael asks, and now his voice is ominously quiet. A muscle ticks in his jaw. "Did the coach make the girls leave the field?"

"I left," Finn says. He glares at all of us, as if we are the ones at fault, and maybe we are. Maybe we pushed him too hard, or didn't push the school enough. Maybe we handled this whole situation wrong from the start, although I'm not sure how else we could have handled it. All I know is right now I feel hopelessly uncertain—about everything. "And I told the coach I was quitting," Finn finishes. "He understood."

"So these girls," Michael surmises, "just got away with it?"

"Michael..." I can't help but protest at his scathing, certain tone. We don't know who these girls are, what they've been through, what drove them onto that field. We don't know that they *got away* with anything. And yet it still isn't fair to my son.

"No, I mean it," Michael says, looking around at us all. "From day one Finn has been painted as the only bad guy in this situation and no one else has had to have any accountability at all. And now he's been forced off the soccer team, when he doesn't even think he did anything wrong?" He swings back to face Finn. "You don't, do you? You don't think you even touched Bella then. You said so."

"I... I don't know," Finn mumbles, still looking down at his plate. He doesn't want this self-righteous swell of fury from his father, I can tell that much.

"This is unacceptable." Michael slams his palm on the table, startling us all, as he rises from his chair. "*Unacceptable*. And I am going to sort it out right now."

He strides from the kitchen, grabbing his car keys from the counter, while the rest of us simply gape, flummoxed.

"Dad, what are you doing?" Finn calls, in a panic. He rises from the table. "Where are you going?"

"To the Rosses'," Michael calls back, already at the front door.

"The *Rosses*?" This elicits a yelp from Finn, while Henry looks on, his face pale, his mouth agape. "What? Why? Dad, this wasn't even anything to do with Bella. She wasn't there—"

"They're the ones who started this whole thing," Michael shouts back as he wrenches open the door. "And now we're going to finish it."

And on that terrifyingly ominous statement, he walks out into the night, slamming the door behind him.

CHAPTER 22

ROSE

"What the hell does Michael want?" Brad asks, sounding mystified rather than alarmed, as the knocking on the front door continues, a determined, angry hammering that echoes through the house.

"I... don't know." I am mystified too, as well as alarmed. Very alarmed, because Michael sounds as if he is in a complete rage.

Elspeth sidles into the kitchen, looking wary but intrigued by the commotion. "What's going on?"

"Michael Johnston is at the door." I try to say this reasonably, even as the pounding reverberates all around us.

"Dad," Bella asks, her voice wavering, "aren't you going to answer it?"

He glances at me, and I shrug. I'm not about to face down a furious Michael.

"Fine," he says and walks toward the front door. We trail a decent distance behind, curious and cautious.

Brad opens the door and starts to take a step back before checking himself and standing his ground, squaring his shoulders and puffing out his chest, the big man. He's got to have thirty pounds at least on Michael, who has squared up to him, jabbing a finger in his chest.

"This needs to stop," Michael growls. "Do you hear me? It needs to stop right now."

"Whoa, Michael." Brad flings his hands up and I know exactly how he's going to play this—condescendingly compassionate, big enough to humor him but also tone him down. "Let's calm down here, okay? Whatever's going on, we can talk about it reasonably."

"Reasonably?" Michael shouts. "What is reasonable about my son being forced off the field for something he didn't do?"

I know what Michael is talking about, but Brad obviously doesn't, and he simply stares, nonplussed, his hands still in the air.

Michael looks beyond him to us, gathered in the back of the hallway. "Do you know Finn quit the soccer team?" he demands, and I can't tell who he is asking—me, Elspeth, or Bella. Maybe all of us.

Bella lets out a soft gasp. "I didn't know he *quit*."

"He's being hounded and harassed," Michael continues over Brad's shoulder, his gaze on Bella. "For nothing. Because you know, Bella, he says he didn't do it. He says he's sure he didn't assault you, he wasn't that out of it, not to remember something like that. What do you think about that?"

Bella's mouth opens soundlessly. I put my hand on her shoulder, steadying her, although I feel far from steady myself. My mouth is bone dry and my heart is pounding.

"Hey, now," Brad says, uselessly. "Hey, now."

"You are ruining my son's life," Michael declares, swinging around to get right in Brad's face. This time, Brad does take a step back, and I can tell he's annoyed that he did.

"And what about Bella?" I demand. I sound cross rather than reasonable, and it frustrates me. This is too big an issue to engage in a who-trumps-who in the victim stakes.

"What about her?" Michael turns to pin Bella with his angry gaze. "What about you, Bella? Is this what you wanted? Finn, quitting his teams? Refusing to go to school? Ruining his whole future?"

"That's not our concern—" I begin, only to have Bella cut across me.

"I don't want any of that," she insists, her voice caught between a whisper and a cry. "Of course I don't. I never wanted those girls to go out onto the field—"

"But you caused it," Michael cuts across her. "By writing what you did. By turning Finn into the bad guy."

"He *is* the bad guy!" The screech erupts out of me, shocking me as well as everyone else, the emotion in my voice raw and pulsing. "The consequences might be regrettable, but Finn *is* the bad guy here, Michael." I take a step toward him, even though I am shaking. "He assaulted my daughter—"

"He says he didn't!"

"And I'm supposed to believe that?" I scoff. My voice is shaking alongside my body.

Michael's fists bunch. "And I'm supposed to believe Bella?"

"Now wait a minute—" This from Brad, who has decided to insert himself, all pointless bluster. "Wait a minute, Michael."

"For what?" he demands, and jabs his finger in Brad's chest, hard enough for him to stumble back a little. "For you to point the finger at Finn yet again?" Another jab; Michael must be stronger than he looks, because Brad nearly loses his balance and has to grab hold of the doorframe to steady himself. "Claim everything is his fault," he shouts, "without looking at your own daughter's behavior—"

"That's enough!" I shout, the cry ripped from me. I put my arm around my daughter, drawing her close. She doesn't say a word; her body is taut beneath my arm. "Don't blame Bella for Finn's actions."

"I'm not blaming her." Michael takes a step back as a

shudder goes through him and he holds up his hands in defeat, or maybe apology. Brad is still holding onto the doorframe. "I'm not." He glances at Bella, weary now. "I'm sorry for what... what you feel you've been through, truly. But vilifying my son doesn't help anything, surely? They're teenagers." He turns to me. "Kids. Kids you know well. They grew up together—"

"And that's supposed to make a difference?" I ask coldly.

"Mom, don't." Bella squirms out from under my arm. "I never wanted this," she says to Michael. "You have to believe me."

Michael's weary expression softens a little. "I do, Bella," he says. "About that, I do."

And for a second, I think it's all going to be okay, the explosive tension has been defused. Michael doesn't seem so angry anymore, more defeated, and I feel sorry for him. Sorry for Finn, too, if reluctantly.

I open my mouth to say something conciliatory, I'm not sure what, when a car screeches down the road, then up our driveway.

Cara scrambles out of the driver's seat, runs towards Michael.

"Michael, please—" she gasps out, running up to us. She meets my gaze and stops, glancing between us all. "What..." she begins, trailing off. Did she think she was going to be interrupting a brawl? To be fair, she might have. "What's happened?" she asks us, and out of the corner of my eye, I see Brad straighten, dropping his hand from the door, his face flushing a brick red as his chest swells up and everything in me tenses.

"What's *happened*?" he repeats in a sneer. "I'll tell you what's happened. Your lame ass of a husband came storming up here, trying to blame my daughter for what your punk of a son did."

Briefly, I close my eyes. If I thought the situation was de-escalating, I know now that was absurd, wishful thinking. Brad can't stand being humiliated, not even a little bit, and I know that's how he feels right now, and he's not going to stand for it.

"Daddy," Bella whispers, a protest, and one he doesn't hear.

"Do you know what your pathetic husband has done?" he asks Cara, and confusion flashes in her eyes even as her face drains of color.

"Don't," Michael says, and it sounds like a plea, or maybe a warning.

But Brad isn't about to stop. He's on a roll, determined to ride this out, show Michael up. "Your husband asked me for money," he tells Cara. "That night at the beach. That's why he had a tantrum and stormed off, because I told him no. No way."

"What..." The word escapes me in a hiss. I'd practically forgotten about all that, in the light of everything that happened afterward.

Cara doesn't say anything, just stares at Brad and it's enough for him to continue, now with a little swagger. Bella and Elspeth are completely still, silent.

"Said he needed it for an investment, and he'd have it back to me within a week. Thirty grand, he wanted, can you believe it? Of course, it's peanuts to me, but I'm a good judge of character and I knew it wasn't an *investment*." He glances at Michael, his face full of smug derision. "He gambled it away. Didn't you, Michael? What was it? Online poker? Or maybe you don't have the skill for that kind of game. Knowing you, it was probably slots or something stupid like that. You were never going to get ahead, were you? I knew that from the moment I met you. You have 'loser' written all over you."

"Shut *up*," Michael roars, and then, before any of us can do anything or so much as speak, he punches Brad right in the face.

Bella screams and Cara grabs Michael's arm, pulling him away, while Brad doubles over, blood streaming from his nose, and I simply stand there and watch, too shocked to move. To think.

"You dumbass," Brad says as he holds one hand to his nose. "You know I could sue you for everything you have?"

"Brad." My voice is quiet and sounds far more controlled than I expected it to, considering how shocked I feel. "Don't."

He glances at me, florid-faced and bloody. "Are you *defending* him?"

"You were a jerk to him," I state. "So maybe, yeah." I take a deep breath and then I turn to Cara and Michael. She is still holding onto his arm, and he is looking winded, cradling his hand. I wonder if he's ever punched anyone before. I doubt he expected to punch Brad. "I think you should go home," I tell them. "The police investigation has been dropped, so we all need to move on with our lives, as best as we can." And for the first time, I genuinely mean it. This has gone on long enough. Too long, and with no satisfactory results for anyone—not Finn, not Bella, not our families, not the school. No one has benefitted from any of this, I realize sickly, and it all feels so pointless and sad and unfair. Bella is still hurting; so is Finn. Where is the justice? Where is the mercy? I was so focused on the former I forgot about the latter... maybe the most important part. "I'm sorry," I tell Cara and Michael, and even though I mean it, I'm not sure what I'm saying sorry for. Simply that it all happened this way, perhaps. For everything.

Michael looks like he wants to say something, but Cara tugs on his arm and after a few seconds he lets her lead him back to the car. I watch from the doorway as Cara reverses down the driveway and then turns into the road. Michael's car is still parked on the street, but they can sort out their own transport. I close the door while Brad glares at me.

"Nice show of support," he says, wiping the blood from his nose.

"I could say the same to you for the last twenty years," I

reply. I glance at Elspeth and Bella, who are both wide-eyed, transfixed. "Could you please go upstairs? I need to talk to your father."

My tone must be that grave, because neither of them protest, just head silently upstairs.

Brad straightens, his eyes narrowed as he looks at me. His nose has stopped bleeding; it wasn't that hard a punch, really. "What's this about, Rose?" he asks.

"Let's go into the kitchen." I don't want the girls to overhear.

With a long-suffering sigh, like I'm asking so very much of him, he follows me to the kitchen. I take a sheet of paper towel and dampen it under the sink, then hand it to him. He takes it without a word, and I open the freezer for an ice pack—the only kind we have is the one we used for the girls, when they were little, in the shape of a teddy bear. I hand it to Brad and he puts it on his nose; the sight would almost be funny if I didn't feel so serious, so sad.

"I'm leaving you, Brad."

He lets out a huff of sound that maybe is meant to pass for a laugh. "Are you serious?"

"Very much so." I fold my arms to anchor myself because I can't believe I just said what I did, and it's making me shake again. I know I mean it, I mean it utterly, but saying it out loud still rocks me right through, especially now, with everything else that has happened.

"Come on, Rose." He shakes his head, the teddy bear ice pack still pressed to his nose. "This, now? Why? Because of last week?"

"You mean when you stayed out late with your clients while I took our daughter to make a report to the police?"

He rolls his eyes. "You know I can't just leave clients on their own. We went to a bar, anyway, that's it."

A bar that offers lap dances, no doubt, but I don't even care about that now.

"It's not about that, Brad," I tell him. "At least, it's not just about that. It's about the fact that we have completely different ideas about what it means to be married."

"It's just business—"

"No," I cut across him. "It really isn't. I tried to convince myself that it was, because I loved you once, or at least I thought I did, and I didn't want to walk away from my marriage. But for twenty years you've been treating me like that man did, back in college—" Even now I can't say his name.

Brad lets out another one of those huffs. "You're seriously comparing me to a rapist?"

"At least you acknowledge it was rape," I reply levelly, "when you seem to not believe that Bella's case was assault."

"I've never said it—"

"You have, actually," I cut across him, "but in any case, it doesn't matter. It's all of it. I won't be disrespected and dismissed anymore. I won't be told, in a thousand different ways, that my feelings don't matter. That I don't matter, that our marriage doesn't matter."

Brad rolls his eyes. "You sound like you've been reading a few too many self-help books lately—"

"Actually, I haven't, but I wish I had. I wish I'd come to this realization sooner, but I couldn't when it was just me, because I know you love the girls, and they love you. And I didn't want to take that away from them. But it's different now, because you've treated Bella the way you've treated me. Dismissing her concerns. Telling her it's not a big deal."

Brad straightens, lowering the ice pack as he looks at me in cool-eyed assessment, with nothing of the husband about him now; he is a businessman negotiating a deal. "So what are you going to do, Rose? Walk away from all this? This house, the perks, the staff, the clothes—"

I straighten, tilting my chin. "I never cared about any of that nearly as much as you thought I did."

"You might care about it when you don't have it anymore," Brad returns on something close to a snarl. "Connecticut may be a no-fault state, but I'll make sure you don't get a penny more than you deserve, and with the girls almost grown up, there won't be much for child support, either."

"Is that a threat," I ask, "or a promise?"

"Both," he snaps back, before he suddenly deflates, looking almost as if he might cry. "Rose, come on, really? Let's not fight about this. What about the girls?"

"I think the girls will be okay. I'll make it my priority that they are."

"You said you loved me once." He gives me a little-boy look, made more pathetic by the blood still on his face, and for a second my sympathy stirs.

"I did," I tell him quietly, "and in any case, it's not really about love. Love comes and goes, and I would have stayed married to you if it was just a question of that. I took my vows seriously, Brad, more seriously than you did."

"Come on—" he exclaims, no doubt annoyed that I'm harping back to the laundry list of his indiscretions.

"It's because of our daughters, and what I want for them," I tell him quietly. "I want them to grow up believing that they deserve respect, that they're worthy of love. That they will be believed and protected. If I stay married to you, that won't happen, and I'll be setting them an awful example of what a woman should put up with. Well, I'm not putting up with it anymore." Strong words, but they fill me with terror. I know Brad will do his best to make sure I get as little alimony as possible. How am I going to survive?

Then I tell myself it doesn't matter. I will. Somehow, I will.

"I mean it, Brad," I say, and my voice rings out, certain and true. "It's over."

CHAPTER 23

CARA

As I reverse out of the Rosses' driveway, neither Michael nor I say a single word. I focus on driving, because my body is shaking from the shock of that whole encounter and the last thing I want to do right now is crash the car, while Michael sits abjectly in the front seat, his hands in his lap, his head lowered. The tension between us is thick, palpable.

As I pull out into the road, the Rosses' front door closes and I see Michael's car parked haphazardly on the side of the street. I pull in behind it, turn off the car, and then take a deep breath.

"Is it true?" I ask into the taut silence between us. I'm not sure why I ask; I already know it is.

"Yes," Michael answers, after a brief pause. He raises his head to stare blindly out the window at the darkened street. "If you mean the part about the gambling. Is it true that I've got loser written all over me? I suppose you have to decide that one for yourself."

I draw a sharp breath, surprised at how angry I feel suddenly, like I've slammed into a wall of fury. "Don't play the self-pity card right now, Michael," I bite out.

He turns to look at me, shoulders slumped, head bowed again. "You're right. I'm sorry."

I nod, and we sit there in silence for a few minutes, the only sound our breathing. I don't know what to say, where to begin. My head aches and my eyes feel gritty. I left the boys in a panic, following Michael out of the house to keep him from doing something stupid, which I obviously didn't. Finn followed me, asking what I was doing, and Henry simply stared at me, stricken. I told them I'd be back as soon as I could, but I can't go back to them with this unresolved between Michael and me. And I don't want to have a conversation this important, this painful, in a car, parked in front of the Rosses' house.

"Let's go somewhere," I tell my husband. "Get a coffee or a drink and talk—really talk, okay?" The confrontation I've been avoiding for a year is finally here, and to my surprise I want to have it. I am ready. "Because I think we need to be honest with each other," I say, "about a lot of things."

Slowly, Michael nods.

"Let me text the boys, to tell them when we'll be home."

Michael waits silently while I type out the same text to both Henry and Finn, saying everything is fine and we'll be back in an hour and they should do their homework, have showers. I want things to be normal; I want to be back in the comforting world of rules, of protective boundaries, even though we feel so far from that now.

As I slip my phone back in my purse, I turn to Michael. "Where do you want to go?"

He shrugs. "Sherwood?" he suggests, and I nod my acceptance and start the car.

Sherwood Diner is practically a Westport institution, a family-owned, old-fashioned place that serves up enormous breakfasts and unlimited coffee, plus the usual evening fare of burgers, fries, milkshakes, and huge salads.

We drive the short distance in complete silence; in

complete silence we park, leave the car, and head inside. At nearly eight o'clock at night, the place is pretty empty; the waitress warns us that they close at nine.

"We just want a drink, if that's okay," I say and she takes in our weary, defeated expressions before she nods and leads us to a booth in the window, away from the few other customers.

I scan the options on the menu without interest; I have no appetite at all, even though I barely ate half my dinner before Michael stormed out. Michael clearly doesn't, either, because we both just order coffee, waiting for the waitress to return to fill our cups from the pot behind the counter before she leaves, and finally, we speak.

"Where do you want me to start?" Michael asks wearily.

"At the beginning," I answer after a moment. "Whenever that is. When did the—the gambling start?"

Gambling. I haven't got my head around the concept yet, even though I am not actually surprised. I know I suspected it was something like this, even if I refused to articulate it, when he acted so strangely about the accounts, maybe even before then. I knew something was wrong, but I didn't want to guess what it was, and so I managed not to think about it for an entire year. For that, I know I am to blame.

Michael lets out a heavy sigh. "About a year ago. It was just for a laugh, at the start. A guy at work mentioned a website; if he referred people to it, he got some free gold coins, you know, to use online. It seemed no big deal—he said it was just for fun, a hobby. He never spent more than a couple hundred bucks." I nod, accepting, willing him to go on. "So I played—I only put up a hundred, told myself I wouldn't go over that, and I didn't. But in a game of roulette I won a thousand dollars. I *know* that's how they reel you in, I'm not stupid," he adds, in a tone that makes it seem as if I just said he was. "But I figured I could spend that thousand, or at least nine hundred of it, and I'd be back where I started, no problem." He lets out a shuddery breath and then takes a sip of coffee.

I take a sip of mine, put the cup down. "And then?" I ask.

"And then I kept going. It felt like such a *release*—work has been, well, it's been like Brad said. I'm stuck in middle management, I've never gotten any really big deals, but they don't want to fire me. I'm too expensive to let go with a redundancy package, so they keep shunting me sideways until I'm practically irrelevant. I've seen it happen to other guys. I know that's what's happening to me."

I open my mouth to say I wish he'd told me that, and then close it again. Such a remark isn't helpful now, and I know full well that I never asked. I didn't want to know, not really. "And then you started losing money?" I surmise. I need to steel myself to ask how much we've lost.

"I started playing poker," Michael admits. "And I was doing well. I put all the earnings in a separate account, so I could see how much money I was making. It felt good," he tells me with feeling, "and I know this is pathetic, I do—but it felt really *good*, to be seen as good at something. To feel like I was at the top." He shakes his head and looks down at his coffee cup. "Brad was right. I do have—"

"This isn't about Brad," I interject sharply. "Or what he thinks of you. I don't care about Brad, Michael. He's insufferable at the best of times. I care about you." I lean forward, over the table. "For the last year you've been so distant from me," I tell him, the words coming painfully, because even now it's hard to say them, and they hurt. "Was it just because of this, or something else?"

Michael looks away before resolutely swinging his gaze back to me. "I know I have been," he says, and my breath comes out in a sigh of something almost like relief. I realize how much I needed him to say that, to admit it. I'm not crazy. What I felt was real—but was gambling the only source? Or is there something else, something even worse? "At first, it was just because I felt like I was living this double life," he continues. "I knew you'd be completely scathing about it if you knew I'd been gambling."

"I wouldn't—" I begin, only to fall silent at Michael's skeptical and knowing look.

"Come on, Cara. Gambling is stupid. We both know that, and you have never suffered fools gladly."

"You think I'm judgmental?" I ask quietly.

"Maybe a little," he concedes, "but maybe that's because you're afraid of being judged yourself. Because of your mom. I know her... her coldness has always hurt you." A lump forms in my throat as I see the compassion in his face, a remnant of the man I remember, the man I love. "And you're always so determined to do everything right," he continues. "It's part of what I've always loved about you—you're fierce, you work hard, you *mean* things." The little glow of pleasure his words give me is dimmed by what he says next. "But when I couldn't match it, when I felt like I was failing you? Well, it made it hard to be around you. I'm not saying that was your fault—it was mine. I was the one who was messing up. But that's why I started keeping my distance. And the more I did it, the easier it became." He gives a little shrug as he looks away. "I'm sorry. I've messed everything up, I know that."

I knot my fingers together on the table, my stomach and mind both swirling. What is he saying, exactly? Is this the end—or the beginning? Where can we go from here—and how can we get there? I don't know the answers to any of those questions.

"And the thing with the accounts?" I ask after a moment.

A long, telling pause. "I lost a big game. It seemed like such a sure thing. A full house..." He must hear the shaming eagerness in his voice, the plaintiveness, because he subsides with a sigh. "I bet it all, and..." He draws a quick breath. "I couldn't cover it without you knowing about it—that's why I asked Brad for the loan. It was just for a week, until I got paid, but he was so smug about it, telling me he was saying no for my own good, like I was some little kid who'd gotten in trouble. It was a low moment, believe me."

"I'm sure," I reply coolly, because, as it turns out, I don't have *that* much sympathy.

Michael grimaces. "I know, I know. I'm sorry."

I lift my head to look at him squarely in the face. "How much?"

He stares at me for a moment, his expression wary and still, and I lean forward.

"Please, Michael, however bad it is, just tell me the truth. That's all I want now. How much have we lost?"

"All our savings," he admits in a low voice. "And some of our investments. Things will be tight, really tight, but we're not in debt. Exactly."

So, that healthy amount that always gave me so much reassurance is gone. I find it doesn't hurt nearly as much as I expected it to.

"How much exactly?" I ask, because I still need the certainty of a number.

"About eighty-five grand."

A shocked breath escapes me in a rush and I look down at my hands. Okay, that does sting. That is *so* much money. A year of college tuition, I think numbly. A year of Finn at Princeton.

"How did you cover it, when you lost that big game?" I ask. Because eighty-five grand is more than we ever had in our savings account, I know that much.

Another hesitation, and I tense.

"I sold a stock," he admits, "but just one, I promise. And I used most of my pay check for the last few months, more than I normally would have. I hoped you wouldn't notice, as long as the balances stayed healthy, and we don't spend that much money, anyway, not really. I thought I could recoup it over time, by watching our pennies."

And to do that, he would have had to stop gambling.

Eighty-five grand. It could be so much worse, I tell myself, and yet it's bad enough. Things will be more than tight, I know. We'll have to make some tough budget cuts, at the very least.

I look up. "When's the last time you've gambled?" I ask him. "The truth, please, if you want me to trust you."

Another long hesitation. I have to brace myself.

"Three days ago," he admits. "I won six hundred bucks."

I let out a huff of hard laughter. "Am I supposed to be impressed?"

For a second, annoyance, or maybe hurt, flashes in Michael's eyes, but then he shakes his head slowly. "No," he says quietly. "Of course not."

I let out a breath and we both sit in silence. In the distance, someone thanks the waitress, and on a flurry of cheerful good-byes, a couple leaves the diner, the door swinging behind them with a merry tinkle of bells.

I close my eyes. I am so, so tired, but I am not going to back away from this. I've done that too many times—chosen not to force a confrontation, because I'm afraid of the answer. I did with Michael, with my mother, with both Henry and Finn. I won't do it now, not when my marriage is at stake.

I open my eyes and stare at Michael. "What do you want right now?" I ask him, and he looks surprised, discomfited, fidgeting a little in his seat.

"What do I want?"

"Yes."

"I don't know," he admits. "To go back and never have gone on that stupid site, I guess."

"What do you want," I repeat clearly, "that's feasible? Do you want to stop gambling? Do you want to stay married to me?" I can't believe I finally have the guts to ask those questions as clearly as that, and even though it's hard, I'm glad I did.

"Stay married..." For the first time, Michael looks alarmed. "What are you saying, Cara? You want to get *divorced*—"

"For the last year you've frozen me out." The hurt vibrates in my voice, and I realize I need him to hear it, to understand it. "I didn't know what was going on, Michael. I barely let myself think about it, but I always felt so... so alone. Maybe I should have confronted you about it, but the truth is, I was scared. Scared you were going to tell me that you were tired of me, that you were leaving me and the boys."

"I wasn't tired of you," he protests in a low voice. "I didn't want to leave."

"But you *were* tired, sort of, weren't you?" I counter, striving to sound logical. "You were tired of the way I am—driven, focused, maybe a little judgmental. Maybe more than a little judgmental." I think of the invisible flock of mothers who have perched on my shoulder and judged me—hissing that I wasn't buying organic, that my son hadn't gotten an A, that I wasn't a good enough mother. Those mothers weren't real, I realize; *I* was the one who was judging. Not just myself, but everyone else, too. Rose, my mother, my husband. "I understand it," I continue, "in a way. And I hope that if you'd told me what was going on, even if I was angry or surprised, I would have been supportive, too." I take a deep breath. "But the point is, for a whole year I felt like our marriage was hopelessly floundering. And I need to know if we can move on from this, if we can change. Be honest with each other, no matter what. And," I finish, trying to hide the tremble in my voice, "I need to know if you even want that. If you want to stay married to me."

"Cara, I've always wanted to stay married to you." Michael reaches across the table for my hand; I let him hold it, one icy palm pressed to another. This is hard for both of us. "I'm sorry I did what I did. I was stupid, I knew it, and I doubled down on my stupidity. I just felt like such a failure, and that's not me throwing a pity party, it's just being honest. I really did—a failure on so many fronts. And it made me act in ways I shouldn't have." He pauses and then continues raggedly, "Not just with you, but with Finn. I loved seeing how successful he was. I encouraged it, because it made me feel big. Like I could take some credit for his accomplishments. And I know that probably got out of hand. I probably let him get away with some attitude, I got obsessed about the Ivies. I don't know." He shakes his head slowly. "Maybe it led to the mess we're in now. Maybe I'm the one to blame."

I think back to that night—my own insecurity, Michael storming off, Rose and Brad drinking too much, the kids alone on the beach, Finn feeling confident, Bella flirting...

"I don't know," I say heavily. "I think we all had a part to play, in a way, but at the end of the day, the person to blame is the one who assaulted Bella." I close my eyes as the realization I've been so desperate to avoid for the last three days thuds through me. "And I don't think that was Finn."

Michael's hand tightens on mine. "What are you saying..."

"I think," I begin, letting the shadowy fears coalesce in my mind, "that it was—" I stop, because my phone is buzzing like an angry bee in my purse. I slip my hand from Michael's to take it out, intending only to silence it, but then I see it's from Finn and some mother instinct rears up in me and I swipe to take the call. "Finn—"

"Mom?" He is crying, sobbing, the word torn from him. "Mom, you've got to come—"

"What's happened, Finn?" Michael straightens at the sharp sound of my voice, panic flaring in his eyes.

Finn is crying too hard to answer, and my stomach swoops, drops, and my vision tunnels.

"Finn," I say faintly, and between gulping sobs, he answers.

"You've got to come, Mom," he chokes out. "It's Henry."

CHAPTER 24

ROSE

After our conversation, Brad, in typical fashion, goes into his study in a wounded huff, as if we've had nothing more than an argument rather than an acknowledgement our marriage was already over. I don't actually mind; in the end, there was nothing more to say, and I wasn't ready to talk particulars about custody or alimony or who gets the house.

Nothing has been decided beyond that one simple fact, shining and true—I am leaving him. I really am. I have to remind myself, because it feels so surprising, a prospect that fills me with both terror and wonder—and a flickering of hope. Finally, I am taking action. I am taking back control of my life, or at least starting to.

With Brad in his study, I go upstairs to reassure my daughters. I'm not ready to tell them everything, but I know I need to make sure they're okay. I go to Bella first, because talking to Elspeth will be more complicated; when I go into her bedroom, she's sprawled on her bed, staring up at the ceiling, her phone flung away from her.

"You okay, sweetheart?" I ask softly.

"I just wish none of this had ever happened." Bella lets out a gusty sigh. "*None* of it."

"I know."

She lifts her head from the bed. "Is Dad okay? Did Mr. Johnston break his nose?"

"Dad's fine." I wait for more questions, but she drops her head back onto the bed without saying anything more. Now is not the time to tell her I'm divorcing her father, although that time will come, and soon. I perch on the edge of her bed. "You are going to get through this, Bella. You're going to be okay. Eventually. I know it will take time, and that's hard, but it will happen." It is happening, even, for me.

Another sigh gusts through her. "I still wish the whole thing had never happened." She glances at me. "Not just... you know, with Finn, but all of it. I never meant for it to be like this."

"I know you didn't," I tell her, "but... sometimes it's the hardest things that can help us. They can make us stronger, if we let them, if we choose for it to." I hesitate and then I continue gently, "Maybe this whole experience can do that for you... if you let it."

She raises her head to give me a disbelieving look.

"You could get involved in some social action," I suggest, warming to my theme, a cautious enthusiasm creeping in. "For the rights of women and girls. Or maybe do some volunteer counselling—you'll have so much more empathy now, because you've been through it."

Bella's forehead crinkles, and I realize I am probably sounding too earnest, too much like a PSA. I dial it back.

"Just a thought," I tell her, patting her knee. "Just a way to think about this differently, more positively, in time, when you're ready."

"Maybe," Bella says, sounding dubious as she drops her head back onto the pillow. I pat her knee one more time and then I go to find Elspeth.

Like Bella, she is on her bed, but huddled up, her arms wrapped around her knees. "Are you and Dad getting divorced?" she fires at me the instant I step into her bedroom. Of course she leads with that.

"Dad and I are talking through some things, Elspeth," I say carefully. I'm not ready to issue ultimatums to Brad just yet, to upend my daughters' worlds. Not until I've thought through things more, how to tell them, what it might mean. "But the important thing to remember is that we both love you very much, and we want the best for you."

My daughter rolls her eyes. "But are you?" she asks, and I almost smile at that, because clearly she sees right through the greeting-card sentiments.

"I want to talk about something else with you," I tell her seriously.

She narrows her eyes, hugging her knees tighter, and I sit on the edge of the bed. I don't want to have this conversation, but I have to. I have to start facing things. Dealing with them.

"I know you were the one who posted that photo of Bella," I say quietly, "but I'd like to know why you did it."

Elspeth stares at me for a few taut seconds, her face expressionless, her body still, and then she looks away.

"Elspeth?" I prompt gently. "Why?"

She hunches her shoulders, bending her head toward her knees, and doesn't reply.

"Elspeth." I try to speak gently, but some of my impatience and frustration bleeds through. This parenting thing, when you try to do it properly, see it through? It's *hard*. Elspeth's body is tucked up, tense, her head angled away from me. "Can you please tell me why?"

"It was just a joke," she whispers, her voice so low I have to strain to hear it, even though I am sitting right next to her on the bed.

"A joke..." I am at a loss. How could she have possibly

thought it was a *joke?* I realize I should have considered what I was going to say, how I was going to say it. "Elspeth, you must have known that it wasn't going to be funny." Again, I try to speak gently, and again the frustration creeps in, peeks through.

She looks up at me, her shoulders still hunched, her eyes flashing. "Maybe I didn't want it to be *funny*."

I stare at her for a long moment, noticing her skinny arms, wrapped around her knees, her bony shoulders. The long, strawberry blond hair, straight and thin, the round, childish curve of her cheek. Despite her smarts and sass, she's just a child. A child who couldn't possibly understand the ramifications of what she did. A child, I also know, who struggles with insecurity, with envy, with shame. *My* child.

"What were you hoping would happen, then?" I ask.

She shrugs, her hair swinging in front of her face, unwilling to reply.

I count to ten, and then twenty. "*Elspeth.*"

"I don't know," she bursts out, hunching harder. "I just... I wanted Bella to feel like people were, I don't know, laughing at her, I guess, because no one ever does. It's like, *whatever* she does, no matter how stupid it is, it's perfect. She's perfect. She's *always* perfect." This last comes out on a breath that sounds close to a sob, and then once more she burrows her head in her knees.

I gaze at her in dismay, because while I have known Elspeth has been jealous of Bella's easy popularity, I never realized it ran this deep, was felt this hard, and now I'm not sure how to respond. What punishment fits this kind of crime? Or has she been punished enough, feeling so guilty, terrified of being found out? As sympathetic as I am, somehow I doubt it.

"How did you get the photo from Finn's phone?" I ask after a moment.

She shrugs. "That was easy. He wanted to airdrop them to Bella and he was so drunk he couldn't figure it out, so I did it, instead, to my phone." She speaks so scornfully, I find myself cringing. Not a single one of them comes out of this in a good light, I realize, except maybe for Henry.

"Why?"

She shrugs. "I don't know. I thought it would be funny."

Funny. That word encompasses so much, tells so little. "That was before you left them, then."

"Yeah." She lowers head, picking her nails, not wanting to look at me.

"And when it got out of hand?" I ask. "When everyone started calling Bella names, teasing her?" *Making her life a misery? Shaming her for someone else's cruelty?*

Elspeth presses her lips together, her gaze darting away from mine. "I didn't expect it to happen like that. I just..." She looks back at me, tears in her eyes. "I don't even really know why I did it. I wasn't going to, I was just messing around with the photos, but then Bella always ignores me, and acts like she's so much better than me, and so I just... posted it. I didn't think anyone would actually *see* it." The plaintive cry of so many teenagers who somehow forget that posting something on social media means it's public. "And then I thought I'd take it down really quick, like after an hour maybe, but by then lots of people had seen it." She sniffs and gulps, her wide-eyed gaze beseeching now, begging me to understand. "I didn't think it would get so... But then when it all got really big, I went to the police, and I told Henry to, too. I was trying to make it better." When what she really should have done is come to me. Confessed, although what would I have done? I don't even know.

This was all part of the reason, I suppose, that Finn was questioned so publicly, suspended from the soccer team, and ostracized at school. *Oh, Elspeth.*

"You shouldn't have interfered at all," I tell her, trying not to sound too severe, even though part of me feels like throttling her. "The situation was volatile enough without you contributing to it."

"Of course you take her side," Elspeth cries, and I want to groan, roll my eyes, and hug her all at once. And yes, throttle her still, too.

"This is not about taking sides," I say quietly. "I love both you and Bella, and I always will, and so will Dad." She huffs and I continue, "And I love Bella for being Bella, and you for being you. You don't need to be like Bella, you know, Elspeth—"

"As if I'd want to," she scoffs, but there is a waver in her voice, and my heart aches. No, she doesn't want to be like Bella, but I'm pretty sure she has wanted to be as popular as she is. She wants to be liked for her own sake, and yet the cruel world of high-school popularity is both shallow and fickle. I fear Elspeth might go through life always feeling frustrated and alone, while Bella will traipse along, liked by many simply because she is good-looking and easygoing. It's not fair, but it still is.

"You aren't... you aren't going to tell Bella that I did it?" Elspeth asks tremulously.

"No," I say after a moment, because that could be the death knell of any sisterly relationship they might have. "But I hope this whole situation makes you realize that Bella's life isn't as easy and golden as you seem to think it is. You two are different, and that's okay. Focus on being your best self, rather than comparing yourself to Bella."

Elspeth makes a face at my sappy, if heartfelt, sentiments. "Okay, thanks for that, Mom."

"Right." I hold out my hand, because she's not getting off that easily. "And I'll take your phone, please."

"What—"

"Your actions have consequences, Elspeth. You've used your phone irresponsibly, *very* irresponsibly, and so now I'm going to confiscate it."

She looks both shocked and wounded, because I have not been the kind of mom who confiscates phones. I might wag a finger, adopt a stern tone, and then let it go—all under the guise of laidback, child-focused parenting, but really, I acknowledge now, because it's easier.

My hand is still stretched out. "Elspeth."

Grumbling under her breath, she takes it out of her pocket and slaps it into my palm. "For how long?"

"To be determined," I tell her sternly. "We'll start with a week."

"A *week*—"

"Yes, a week." I slip the phone into my pocket before I surprise Elspeth by putting my arms around her and drawing her close. "I love you, Elspeth," I tell her, my lips against her hair. "I love you for exactly who you are—smart and funny and passionate. I don't want you to be anyone but yourself."

For a second, I think she is going to resist—squirm away and roll her eyes, telling me not to be so cringy. But then her arms come around me, skinny and strong, and she hugs me tightly for a few seconds before she twists away, flopping onto her bed, her back to me.

"Ugh, what am I going to do without my phone?" she complains in a voice full of melodrama.

I rise from the bed, her phone in my pocket heavy against my hip. "You'll think of something, I'm sure. You could always read a book."

"A *book*." She sounds both incensed and incredulous.

As I leave her room, I realize I am smiling. I am finally being the kind of mother I've always wanted to be.

The next day is strange in its surprising normality, when my life feels as if its tectonic plates have forever shifted and yet nothing noticeable has changed. Bella and Elspeth go to school, Brad to work. He slept in the guestroom last night, acting like he was the injured party. I was just glad not to have him snoring next to me. I know the sorrow and grief will come; already I feel them lapping at the edges of my consciousness, threatening to sweep and loom, but right now I just feel free, the world, for once, alight with possibilities, and I want to enjoy that sensation for as long as I have it.

I spend the morning updating my resumé—which sadly doesn't take very long at all—and then applying for a handful of jobs in the charity sector. I know I probably won't get so much as an interview, but I have to start somewhere. I also email a few local organizations—a charity for survivors of domestic abuse and a rape crisis center—asking if they need volunteers. I figure I might as well get some work experience, if I can.

I also look up divorce lawyers, and find one that looks promising—a sharp and savvy woman, a bit like Elspeth might be in thirty years. I'm not ready to call her, though, even though I'm sure Brad will already be lining up his own legal advice. He's not going to give me a dime more than he has to, I know that much, but I don't mind. Whatever I get, it will be enough. I will make sure of it.

I think of calling Cara, although I'm not sure what I'd say to her. Apologize on Brad's behalf? Ask how Finn is? Find a way back to some sort of friendship? I'm not sure we can, after everything that has happened.

Then, when Elspeth and Bella come home, the world shifts. Again.

"Finn and Henry didn't come to school today," Elspeth blurts as soon as she comes into the kitchen. Her face is pale and strained, her lip red and swollen from where she's bitten it. "And people are saying something happened."

I am not particularly alarmed, not at first. "Maybe they wanted a day off, after the ruckus of last night," I suggest, and then Bella comes in behind Elspeth, her eyes wide, her expression just as panicked.

"Someone said they saw an ambulance in front of their house last night," she says.

I frown, the first stirrings of unease swirling in my stomach. "An ambulance? Who said that?"

"Just someone at school—"

"It could just be a rumor. You know how people get wound up." I speak placatingly, but I am starting to feel worried.

"What if something has happened to Finn?" Bella's voice is high and thin, her eyes wide and full of fear. Despite everything that has happened, I know she still cares for him—and that's what has made this whole situation hurt all the more.

"I'm sure Finn is fine," I tell her, although, of course, I can be sure of no such thing.

Bella doesn't look remotely convinced, and yet I feel like I would have heard, if something had happened. Then I remember everything that went down last night and realize I probably wouldn't have.

"Can you text Mrs. Johnston?" she asks. "Make sure they're all okay?"

I hesitate, because even though I was thinking about calling Cara earlier, I'm not sure I want to pry into her family's affairs right now. And if something did happen—heaven knows what—what can I really do about it? Texting at this point, after the distance and hostility between us, might seem like some kind of gleeful rubbernecking.

"Can I have my phone back?" Elspeth asks. "To check if Henry has texted me?"

Bella looks surprised. "Why don't you have your phone?"

"She was on it too much," I insert swiftly, not wanting to get into all that just now. "Do you really think Henry would text you, Elspeth?"

"Yeah, he does, sometimes." She gives me a haughty look. "We *are* friends, you know."

Still I hesitate, not wanting to get into the whole messy complication of Elspeth insisting she needs to check her phone when it's been banned, but the girls' sense of alarm has infected me. What if something *has* happened? What if Henry has texted her?

"I'll check it," I say, and Elspeth lets out a howl of protest at this seemingly unthinkable outrage.

"*Mom—*"

I ignore her and hurry upstairs, taking her phone out of the bottom drawer of my bedside table. I don't know her password, but it doesn't matter because the text comes up on her home screen as soon as I swipe. It's from Henry.

This is all my fault. I'm the one to blame. I'm going to make it right. Tell everyone I'm sorry.

CHAPTER 25

CARA

So here I am, in the place I never wanted to be. Sitting in a hospital room next to my son, wondering if he'll live, where I went wrong. When Finn called us, sobbing and hysterical, I told him to call 911 and we drove home immediately, blind with panic, our bodies pulsing with the worst fear a parent can ever know.

What if...

Neither Michael nor I finished that sentence. We did not want to ask the question; we did not want to consider the answer.

By the time we got back, an ambulance was already there. They'd loaded Henry into it, strapping him down; he was unconscious, but I saw the awful red welt around his neck and I let out an anguished cry. My fourteen-year-old son had tried to hang himself.

Those first few hours were all about his treatment and prognosis; I couldn't think about everything that had brought us to this moment. At the hospital in Bridgeport, the doctor told us that while it was good Finn had found him when he had—just a few minutes after he'd attempted suicide—Henry's condition was still very serious. He used terms I didn't fully understand, or maybe I simply didn't want to—cerebral edema, severe hypoxia. I knew they were bad, though; of course they were bad.

"The risk, of course," the doctor told us, "is brain damage. We'll know more in the next twenty-four hours, whether there are neurological deficits, although the extent won't be possible to determine for some time."

"But he'll live?" I asked desperately, curling my hands into fists to keep from grabbing his sleeve, begging.

The doctor hesitated, not quite meeting our gazes. "I can't make any promises. While his body has survived the trauma, his brain has been starved of oxygen for some time. It remains to be seen whether the neurological impairment has, functionally, made him brain-dead. We'll do a scan when he's stable enough." He patted my arm, the barest show of sympathy, and left us alone, shocked and reeling.

Michael went back to be with Finn, who we knew shouldn't be alone. He'd been utterly distraught as we'd stood, shocked, by the ambulance, sobbing and begging us to forgive him.

"I didn't know... *I didn't know!*"

None of us knew, but maybe we should have guessed.

The story came out in bits and pieces, first from Finn, who told Michael, who told me. After I'd left the house to follow Michael to the Rosses', Henry had become hysterical and confessed to Finn—*he'd* been the one to assault Bella. He hadn't remembered at first, since he'd been so drunk, and it wasn't until the police had told him when the assault had happened, that the memories started to come back and he realized he might have been the guilty one, not Finn. By that point, he'd been too terrified to tell anyone, although I realized he had been trying, in his own, frightened way, to tell me.

Finn, understandably, had been completely furious, and he had tried to punch Henry, who had run up to his room. When

Finn heard the thud of his chair being kicked over, he didn't go up at first—a delay of a minute or two that now fills him with a terrible guilt. Then, perhaps with some brotherly instinct he didn't even know he possessed, he went up to check on Henry and found him in his bedroom, hanging from the ceiling fan by his belt.

My Henry. My poor, poor Henry.

I stare at him now—his pale, slack face, the deep red welt encircling his neck, and more tellingly, the claw marks on his throat. He'd had second thoughts, which apparently is very common, but also gives me a strange sort of comfort. My little boy didn't truly want to die.

Now he simply needs to survive. He *must* survive, because the alternative is unthinkable. Unbearable. I've told myself I can accept anything except my son's death. Neurological deficits, however deep or lasting those may be... but, please God, let him live. And yet the hours tick on through the night, and there is no change.

It gives me time to think, though, too much time to let my mind drift through the days, the months and the years, and wonder what I could have done to keep Henry—and all of us—from this moment. I can't help but believe, with a deep, gut-level instinct, that it wasn't one mistake that led us to here, but a series of steps and missteps, of good intentions as well as wrong decisions. Was it my need to be strict, to set boundaries? Was it Michael's adulation of Finn and his success? Was it Henry's insecurity, Finn's low-grade yet relentless bullying, my fractured friendship with Rose, that made us leave them there on the beach in the first place, hoping they could get along?

Perhaps it was everything, the perfect storm, or maybe it's simply the way life is: continually messy, complicated, difficult, no matter how determined you are, how hard you try.

I have no answers. I only have a longing for my son to be well, for the opportunity to do better. I'll be such a better mother, I think, desperately. I won't make him practice piano anymore. I won't stress about grades. I'll slow down, maybe even work part-time if we can afford it, remember to breathe and smile and enjoy life in a way I haven't in a long, long time. I will, I think with a soft huff of humorless laughter, be more like Rose. If only I am given the chance. If only we all are.

The morning after Henry's suicide attempt, a night where I sat by his bed, gritty-eyed and refusing to sleep, he wakes up. Sort of. His eyes open, remaining unfocused, and he opens his mouth as if to speak, but the only sound that comes out is a sort of wordless gargle.

The doctor tells us this is a good sign.

I call Michael, who is still home with Finn, and he says they'll come in this afternoon, when Finn is ready. I wait by Henry's bed, scanning his sleeping face, hoping for another sign. He'll open his eyes, he'll speak. *Please...*

The hours pass so slowly when you're waiting. Time spent in a hospital is strange, a sort of suspended reality of halogen lights and squeaky wheels, sudden beeps and murmured voices. Sitting next to Henry's bed, it feels hard to believe that there is a whole world out there, going on and on; children going to school, people to work, reading the news, checking their phones, dealing with petty irritations, wondering what to eat, the sun rising, shining, setting on us all. A simple, faraway world that feels utterly remote to me now.

Finn and Michael come by after lunch; there has been no change. I hug my oldest son tightly; I haven't had a chance to talk to him since this all happened, and I see how haggard he looks—his lips bitten raw, his face so pale, dark circles under his eyes.

"Is he going to be okay?" he asks hoarsely.

"They don't know yet, but there have been some hopeful signs. He's going for a scan soon." I smile encouragingly at Finn, which feels like the hardest thing to do, because inside I feel as if I am breaking into pieces. I am making promises I do not have the power or control to keep.

"It was Henry," Finn says slowly as he sinks into a chair. "All this time, it was *Henry*."

"Yes." I should have realized, I think now. Looking back, I can see all the signs clearly—his anxiety, his agitation, wanting to speak to me, insisting Finn hadn't done it. I'd started to wonder, like a buzzing in the back of my brain, but I hadn't let myself guess. If only I'd talked about it with Henry, gotten him to trust me, tell me.

If only. If only.

The two most pointless words in the world.

Finn shakes his head slowly. "I still can't believe it. He told me last night... he said he didn't remember at first. It was only when he started to think about it, when he found out it had happened later that night... he started to remember, but it was always blurry. He was so drunk, because of the beers we gave him, Bella and me..." He swallows convulsively, his head bowed. "I made him feel bad, that night. I was teasing him right before he ran off, calling him a geek. I just wanted to seem cool to Bella. It sounds so stupid now, but—"

"Finn," Michael says gently, putting his hand on his son's shoulder. "This is not your fault."

"But maybe he wouldn't have if I..." Finn gulps. "He said he came back and I was pretty much passed out. Bella was too, but then she opened her eyes and smiled at him or something. She asked him to help her up, and he came toward her, and then..." He shrugs helplessly and I try to imagine the scene—Bella smiling, seeming warm and inviting, Henry befuddled by drink, raw from his older brother's bullying. He took her hand and then what? I know what Rose would say. He assaulted her, plain and simple. And yes, he did. He must have, and it was as wrong as it was before, I know that, absolutely, but... It doesn't feel nearly as clear as I would expect it to be. "If he survives... will the Rosses..." Finn asks, trailing off uncertainly, and I am jolted by what he doesn't want to put into words. This nightmare could continue, Henry could be taken to the police, vilified by the school, questioned, prosecuted, judged. He's as guilty as everyone thought Finn was, after all.

"Let's just take one day at a time," Michael advises. "We've got enough to worry about right now."

"I'm sorry," Finn whispers, his head bowed. "I'm so sorry."

I put my arm around him and he leans his head against my shoulder. There is no need for any more words.

A little while later, they take Henry away for a scan. We head downstairs to the coffee shop for something to eat, even though none of us is hungry. We need something to do, to distract us, but there is no distraction from the fear eating away at my stomach, lodging like a stone in my gut.

An hour later, Henry is back in his room, and the neurologist who has been handling his case is smiling, although I can't tell if it is a reassuring smile or a sympathetic one. I feel my legs give beneath me and Michael takes me by the elbow, holding me up.

"Is he..."

"The scan showed some brain activity," the consultant tells us without preamble. "So that is good news."

He ushers us into his office, takes us through it all in a way I can't understand—"hypoxic ischemic injury" is the term he uses, but after going through all the jargon, the end result is that Henry will live, that he will recover, but there will definitely be some damage. How much is impossible to say at this point; he is hopeful for a "very good partial recovery," whatever that means. Will Henry be able to go to school? Live a normal life? The neurologist has no answers, not yet, although he says encouraging things about neuroplasticity and brains being able to recover from trauma "more than anyone actually realizes."

I don't know whether I can bear to believe him; to hope, only to have it taken away. For, while I am filled with relief that Henry will live, I also feel a fresh grief. He will not be the same. I didn't let myself think about what that could mean before, but now the reality of it slams into me. Life, for all of us, and most of all for Henry, has been forever changed. We have lost something—someone—today, and the magnitude of that loss is as yet unknowable. It is hard to deal with that, on top of everything else, and in truth, I can barely think about it. Today's pain is enough of a burden to bear.

After the scan, Michael takes a turn to stay with Henry and I take Finn home to get some rest. I check my phone for the first time in what feels like days, to see if there are any messages, but there are none. Who, I wonder, has heard about Henry? Has Rose? Would she call? It doesn't matter anymore; I know our friendship is over, but I still feel a flicker of sadness for what was, and what will never be again.

The next morning, Finn goes to school—we both agreed it was better for him to be busy—and I head back to the hospital. Henry opened his eyes during the night, tried to speak. Michael is encouraged, almost buoyant with hope; I feel more cautious. When I arrive, he is sleeping again, slack-jawed, silent. I sit by his side.

Again, the hours pass with bittersweet slowness, because they give me so much time to think. To remember Henry as a baby—wide-eyed and serious; as a little boy, dark-haired and watchful. I recall how his whole face would light up when he was playing one of his adventure games with his friends, the laughter that would erupt from him like hiccups, seeming to surprise him. I picture him sprawled on the sofa, deep into some manga comic or other; I remember how we used to bake, elbow-deep in flour, and how he would never sneak a taste the way most children would because he wanted, as he did with just about everything, to do the thing properly.

Oh, Henry. I miss you, I think. *I love you. Wake up, wake up please, my darling boy. Wake up and let me show you how much better I'll be this time around. How much harder I'll try.*

Early in the afternoon, I have a visitor. I sense her presence before she speaks, and then I smell her perfume—that expensive, flowery scent. I tense but don't turn, because I'm not sure how to handle this moment, or what mood she'll be in. Repentant? Vindictive? Effusive? I never was able to guess, to tell.

"Cara?" she asks softly, and finally I turn, steel myself.

"Hello, Rose."

CHAPTER 26

ROSE

Cara looks awful—dark circles under her eyes, lank hair, grief etched deeply onto every line of her face. I stare at her, staring back at me so resolutely, and I realize I have no idea what to say. The usual sentiments feel paltry and weak, even if I know that I'll mean them. I came here because I knew I needed to, and also because I wanted to, but that doesn't mean the moment is easy.

I wouldn't blame Cara for blaming me for this; if I'd just let it go, way back at the beginning, we might never have got to this point. Henry would have kept quiet, Bella would have recovered, all four of them would have gone about their lives, some of them with scars, yes, but mostly okay. Hopefully. And yet that wasn't the right thing to do. I know that now just as I did before, utterly and absolutely, and yet I am still full of grief.

"I didn't know if you knew what happened," Cara finally says, her tone lifeless, her face turned away from me.

"Henry texted Elspeth, and told her. Before he..." I pause, because I don't know the exact details, and it feels cruel to mention what I do know, what Bella and Elspeth have learned from the rumors swirling about the school.

"Before he hanged himself," Cara finishes flatly. "Did he? We haven't looked at his phone."

"Yes, he said he was sorry, that it was all his fault. That he... he was the one who assaulted Bella." Even now I can't believe it. Neither can Bella, yet we both know it's true. Henry. Of all people, *Henry*.

"Are you here to tell me you're going to go to the police?" Cara suddenly spits as she turns to me, screwing up her face in something that would be fury but is too much like grief. "Because if you are, fine, go ahead, but you didn't need to come here and let me know."

"What?" I gape at her, shocked by her bitterness, the wildness of her grief. "Cara, no. That's not why I'm here, I promise." Once I was so determined to involve the police. That feels like a long time ago, now.

"Why are you here, then?" she asks, lifting her chin. "Because we're not friends anymore, are we? We haven't been for a long time. I realize that now. I realized it a while ago."

I stare at her for a moment and then I lower myself into the chair opposite her; the vinyl squeaks under me, the only sound in the room besides the steady beeping of the machine next to Henry. "We have been good friends, though," I say quietly. "In the past. You were my best friend. My only friend, actually. At least, my only real friend."

She angles her face away from me, toward her son. "I'm not sure it matters now."

"Doesn't it?" I realize, quite suddenly and urgently, that I don't want to lose Cara's friendship. That I've taken it for granted all these years, rolled my eyes at her intensity, felt her emotions were too exhausting. But right now I am remembering how she was always, *always* there for me—birthday cards every year for the girls, more than willing to have them over at a moment's notice, or to babysit at ours when we couldn't find a sitter. I think of how many times she sat at my kitchen table and listened to me moan about my seemingly boring life, or cleaned my kitchen when I felt overwhelmed, or took my teasing, some of it a bit mean-spirited, in smiling stride. "You've been my best friend," I tell her honestly, "but I don't think I have been a very good friend to you."

"Oh, Rose." Cara shakes her head wearily. "You were. You helped tone me down a bit, made me laugh, which I know I needed. I was always grateful for your attention."

Something I think I always knew. I know I felt superior, even if now I am wondering just why I did. "Still," I say. "I wish I'd been a better friend."

"It really doesn't matter." And I know that for her, it doesn't. Her son is hovering between life and death; why would she care about being friends with me? It was stupid and selfish to mention it now, and yet I want to help. I want to be there for her, now. At last.

"I'm sorry for the way everything happened," I tell her quietly. "Not just since the barbecue, but even before." I want to tell her that I lost myself over the last twenty years, that I've been playacting for so long I don't know who is real anymore, that I've always admired her dedication as a friend, as a mother, as a person. I want to say that I am trying to be more like her, taking control of my life in the way she always has, but I don't, because now is not the time. I hope that a time will come when I can say those things to her, when I can show her that I mean them, and that they will matter to her. "Do you know how he is?" I ask instead.

"He's going to live." Cara speaks matter-of-factly, but there is a tremble to her words. "But the neurologist said there will almost certainly be some brain damage. They don't know how that will manifest itself—speech, memory, mobility, maybe all three. It could be anything. They gave me a brochure..." She lets out a high, wavery laugh. "'How To Deal with Your Child's Traumatic Brain Injury.' That's essentially what he has,

because of the oxygen deprivation to his brain, when he was..."
She swallows, gulping back the words. "Makes for great reading, let me tell you."

"Oh, Cara." My eyes fill with tears, and I make myself blink them back. I ache for them all: for Henry, so injured, for Finn, so wronged, for Bella, so violated. They've all suffered in their own ways, perhaps Henry most of all.

"Sometimes, after the brain has been deprived of oxygen," she continues in a high, false, isn't-that-interesting sort of voice, "they can have a complete personality change. It happens in stroke victims, sometimes. Wouldn't that be strange? What do you think Henry would be like, with a totally different personality?" She lets out another one of those strange laughs, but then it turns into a sob, the deep kind from the gut, and she bends over, her arms wrapped around herself as the sobs tear out of her.

"Oh, Cara. *Cara.*" I cross the room, kneeling in front of her as I put my arms around her, and she presses her face against my shoulders and sobs like she'll never stop, like she's being torn right in half. It is the sound of pure, raw grief, coming from deep within, and it makes tears run down my face unchecked because there is simply too much sorrow in the world, and neither of us can bear it. "I'm so sorry," I say, over and over again, because I'm not sure there are any other words right now. "So sorry."

"I know," she says at last, easing back as she wipes her face. A shuddering breath goes through her and she straightens her shoulders. "I know you are. And I'm sorry, too. Henry..." She shakes her head, pressing her lips together to keep from crying again. "I never would have thought he'd do something like... but he assaulted Bella. We know that much. He didn't remember it right away, Finn said, and by the time he did, he was too frightened to say anything. But I'm sorry for Bella's sake, I truly am. How is she coping with it?"

My heart aches, that she has the strength and compassion to

ask about Bella, when her own son is hooked up to machines, his life forever changed. "She's okay," I tell her. "She was shocked when she found out, because she'd really convinced herself it was Finn, but she's okay." Nothing compared to how Henry is, of course, though it hardly needs saying. Bella will recover—with time, with help, with healing. She already is.

A sigh escapes Cara and briefly she closes her eyes. "What is this world?" she asks, her eyes still closed. "That these things can happen? That we let them?"

"I don't know if any of us could have stopped it." Although I've already gone over in my mind, time and time again, what I could have done differently. How I could have prevented this. If I'd drunk less, if I hadn't been fixated on myself, my marriage, if I hadn't given Bella those beers. So many little decisions, but in the end would any of it have gone differently?

"I just *feel* for them all," Cara says sadly as she opens her eyes. "Each and every one of them. Our teenagers. I think about when they were little, when it was so easy, and yet so exhausting. Nothing that couldn't be solved with a Band-Aid and a kiss, or maybe some ice cream, a good night's sleep." She smiles at me, full of sorrow. "We had no idea—no idea at all—what was in store. For them and for us." She shakes her head slowly as a weary sigh escapes her.

"I don't think anyone has," I reply feelingly. If we had, would anyone dare to have children, raise them up with love and care, sweat and sleepless nights and so many tears, only for them to be hurt, worse than ever before, and in a way where there is absolutely nothing you can do about it? And yet that is what parenting is all about.

"I want something to change," Cara states, turning to look at me. "I don't know what. But all of it—the bullying, the peer pressure, the social media, the sheer *toxicity*... all of it led to this, here, in a way. I know Henry has to be responsible for his own actions, I do, truly, but the culture, the *climate*..."

"I know," I say quickly, because I do. If even *Henry* could have fallen into this kind of behavior, what hope is there for any teenaged child?

"I want something to change." There is a spark of challenge in her eyes that has an answering flare in me.

"So do I," I tell her, and I mean it. Utterly.

We stare at each other for a moment, as if taking each other's measure, entering an agreement, perhaps, although I'm not sure what it is. Then Cara smiles, so very faintly, and looks away.

"I've left Brad," I tell her suddenly, and she lets out a huff of surprised laughter.

"Have you? Good."

I laugh back, also surprised, and when she turns back to me, her smile has widened, although there are tears in her eyes.

"Thank you," she says softly, and I nod, unsure what she is thanking me for, but grateful, so grateful, that we have found our way here, even as so much—far too much—remains uncertain.

Then Cara lets out a muffled gasp, and I turn to see that Henry has opened his eyes.

EPILOGUE

CARA

NINE MONTHS LATER

It's the fourth of July weekend, and we've come to the beach. It's the first time I've been here since it all happened, and the sight of the Sound, burnished under the setting sun, brings a rush of memory that is painful but bittersweet, because I am not just remembering last summer, with all of its sorrow and regret, but all the summers before that, the ones that were wonderful. Finn and Bella, holding hands as they ran squealing into the water. Elspeth and Henry building an epic sandcastle, with Elspeth as architect, Henry her laborer. Rose and I sprawled on a blanket on the beach, Michael and Brad by the grill.

Brad is not here. His and Rose's divorce was finalized several months ago. She got a decent settlement; they sold the big house in Green Farms, and she lives in a split-level just a few blocks from me. Brad took an apartment in the city. Rose has the girls the majority of the time; Brad swoops in for the occasional grandiose weekend.

She's got a job too, as an administrative assistant for a law office. Bella and Finn are both starting at UConn next month;

in the end, Finn didn't apply to any Ivies, and Michael accepted his decision. Finn and Bella are still friends, maybe even something more, or at least could be one day, although neither Rose nor I have yet dared to ask. Bella has taken her own steps to recovery, has found ways to use the experience for good, speaking out about social media, about peer pressure, about all that has gone wrong with our teenagers' lives.

Elspeth is about to start tenth grade, still sassy but sometimes subdued, which is no bad thing. And as for Henry? Henry has been so brave, so determined and strong. He hasn't made a full recovery, but then we never expected him to. Every small milestone has been a success, every tiny victory an epic win. He's had issues with speech, with mobility, with memory; he gets headaches often and staring at a screen or book is hard. He walks with a slightly strained, lopsided gait, although that's coming on, and he can speak clearly now, if very carefully. He forgets things—occasional words, how to tie his shoes—but he is learning all the time. He is determined to improve, to succeed, and I know that he will.

After the accident—which is what we call it, what it felt like—his friends rallied around. They visited him almost every day in the hospital, and then later at the rehab center, even bringing along the Dungeons and Dragons-type board game they all loved, and playing it in the day room for as long as Henry could, setting up all its pieces and cards and colored dice. Finn rallied too, and even agreed to play the game with them a few times, enjoying it, I think, far more than he expected to. Apparently, he likes attacking orcs.

Their brotherly relationship has suffered a fracture; perhaps it will always have a hairline crack, a point of weakness, but at least it is whole again, and growing stronger. They are both trying to make amends, grow together rather than apart. And Bella and Henry have reconciled, as well; Bella has been amazingly understanding toward Henry, and Elspeth has become almost fiercely protective of him.

As for Michael and me... that has been hard, too. Michael joined Gamblers Anonymous, attended the meetings regularly, agreed to hand over his laptop and phone, so I could check if he'd been to an online casino. Money has been tight and there have been a few blips, but none recently, and while we have those cracks too, we are whole. We are solid. That doesn't, I've come to learn, mean it's easy, but most things that are worthwhile aren't. Something Rose has taught me, when she learned it herself, with me.

"How about over here?" Rose calls, gesturing to a spare patch of sand fairly near the fireworks. The sun is already starting to set, the first stars coming out in a sky fading to lavender, then indigo. The air is heavy and humid, but at least the breeze from the Sound is cool. We agreed this year that instead of a Labor Day beach barbecue, when Bella and Finn would have already headed off to UConn, we'd do a Fourth of July one instead—something different; a new tradition.

I take Henry by the arm as I help him over the undulating sand, and Elspeth takes his other one, teasing him about being a slow poke, but with a smile on her face. It's her way of coping, and Henry likes it; he grins back. They exchange banter now, of a sort, which they never used to do. In the midst of the trials, Henry has found a strength and a courage neither he nor we knew he possessed.

Bella and Finn are walking ahead of us, heads bent together. I hear their voices drift over the sand, the lilt of laughter, and I smile, because like Rose said all those years ago, they really are suited to one another.

"So I've looked into charity names for a website," Rose says as she falls into step alongside me. "Truth Speaks is free."

"That's great," I reply as she spreads the blanket and I help

Henry onto it. I straighten, one hand to the small of my back. "Have you registered the domain name?"

"I wanted to ask you first."

"I think you should."

We smile at each other, then, because it feels pretty big to have gotten to this moment. Rose was the one with the idea, after I'd said, back in the hospital, that I wanted things to change. She suggested we start a charity, to raise awareness of the issues that teens are facing—issues around social media, sexual assault, peer pressure. There are plenty of charities that are already around, helping the kids themselves, but not so many educating parents, relatives, teachers. That's where we might come in, at least one day. This is the beginning—of what, neither of us are exactly sure, but something. Definitely something.

Michael sits next to me, reaching for my hand, threading his fingers through mine. On the other side of me, Henry settles onto the sand, giving me his now-lopsided smile that I love. I'm so fiercely proud of him, for overcoming so much, acknowledging his guilt yet moving past it; sometimes it feels like my pride and love beams out of me, fill me with light.

In the sky above us, the first fireworks explode in dazzling pinwheels of color, red and green, pink and blue, and Henry lets out a laugh, a sound of pure joy, while I tilt my head back, breathe deep, and smile.

A LETTER FROM KATE

Dear reader,

I want to say a huge thank you for choosing to read *That Night at the Beach*. If you found it thought-provoking and powerful, and would like to keep up to date with all my latest releases, just sign up at the following link. Your email address will never be shared and you can unsubscribe at any time.

www.bookouture.com/kate-hewitt

This book was born out of a desire and even a need, as a mother of both teenaged daughters and a son, to explore a difficult, painful, and complicated issue with, I hope, compassion and sensitivity. As I wrote it, I was struck afresh by how there are no easy answers, and yet, like Rose and Cara agree at the end, that something needs to change. I hope this story challenged and inspired you, as it did me when writing it!

I hope you loved *That Night at the Beach* and if you did, I would be very grateful if you could write a review. I'd love to hear what you think, and it makes such a difference helping new readers to discover one of my books for the first time.

I love hearing from my readers—you can get in touch on my Facebook page, through Twitter, Goodreads or my website.

Thanks again for reading!
Kate

KEEP IN TOUCH WITH KATE

www.kate-hewitt.com

 facebook.com/KateHewittAuthor
twitter.com/author_kate

ACKNOWLEDGEMENTS

There are so many people to thank when writing a book, from the friends who cheer on the sidelines, to the family members who put up with me living in an alternate reality for a good part of every day, to the amazing team at Bookouture who help bring my story out into the world. Most of all, though, I'd like to thank my editor Isobel, who has worked with me for the last five years. She has been such a wonderful editor, encourager, and friend, and I'll miss her so much as she goes onto a new position. Thank you, Isobel, for being the absolutely best editor I could ask for! I have so appreciated your insights over the years. And thank you to everyone else at Bookouture who help bring my books to light —Alex, Kim, Sarah, Jess, Saidah, Iulia, Richard, Mel, Occy, Natalie, Lauren, Peta, Alex, Laura, and my new editor, Jess, along with many others.

Thank you also to my good friend Katy, with whom I've had many interesting dialogues and debates during our country walks, and Emma, who has been such a great writing retreat partner. Thanks also to Jenna, who is always on the other end of a text to listen to me moan about my plot.

Lastly, thanks to my teens—although two of you are in your

twenties now! Caroline, Ellen, Teddy, and Anna—you've given me some grey hairs, it is true, but also an abundance of laughter, love, and joy. I am so grateful for all of you. And thanks to my youngest, Charlotte—you may only be nine but you have a lot of emotional maturity already, so please, please don't be too crazy a teenager!! I love you all.

Made in the USA
Coppell, TX
16 February 2023

12936492R00184